Use You

Us
And Not Your Eyes

MW01136280

A novel by

Natavia

SOUL Publications

Use Your Heart and Not Your Eyes

Use Your Heart and Not Your Eyes

I am not perfect, but I'm all me.
I would never change myself for the world.
Sometimes I might look in the mirror to discover a new flaw,
but I would never change it for the world.
I have been told many hateful things, but
I still love me and I can't change it for the world.
If you love me, you will have to look above my flaws,
If you love me, you will have to use your heart.
If you use your eyes to love me, then you may never.
I will always love me, and I won't change that for the world.
If I do change, then it will be for me but the problem with that is,
I love me just as I am.

~Natavia

Gautier
Curvy and Chic

I roamed through the racks inside of Forever 21 frustrated because they didn't have shit I wanted. I hated their plus size section because their sizes were cut small. I was a size twenty around my hips and ass. I had too much ass, and was often asked if I had fat transfer surgery. I received a lot of negative comments on Instagram and Facebook under my pictures because of my confidence. There was always a debate on what I should or should not wear. I didn't give two fucks about it because if I did, I wouldn't have posted a picture of me in a two-piece bathing suit. My breasts were round and full; my stomach wasn't that bad but a few sit-ups wouldn't hurt. My thighs were meaty, but nonetheless, I was beautiful. I had pecan-colored skin and my eyes were slanted. People mistook me for another race, but I guess you couldn't be an exotic-looking black woman without being mixed. I was popular around my city but I hated it at times because everyone was always questioning my love life. Some thought I was acting out in desperation for a man and others thought my man didn't love me because he wouldn't allow me to post certain things. Well, I was single and did whatever I wanted. To make my life easier, I deleted and blocked the people who left negative comments under my pictures.

"Hey, are you the Curvy and Chic girl on IG?" a white girl asked me. She was shopping in the plus size section, too. My name is Gautier Sadosa, but on social media I'm Curvy and Chic.

"Yes, I am," I answered.

"OH, MY GOD! I LOVE YOU!" she screamed in excitement. The people in the store looked at her like she was crazy and so did I.

I hated the bullshit because I didn't want to be like a celebrity. I just wanted to comfortably be myself.

"Awwwww, thank you," I replied.

"You just don't understand how much you help other women like us out. Your beautiful pictures are the highlights of my day. Look what I wore to the beach yesterday," she said. She pulled out her phone and showed me a picture of her standing on the beach wearing a bathing suit similar to the one I posted a few weeks prior.

"This is cute! I need that cover-up," I said.

"Ashley Stewart has them," she replied.

I admired the neon pink cover-up she wore over her lime green two-piece suit.

"Keep up the good work," I replied.

"Oh my God! I sooo can't wait to brag to my friends about this. Can I take a selfie with you?" she asked.

"Sure," I replied.

After we took selfies as if we were best friends, I waved her goodbye when she left out of the store. I lost my train of thought and left the store, too. I just wanted to be like everyone else. Why was my confidence a big deal? I lost my good paying job because of my pictures. An evil bitch at my old job showed our boss the pictures on my page, and she thought it wasn't a good look for the company. I worked at a high-end makeup company. I was also a stylist and anything else that had something to do with being fabulous. I started my own company after I was fired which worked out for me because I kept my clients. I also brought on my friends. One was a hairstylist and the other one was a nail tech. The three of us together was a team to work with. I unlocked the door to my black-on-black Jeep Wrangler and climbed in. I turned the radio up because "Money Showers" was playing. I pulled out of the parking lot and headed home.

****

A jump off, which was someone I had occasional sex with, was standing in front of my building when I pulled up to my neighborhood. He was my personal trainer but it didn't last for long. One week later, we ended up fucking. My love life was the worst. I was one of those women who couldn't keep a man. A few of them only wanted me behind closed doors but hated to be seen with me in public because of some of the negative talk about me. It used to bother me so much that I went into depression. But I quickly got over it because I figured out a plan. The plan was to never fall in love and get a couple of orgasms out of them.

"You're late," Aniston said to me.

"Why in the fuck is you clocking me? I'm ready to charge you rent because you are here more than me," I fussed. I pushed him into the wall on my way up the stairs. I lived on the third floor in my building because a year ago when I lived on the second floor, someone broke into my condo and trashed my home. I had a feeling it was one of the guys I messed with in the past because nothing was taken. After I unlocked the door to my condo, Aniston walked in like he owned it. It was time for me to lay down some ground rules.

"I need my space," I said.

"Are you dumping me?" he asked.

"We have only been fucking for four months!" I yelled at him.

"It's that internet shit that's getting to your head, huh? You think you're a celebrity or something? They are laughing at you and making memes out of you. You should be glad someone like me wants to spend time with you," Aniston said.

"I'm going out tonight. It's the weekend, so you know what time it is. You won't be hearing from me until Monday and that's a maybe," I spat. Aniston was sexy until he started talking because he whined a lot. He was known for having the best weight training and physical therapy in the city. He had his own gym and was successful at it. He was thirty years old and didn't have any kids. He was tall, dark, and tatted. I liked my men how I liked my liquor, dark with no chaser. Aniston also modeled for different franchises, so his brand was steady growing. Women went crazy over him and I think that's why I kept him around. The same women that tried to ruin my name were the same ones who wanted the niggas I had in my back pocket.

"Let me get this shit straight. I drove all the way here to spend time with you and this is what you give me? A kick out of your home?" he asked. He was beyond pissed off and the vein in his forehead was threatening to burst.

"Yup, toodles," I said.

"Lose my number this time and I mean it, bitch!" he yelled at me again. I figured it was the power of my pussy because breaking up with a man was hard for me to do. It never ended well and it didn't matter how hard I tried to be nice about it. Everyone I had dealt with hated my guts.

"Bye, Aniston before I have your stalking ass removed from here!" I said to him. He charged into me then wrapped his hand around my neck. He knew I liked it rough but he wasn't playing fair. He slid his hand up my dress and snatched my panties off.

"Shut the fuck up! I've been wanting this juicy shit all day," he groaned. Before I could respond, he had a condom on and was ready to enter me. I moaned when he rammed his big dick inside of me. He roughly fucked me against the wall for twenty minutes before we both exploded. He walked into my bathroom to flush the condom. My legs felt like noodles which was the other reason why I kept Aniston around. He had a big dick and he knew how to work it. What I didn't like about him was that he made it seem as if it was an honor for a girl like me to be with someone like him. Aniston didn't know much about me and I didn't know much about him other than the fact he was paid, arrogant, fine, and single. I heard the toilet flush as I walked down the hall.

"Call me next week," I said to him before I walked into my bedroom. Aniston stood in the doorway of my room with a scowl on his face.

"What are you wearing tonight?" he asked.

"My birthday suit," I replied.

"You don't respect yourself. The shit you do on the internet isn't attractive. I think you'd look better if you wore something that kind of hid your thighs," he said and I laughed.

"Are my thighs an issue when you're between them? Is it hard for you to fuck me? It can't be because I don't hear you complaining when I make you nut. You have a big girl fetish. I see it all the time. It's sorta like being a down low nigga. The type to bash gay men on the internet but will be quick to fuck one when the opportunity presents itself. You're like many others I came across. I was big when you met me, big when you fucked me, and big when you begged me to stop seeing other men. You're confused, baby, and it's okay but you can get the hell out now. You served your purpose," I replied. Aniston stormed out of my condo and the door slammed behind him. I took a nice hot bath inside my bath tub that was big enough for three people. I dozed off and woke up to the sound of my cell phone ringing. It was my mother calling me.

"Hey, Ma," I answered.

"I'm just calling to let you know we'll be back home in a few days," she said. I heard laughter in the background and water splashing. She was in Jamaica on a family trip with her sisters and nieces.

"What is Brooke doing?" I asked about my daughter who was four years old.

"In the pool. She doesn't want to leave," my mother said.

"She's spoiled, Ma. I really appreciate you taking her with you. I kind of needed the break," I said.

"Anytime, baby. Now, don't party too hard and I mean it. Brooke will call you before she goes to bed," my mother replied. My mother was sixteen years older than me but I still respected her. I didn't say or do certain things around her although she still acted a little young. I washed up before I got out of the tub. I sat on my bed with a towel wrapped around me. I was excited about going out with my friends later on, but sadness came over me. I grabbed my phone and went to Salih Jones's IG page. He was a professional baseball player for the Orioles. He had smooth dark skin, and pretty thick waves that somewhat curled around his head. His beard was shaped-up nicely. On one of his pictures he was sitting in the driver's seat of a white Lamborghini with the suicide door up. He was six-foot-four and his arms were full of tattoos. He was considered one of the finest men on Earth. His teeth were pearly white and he had two diamond golds in the top row of his mouth. He was young and rich. He was also my daughter's father. Everyone knew he had a daughter but they didn't know I was her mother because I didn't post her. Next to him in the car was his Panamanian fiancée. She was gorgeous although she had a lot of surgery done. I wanted to scream but I held it in. Salih had his lawyer contact me for confidential reasons when he got drafted. I agreed to not mention his name to anybody because of his career. He paid me twelve thousand dollars a month in child support but there were rules behind it. I couldn't take her to local places, I couldn't post her, and I also couldn't tell anyone she was my daughter. It was written up as some kind of safety agreement so no one could kidnap her and etcetera but I knew the real issue. Salih didn't want anyone to know I was his daughter's mother. I only agreed to the rules because I didn't have any money at the time. I was also afraid of the exposure me and my daughter would have if I took it to court. I didn't want her to go through that so I agreed to kept quiet. I didn't want my baby to be in the middle of a nasty battle leaked to the media. I would've looked like the fat baby mama that trapped him. I had to salvage the little bit of dignity I had left. My friends were the only ones who knew about Brooke because I knew I could trust them to keep quiet.

Moments later, I got dressed in a long flowing multicolored maxi dress. I wore a pair of pink and gold studded Givenchy heels. It was hot outside so I styled my long weave up into an updo. I wore a little makeup because of the weather but I made sure my eyebrows stood out. I headed for the door after I checked myself in the mirror again to make sure I was intact. I hit the alarm to my brand new BMV. I didn't drive it much because I did a lot of driving for work and I didn't want to put the mileage on my car. I lived in a decent neighborhood but with the money I had you would've thought I lived in a big house. I saved the majority of the money Salih gave me and used the money I made from my shop. I prepared myself just in case Salih decided to stop being a father. He was a good father but his actions toward me were unexplainable. I feared one day he'd get mad at me and cut Brooke off, he hated me that much.

I pulled up to my best friend, Tyshae's house and she strutted out with a cute two-piece outfit on. Her hair was cut very close to her head and dyed platinum. I called her Amber Rose because of her boy cut. She was light-skinned with hazel eyes and had a piercing in her cheek. She was tall and considered "slim thick." She had a fat butt with a slim figure and nice breasts that sat up perfectly. Tyshae was like my sister; she was there for me through the toughest times. She was also Brooke's godmother.

"I just love these!" she said squeezing my breasts. I smacked her hand away and she giggled.

"Cut that shit out," I laughed.

"Is Saz coming out, too?" Tyshae asked.

"Yes she is and please behave," I said.

"I will but you know how she gets when she drinks. I love her to death but she almost got her ass whipped last weekend. Her attitude is bad," Tyshae laughed.

"Saz just doesn't know how to control her liquor," I replied.

My phone rang while I was pulling off; Salih was calling me and I hated answering his calls because we argued a lot. He always found a way to get under my skin. It seemed as if he planned his days on making me miserable.

"Hello," I answered dryly.

"When is Brooke coming back?" His deep voice blared through the phone.

"In a few days," I replied.

"When is she coming back? In a few days means what? Monday, Tuesday, Wednesday? I need a specific day," he said.

"I said in a few damn days! It doesn't fucking matter when!" I yelled into the phone.

"Shut the fuck up! You ain't shit but a bitter chicken head that needs attention. I see your shit floating around the internet and you know better. My daughter doesn't need to be around that shit. I think I should get full custody," Salih said. I almost swerved off the road.

"WHAT!" I yelled.

"You heard what I said and you know I can do it. I'm actually tired of being nice to you. How many niggas be around her anyway?" Salih asked. Salih claimed he didn't want me but he got mad every time I posted a sexy picture. He called me and made threats because of how tight something was on my body. He always said he was going to take Brooke and raise her properly because I was a whore. I believed he stalked my page. I blocked him but I figured he had another secret account. He also found out about every guy I slept with. I knew it wasn't Brooke who told him about the guys I had over the condo because I didn't bring them around her. Salih was a baby father from hell but the world would've never known. He was always at fundraisers, speaking at schools, and giving to charity. Everyone loved Salih because of his smooth, cocky but nice attitude. If only they knew how fucked up he was in the head. The only person who saw the monster was me.

"What I do is my business as long as I don't do it around our daughter," I replied.

"You better not have that nigga, Aniston around her neither and I mean that shit. I don't trust none of those niggas you fuck from the internet. They might kidnap her for ransom because of me," Salih said. I wanted to laugh but it wasn't funny. He was actually sick in the head.

"Because of you? Nigga, they don't even know you're her father! They also don't know I have a daughter, so what are you trying to say?" I asked, getting pissed off. He got quiet on the other end of the phone before he hung up in my ear.

"Girl, smoke this because you need it. I'm surprised your ass ain't fifty pounds behind his black ass. He complains about every damn thing you do. That man is just jealous over you," Tyshae said.

"What the hell for? He has a perfect Build-A-Barbie at home. He is not concerned about my fat ass. He just wants me to be miserable," I replied.

"Well, we know he wants you to be miserable. I'll have Eron talk to him when he gets back from Spain," she replied. Eron was a professional basketball player and he was also Salih's best friend. All four of us grew up around the same hood. I missed those times but the fame changed it all.

"How many times has Eron tried?" I asked.

"You do have a point. I'm sick of Salih's ass trying to run your life. I cursed him out last week when he came over. He thought it was funny. The bastard is looney," she said and I agreed.

My last stop was at Saz's house. She was waiting in front of her building with her arms crossed because I was late picking her up. Saz acted like she was a celebrity but it didn't bother me; I actually thought it was hysterical. She rolled her eyes at me when she got in the back seat of my car.

"Salih must've called you," Saz said.

"Well, hi to you, too," I replied.

"I was waiting outside for twenty minutes. I was ready to change my mind," Saz said. Saz had the worst attitude and she thought the world owed her something because of the rapper she was messing with. He spoiled her but I figured it was hush money because he was married.

"Next time call a limo," Tyshae joked to get under her skin.

"Next time I just might because I got the money to do it," Saz said.

Saz was beautiful, too; we all were beautiful girls. She was dark-skinned with long, beautiful hair which was all hers. She had an island look to her and her body was amazing. She was about a size sixteen around the hips. Saz's attitude was too diva-like and it made it hard for anyone to get along with her. I met her a few years ago when I did her makeup for a party. We instantly clicked and we have been friends since. Saz wasn't an easy person to understand but underneath it all, she was still a sweet girl. Tyshae has been my friend since ninth grade. We had a solid friendship and I wouldn't trade them for the world.

"We are going to have fun tonight!" I screamed out in excitement.

"My bitch," Tyshae said.

I shook Salih off my shoulder as I headed to the party. All I wanted was to have fun for a little bit without being stressed. I put Salih's number on the block list and blocked his messages. It pissed him off when I ignored him and I planned on doing just that.

Salih
Old Flame

I was chilling in the VIP section with a few of my teammates. The summer pool bash was always the party of the year in Maryland. I tried to call Gautier back but she blocked me. She knew how to get under my skin and at times I wanted to choke her. She played the innocent role but she knew the real reason why I wasn't feeling her. She was popular because of her confidence but she was always that way. I used to tease her in school but it wasn't because of her thick legs and big butt. I liked her but was too embarrassed to admit it because the guys used to talk about her in the locker room. There were also rumors about her being a hoe because she was messing around with older guys around the neighborhood. The rumors didn't stop me, though, because there was something about her I couldn't shake…

Eleventh grade, 2010…

"Nigga, did you see what Gautier had on today? That bitch looked like a Pillsbury doughboy with all of those rolls hanging," one of my friends said.

"She's pretty, though, and y'all are lying. She's not even fat. Her ass and titties are," Eron said.

"Nigga, stop lying. You got the baddest girl in this school, so you don't need to be in this conversation," Eddie replied. They kept talking about girls and who was bad and who wasn't. When I walked out of the locker room, I headed to my class. Gautier was standing in the hallway talking to the same boy that ragged her out in the locker*

room. He was smiling in her face and she was smiling back at him. My blood boiled and I felt myself walking over to them. I pushed Eddie into the lockers and Gautier looked at me like I was crazy. Eddie made it seem as if it was wrong to like her, but he only dissed her because he wanted her to himself.

"What did you do that for? Yo, you are bugging!" Eddie yelled at me. I slammed my fist into his face and Gautier ran to the office to get the principal. I was suspended for five days and that's when I knew I was jealous over her. I was so jealous that I hated her. I told my friends I beat up Eddie because he stole my Jordan's out of my locker. I wasn't going to tell them it was because of Gautier but Eron knew I was in love with her.

"I know Eddie didn't take your Jordan's. You beat him up because he was talking to Gautier," Eron said. It was the weekend and we were sitting in front of my house. I wasn't supposed to be outside because I was punished for fighting in school but my mother was at work. My brother, Damien was supposed to watch me to make sure I didn't go outside or play the game but he was running the streets.

"Nigga, you are bugging. Fuck that bitch, and why do y'all niggas keep talking about her like she's sexy or something?" I asked.

"Some of us think she is, though. Even the ones who talk about her think she is, too. Eddie is her boyfriend. I found that out earlier," Eron said.

"WHAT?" I asked.

"Tyshae told me today that Eddie is Gautier's boyfriend," he repeated.

"Why does he talk about her?" I asked.

"For the same reason you do. He thinks it's cool," he said.

Gautier lived down the street from me. I knew she was outside because she was always outside kicking it with Tyshae or some of the other girls in the neighborhood. I went in the house to put on my shoes and change my shirt. I brushed my waves before I left back out of the house.

"Where are you going?" Eron laughed.

"None of your business," I replied.

We walked down the street and I saw her talking to a few girls. I called her over to me but she didn't want to come.

"Get the hell away, psycho!" Gautier said to me.

I grabbed her by the arm and pulled her away from her friends. She snatched away from me and balled her fist up. I was way taller than her so she couldn't hit me in the face if she tried.

"Why are you messing with that punk, Eddie?" I asked.

"Awww, the most popular boy in school is questioning me," Gautier teased.

"You can't talk to him anymore," I replied.

"Why not?" she asked.

"Because I said so, plus he's a nobody. I'm your boyfriend now," I replied.

"Ewwww," she said.

"You know you like me," I replied.

"Until you started fucking with me in school," she said.

"Okay, I'll stop, but don't talk to nobody and I mean it," I said.

"Be here at seven in the morning to walk me to school. Oh, and you better carry my books, too. I'm not playing, either," she replied...

It wasn't the best way to ask someone out but it worked for me because I knew Gautier liked me. One day, I snatched her journal from her and read it out loud in class. She didn't come to school for a few days afterwards because they teased her. It was childish what I did but I was only sixteen at the time and couldn't handle having a crush on someone everyone talked about. Our teenage love blossomed into something deeper. We were together for four and a half years until she betrayed me. I didn't think my daughter was mine when she was born and didn't acknowledge her until I got drafted into the baseball league. I wanted a blood test after I went pro because I couldn't risk it coming out while I was in the spotlight. Too many people looked up to me and custody battles were always in the public eye. The media normally took the mother's side not knowing the full story. I had reasons why I thought Brooke wasn't my daughter. Gautier wanted everyone to feel sorry for her, so she could justify the number of niggas she fucked. I figured she did the things she did because deep down she was insecure. She was older and still doing the same things she did when she was younger. I thought the love she had for me would've caused her to change but she was worse. Judging by her social network, she stopped caring about herself and still didn't give a shit about me. I was chilling and clowning with my homeboys in VIP until Gautier walked in. The liquor I was drinking went down the wrong pipe. I didn't want her in the same spot as me.

"Bro, are you aight?" one of my teammates asked me.

"Ummm, yeah. It went down the wrong pipe," I replied. I got up and left the section, heading to Gautier. Tyshae tapped Gautier's shoulder to warn her that I was coming. Gautier turned around in shock as if she saw a ghost. Her drink slipped out of her hand and spilled on my Giuseppe sneakers.

"Go the fuck home or I'll drag your dumbass out," I gritted.

"Here we go," Saz said.

"You should know by now how it always goes. She leaves because I said so. Mind your hoe-ass business anyway and Tyshae, you better not say a damn thing to me," I said to Gautier's friends.

"You don't run her life," Tyshae spat.

"Gautier can show you the receipts for that because technically I do. She knows it, too, which is why she isn't saying shit. You have ten minutes to leave before I have someone escort you out," I said to Gautier.

"Ohhhhhhh, I hate his ass," Saz said.

"Let's just go," Tyshae said.

"No, we are staying here. There's too much eye candy in here, so let's party like we came to do," Gautier said.

"Oh really?" I asked.

"Don't cause a scene, Salih. I know you don't want to end up on IG talking to me. They might get the impression that you are a nigga that's on the DL for a chubby girl," Gautier said and her friends laughed.

"This isn't over," I replied before walking away.

I went over to my section and chilled for the remainder of the night. Gautier turned down a few men that wanted to talk to her. Maybe she was getting better with reserving her pussy or maybe it was because I was in the building.

"Is that the girl everyone is making a buzz about?" my teammate, Andy asked. Andy was a straight-laced dude and was a few years older than me. He was mixed with a little bit of everything but I thought he looked Hispanic.

"Yeah, why?" I asked.

"I heard big girls are freaks. I bet she can swallow my dick," Andy said. He was married with two kids but had a record of sleeping with random women. He was always caught up something but his wife was okay with it as long as she could spend his money.

"I think you had too much to drink," I replied and he laughed.

"Come on, bro. I know she's a freak. I know she would love to get fucked by a star. We are in the big leagues and we can do what we want. Who will tell us no? Who would resist being famous for a few minutes?" Andy asked.

"Nigga, I'm not your bro and watch your mouth," I said getting pissed off.

"Just chill out. He's only fucking around," Yudai said.

Yudai was the only one on the team that I considered a homeboy. Everyone else was just a teammate. I didn't invite them to the party but a teammate named Jason did. Andy thought he could say what he wanted to everyone because he had been on the team the longest, but I was waiting for the day to knock his bitch-ass out.

"Go over there and tell that fine slut I want her to come to my room," Andy said to Yudai. I wrapped my hand around his throat and slammed him onto the table that held our drinks. The liquor spilled everywhere and the bottles rolled out of our section. I punched him in the face before three of my teammates pulled me off him.

"Keep running your mouth, muthafucka!" I yelled as they tried to calm me down.

"This is what happens when they let ghetto trash on our team!" Andy said as he wiped the blood off his mouth. I broke away from my teammates and tackled him onto the floor. We fell over the rope and into the crowd. I sent body shots to his face and midsection. Security pulled me off Andy and escorted me out. I knew I was going to sit on the side for the next few games, but Andy had it coming. He was a straight up asshole and niggas was scared to speak up. He was the best player on the team before I came in. He couldn't believe a nigga from the hood came on his team and took over. We always bumped heads but that was the first time I put my hands on him. He had it coming one way or another.

"I'm straight, now get the fuck off me!" I yelled to the bouncer. Yudai told them he was going to make sure I get in my car before they walked away.

"Bruh, we have a big game coming up and this shit is unacceptable. The kids look up to you and they can't see their favorite player fighting a teammate," Yudai said.

"I'm sick of that muthafucka saying shit to me. He had it coming," I replied. I checked my wrist and neck to make sure I had all of my jewelry on. Someone would've gotten lucky with one of my pieces.

"He asked about the Curvy and Chic girl and you went postal. Do you want to tell me what that's about?" he asked.

"It's none of your business," I replied and he held his hands up.

"Aight, cool then, muthafucka," he laughed.

"My bad, bruh. I'm just tripping for no reason. I got a lot of shit going on in my life," I said.

"You nervous about your wedding in a few months?" he asked.

"Yeah," I lied.

My fiancée, Pita, was somebody I ended up with just because. I met her how some other players met their wives. I saw her at a club and I fucked her on the same night. I was new to the league and my name was buzzing. I was young and paid, so it didn't take no time for her to fall in love with me. I didn't feel the same way about her, though. I felt pressured into proposing to her. My fans and everyone else I knew wanted me to marry her and didn't waste any time telling me. One day, we were at the mall and Pita wanted to stop at the jewelry store. She started trying on rings and a fan took pictures of us. Seconds later, people in the mall were surrounding us and asking me if I was proposing. We were being recorded on live, so I proposed. It was a screwed-up situation because I didn't want to get married but I didn't want to embarrass her and look like the bad guy.

"Hit me up in the morning. We still on for the gym tomorrow, right?" he asked.

"No doubt," I said then slapped hands with him.

I got inside my Lamborghini then sped off. Future's song "Used to This" played on the radio and I turned it up. It reminded me of my life. I thought Gautier was going to be by my side when I went pro, but I couldn't forgive her for what she did to me—to us. Not even if I wanted to.

****

I punched the code in to the gate at my mansion before I drove up the hill. I pulled up to the front of my house and sat in my car. I didn't want to walk into my house right away. Gautier sent me a text message asking me if I was okay. I stared at the message for two minutes before I texted her back. My response wasn't a good one but I got into a fight because of her. She should've left when I told her to.

Your hoe-ass should've went home when I told you to! I texted back.

Use Your Heart and Not Your Eyes

She sent me the middle finger emoji and told me that she should've helped Andy kick my ass. I roared in laughter because she always had a comeback. I sent her another message and we went back and forth for almost an hour. She threatened to tell my fiancée how much I harass her. I was ready to respond but there was a knock on my window. Pita was staring at me with her hands on her hips when I looked up.

"Get the hell out of the car!" she yelled at me. I stuck my phone inside my pocket before I stepped out the car.

"What's up?" I asked.

"Andy's wife just called me. Why did you fight him?" she yelled at me. Pita's face barely moved because of the plastic surgery she had. She was gorgeous but she ruined her body. She was only twenty-five years old but looked way over thirty. She had a lot of confidence until I introduced her to the baseball wives. They filled her head up with a bunch of groupie nonsense so she ended up changing herself to keep me from cheating. I dabbled with a few women and I was lucky that they didn't expose me. One of them had a pregnancy scare and I cut her off after that because she was looking for a come-up. Pita loved the attention she got from her new body. A lot of niggas wanted her and a few rappers mentioned her in their songs but I wasn't impressed or jealous.

"The nagging shit is getting old!" I yelled back at her.

"I don't have to be here, Salih! You will respect me and your teammates," she replied.

"What's the worst that can happen if I don't? I can replace you and I can replace my team. Do you know how many teams want me?

Use Your Heart and Not Your Eyes

I don't give a fuck about neither one of y'all right now," I said. I walked out of her face and into the house. She followed behind me yelling and screaming. I went into the kitchen and poured myself a drink. She stood next to the kitchen island with a scowl on her face.

"Did you look over the pre-nup?" I asked.

"Why do you want me to sign it? You want to cheat on me after we get married?" she asked.

"You think I want to lose everything I achieved for myself? I have a daughter that depends on me. None of my shit belongs to anybody! You either sign or no wedding," I said.

"I have my own money!" she screamed and I chuckled.

"Yeah, I'm sure selling waist trainers and skin care products equals to everything I have. No signature, no wedding," I said. I pulled my phone out of my pocket and saw that I had five messages from Gautier. The last message was a picture. It was a picture of her pussy. My phone almost slipped out of my hand but I hurriedly caught it so Pita's nosey ass couldn't see it.

"Who is texting you this late?" she asked.

"Yudai was just checking up on me," I lied.

Gautier sent me another message and she told me she meant to send that to her man. My blood boiled and Pita was giving me a headache. I had to hurry up and get away from her before I caught a domestic violence charge.

"I'm tired of competing with a dead woman," Pita said. For some reason, she thought Brooke's mother was dead because my mother was helping me with Brooke. My schedule got crazy at times and I knew I couldn't rely on Pita to watch Brooke. Pita never met Brooke and never asked to meet her. That's how I knew our relationship was a fraud.

"Goodnight," I replied. I could've corrected Pita but I didn't want to. It would've made my life at home depressing if she knew Brooke's mother was alive.

I went to the basement and locked the door. I took off my clothes and sat on the couch. I wanted to smoke weed but I couldn't until baseball season was over. I needed something to take the edge off and I knew what could. I looked at Gautier's pussy picture and my dick got hard. I tried to think of something else so it could go down but it didn't. I felt like I popped five Viagra pills. I closed my eyes and stroked my dick as I thought about banging Gautier's back out like I used to do. I stroked my package until sperm shot across the room.

"What are you moaning for? Who pussy is wet? Open the damn door, Salih! What the hell are you doing in there? Did you sneak a bitch in my house?" Pita screamed and banged on the door.

"I'm jerking off in peace! Knock on the door again and I'll cancel the Botox appointment you have in the morning!" I shouted back to her.

"Fuck you!" Pita yelled.

The press thought we had a perfect relationship but pictures lie because it's never what it seems. I only slept next to her when I wanted some pussy but most nights I slept in the basement which was set up like an apartment. I had everything I needed: bed, couch, kitchen, bathroom, and Jacuzzi.

I dozed off after Pita stopped crying and knocking on the door like a spoiled brat. I thought about my relationship with Pita and how it wasn't going anywhere. I made my mind up that I wasn't going to marry her. I knew some of our fans would hate me because Pita was going to be a scorned woman. A man can be unhappy and do the right thing by leaving but it still made us look like no good niggas. I wasn't sure if I was ready for all that but I couldn't do this shit anymore. I hated to pull her along and treat her like trash but I wanted her to leave me so I wouldn't get shamed for it. I also wanted her to respond to the thousands of niggas that DM'd her.

****

Me and Andy had to sit out for the next two games. I wasn't tripping over it because it felt good whipping his ass. That nigga said what he wanted and when he wanted. I heard he slept with a few teammates' wives but I didn't know how true that was. I didn't care who he fucked as long as he stayed away from Gautier. Brooke was back home from her vacation and I couldn't wait to see her. As soon as I left my barber, I called my mother. I almost hung up on her when she told me she wasn't home and I had to pick Brooke up from her mother's house.

"You're supposed to be home," I said to my mother.

"Nigga, shut the fuck up. You don't know where I'm at! I could be home but you don't need to know," she spat. My mother was still as hood as they came. She was the opposite of Gautier's mother. Gautier's mother was a decent woman, so I couldn't understand how Gautier turned out to be a thot.

"I swear you know how to fuck up my day," I spat.

Use Your Heart and Not Your Eyes

"You know how to fuck up my sex life. I love my granddaughter and all but I'm tired of this bullshit now. It's getting old and so are you! Grow up and be a man for once. Gautier is a sweet girl and you treat her like she ain't shit. What if Brooke grows up and meets a man like you? How would you feel?" she asked.

"I wouldn't care because Brooke ain't messing with nobody until I'm dead. Stop playing, Ma, and tell me where you at," I said.

"I'm at a hotel room. I been here all weekend. I have a life, too, and it doesn't revolve around yours or Gautier's. I cursed her ass out this morning, too. She told me she didn't want you to come to her house," my mother said. My mother was sleeping with the mail man and she thought nobody knew. Mail men don't deliver mail at midnight. She lied and told me he was running behind on his deliveries the night I caught them in her house.

"She laid up with a nigga or somethin'?" I replied.

"I hope she is so it can send your black ass to the hospital. You need to be anywhere but on my phone right now," my mother said. She hung up in my ear and I made a U-turn in the middle of the street.

"I'm going to merk Gautier's dumb ass and the nigga she's laid up with," I said to myself as I drove to her home.

Gautier
Tell Me You Still Love Me…

"**M**ommy! Daddy is ringing the bell," Brooke shouted from the living room. I was nervous and didn't know what to do. It was Salih's first time stepping foot inside my house. I had to work so I wore a black maxi dress with turquoise accessories. I washed my weave and it air dried. My weave was full and had bushy curls. My makeup was done to perfection and my Tory Burch perfume lingered in the air. Butterflies formed in my stomach when I told Brooke to open the door. I looked in the mirror in the hallway to make sure I looked delectable.

"Hey, Daddy," Brooke said when her father stepped in. Salih was showing off and he knew it. He had on a black fitted tank-top, shorts, and a pair of all black Yeezy's on his feet. His chocolate tatted arms caused me to lick my lips. His cologne filled my nostrils and my nipples turned to pebbles. I hoped he didn't notice because the last thing I wanted was for him to know how much I still loved him. It's hard not loving someone who accepted you for you. Salih is the biggest egotistical asshole on Earth but he wasn't always that way. He teased me when we were younger but he ended up being a sweetheart—well, toward me that is. He was always a jerk to everyone else.

"How was your trip? You didn't call me. I was crushed," Salih said to Brooke. Brooke looked so much like her father it was ridiculous. She had his complexion, his good grade of hair, his nose, eyes, lips, and his smile. He denied her for a whole year before he took the DNA test. It crushed me because he wasn't there when I gave birth to her. I remember the day like it was yesterday…

Use Your Heart and Not Your Eyes

I left cosmetology school early because Salih had been ignoring me and I needed to talk to him. Two hours later, I pulled up to Salih's college and waited for him to walk out. Our relationship became a little distant in his third year of college but him ignoring me was a new behavior and I couldn't deal with it. I got out of my car and sat on the bench. I knew his school schedule because I visited him a few times when we were on good terms. Thirty minutes later, students began walking out of the main door. My heart dropped when Salih walked out with his arm around a girl. The girl was pretty but of course she was. Salih knew what he liked and didn't mind going after it. I stood up from the bench and fixed my jacket. I didn't want to look sloppy in front of his new friend.

"Salih, I need to talk to you," I said. He looked at me like a deer caught in head lights. The girl he was with looked confused, too. He told her to wait by his car while he talked to an "old friend." She smacked her teeth before walking away.

"What in the hell is that?" I asked.

"What are you doing here?" he asked.

"We need to talk," I said.

"What the fuck do we have to talk about?" he snapped at me.

"Where is this coming from?" I asked.

"You are a hoe! You know what the fuck you did!" he yelled at me and I jumped. Tears fell from my eyes because I didn't know what to do. I was nineteen years old and pregnant. It happened during spring break when he came home from school. I was six

weeks when I found out. I kept getting sick and when I went to the doctor's they took samples of my blood. I tried to get in contact with him, but it was hard.

"I understand what happened to your brother but you don't have to treat me like this. You have been treating me like shit since he was killed," I said. Salih's oldest brother was killed at their grandmother's house. His brother was heavy in the streets and got caught up. Salih was angry at the world afterwards. Salih yanked me off the sidewalk and pulled me behind the building. He wrapped his hand around my neck and choked me.

"Bitch, I hate you! I fucking hate you so much that I want to kill you!" he yelled at me with tears in his eyes.

"I loved you and didn't care about what everyone else thought but I should've listened. I should've listened when they told me you were a hoe!" he yelled at me. Tears fell from my eyes as I felt my body go limp. Salih wanted to kill me and I didn't know why. I fell to the ground gasping for air after he let me go. I couldn't catch my breath and he stood over me and watched me with hate-filled eyes.

"I'm pregnant," I said.

"I'm not the father. You just want to pin a baby on me because you know I have a few scouts looking at me for the big leagues. That's not my baby, so stop calling me. You are going to wish that I killed you if you call me again. I have a new bitch now and guess what? She isn't a fat hoe like you," he said and walked off. I cried so hard on my way home that I got into a car accident. My car tipped over and caught on fire. Someone pulled me out in time before it blew up. I broke my arm and leg. The glass from the window was embedded in my skin. A piece of glass was stuck in my cheek and it left a scar. I didn't lose my baby but I lost Salih that day…

"Are you okay, Mommy. Why are you crying?" Brooke asked me. Salih looked at me as if I was crazy and I was. I still loved him though he still hated my guts.

"Yes, I'm fine. I think an eyelash is in my eye. I'll be right back," I said and stormed off. I went into my bedroom and burst into tears. I couldn't get over that day even when I tried. Why did he hate me? Why did he stop loving me? Why did he allow me to be a single, struggling mother for a year before he stepped up? Those were the questions I asked myself every day when I looked at our daughter. My door opened. I forgot to lock it.

"Mommy is fine, Brooke," I said with my back against the door. I came face-to-face with my nemesis when I turned around.

"Brooke wanted me to check on you," Salih said and I rolled my eyes.

"I'm still living so you can get out of my room," I replied. He walked around my room as if he was looking for something. He went inside my walk-in closet and I shook my head. Salih was every bit of looney and he didn't hide it.

"Your ego wouldn't be in my closet if that's what you're looking for," I said.

"I'm sure I can find it between your legs like how every nigga that fucked you found theirs," he fired back.

"Brooke is waiting for you," I said. He leaned against the doorway of the closet and crossed his arms.

"What nigga is fucking you now?" he asked.

"Your father," I said and he flinched.

"Bitch," he mumbled.

"A beautiful one at that and that's why you troll my damn page. You got to be careful because your thirsty ass made a mistake and liked one of my pics. You think I don't know who 'Brooke is number one' is?" I asked and he smirked.

"There's a lot of Brookes in this world. It could've been one of your admirers. I would rather lose my finger than like any of your thirsty pics. I did go on Craigslist, though. I had to make sure you weren't selling your pussy on there," he said.

"Bye," I replied.

Salih's eyes fell upon my legs and he slightly bit his lip. It was a habit he had when I used to strip for him. He still had it, so I knew he was still attracted to me. I lifted my dress and showed him my pink lace panties. I opened my legs for him and he couldn't move. I was taunting him instead of seducing him. I knew that him wanting me made him mad for whatever reason. I just wanted him out of my room and I knew what could shut him up.

"It's still tight and wet for you," I said.

He walked over to me and placed his hand inside my panties. His thumb brushed across my clit and it jumped. She was awakened by that familiar feeling. My body never responded to anyone else the way it did for him. A moan escaped my lips but I didn't mean for it to get that far. I didn't think Salih was bold enough to touch me. He hadn't touched me since he choked me but we also hadn't been alone in the same room since then. He pulled his hand away from me and smelled it.

"I'm good on that shit. I'll bring Brooke home tomorrow morning," he said. He called out to her and she came out of her bedroom. She yelled out "goodbye" to me before they left the house. I rushed to the bathroom and took my panties off. I smelled them and smelled the scent of Dove soap. I slipped a finger inside of my pussy and sniffed and I didn't smell anything.

"BITCH!" I yelled out.

I grabbed my purse and the keys to my truck before I left my condo. It took me an hour to get to my building because of morning traffic. I was greeted by Tyshae and Saz when I walked into the shop.

"Good morning, doll," Tyshae said to me before she kissed my cheek. Saz kissed my other cheek and I was wondering why they were being extra nice. I placed my purse on the counter and crossed my arms.

"Why are y'all being so nice?" I asked.

"I think we should hire someone else to run the boutique upstairs," Tyshae said. We had a boutique that sold clothes for women of all sizes, but everyone's favorite was our lingerie and maxi dresses.

"It's just the three of us and I'd like to keep it that way," I replied.

"My appointments are getting out of hand," Saz said. She was the hairstylist and her clientele was through the roof. She did frontals, cuts, braids and everything else. Tyshae did nails, tattoos, and piercings. Nobody in the area did nails like Tyshae. She had everyone in the city walking around with 3D nails and other crazy but fabulous designs. Our business was called Luxury Tea.

"Dealing with the two of you is enough. We don't need new bitches in our circle," I said.

"I knew her ass wasn't going to like the idea. I should take my kiss back," Tyshae said. The shop was beautifully decorated. The colors were pink, black, and gold. I had black marble floors with gold designs across them. The furniture was black and pink and the chairs were gold. It felt like home and I always made the customers feel welcomed. I had a small bar in the corner of the shop which had the best liquor money could buy. I grabbed my vest with my IG name on it in blinged-out letters. All of our vests had our IG names on them because we did a lot of advertisements on our pages. I went into the kitchen in the back to fix us a cup of coffee to get the morning started. I heard a man arguing, so I left out the kitchen. I knew exactly who it was.

"Why you ain't answer the phone last night? I know you seen me calling your dumb black ass!" Cash Flow yelled at Saz. I rolled my eyes at him and Tyshae smacked her teeth. Cash Flow was a rapper and he was an ugly one at that. He had tattoos on his face and his style was hideous. He wore a pair of shorts with bleach stains and holes. He had on a pair of tennis shoes that looked like silver moon boots and his purple ripped shirt was two sizes too small. Saz was too prissy for Cash Flow so I didn't understand what the hell she saw in the bastard. He was disrespectful and he made a rap song about her called "My Fat Bitch," which topped the charts. It was degrading to women like us but he made a lot of money off it so she wasn't worried. Although Salih was disrespectful, too, Cash Flow took it to a whole other level. He leaked some of Saz's naked pictures but blocked her face. Nobody knew it was her but we found out about it was because she came to work crying one day.

"What are you doing in my shop, punk? And why are you dressed like a runaway teen? Bitch, do you need Dr. Phil or something? This is my place of business and you need to respect it," I said to him.

"Tame your wildebeest, Saz. I know a family in the hood that would love to roast that pig," Cash Flow laughed. Tyshae was frightened by Cash Flow because he rapped about chopping people up and serving crack to his mother. He was the worst guy in the music industry and I hated him.

"Why are you talking to my friend like that?" Saz asked him.

"Your friend? That bitch ain't your friend. She's your boss and I keep telling you to stop working in this bootleg ass store, mall, salon or whatever the hell it is," Cash Flow fussed.

"Take your trash outside and talk to it, Saz. I have an appointment in a few minutes," I said.

"Bitch, do you know who I am?" Cash Flow asked me. I would've slapped his face if his bodyguards weren't guarding the doors from outside. I stared at the laughing emoji tattoo on his face and I couldn't take him serious. I couldn't argue with a grown man with a laughing emoji on his face. It was right underneath his left eye and it was the size of a quarter. I hated the Flavor Flav look-alike.

"Oh, look, it's a shit fly. I wonder why it follows you around," I said and Saz giggled. We always joked about Cash Flow resembling the pile of shit emoji.

"Be at my penthouse tomorrow night at eleven and don't be late. I'm trying to fuck," he said to Saz. He placed a rubber band full of money on the counter in front of her before he left the shop.

"I don't want to hear it," Saz said as I stared at her.

"You let him make a fool out of you. He calls you fat and ugly! Why do you allow that shit?" I asked, getting pissed off.

"I guess Salih has shiny armor," she replied.

"Salih ain't my damn man! I'm not screwing him so he can say what he wants. You are faithful to that piece of shit and he's married for Christ's sake. Not only is he married but he talks about you in his songs," I said.

"He was neglected when he was baby," Saz said.

"We know that by looking at him but that doesn't give him a right to degrade you," I replied. Saz wanted to cry but she held it together. Honestly, it wasn't easy for girls like us to date. I sympathized with gay men because we were in the same boat. I had a few gay friends who dated celebrities but had to keep it a secret because their lovers were ashamed. The media constantly reminded us of what is defined as beautiful and I guess we didn't make the cut. People think it's not a big deal and don't understand why I make a big deal about it, but it's cyber bullying. I could lose the weight but I wanted to make that decision myself, not because of someone else's opinion.

"You deserve better," Tyshae said to Saz.

"What do you know? You don't know what it's like to be like us," Saz snapped at Tyshae.

"I'm not going to argue with you today because you clearly let that punk say what he wants to you, but you always find a way to attack us," Tyshae said to Saz.

Use Your Heart and Not Your Eyes

"You don't understand. You're perfect and you don't know what me and Gautier go through sometimes, so just shut up," Saz replied.

"I'm going to the back to enjoy my coffee. You can stand there and cry over that bug! I'm just being a friend," Tyshae said. She stormed off to the back and slammed the door.

"What the hell was that about?" I asked Saz.

"She doesn't understand our problems, so she shouldn't speak on them," Saz said.

"You need to apologize," I replied.

"I know I do. I'm just so stressed out," Saz said.

Two young Caucasian men walked into my shop with two huge pretty vases of my favorite flowers. I also had a big edible arrangement basket with chocolate-covered bananas. I loved chocolate-covered bananas.

"I'm looking for Gautier," one of the guys said.

"That would be me," I replied.

"These are for you. Can you sign here for me?" he asked after he sat everything down on the counter. He gave me an iPad so I could sign with my finger. I thanked the two gentlemen and gave them a business card before they left. I searched the flowers to see if they had a card but I didn't see one. I figured it was Aniston apologizing to me for being an asshole. I called him and he answered on the fifth ring.

"Thank you for my edible arrangement and my flowers," I beamed.

"What are you talking about? I didn't send you anything. Do you think I would after you treated me like some random guy a few days ago?" he replied.

"Stop playing, Aniston," I said.

"I'm sure one of your other men sent them," he said.

"Have a good day," I said before I hung up. He called back again but I declined his call.

"Who sent them?" Saz asked.

"Salih probably sent them," Tyshae said when she came out the back room.

"Really? You know damn well he hates my guts," I said.

"What man besides Salih knows what kind of flowers and fruit you like? The men you deal with can't get close enough to you to find out what you really like," Tyshae said.

"Aniston probably did it but is being a jack-ass about it," Saz said.

"Yeah, you're right," I replied.

"Good morning," said a voice from behind me. When I turned around, it was Yudai. Yudai was on the same team as Salih. I didn't know much about him but I knew he did a little modeling for Versace men's underwear. He was tall with a caramel complexion.

He was lean but muscular. He had perfect white teeth and his hair was tapered on the sides with a mass of curls in the middle. He looked younger than Salih but I wasn't sure of Yudai's age. All I knew about him was that he was the newest member on the baseball team.

"Good morning. What may I help you with?" I asked.

"Is Saz here? She's supposed to give me two braids. I'm kind of in a rush. I have practice in a few," he said.

"So, you're the one who called an hour ago? I knew your name sounded familiar," Saz said.

"I saw you at the party a few days ago," Yudai said.

"Yup, I was there. Do you need your hair washed?" Saz asked Yudai.

"Yeah," he answered.

"Follow me," Saz said to Yudai.

She strutted to the back of the shop with her ass bouncing in her silk jeggings and it seemed like Yudai enjoyed the view.

"He's a chubby chaser," I whispered to Tyshae.

"How do you know, detective?" she laughed.

"Just watch how he looks at her. Google his ass," I said to Tyshae and she did.

"He's a damn baby, bitch," Tyshae said while scrolling down her phone.

"How old?" I asked.

"He just turned twenty," she replied.

"And he plays baseball in the big leagues?" I asked.

"Julio Urias who plays for the Dodgers was signed after his sixteenth birthday," Tyshae said.

Me and Tyshae stood behind the counter and watched Yudai lust over Saz. Saz dropped a comb on the floor and she reached down to get it. Yudai grabbed his dick and bit his bottom lip while getting a full view of Saz's ass.

"Oh no he didn't. Who taught his young ass how to do that? I bet he's very nasty, too," Tyshae asked.

"I don't know but Saz knows damn well she dropped that on purpose," I laughed. I loved my girls and they got me through the toughest times. Salih pissed me off earlier but it was all forgotten as I laughed and joked around with Tyshae. Yudai paid Saz after she was finished with his hair.

"Can I take you out tomorrow night?" Yudai asked Saz.

I was angry for him because I knew she was going to turn him down. She had to be at Cash Flow's penthouse so he could screw her any way he felt like it.

"I can't mix business with pleasure," Saz said and I rolled my eyes.

"Who said anything about that? Maybe I just wanted to talk to you," he said and Tyshae fanned herself. I elbowed her because she was making it obvious that we were listening.

"I have something to do tomorrow night but I'm free the day after," Saz said.

"We can do that," he replied with a smirk on his face. They exchanged numbers before he left the shop. Saz looked out the window to see what he was driving.

"He's driving a Porsche Panamera," Saz beamed.

"Stop it, Saz," I said.

"You know the car game gotta be proper in order for Saz to cruise the streets in it," she replied.

An hour later, the shop got busy. It was so busy that we didn't close until midnight. I finally broke down and decided to get someone else in. I wasn't into doing hair but I helped Saz out when she overbooked herself. I did the shampooing and other small things for her. I also had to ring up the customers in the boutique and I had six clients that needed their makeup professionally done. I really couldn't complain because the money was better than ever. My feet were sore and my eyelids were heavy as I drove home but it was just another day at the shop.

****

I fell out of bed when I heard someone knocking at my door and ringing my doorbell. I looked at the clock and realized I overslept. I didn't have any morning appointments but I still had to go in early to help Saz and Tyshae. I grabbed my robe and rushed to the door. It was Salih and Brooke. I had a scarf tied around my head and I didn't wash my face.

Ugghhhhh, why did he have to catch me like this? I asked myself. I covered my mouth to keep from laughing because Brooke's ponytails were a mess. Salih tried to do her hair and it was a huge fail but I thought it was cute. I told Brooke to go to her room so I could talk to her father in private.

"I think it's time we are adults about this situation," I said.

"Pause this conversation until after you brush your teeth. I ain't got shit else to do, so I'll wait," Salih said. I walked away and headed for my bedroom. I did more than brush my teeth. I took a shower and got dressed. I wore a black linen romper with gold and black zebra print ballerina shoes. I had to be comfortable for the long day ahead of me. Brooke was in the living room watching TV with her father.

"Who combed her hair?" I asked Salih although I knew he did.

"Who else?" he replied.

"Your fiancée should learn how to do little black girl's hair, right?" I asked.

"I think Daddy did a good job," Brooke said and Salih smiled. She was happy about her Alfalfa hairstyle.

"Daddy got this," Salih said and Brooke slapped hands with him. My cell phone rang and it was Aniston calling me. I hit the *ignore* button and he called again. I answered because he was going to keep calling if I didn't.

"What is it?" I asked.

"I'm outside of your building. Whose Lamborghini is that?" Aniston asked.

"I don't know but what did I tell you about popping up unannounced. My daughter is home and you cannot meet her. We had this damn discussion before. We fuck each other and that's it. Why do you feel the need to pop up whenever you feel like it?" I whispered into the phone as I walked down the hallway.

"We need to talk about this relationship," he said.

"What relationship? You are embarrassed by me, so what do we need to talk about?" I asked.

"If you think that then why do you let me fuck you?" he asked.

"Because that's all I want from you, so therefore I don't give two fucks about how you feel about me. Did that answer your question?" I asked.

"This conversation isn't over," he said and hung up. Salih was standing behind me when I turned around.

"You still haven't changed one bit. Why is my daughter exposed to this shit? Do you think it's safe for her? Your niggas are not supposed to know where you live at all! Meet them at a hotel or something," Salih whispered.

"Stop trying to run my life," I replied.

"Who else is going to run it for you? You do stupid shit," he fussed. I peeked around him and Brooke was still watching TV. Salih made it so hard for me that at times I wished I was a single parent. He treated me like I was a deadbeat mother.

"Let's not forget how you were absent from her life for a year. I guess you're parent of the year," I said. I struck a nerve because he pushed me into my bedroom and locked the door.

"I wouldn't have had to be gone for a year if you didn't fuck another nigga! The same nigga that killed my brother!" Salih yelled at me.

"I didn't know he did it!" I yelled back at him.

"Which could've been avoided if you kept your legs closed. You fucked him and I saw it. I was away at school thinking I had a loyal girl. I came to your house thinking you missed me but I caught a nigga fucking you," Salih said. Sisco was a guy that I started talking to while Salih was in college. I let my insecurities get the best of me and I was stupid. Sisco was an older street guy and he was always into something. I didn't know he was the one responsible for Damien's death. I didn't know Salih saw us until he took a DNA test...

"Why do you hate me so much?" I asked Salih while holding Brooke in my arms. We were standing outside of the paternity test building.

"You really don't know what you did?" he asked.

"Tell me," I said.

Use Your Heart and Not Your Eyes

"I can't believe your hoe ass. That baby is saving your life right now because you would be dead if you weren't holding her," Salih said.

"What are you talking about?" I asked.

"May 8th," he said.

"What about it?" I asked.

"Yeah, you're a hoe if you don't remember you fucked a nigga that day. I came home to surprise you and I caught one alright. It was feeling good to you, too. It was so good that you didn't notice I was in the fucking room! I wanted to hurt the both of y'all, but I wasn't trying to sit behind bars over loose pussy," he said. Salih knew where my mother kept the spare key hidden outside of the house for emergencies. He also used it to sneak in while my mother was asleep.

"I was already pregnant when I slept with him," I said with my head down.

"More of a reason why I hate you. I hate myself for even loving you. I don't want shit to do with you and I mean it. I hope that baby isn't mine. Matter of fact, she looks like that nigga, Sisco," Salih said. He cursed me out and caused a scene as I walked to my mother's car. Brooke was sleeping peacefully in my arms. I drove home in tears but I made sure to focus on the road. My mother was standing on the steps waiting for me to pull up. I ran to her and cried on her shoulder when I got out of the car.

"He hates me," I cried to my mother as she rubbed my back...

Use Your Heart and Not Your Eyes

"When will you forgive me? I'm begging you to just forgive me. I can't live like this anymore. It's not right for Brooke and you know it," I said.

"Give me full custody then it might go away. I don't want her to see a bunch of niggas in and out of her life. I don't want her to be like you," he said and it was a low blow.

"You think I'm a bad person for that one mistake? I was young and I was going through a phase," I replied.

"You were supposed to be there with me when I got drafted. We made plans together and you fucked it up for a nigga that didn't love you. He told everybody what he did to you and how easy it was. It was on Facebook! He had a naked picture of you on there. Another picture of you sucking his dick. The whole time you were carrying my daughter. I get so mad when I think about what you did. I couldn't allow your fuck-ups to be attached to my career so I disowned you. It's no hard feelings, though. I'd rather chase a check instead of chasing an ungrateful slut," Salih said. I sat on my bed and stared at the wall. Salih kneeled in front of me.

"Did you know Sisco was going to kill my brother?" Salih asked for the hundredth time.

"I didn't know they had beef. I loved Damien as a brother and you know that. I didn't know Sisco was responsible until after he was caught. Please believe me," I said. Salih stood up with anger on his face. Sisco killed Damien a little after we slept together. I met Sisco at a house party and he seemed like a cool guy. Salih was away at college and I let my insecurities get the best of me. I slept with Sisco one time and it was the day Salih saw us. It was my first and only time cheating on him and I was still paying for it. If I knew Sisco and Damien had a drug war going on, I wouldn't have gotten involved with him. I was so naïve to a lot of things but I would never intentionally cause Salih's family any harm.

"I don't believe you. You straight up played me," Salih said. He left my bedroom then out of my condo.

God, please forgive me for turning Salih into the devil, I thought. I walked into my closet and pulled out a box from the top shelf. I opened the box and there was a picture of me and Salih at Six Flags. He had his arm around me and I had the biggest smile on my face. My hair was bushy because of the water ride we had just gotten off of. I still had the note he wrote me when he was in twelfth grade...

My Boo,

I know I wasn't the nicest person to you but that's because I liked you. I don't care what we go through just don't change nothing! I like everything about you but your personality is my favorite trait. I know I sound corny so don't show Tyshae this shit. We have been together for over a year now and I still can't believe how I asked you to be my girl. You just went with the flow but I'm glad you did, though. I was going to tell you last night when we were at the movies but I didn't know how to say it. I just want to tell you that I love you and I want you to be mine forever. I want you with me wherever I go. I love you with my heart and not my eyes, although you are beautiful. You got me forever.

Your nigga,

Salih

P.S. You better not show Tyshae this shit, neither. I still gotta keep my swag up and I can't be out here looking like Shakespeare and shit. You can tell her I love you, though, with her nosey ass.

The letter had missing words because my tears made the ink run. I read it so much that I could say it backwards. I had true love but I didn't have true love for myself at the time. I thought Salih was going to go off to college, become famous, and forget about me, so I hurt him before he could do me. Sadly, I didn't know how insecure I was until Salih stopped coming around. I messed up a good thing and I prayed I could be forgiven. It was almost five years ago but the hurt and pain was still fresh. It was because we were still in love with each other and the pain wasn't going to go away until we found peace.

Saz
Finding Myself

I watched Cash Flow pace back and forth in his living room with a blunt hanging from his mouth. The sight of him made my stomach turn and I couldn't understand how I fell in love with him. I met him a year and a half ago at a club. I walked past his VIP section on my way to the bathroom and he spotted me. I knew about the rapper but I wasn't checking for him or his music until his assistant contacted me the next day. I don't know how he got my number, but he found me. At first, I thought it was a prank because I didn't expect a rapper on his level to look my way. When he told me to FaceTime him, I knew it was real. Let's just say Cash Flow had a secret obsession with plump girls. Gautier called them DL men because some of them were embarrassed about liking big girls. The media had a way of destroying us and making us feel like outcasts. Gautier broke through it because of her confidence. I wish I had the confidence she had—I take that back. I used to have the confidence she has until I got to know the real Cash Flow. He was nice in the beginning but he got used to me. Let's just say he used to treat me like a queen but that all changed. He became obsessive, violent, and out of control.

"I keep telling you to stay away from that bitch, Gautier! She just wants you to be like her by showing your body and all of that shit. She wants people to make fun of her. I guess she ain't tired of the memes," Cash Flow fussed. He was insecure because I had a friend like Gautier. He would've been more comfortable if I didn't have any friends at all. Cash Flow hated anyone who I confided in.

"My friend is not a bitch!" I yelled at him. He slapped me in the mouth and yanked me by the hair.

"I'll kill you if you ever in your life disrespect me again. I made you and I can break you! I want you to quit working at that trashy shop. It's taking too much of your time. I told you to be here at eleven and you got here three minutes late," he gritted. I snatched away from him and grabbed my purse.

"I can't do this anymore," I said. He snatched my purse from me and dumped everything inside on the floor.

"Carry that shit in your pouch with your kangaroo stomach. I bought this shit and you ain't leaving here with it," he gritted.

"I bought that purse with my money, so give it back!" I yelled at him. He slammed it into my face and the strap cut across my lip. I tasted blood in my mouth and my bottom lip went numb. I held my mouth as water filled my eyes.

"Why do you have to make me so mad? I only want to spend time with you before I catch my jet tomorrow morning. I'm sorry, Saz. I just love you so much and sometimes it makes me go crazy. I don't want you showing my goods off and acting all cute about it. You might leave me if you figure out how beautiful and perfect you are. I got to do this so you can know your place," he pleaded.

I knew at that moment how pathetic I was for him to feel comfortable saying that shit to me. The money, the shopping sprees, and the good sex meant nothing to me anymore. I wanted my old life back but it seemed as if I couldn't get rid of him. He had enough money to ruin my life, so I was afraid. He did it before when I left him. He leaked pictures of me and did a diss song about me. I had to go back before he leaked more photos or videos of me. One video was of me tossing his salad. The thought of it almost made me vomit.

Why did I do this to myself? I thought.

"I don't feel so good," I said.

"Baby, what's wrong? Talk to me? I'm so sorry! What do you want me to do? I can buy you that new Birkin bag if you want it," he said. I fell out on the floor and pretended I was having a seizure. I managed to drool as my body shook uncontrollably. Cash Flow began to panic as my body convulsed.

"Wake up! I didn't hit you that hard. I can't call the ambulance up here! Everybody would know that I have a side-chick. My wife would take all of my money," he said. I had him shook so I stopped after a few seconds. He kneeled next to me and hugged me.

"I'm sorry, baby. Do you forgive me?" he asked.

"I need to go home and rest. You don't want me to get sick up here again, do you?" my voice dragged.

"Yeah, you might want to go home and hurry up. I can't have this type of heat on me," he said. He put everything that fell out of my purse back and helped me put my shoes on. He walked me to the door and told me to call him as soon as I got home. I caught the elevator from the sixteenth floor to the lobby and walked out the main entrance. The valet driver pulled up in my black 2017 Tesla. It was a gift from Cash Flow after I had an abortion. I had an abortion after he got married. I thought him and his girlfriend was broken up at the time when we started dating. Months later, he popped up married. He had a secret wedding in Dubai. I was so humiliated and I should've left him then but I was already in love. Judge me if you want, but every girl dreamed about experiencing that lifestyle. Cash Flow showed me a world that I thought didn't exist for girls like me. I wasn't a singer or an actress, so how else was I going to experience the lavish lifestyle? I learned what glittered wasn't gold the hard way. Gautier tried to warn me but she had issues herself. She didn't care about love. She didn't care how men felt about her because she said they were only good for sex. Gautier was headstrong but she allowed Salih to crush her spirit. I didn't know much about their past because she didn't like talking about it. All I knew was that Salih to Gautier was like salt to a slug. I checked my lip in the mirror and I had a small cut. I used a wet wipe to clean it off before I put on dark, red lipstick.

I headed to MGM casino in Fort Washington which wasn't far from Cash Flow's secret home. I needed a drink and I also wanted to gamble. I didn't call my friends because I didn't feel like hearing, "I told you so." It was easier said than done. I was afraid of being exposed to the point where my whole existence would become non-existent. Being leaked and dragged on social media was the hardest thing to recover from. A few people even committed suicide because of the pressure. I had to figure out something and fast before I became a woman who was permanently stuck with an asshole. I pulled up to valet parking and stepped out of my car. I strutted inside the casino with a sense of relief. I wore a pair of black palazzo pants with slits in the middle. My pink off-the-shoulder wrap top showed a perfect amount of cleavage. My black and pink studded-toe stiletto heels clicked across the floor. I added an extra sway to my hips so my voluptuous backside could bounce. My hair was styled with flexi rods. I had a curly bang which stopped above my eyes with platinum tips. I sat at the bar and ordered a drink. A guy came up to me and he smelled like cigarettes. I was automatically turned off.

"I'm married," I said to the stranger.

"My bad, shorty. I can still buy you a drink, though," he replied.

Use Your Heart and Not Your Eyes

"No thanks, my husband wouldn't like that," I replied and he walked away. The stranger was cute and had on clean clothes but cigarette smoke seemed dirty when it lingered on your clothes. I loved to smell a man who wore nice cologne. Gautier texted me to check up on me. She treated me like a child. Matter of fact, her and Tyshae both did. Maybe it was because I was younger than them by a few years. I was only twenty-one but I liked older men. I didn't like to date guys my age, but then again, I should've. Cash Flow was almost eight years older than me and he was the worst.

"Can I sit here?" someone asked me and I smacked my teeth.

"I guess so," I replied.

"So, you skipped out on a date with me to hang out here?" he asked. Yudai was staring down at me when I glanced up. He looked like a snack! He looked good when he came in the shop the day before but he was looking better than that. His cologne was enough to send me into an orgasm.

"This was last-minute. What are you doing here?" I asked.

"Kicking it with my cousins before my away game in a few days," he said. His eyes roamed over my body as he smirked.

"I dig your style. It's hood but classy. Your hair is beautiful by the way. I love when a female can sport her real hair," he said.

"Who said it was real?" I asked.

"I have sisters. I know lace fronts and all that other shit when I see it," Yudai said and I laughed.

"I make my own hair products so that it can be healthy without a perm. I'm thinking about selling them but I don't know if it would work for everyone else. I'm nervous about it," I said.

"We all get nervous about something but you won't know the results if you don't take a chance. You can test it on my hair if you want to," he said.

"How old are you?" I asked.

"Come on, Saz. Don't fuck with me. You know my age and my whole name. It's in my Wikipedia," he said and I rolled my eyes.

"I guess because you are mature for your age," I replied.

"I gotta be. I'm not trying to get into anything that can ruin my career. I'm a young nigga from Baltimore who got lucky by getting drafted into MLB. Too many of us are dying, so I thank God every day that I made it and pray for others to do so, too," he said. I ordered another Patrón on the rocks but I noticed Yudai didn't order anything.

"You don't drink?" I asked.

"Not when I have practice in the a.m.," he said.

"I will drink for the both of us then," I replied.

"Excuse me, are you Yudai Hasan?" a Caucasian woman asked. She was with a group of girls, and they all had the name "Groupie" written across their foreheads.

"Yeah," Yudai replied.

"Can we have an autograph?" she asked and lowered her shirt. I wanted to say something, but I couldn't because he wasn't my man. I turned my head and continued to sip my drink. I was bothered that the dumb bitch didn't know if I was his woman or not, but groupies don't care.

"I want one right here," her other friend said. All of them pulled their shirts down. Yudai took a few napkins off the bar and signed them. If looks could kill, he would've been dead. He passed the napkins around to the small group of girls.

"Can you take our picture?" the blonde ringleader asked me.

"Sure," I replied.

They stood around by Yudai as I took the picture. I gave the phone back to her and she scurried away.

"She can't wait to post it on social media. Why didn't you sign the boobs?" I asked Yudai.

"Salih told me not to. He said groupies be filing sexual harassment reports for money. I don't touch them and I keep my hands in front of me when I take pictures so it can look friendly. I don't got time for that shit," he said.

"Interesting," I said.

"I might take a chance with you, though," he flirted.

"Do you have a girlfriend? I know you do," I said.

"Naw, no shorty at the moment. What about you? Are you single? I wouldn't care if you weren't, though. I'll be the perfect side-nigga. I'm always on the road, so I won't be in the way," he said. I doubled over in laughter.

"I'm serious, though, and you playing," he said.

"I'm single," I replied and he nodded his head.

"What type of women do you like?" I asked.

"Down to earth, pretty face, pretty hands and feet. She gotta be street and book smart. I love a good personality, too," he replied.

"What don't you like?" I asked.

"A woman who acts tough like she doesn't want a nigga or push a nigga away for something another nigga did. That shit burns me hot. Why am I being punished for something another muthafucka did?" he said.

"What about insecure women?" I asked and he chuckled.

"All women are insecure. Some just got it worse than others. Are you insecure or something?" he asked.

"Am I supposed to be?" I spat.

"No need for the attitude, damn. Are you insecure? You can tell me. I won't tell nobody," he chuckled.

"I wish I was a little smaller," I said and he laughed. I was ready to slap him off the stool because he was pissing me off.

"That is not funny!" I said.

Use Your Heart and Not Your Eyes

"Naw, it's not funny. I'm just surprised you said that shit. I'm going to be honest with you. I was watching you from across the room before I came over here. I saw this thick lil' shorty with a fat ass and I told myself I know that walk from somewhere. My cousins were looking at you, too. Shid, the whole table was looking at you. You don't seem like an insecure woman to me. You walked in this casino like it was yours," Yudai said.

"I don't know what's wrong with me. I just haven't been feeling like myself," I said. I was surprised at how easy it was for me to open up to Yudai, but he was easy to talk to. I didn't have to explain myself as much I had to with Gautier and Tyshae.

"Just don't stop looking sexy for me," he said. My stomach growled. I needed to eat something. It was late and not many restaurants were open.

"I need to feed my face. I can't drink this on an empty stomach," I said.

"Are you inviting me?" he asked.

"Of course," I replied.

"Aight, cool," he said.

People stared at us as we headed down the escalator, mainly women. Yudai wasn't focused on anyone but me and I liked that. It had been a while since a guy seemed more interested in conversation than what was between my legs. I headed to the burger spot which had the best burgers. I wanted one with cheese fries on the side. Yudai ordered my food for me while I waited at the table. My phone rang and it was Cash Flow calling. The ringtone was his latest song, "Cash me in the Club."

"You listen to Cash Flow?" Yudai asked when he sat across from me.

"Yeah, sometimes. Do you listen to his music?" I asked.

"Fuck naw. I tell my teammates not to play that shit around me before a game. His music is bad luck. I hate to diss another nigga's talent but he turned rap into a joke. Nigga be wearing leggings and shit. His bars are trash and the only thing that's catchy is his beats," Yudai said.

"Who do you listen to?" I asked.

"Kendrick, J. Cole, Yo Gotti, Jeezy, Drake, and my big homie Ross," Yudai said.

"Great taste," I replied.

We made small talk until my food was ready. Yudai came back with two trays. Two big burgers and two cheese fries were on his tray.

"You can eat all that?" I asked.

"Yeah. I'll burn it off tomorrow and I only do it once a week," he said.

I placed hot sauce on my burger before I cut it and Yudai chuckled.

"Girl, if you don't eat that shit properly. Let me try some of this," he said and took the hot sauce. He drenched his burger in it. He choked after he bit into it.

Use Your Heart and Not Your Eyes

"Damn, this is spicy but it's good," he said.

I sat back in my chair and rubbed my stomach; I was bloated and full.

"I'm going to burst," I replied.

"Want me to rub your stomach for you?" he asked.

"Your fans might get the wrong idea. They might think I'm carrying a baby or something," I said.

"I don't care what people think because I don't have to answer to that shit," he replied.

"My friend, Gautier is the same way," I said.

"The girls at the shop are close friends of yours?" he asked.

"They are my best friends. Sorta like my older sisters," I replied.

Yudai walked me outside an hour later. We talked about a lot of things and he was a big flirt. He flirted so much that it gave me a bad case of butterflies. I couldn't stop blushing if I wanted to. I gave my ticket to valet and Yudai waited with me for my car.

"I enjoyed my time with you," I said.

"We still on for tomorrow night, right?" he asked.

"Yup. I'll be ready by nine," I replied.

"What do you want to do?" he asked.

"I want to see the new Transformers movie," I said.

Use Your Heart and Not Your Eyes

"Awwww, shit. You like the Transformers, too?" he asked.

"I love them! Me and Bumblebee are together in the world of Cybertron," I said and he laughed.

"Now I gotta be jealous of that nigga?" he asked and I giggled. The valet driver pulled up in my car. I didn't want to leave but I couldn't seem thirsty either.

"Hit me up and let me know you made it home safe," Yudai said.

"Okay," I replied and stepped off the curb. He grabbed my arm and I turned around.

"Can I get a hug?" he asked.

You will get more than a hug if you keep looking at me like that, I thought. I stood on my tippy toes and wrapped my arms around his neck and he squeezed me.

Clean up in aisle seven! There is a spill in the aisle, my panties said.

"Damn, you feel good," he whispered in my ear. I pulled away from him and he winked at me.

"I'll be waiting for that call, beautiful," he said.

I waved at him as I got in the car. I called Gautier as soon as I pulled out into traffic.

"Hello," she yawned into the phone.

"Wait a minute, I have to call Tyshae," I replied. I called Tyshae on three-way. After their calls merged, I screamed into the phone.

"Here she goes with the dramatics. You know you should be an actress," Tyshae laughed. I told them every little detail about my run-in with Yudai.

"Bittccccccccchhhhhh, give him the eggs!" Tyshae said.

"It's too soon," Gautier said.

"Who cares? I just want a reason for Cash Flow to commit suicide," Tyshae said and Gautier screamed in laughter.

"I was ready to give him the whole dairy aisle when he hugged me. His cologne is still on me," I said, sniffing my shoulder.

"That's what you call a man! Cash Flow smelled like lollipops and strawberry bubbles earlier," Gautier said.

"That nigga's nails were painted to the gods," Tyshae said.

"Enough about him. I called to talk about Yudai," I said.

"Spill the tea," Gautier said.

"So, we're going to the movies tomorrow night. What should I wear?" I asked them.

"A maxi dress. Matter of fact, a few were just shipped to my house. I want you to model them for me so I can post it on our IG business page," Gautier said.

"Maxi dresses are a man's best friend. Don't wear any panties underneath it," Tyshae said. I talked to my friends until I arrived home. Cash Flow called my phone as soon as I hung up with them.

"Hello," I groggily answered.

"I thought you were sick?" he asked.

"I was," I replied.

"Why in the fuck is there a picture of you hugging that punk-ass baseball player, Yudai?" he asked.

Damn, that was fast! I thought.

"He's a client of mine. I ran into him at the casino," I replied.

"Naw, that nigga was hugging you like you're his woman!" Cash Flow screamed into the phone. I wasn't as popular as Gautier but I did have a decent number of followers on Snapchat and IG. Everyone in the DMV area knew we were the girls with the popping shop, so it didn't take any time for someone to identify me.

"I have a headache," I replied.

"Bitch, I'm going to give you a real one if you don't stay away from that nigga. He ain't shit but a pretty boy anyway. I'll have one of my niggas fuck his bitch-ass up so he can't play baseball anymore," Cash Flow said.

"Is that all you wanted?" I asked.

"I will kill you! I will fucking kill your non-worthy piece of ass!" he yelled into the phone.

"Goodnight," I replied. I hung up the phone and he called back ten times but I didn't answer. I was too emotionally drained and I couldn't deal with him. I took a long hot bath with a bottle of wine. I couldn't believe how much I lost myself in a man—a man who didn't appreciate me.

The next day...

I walked into the shop the next morning and there was a vase of flowers sitting at my station. Tyshae looked at me and chuckled.

"What?" I asked.

"You really need to leave Cash Flow alone. He does this all the time. He treats you like garbage and you deserve so much more," Tyshae said. I read the card next to the flowers and it was nothing but a weak-ass apology. I dropped the flowers and the card in the trash can.

"We got your back," Tyshae said.

"I know, but I need to start having my own back. How can I love myself but let this happen to me? I'm just fed up," I replied.

"Nothing lasts forever," she said.

The bell above the door chimed and it was Gautier. She walked into the shop with iced coffees from Starbucks. She looked pissed off about something. She slammed the coffees down on the counter and threw her purse into the wall.

"What's up with you?" I asked.

"I want to fucking scream! I want to kill him!" Gautier said.

"Salih?" I asked.

"Yes, that nigga! Why is he making my life a living hell? He told me I had to move from my condo this morning. He said it wasn't a safe place for our daughter. I don't want him to take me to court, so I'm going to move, but why is he controlling my life?" Gautier asked.

"He still loves you, but I honestly think he cares about your safety. He doesn't want you to know he does, so he says things to hurt you," Tyshae said to Gautier. Gautier was ready to respond but the door to the shop swung open. Salih stormed in wearing gym clothes. I remembered Yudai saying they had practice in the morning. It was my first time seeing him at the shop, so I knew he was really mad.

"Talk all that bullshit you were talking over the phone! You want to move my daughter to another state away from me?" Salih yelled at Gautier.

"This isn't healthy for her and you know it!" Gautier yelled at him.

"Healthy? You think fucking random niggas around her is healthy?" Salih asked Gautier.

"This is our place of business," I said to Salih.

"Mind your business, Saz! And Tyshae, don't say one damn word to me!" Salih yelled at us. I sat back in my chair and crossed my arms. Tyshae grabbed her phone and went to the back. I knew what she was up to. She was calling her man which was Salih's best friend to tell on him. Salih was out of hand and it was getting worse. He was too controlling over Gautier.

"Can we talk about this later?" Gautier asked.

"Naw, we can talk now. Is this what you wear to work?" he asked Gautier.

Niggas, I thought.

Gautier wore a white pencil skirt with a sleeveless jean top that showed her cleavage. The outfit looked great on her and the red pumps she wore made it pop. Gautier was breathtakingly beautiful and Salih couldn't help himself. I could sense the attraction and the love they still had for one another. Gautier didn't want a man and Salih had everything to do with that.

"Again, you're worried about the wrong woman! Your fiancée is always half-naked. Worry about her and leave me the fuck alone before I expose your black ass," Gautier fussed.

"You got thirty days to be out of that condo and I mean it. I don't mean in another state, neither. Don't make this turn ugly," Salih warned Gautier. When he turned to leave, Gautier threw her iced coffee at the back of his head. I covered my mouth to keep from laughing.

"I'll move when I'm ready, punk," she yelled at him. Salih angrily snatched the door open and left the shop.

"Now that's how you handle a disrespectful man," Gautier said.

"I see Salih is not caring anymore. He came to the shop knowing this place gets popping and someone could've seen him," I said.

Use Your Heart and Not Your Eyes

"Salih is crazy. He doesn't think when he's mad. He has always been that way," Gautier replied. She grabbed a mop to clean up the mess she made from throwing the drink at Salih. The door opened and a blonde-haired Asian girl walked in.

"I was wondering if y'all needed help? I lost my job this morning," she said.

"What's your name?" Gautier asked her.

"Lisa," she replied.

"What do you do, Lisa?" I asked.

"Hair, nails, makeup, and anything else you want me to do. I don't know how to braid but I do know how to use a curling iron really good," she replied. It was perfect because we needed someone to help us around the shop.

"You can hang around here for the day. It doesn't mean you got the job yet. I need to see your work," Gautier said. I introduced myself to Lisa. I walked to the back room to tell Tyshae about Lisa but she was arguing with someone on the phone.

"I know you are cheating on me! Tell me the truth, Eron! Is it Latasia again? Your Russian lover?" she asked. I backed away from the room because I didn't want to hear any more. I didn't know Tyshae was having problems with her fiancé. They seemed like the perfect couple but that's only because I was on the outside looking in. I wanted to know why she didn't tell us about their problems. She was always playing the relationship doctor but she didn't have the perfect relationship herself.

"Earth to Saz," Gautier said while I was in deep thought.

"Sorry, I was thinking about what I wanted to wear for my date tonight," I lied.

"That's right, I want you to try on the maxi dresses so I can post them on our page. I know they are fittin' to sell like hotcakes. Tell Tyshae to come on because I want to show how they look in different sizes," Gautier said. Tyshae came from the back room with red eyes.

"Are you okay?" I asked.

"Yeah, I was spraying air freshener and it got in my eyes," she lied.

"My name is Lisa and it's nice to meet you," she said to Tyshae.

"She's going to help us today. I want to see her work before I hire her," Gautier said to Tyshae. My phone beeped and it was a text message from Yudai. I blushed as I read it; he wished I had a great day and he couldn't wait to see me later. I laughed when he texted me and told me to put sandwiches in my purse for the movie. He was so down to earth that it attracted me to him even more. I texted him until my clients came into the shop. It was a usual busy work day for us and Lisa wasn't bad at all. She did nails and a few blow-outs. If I closed my eyes and listened to her talk, I would've thought she was a black woman. Gautier gave her a job within a few hours because she was impressed. Tyshae was antisocial and I couldn't hold it in any longer. I pulled her to the corner away from everyone.

"I don't want you to think I'm being nosey but I heard you yelling at Eron. Why didn't you tell us he was cheating on you?" I asked.

"Because he isn't. I just keep accusing him of things because he's always away. Eron is a good man, so forget we talked about this," she said and stormed away from me.

What in the hell just happened? I thought.

Hours later...

Yudai pulled up to my building in his yellow Camaro. I opened the passenger side door and the scent of his Givenchy cologne filled my nostrils. *Damn, he always smells good,* I thought. I wore a Transformers shirt with a pair of distressed jeans, and on my feet were a cute pair of Yeezy's. It was nine o'clock and Yudai was on time. *And he's punctual. Damn, he's perfect,* I thought.

"We are nerds," I said. I saw two platinum diamond caps in the bottom row of his mouth. Diamond grillz was a big thing in the Maryland area and everyone had them. I even had a set but I wore them when I wanted to be extra.

"Do you have my sandwiches?" he asked.

"Yup, I made us soft crab sandwiches. I also have a container in my purse with shrimp salad," I replied.

"Awwww, shit! A shorty that ain't selfish," Yudai said. My phone rang and it was Cash Flow calling me. I went to his contact and blocked him. I didn't need him disturbing me while I was on a date—a real date.

"How was practice?" I asked.

"It was cool. We had to practice for an extra hour because Salih wasn't focused. I don't know what's up with him," Yudai laughed.

He was probably in his feelings about Gautier, I thought.

We talked until we reached the movie theater at Arundel Mills mall. I was skeptical about it because I was expecting something low-key since Yudai was a professional athlete. I was aware of the consequences of being out with him, so I enjoyed it while it lasted. Cash Flow wasn't going to be happy about it but I deserved happiness although it was only temporary. Yudai used valet to park his car in front of the theater. After we stepped out of the car, he grabbed my hand. We walked inside the mall hand-in-hand like a couple. He wasn't afraid to let people know who he was interested in; he scored more brownie points with me. Yudai seemed perfect but I knew he had a flaw. He was too good to be true. The movie had already started but our seats were reserved in the packed theater.

"Crack that bag open. A nigga is starving," Yudai said when we sat down in our seats.

"Wait until security leaves," I laughed.

"Shit, for what?" he asked. I went inside my bag and pulled out two containers with lids. I gave Yudai his container and his food was gone in five minutes.

"Really?" I asked.

"I was starving," he chuckled.

My phone beeped and it was a message from an "Unknown" number. I knew it was from Cash Flow. I couldn't understand how he loved me but hated me. I turned my phone completely off to focus my attention on Yudai.

"Would I be a creepy nigga if I kiss you?" Yudai asked me.

"Really?" I asked.

"Yo, your lips are so sexy. I won't get mad if I can't," he said. I pulled his face close to mine and planted a wet kiss on his lips. He gently bit my lip and my nipples stabbed at the fabric of my shirt. I pulled away from him before it turned Rated-R. I wiped my gloss off his lips and he sexily winked at me. I caught a glimpse of his hard-on against his leg; Yudai's dick was long and thick. I hurriedly sat back in my seat and focused on the big screen.

What can I do with that? He's huge, I thought.

"Oh, my bad," Yudai said and fixed himself.

"You knew what you were doing," I said.

"I can't help how much I'm attracted to you. I kinda feel like a nerdy nigga in high school who got a crush on the popular girl," he said.

"I feel the same way about you, too," I admitted. He leaned over and kissed my forehead. I have never blushed so much in my life.

He lifted his armrest and I laid on his shoulder. I was hypnotized by the scent of his cologne. He occasionally rubbed my thigh but not in a sexual way; it was soothing. Being around Yudai was comforting but I was afraid he'd turn out like Cash Flow. Cash Flow was a gentleman when I first met him but he turned into a demon a few months later. I didn't want to see Yudai's ugly side if he had one because I didn't want to lose hope on finding a good guy.

"Yo, that movie was whack!" Yudai fussed when the movie was over.

"I fell asleep," I replied.

"Out of all the Transformers movies, that one was my least favorite. The whole King Arthur thing just took that shit out of element. I'm pissed off about this shit," Yudai fussed.

"I grew two inches of hair during that long ass movie," I joked and Yudai chuckled. We stood on the curb flirting while he waited for the valet driver to bring his car. He wrapped his arms around my hips and kissed my neck. Yudai was playful and flirtatious and I enjoyed every bit of it. Maybe it was because he was only twenty and wanted to have fun.

"Excuse me, can I have an autograph? My son would love it," a white man said to Yudai.

"Sure," Yudai said. The stranger pulled out a business card and Yudai signed the back of it. He shook hands with Yudai before he walked off.

"You're so down to earth," I said.

"I started from the bottom so I gotta' be appreciative of the support," he replied. Seconds later, the valet driver brought him his car. After we left the mall, we headed to D.C. We went to a hookah bar in Adams Morgan. We received a lot of stares and pictures were taken of us. I was having so much fun, I forgot about the past miserable year of life, it was a distant memory.

"Can I keep you tonight?" Yudai asked me after we left the lounge.

"Keep me?" I asked.

"Stop playing. You act like you're not going to be my lil' shorty," he said.

"Oh, so I'm going to be your girl?" I asked.

"Yeah, you are," he replied arrogantly. I playfully pushed him and he smirked at me.

"Don't get fucked up on these streets," he said. It was something about his Baltimore swag. He was hood at heart but knew how to turn it off when he needed to.

"I'm waiting for it, Zaddy," I replied and he burst into laughter.

"Yoooo, you called me Zaddy? See, that's the talk that'll put your lil' ass into some grown nigga shit that you won't be able to get out of. Don't say shit to me after I put you in a chokehold, and it ain't the violent kind," he bragged.

I'm fittin' to fall in love with this pretty muthafucka, I thought.

"You don't want these big girl problems," I joked.

"Y'all thick girls always talking shit. I got the equipment and strength to handle every single last one of your curves," he replied. We left D.C. and went to my home. Yudai walked around my house nodding his head in approval.

"Nice crib," he said.

"Thanks," I said.

Use Your Heart and Not Your Eyes

I took my shoes off and grabbed a bottle of wine. I sat on the couch and turned the TV on. Yudai took his shirt off to get comfortable and I almost had a seizure—a real one. He was lean but he his arms were toned and he had a six-pack. He had tattoos everywhere and a few led to the V-shape of his pelvis. I had dirty thoughts of him as I poured him a glass of wine. I snuggled against him and he wrapped his arm around me.

"Tonight was the first time showing the public my personal life. I mean I had a few chicks I did my thing with but this is the first time I was open about someone I'm interested in. If you got something that can affect us, then you need to tell me now. I'm a good dude but I have a big flaw," he said and I perked up.

I knew it, I thought.

"What is it?" I asked.

"I don't forgive at all. Life is too short to hold onto people who will hurt you. I'll cut a muthafucka off quick and won't look back," he said. I wanted to run for the hills but I liked Yudai. I should've told him about Cash Flow and the video he leaked of me but my face was covered so nobody knew it was me. Cash Flow had more videos of me and I should've told Yudai about those, too. I was stuck and didn't know what to do. Yudai would've cut me off for not telling him but I liked him too much. What man would keep a woman if her business was all out in the streets? Especially a man like Yudai because he had a public career.

"There is nothing going on with me," I replied.

"Yo, I swear your lil' thick ass is perfect," Yudai said.

I'm far from it, I thought.

Gautier
What Dolly Wants, She Might Get

Two weeks later...

Everything was going great at the shop. Lisa was a big help, so the clientele spread. I went on Instagram as I sat on the plush leather couch inside my shop. I replied to the positive comments underneath the picture I posted a few hours prior. A few told me I was too fat to wear what I had on although I was fully covered. I guess the stretch material made them envious of my body because it hugged my curves. I didn't respond to negative comments—I blocked them instead. I went on Salih's page and there was a picture of him and a few players from his baseball team in Club Bliss which was in D.C. I wished things turned out better for us. Salih's smile was heartwarming but who would've thought an evil person hid behind that smile?

Saz walked into the shop smiling. Yudai just dropped her off from a brunch date. I smiled at Saz because I was happy that she was happy. Cash Flow needed to burn in the pits of hell.

"Are you stalking Salih's page again?" Saz asked and I rolled my eyes at her.

"Nope," I lied and she crossed her arms.

"Do you think y'all should seek counseling?" Saz asked.

Use Your Heart and Not Your Eyes

"Hell no! I don't want to be in the room with that demon. I might kill him and the counselor, but enough about me. I want to know what's going on with you and Yudai," I said. She sat on the couch and fanned herself.

"Well, we are just dating. I just want to have fun. I know Cash Flow will eventually ruin my image but it will be all worth it. Yudai wouldn't want a girl like me anyway, so I'm just enjoying it while it lasts," she said.

"Okay, so why not just tell him?" I replied.

"I want to be happy for the moment. I did things with Cash Flow that I'm not proud of. I mean, it's so bad that you don't know half of it," she said and I sat up on the couch.

"What happened?" I asked.

"I went to a party with him a few months ago. I was drunk and I mean pissy drunk. I actually think I was drugged. Matter of fact, I know I was drugged. Cash Flow's manager and a few guys under his label ran a train on me. I was sodomized and I know this because Cash Flow recorded it and sent it to my phone. He said he owned me because I'm a cow and nobody wants me. He said I should be lucky to get fucked by rich niggas. Why is this happening to me?" Saz asked. I was pissed all the way off. Tears fell from my eyes because of how mad I was. I knew Saz agreed to some of the things Cash Flow wanted her to do but that was just a low blow. He purposely wanted her to be worthless so nobody else could appreciate her. I hated him more than I hated the person that killed Salih's brother.

"I can't go to the cops. Do you think the world would believe me? They will say I made it up because I'm not desirable. They'll take one look at my black, fat ass and tell me that I'm a liar. Why would successful men target me? This is what I have to deal with.

Use Your Heart and Not Your Eyes

I'd rather keep it to myself instead of being called a liar. Either way, those niggas will live a happy life. Yudai is a breath of fresh air but he doesn't deserve my past. He's a good influence on a lot of people and it just isn't a good look," Saz said. I understood how she felt because people were cruel. They wouldn't believe her; I had seen too many cases like that. Some men preyed upon bigger woman because they thought they were weak. They figured they could do what they wanted to them because no one would believe them.

"We will figure this out but what if Yudai catches feelings?" I asked.

"I don't want to think about that right now but don't tell Tyshae. I'll be damned if she knows all of my secrets while she's hiding her own," Saz spat.

"What are you talking about?" I asked.

"I'm just saying," she said. I was ready to respond but my cell phone rang. I rolled my eyes as I answered the phone.

"What the hell do you want?" I asked Salih.

"Who is this?" a woman's voice came through my phone. It didn't take long to figure out it was his fiancée.

"Who are you looking for?" I asked.

"I don't know! I see this number in my fiancé's phone a lot!" she yelled.

"Okay, so why didn't you ask him?" I asked. I wanted to reach through the phone and snatch her plastic lips off her face. Salih had no business being engaged anyway. He only did it to hurt me but I noticed he wasn't posting pictures of his fiancée lately. I wanted to know if they were having issues since she was going through his phone.

"Bitch, I'm asking you! Are you one of his groupies?" she screamed into the phone.

"You must be crazy if you think I'm going to answer questions from a delusional bitch! Get the fuck off my line, plastic face!" I said before I hung up. She called back four more times but I didn't answer. *When were me and my friends going to catch a break?* I thought.

Lisa walked into the shop smiling. She had hickeys on her neck and her skirt was twisted.

"What the hell happened?" Saz asked her.

"Me and my boo had a quickie in the car around the corner," she replied.

"Who is your boo?" I asked out of curiosity. Lisa was a cool person but I wouldn't trust her around my man. She was a real Instagram thot. She posted nude pictures and all kinds of other pictures. One time she posted a picture of a guy going down on her but you couldn't see his face. People loved her because of how open she was with her sex life. She talked about writing a book on the celebrities and athletes she had been with but she wanted to write it under a fake name.

"This athlete. I can't tell anyone because he has a fiancée. You know how that goes," she giggled.

Home wrecker, I thought.

"The men love me. You know they say Asian girls are extra tight," Lisa joked but it wasn't funny.

"Your appointment just walked in. I think you should fix yourself and hide your hickeys," I said to Lisa.

"I'm already on it but do y'all want to go to the party with me tonight? The rapper Cash Flow is having something for his wife. I was invited by Ice Grill," she said and I rolled my eyes. Ice Grill was almost as bad as Cash Flow when it came to fashion. I assumed all the rappers under that label were fruit rollups.

"You must be fucking Ice Grill if he invited you," Saz said to Lisa.

"He's trying to get in my panties but I'm somewhat in a relationship. I only enjoy spending his money," Lisa said. Lisa was dumber than a sack of rocks. She talked about sleeping with someone else's man as if it was something to brag about. I know we all made mistakes, but she was happy about hers. After I left the shop a few hours later, I headed to Salih's mother's house. Luckily, we weren't that busy so I closed the shop at six o'clock. Salih's mother, Dolly, was sitting in the kitchen drinking a glass of wine while Brooke laid cookie dough on a baking sheet. I kissed both of their cheeks and Dolly rolled her eyes at me. Dolly was a short, slim woman. She was brown-skinned with short hair. Good hair ran in their family and Brooke inherited it. Brooke's hair was silky and curly. Salih's grandmother was Ethiopian and she had a lot of kids. Dolly was the youngest of nine.

"What's up with the attitude?" I asked.

Use Your Heart and Not Your Eyes

"Go in the room, Brooke, so I can talk to your mother," Dolly said. Seconds later, Brooke was out of the kitchen and Dolly was cursing at me.

"How long is this shit supposed to go on for? I woke up a few weeks ago and told myself I was sick of being in y'all's mess. Y'all muthafuckas get on my nerves," she said.

"It's Salih's fault," I answered.

"Ohhhhh, nooooo! Don't put all the blame on my son, Gautier. I know y'all's history and you did your dirt, too. It's the both of y'all! Brooke is getting older and she needs her parents in the same damn house," Dolly said.

"What makes you think I want your son?" I asked.

"Honey, I'm old school. I know a pile of shit when I see flies around it and this is exactly what that is—a big ass pile of shit. Y'all need to work it out because I'm out of this mess. I'm not playing messenger or counselor again," she spat.

"Salih blames me for Damien's death," I said.

"That's because you make yourself look guilty by letting him control your life. I know you made a mistake and I also know you loved this family too much to do that to us. You slept with the enemy but you didn't know. I still love you the same," she said. I sat down next to her and broke down. Tears fell from eyes and I couldn't control it. Dolly was right. I let Salih control me because I felt guilty deep down inside. Damien was like a brother to me, too. Thinking about sleeping with his killer made my stomach turn.

"I'm tired, Dolly. I pretend like I'm this strong and confident woman, but at times I don't even know if I love myself. Women look up to me because of my self-esteem but I'm a hypocrite. I feel so worthless because of that mistake. All I had to do was keep my legs closed, but how was I supposed to know Sisco killed Damien? Salih was distant after he was killed and we sorta fell off. Being young and not able to fully understand, I didn't think he was still grieving over Damien's death. I thought Salih didn't love me anymore," I cried on her shoulder.

"You gotta start loving yourself again. Salih is being a bully because he knows he can take advantage of you. Hurt people hurt people. Never take a man's virginity. They are worse than Satan. He has a bad case of being pussy-whipped," Dolly said to lighten the mood.

"I can't tell," I replied.

"His father was the same way and it took forever for him to get over me. That man got so mad that he stopped seeing his sons because I didn't want him. Some people can't let hurt go, so it grows. I'm having a birthday cruise in a few months and I want you to come. The whole family is going to be there. You have been telling me no for years, but this year it will not happen. I was serious when I said I'm sick of y'all. I need some more grandbabies," Dolly said.

"Salih's fiancée can give him one," I replied.

"Salih doesn't want any more kids but I think he just doesn't want any with her," she said.

"Are you trying to get us back together so he won't marry Pita?" I asked.

"And?" she spat.

"I'm sitting here crying to you while you're plotting on me. You haven't changed a bit," I laughed.

"I'm only plotting because I know y'all miserable without each other. Pita told me their wedding is in six months. You have six months to make my baby a happy man again. My son is so unhappy, it hurts my soul," she said. I was ready to respond but the door opened. I didn't plan on staying at Dolly's house that long because I didn't want to run into Salih. He came into the kitchen wearing shorts and a V-neck shirt that showed his masculine physique. The waves around his head swirled into curls that were tapered on the sides. I tried to look away but I couldn't stop staring. Salih walked past us and went into the refrigerator. He didn't say anything to us. He treated us as if we weren't there.

"Call the police and tell them I have a burglar in my home, Gautier. I know this child of mine didn't just disrespect me," Dolly said.

"You cursed me out last night," Salih said to Dolly.

"So, what! I curse your ass out every day," Dolly replied and I laughed.

"Hi, Salih," I said to piss him off even more.

"I'm coming, Brooke!" Dolly yelled as if Brooke called her. Dolly left me in the kitchen with her demonic son. He sat at the kitchen island across from me and grilled me.

"Walk over here so I can see what you got on," he scolded. I didn't know what it was but I was turned on by the sick asshole.

"Only my man can worry about that and his name ain't Salih," I spat.

"Suck on my nuts then," Salih replied.

"Funny you said that because I thought our cycle was on the same day, Sis," I fired back. Seconds later, he jacked me up by the neckline of my dress. His nostrils flared as he looked down at me. I closed my eyes because I thought he was going to hit me.

"Ouch!" I yelled. Salih pinched my breast so hard I had tears in my eyes.

"Keep insulting my manhood," he spat before he walked out of the kitchen. Dolly wanted us back together but did I want the same thing? The thought of raising Brooke together crossed my mind but I still had my doubts. I wondered if he still loved me and if he did, was it enough for him to forgive me? What Dolly wants, she might get.

Salih
Loving a Ballplayer

"Stop, Daddy! That tickles," Brooke yelled while I held her feet and tickled them. She balled up her small fist and punched me in the stomach. I doubled over and fell on the couch holding my stomach while pretending I was hurt. She stood up on the arm of the couch and elbowed me in the chest. My mother was screaming and cursing about her furniture.

"Ain't nobody worried about this stale furniture, Ma. This stuff has been zip-locked for years," I laughed. She threw a plastic-covered pillow at me.

"Kiss your grandma and father goodbye, Brooke. It's time to go home now because I don't want to be stuck in traffic," Gautier said when she came into living room. I kissed Brooke's cheek and she hugged me.

"Can Daddy come with us?" Brooke asked her mother and it caught me off guard. I wondered what made her ask that because she never asked that before. After I thought about it, it made sense. She never asked before because for years me and her mother were never in the same room. Brooke was getting used to us being around each other.

What is going on around here? I thought.

"No, sweetie, your father has practice early in the morning," Gautier answered.

"I can speak for myself," I said to Gautier.

"Well, you weren't speaking fast enough," she gritted and I shook my head. She was probably still mad about me pinching her breast. Honestly, I wanted to touch them anyway. They sat up so perfectly in her dress that they deserved to be licked. I didn't mean to take my frustrations out on my mother but I figured she was up to something. All of a sudden, I had to communicate with Gautier after not having had to for a few years. I was seeing and talking to Gautier more and more. I didn't want to move backwards in life, but Gautier's presence was just that strong. If only she knew how much she humiliated me. I thought her mind and body was mine but she showed me I was replaceable. She showed me the ugly side of loving someone. I wanted to get over it but I didn't know how to. She was the first girl I did everything with, including giving me a daughter. I even felt guilty for crying harder over her than I did when my brother was killed. The pain was different because Gautier murdered my ego. I had mixed feelings about the bitch and it was giving me a headache.

"You better hurry up before you get stuck in traffic. I'll gladly walk you to the door," I said but I was really telling her she needed to hurry the fuck up and leave. Gautier rolled her eyes at me as she was leaving. My mother turned her nose up at me when I closed the door.

"What's that look for?" I asked.

"When are you and Gautier going to stop this foolishness? Don't you think it's time to let it go? She was young and wasn't thinking about the consequences," she said.

"It's still fresh to me. I gotta go because I see where this conversation is headed. I'm ready to meet up with the fellas," I replied.

"Gautier still loves you," she said.

"She'll be aight. She entertains too many niggas and she's always on the internet being extra. Who is she trying to look good for?" I asked.

"She's a woman with confidence. A lot of women love her and are always talking about her. You gotta respect her strength when it comes to people on the internet. Hell, I'm thinking about posing in my two-piece bikini set with my nasty-looking stomach. My body was fine after I had your brother but when I had you, you messed me up. My stomach looks like a bowl of uncleaned chitterlings," she said.

"Y'all are trying to kill me," I replied.

"I invited her on the cruise for my birthday," she blurted out.

"WHAT!" I said.

"Nigga, don't 'what' me! You think you're too good to get an ass whipping? I'll beat the damn black off your ass so good, Pita will be picking her plastic lips off the ground. I invited Gautier to the trip as I have been doing it every year, but this time she's going," she said.

"Pita is going," I replied.

"That's your problem. Lock my door on your way out," she said. She lit another cigarette as I stared at her.

"I said lock my damn door, Salih!" she yelled.

"Crazy-ass," I mumbled as I left the living room.

"OUCH!" I yelled out. My mother threw a photo album at the back of my head.

"Nigga, say something else. I bet you'll be out the games for the rest of the season. I told you I got good ears, Salih. I can hear a mouse fart from underneath the dirt," she fussed. I hurriedly left out of her house. Pita called my phone as I was headed downtown. I didn't want to answer but I knew she would've called back-to-back if I didn't.

"Yoooo, what do you want?" I asked annoyed.

"I'm at the Bentley dealership and I was wondering if you could come down here," she said.

"Come down there for what? I already got a Bentley," I replied.

"I have been talking about the car for months! It's a pretty red with white leather seats. It just came off the truck and I want it," she said.

"Buy it then," I replied.

"I don't have the money, Salih! That's why I'm calling you. Get your ass down here and do it or else," she threatened.

"Look here, shorty, my money is my money and I don't owe you shit. Take your ass, titties, lips, and hips back to Miami and give them to the doctor who gave them to you if you want a Bentley. We talk about this kind of shit every day. I keep telling you to do something else with your time. All you do is post on IG, sell shit that doesn't work, and nag me all day. The baseball wives do things for their community all the time and what do you do? NOTHING! You can't even suck my dick with those plastic lips. Start a GoFundMe or something, shorty, because I'm tired of this shit. You ain't using me for my bread anymore," I spat. I knew it was harsh but Pita's looks weren't going to get her too far because she didn't have anything to offer. I got caught up with her when I first met her because I thought she was going to make something out of her life instead of just wanting to be a baller's wifey. She dropped out of law school and didn't tell me. I think that was what started our problems because she started showing me her true colors. I came too far from the hood to let an Instagram model empty my pockets.

"It's that bitch you have been talking to, huh? I called her phone earlier and I talked to her. She told me everything," Pita said.

"Now you are talking stupid. Did you even cook today?" I asked.

"I was busy," she spat.

"Busy doing what?" I asked.

"A workout tutorial with my new sweat vest," she said.

"How are we supposed to get married if you can't do anything for me?" I replied and the line went silent.

"What do you want me to do? Go back to school or something? I'm too pretty for that and you know it. I'm still young and I have three million followers who look up to me. I'm not going to let you spoil it for me. I'll buy my own Bentley!" she said and hung up on me. I met my boys downtown at a low-key restaurant. I wanted to relax and clear my head and that particular spot was what I needed. I didn't want to sign any autographs or be asked about my Instagram famous fiancée. I pulled up behind my right-hand man, Eron's Bugatti. Eron was in the NBA and we have been homeboys since the first grade. Our mothers were best friends but his mother died when we were in fifth grade. She had a seizure she couldn't come out of. My mother became a mother figure to him because his grandmother worked too much to take care of him. We used to sit on the steps of my mother's house talking about our dreams. I didn't think our dreams were going to come true because we were two young black boys from the hood. Drugs and violence surrounded us but we made it out the trenches. I wasn't as happy about my success as I should've been, though; I wanted to share it with Gautier. Being young and rich was a fantasy everybody had but it didn't mean nothing if you couldn't share it with someone you love. Gautier did something dangerous to me because I didn't look at life the same way anymore. It was all about me and Brooke. The valet driver knocked on my window while I was in deep thought.

"Are you okay, sir?" the young Chinese boy asked.

"Yeah, I'm good," I said as I stepped out.

I walked into Moe's Seafood and headed straight to the back. Yudai, Eron, and Eron's teammate, Davian was sitting at the table. I slapped hands with them before I sat down.

"About time, nigga. How are you going to invite me somewhere and not show up on time?" Yudai asked me. Yudai was cool with Eron but he didn't know much about Davian and it made him uncomfortable. I couldn't blame him because I couldn't be around niggas I didn't know like that, neither. It was a trait most hood dudes carried throughout life.

"My bad, I was over Ma Dukes' crib and she was tripping," I replied.

Use Your Heart and Not Your Eyes

"I need to stop over there before I head home. Shidddd, I don't even know if I want to go home tonight. Tyshae keeps nagging me about irrelevant shit. Why can't she just be happy with the life I provide for her? I'm still a young man, she thinks I'm supposed to be faithful or something? That bitch crazy, man," Eron vented. *We are young, but does being twenty-four justify someone to cheat?* I asked myself.

"My baby mama is the same way. I bought her a Mercedes G-wagon and she still complaining about me not being around. I'm making moves for us. Fuck what the media says, it's what I say," Davian chimed in.

"Y'all ain't shit," I said.

"You're acting like you never stepped out on Pita. Come on, bruh. I know you know what we're talking about," Eron said.

"I don't love Pita but you love Tyshae. You have been with her nagging ass for a minute and she was with you when you were broke. I don't know what you're complaining about but I damn sure didn't come here to talk about this mushy shit," I replied.

"What's your input on this, youngin'?" Davian asked Yudai.

"I don't know. I ain't never been in love before. Y'all old heads got more experience than me. I'm just out here enjoying my life while I can," Yudai answered and I slapped hands with him.

"What's up with you and Saz, though? Bruh, those pictures were all over the internet," Eron said.

"She's a cool little shorty. I'm enjoying her company," Yudai answered.

"You like big girls? Mannnn, y'all must be feeling sorry for those broads or something. They are advertising obesity. I told my baby mama she better not follow that mess because she gotta look good at all times. I don't want her getting any ideas and stop working out because of them big girls in small bikini tops. It's straight-up nasty," Davian said.

"Naw, you're just a clown," Yudai replied. Davian was a clown and was always talking mess on social media. Nobody on his team really liked him but he was cool with me for the time being. A few years back, I knocked him on his ass for saying something about Gautier. He hasn't mentioned her name since. He didn't know who she was to me but he knew not to talk about her around me.

"The fuck you just say?" Davian asked Yudai.

"You heard me, bruh. Don't talk to me like you know me or something," Yudai said.

"Y'all hear this pretty boy talking shit? Nigga, you look like you dance and sing. You ain't gotta get gangsta with me, curly top," Davian replied.

"Yo, shut the fuck up. You stay starting shit. You think because you almost seven feet tall mean something? Nigga, ain't nobody at this table afraid of heights," I said and Davian waved me off.

The waitress came over to our table with two bottles of 1942 Don Julio. She brushed her ass against me and it was phat. I wanted to squeeze it but I didn't know who was watching and taking pictures. She leaned over the table and sat the two buckets of ice down. Her succulent breasts spilled over her white button-up shirt and I couldn't take my eyes off her. It had been a while since I had some pussy and the sight of her made me hard.

"Can I get y'all anything else?" she asked while staring at me. She seductively licked her pink glossed lips. I imagined her wrapping her lips around my dick.

"Not right now," Davian replied. She walked past me and winked at me.

"Damn, she was phat," Eron said.

"Who you are telling. I'll fuck the hell out of her and pay for her to get a new weave," Davian said.

"She was aight in the face but her body was banging," I replied. We ordered everything on the menu and even had a few girls in our section. It was innocent, though. Well, I take that back. Davian had two girls sitting on his lap while one of them was feeding him shrimp. I wanted to talk to Eron about Davian because he was bad news for our image. He was always caught up with groupies and had about five baby mamas at twenty-six years old.

"Aight, it's time for me to roll out. I got business to take care of," Davian said while he eyed the two girls on his lap. We already knew what he was up to. He left with the girls out the back door so nobody would see him.

"I bet paparazzi is waiting in the alley for him," I said and Eron laughed. His phone buzzed and he picked it up.

"It's time for me to roll out. Tyshae crazy ass just took a picture of my cars on flats and she bleached my clothes. Y'all see what I deal with?" he asked.

"Stop cheating," I said.

"I will when she stops acting insecure. The shit is a turnoff. I have been faithful to her until I got drafted. Everything went downhill from there. She cut her hair off, dyed it gray, and now she's starting to wear clothes that show too much. Tyshae was never that way. I mean she was always hood but look at her now. She looks like a fake Amber Rose. I don't know what's gotten into her. I found lightening cream underneath the bathroom sink. She's bleaching her damn skin because I cheated on her with a white woman. She needs help, bruh. But anyways, I'm out," Eron said. He slapped hands with me and Yudai before he left the restaurant.

"I'm scared to have a shorty now," Yudai joked.

"You just gotta fall for the right one," I said.

"No doubt," he replied.

I drove home after we parted ways. I sat outside my house dreading going in. I stared at my mansion and the many cars that were parked in front but felt nothing for it. I pulled out a picture of my brother that I kept in my wallet. We were sitting in front of our mother's house with Eron sitting in front of us on the steps. I chuckled to myself because we were high. Our eyes were red and we had goofy smiles on our faces. Gautier was the one who took our picture and I wanted her to be in it but she said it was a family moment. Who would've thought a few weeks after taking the picture my brother was going to end up dead? I got out my whip and headed to my house. I unlocked the door and heard giggling coming from my living room. I walked into the living room and females were everywhere. Pita walked around serving her guests glasses of wine. It was one o'clock in the morning. My teammates' wives were in attendance and so was a few of Pita's friends. They must've parked in back of the house because I didn't see any unfamiliar cars in front of my crib.

"What's going on?" I asked.

"Hey, baby. I missed you," Pita said. She walked over to me and kissed my lips.

"What's up, beautiful?" I asked.

"So, me and the girls are putting together plans for our very own show. I thought about what you said earlier and you were right about me following my dreams. Well, I'm investing in a show called, *Loving a Ballplayer*. We are going to be on TV!" she screamed in excitement.

Bitch, I should shoot your ass! I thought.

"Ohhh, okay. Congrats," I replied.

"I was also thinking we should have a wedding special on the show for higher ratings since we are getting married in six months. This is going to be very big! I'm going to be the next Mona Scott," she bragged.

Mona Scott will never do a story about her life on her own show, dummy, I thought.

"This is a great idea," one of the girls said.

"I hope we expose my cheating-ass husband. This will be good for me before we divorce. I'm trying to stack my coins. I can see the ratings now," another girl chimed in.

Shorty, you knew Daniel was a cheater before you married him. You were the side-chick at first. Y'all ain't shit but a bunch of gold diggers, I thought.

Use Your Heart and Not Your Eyes

"Excuse me, ladies, I have to holla at Pita about something really quick," I said. I grabbed Pita's hand and pulled her out the living room. I squeezed her hand on our way to the kitchen.

"What do you think you're doing, huh? Get those bitches out of my house and you ain't doing that show. Do you know how messy that is? My teammates are like my brothers!" I yelled at her.

"Too late, I already signed the contract with the network. Earlier at the dealership made me realize I had to follow my dreams. It was something I was thinking about for a long time but I couldn't talk to you about it because you are always busy. Why can't you be happy for me? This is a great money move. All the other celebrities and athletes do it," she said.

"Who probably are having financial problems. Bad enough we have to pretend we are happy with each other and now you want the cameras in our faces?" I asked.

"It's about the money. I don't care what you say because I'm doing this with or without you. I will see you in a few. I have to go over everyone's scripts," she said. I grabbed a bottle of water before I headed to the basement and locked my door.

I gotta' get rid of this broad, I thought.

****

I woke up to banging on the basement door. I looked at the clock and it was eight in the morning. I sat up on the couch and wiped my eyes before I got up. The banging got louder and Pita started yelling for me to open the door.

"I made you breakfast!" she yelled out. I opened the door and she had a tray of food in her hand. Pita was a good cook; she used to cook for me a lot in the beginning of our relationship before she got big headed. She made me a stack of blueberry pancakes, sausages, cheese eggs and grits topped with sautéed shrimp. My stomach growled as I inhaled the food.

"I'm sorry about last night. I think I had too much wine. It's too late to get out of the contract but I won't film any major scenes with you. All I want is for you to make an appearance every now and then. It can be a small dinner date or something. You want me to have my own money, right?" she asked.

"Aight, man, damn. I'm warning you, though, you will get sued if you use material that wasn't approved. You can't go around butting into the players' lives unless they tell you it's okay," I said.

"Okay, fine! Eat up because we have a long day today," she replied.

"What's today? I don't have practice so I'm trying to relax," I said.

"I'm taking you out. It's been a while," she replied.

"Cool," I said. She kissed my lips before she happily ran up the stairs.

I do need some pussy, though. Maybe I can be nice to her so I can get some, I thought. I sat on the couch and ate my food. I stared at my phone wanting to call Gautier but I thought better of it. I didn't have a reason to disrespect her but what could I possibly say without showing her I care about her? It took ten minutes before I figured out the reason for my call.

"What do you want, Salih?" Gautier answered.

"Where is Brooke?" I asked.

"She's with my mother. I had to come to work early because someone tried to rob my store. Your simple-headed ass probably had something to do with it. You just can't stand to see me happy, huh?" she asked.

"Yo, you need some dick or something? What did I do to you?" I asked.

"EVERYTHING!" she yelled.

"It's too early for this," I said.

"What did you call me for? Your fiancée needs to do her damn job so you can leave me alone," she said.

"You trippin'," I replied and she hung up on me. I hurriedly ate my food before I headed to the master bedroom to take a shower. After I got dressed, I stepped into a fresh pair of red Balenciaga sneakers. I walked down the stairs and Pita was coming out of the kitchen.

"Where are you going? I'm not ready yet," she said.

"I gotta check on my mother really quick. I'm coming right back. Somebody was trying to break into her crib," I replied.

"Ohhhh, noooo! Is Mama Dolly okay? Maybe I should go with you," she said.

"NO! I mean, naw you ain't gotta go. You know how much you hate cigarette smoke and you just got your hair done. You don't want that smell in your hair, do you?" I replied as I caressed her face.

"Okay, you're right. Tell Mama Dolly I said 'hi,'" Pita said. I walked out the door and got inside my whip. I headed to Gautier's shop.

Gautier
Unexpected Visitor

I sat on the couch in my shop and cried after the police left. The window was busted out but nothing was missing. The note on the rock that was thrown through the window read, *sloppy whore*. There was only so much I could take. I texted the girls and told them the shop was closed for the day.

"Unlock the door," a familiar voice said. I turned around and Salih was standing in front of the broken window.

"Why are you here?" I asked.

"Just unlock the damn door before I bust the rest of it out. I don't have shit else to do today," he said and I believed him. I got up from the couch and unlocked the door for him. I sat on the couch that faced him and crossed my arms as I grilled him.

"What?" he asked.

"What do you want?" I replied.

"I was in the area and just wanted to make sure you were straight, I guess," he said.

"You are a liar," I replied. He sat across from me and stared at me. I tried to keep my focus off his muscled arms but my eyes landed on them anyway. It was getting too hot all of a sudden.

"This is a nice little spot, though. The area ain't all that good but it's a good investment," he said.

"It's fittin' to snow," I replied because he didn't give compliments.

"Why you gotta be a bitch when I'm trying to be cordial with you? You want me to slap the taste out of your mouth or something? Walk over here," he said.

"If you don't get to the point as to why you are here…" I replied.

"Mannnn, shorty, shut the hell up and walk over here. Hurry up because I'm growing impatient," he said. I got up and walked over to him. I stood in front of him and he smirked at me. Salih was up to something and I was curious about what he really wanted. He grabbed my hand and pulled me down next to him.

"Damn, you are hardheaded," he said and I mushed him.

"You hungry?" he asked.

"No," I replied.

"Stop lying. You stay hungry," he said.

"Did you just insult me?" I replied.

"Naw, but you do. You act like I don't know you or something," he said.

"I didn't eat breakfast yet," I admitted. He pulled out his phone and ordered something from a café downtown which delivered. I smiled to myself when he put my food order in. He knew exactly what I wanted. He ordered waffles with caramel drizzle, southwestern eggs, and fried potatoes. I couldn't wait until my food came.

"Thank you," I said when he hung up. We quietly sat on the couch for a few minutes. Neither one of us knew what to say. It was awkward being around him without fussing. His phone broke the silence. He looked at it and I caught a glimpse of the name. It was his fiancée calling him. I rolled my eyes when he put the phone back in his pocket.

"Go home or something," I said and he laughed.

"You stay poppin' off until I hurt your feelings. You should appreciate this day because I'm still not feeling you, shorty," he said. I scooted closer to him and ran my hand down his leg. I placed my breasts on his arm and seductively whispered in his ear.

"If you want some pussy just say it," I teased. I thought it was going to anger him enough to leave but he didn't. He looked at me with passion-filled eyes instead.

"I do want it, so what are you going to do about it?" he asked.

"But you hate me," I said.

"The pussy ain't got nothing to do with its owner," he replied.

"Get out of my shop," I said. I couldn't give in so easily since he made my life a living hell for the past few years. I stood up and walked away from him. I headed upstairs to the main office which I only used for inventory. I sat behind my desk and tears filled my eyes. I was too emotional being around Salih. It was better when we communicated through Dolly. *Why is Dolly doing this to me*? I asked myself. I didn't want to think about the good times we had together.

Use Your Heart and Not Your Eyes

I was still in love with Salih and it was slowly killing me. The door to my office cracked open and I hurriedly wiped my eyes.

"The fuck is you crying for?" he asked.

"I'm pissed off about the window," I lied.

"It's not that bad, shorty," he said annoyed.

"I thought you were leaving," I replied.

"I'll leave when I feel like it. I'm not bored with you yet. So, what's up witchu'? One of your niggas got mad at you or something?" he asked.

"You sound jealous," I said.

"Naw, never that, but how many niggas are there now?" he asked. I leaned back in my chair and crossed my arms. He stood in the doorway of my office waiting for me to answer. *You are definitely jealous,* I thought.

"How many females are you cheating on Pita with?" I replied and he smirked.

"I'm not a cheater like you, Gautier," he said.

I knew he was lying. Salih's attitude changed over the years toward women. He didn't have any respect for them, especially me. I figured he loved Pita but I wasn't sure if he was in love with her. Butterflies filled my stomach when I thought back to the night Salih entered me for the first time. See, I had a promiscuous side when I was younger. I wasn't a hoe but I wasn't innocent, either. I lost my virginity at thirteen years old to an older boy. From that moment on, I became more curious about sex. I thought I was better than the rest of the girls in school because I was sexually active. I wished I would've known the consequences back then because I was paying for it all.

"Remember that weekend when I stayed over your house? It was a snow blizzard and our mothers couldn't make it home from work? We had so much fun," I said. He sat on the chair in front of my desk and brushed his hands down his waves. A cute smile spread across his handsome face and he almost seemed angelic—almost.

"Yeah, I remember that day. We were in my room chilling and your dumb-ass couldn't keep still because you stole some of my mother's Mad Dog 20/20. You were dancing to Wayne Wonder's song, "No Letting Go." That was your favorite song. I was trying to study for a test but you wouldn't let me," he said. It was a memorable day, a day I'll never forget…

Year 2011…

"Get up, Salih! You have all night to study," I said.

"Yo, chill out. I'm almost done," he replied. I took another swig out of the plastic cup full of cheap liquor I found in his mother's room. I was watching MTV Jams *as I seductively danced to the music video. It had been over a year since Salih told me to be his girlfriend. He turned out to be more than a boyfriend, he was also my best friend. I danced around his room with the TV volume low so he could concentrate. I was only wearing his gym shirt with panties and a bra underneath. I caught Salih eyeing my legs and I teased him.*

"You can touch them if you want to," I flirted.

Use Your Heart and Not Your Eyes

"I know I can but sit down," he said. I laid on his bed next to him and stared at the ceiling. It was his last year of high school and exams were coming up. I didn't want to distract him because the exams were important to him. It was also going to help him get into college. An hour later, he closed his textbooks and placed them on the floor by his bed. He got up and looked out his bedroom window. It was a snow blizzard and my mother didn't want me staying in the house by myself while she was stranded at work. Salih and Damien walked to my house to get me because my heat was broken.

"Damn, I'm studying like we're going to school tomorrow," Salih fussed. He laid next to me on the bed and I laid on his chest. I saw his erection poking through his baller shorts. It was happening a lot lately but he wasn't making a move.

"We can do it if you want to," I said.

"Naw, I gotta focus on my last year of high school," he replied.

"But you are hard. You need to do something so it won't happen a lot," I said.

"Do what?" he asked.

"What do you think?" I replied. I grabbed his thick hard-on and he was embarrassed. Salih was popular in school and in our neighborhood. I was surprised to learn that he was a virgin.

"I don't think about sex," he lied.

"All boys think about sex," I said and I kissed him.

"What if I do it wrong? You have been with older niggas," he said. I slid my panties off and climbed on top of him to straddle him. He grabbed my hips and squeezed them as his dick pressed against

my center. I seductively rocked back and forth on top of him and he slightly moaned. It had been a while since I had sex and being around Salih gave me those strong urges. He was the finest boy I had ever laid eyes on and I was lucky to have him. I leaned forward and placed a kiss on his lips. I moaned against his lips as his fingers dug into my skin. Tired of waiting for him, I reached into his shorts and pulled out his big dick. He was bigger than the boys I had been with—he was very big.

"I don't know about this," Salih said as he sat up. I pushed him back onto the bed and lifted up so I could ease him inside of me. I winced in pain as the tip of him stretched me open. I lost balance and slipped down the length of him. Tears welled up in my eyes. Salih closed his eyes and bit his bottom lip enjoying the feel of wet pussy for the first time. After a few seconds, I moved my hips into an offbeat rhythm. I wasn't good at being on top. Matter of fact, it was my first time riding a boy. In my mind, I thought I had it all down pact because I was more experienced than him. Truth is, it felt like it was my first time, too. He grabbed my breasts and squeezed them through my shirt. He jerked inside me then let out a loud moan.

"It's okay. It will get hard again," I said with sweat dripping down my face. I was actually glad he exploded because I didn't know what I was doing. I climb off of him and kissed his cheek. He got up with anger sketched across his face.

"What's the matter with you?" I asked.

"Yo, I told you I didn't want to fuck," he replied.

"You nutted fast, big deal," I giggled. I playfully reached out to him and he smacked my hand away. He stormed out of his bedroom and went into the bathroom and slammed the door. I heard his brother laughing at him in the hallway.

Use Your Heart and Not Your Eyes

"Bruh, you better go back in there and tear her lil' ass up! The fuck is you mad for? It's normal to nut fast on your first time," *Damien said and I fell over in laughter.*

"You were listening?" Salih asked him.

"Yo, you were loud! I thought it was Gautier moaning at first. I was fucking when I was twelve. You're seventeen years old and acting like a little nigga," Damien said.

"I'll knock your ass out, though," Salih replied to Damien.

"You better hit that pussy into a homerun, baseball player," *Damien said. A few minutes later, Salih came into the bedroom and I acted like I was asleep. He pulled the covers back and got in bed with me. He wrapped his arm around me and kissed my neck.*

"Wake up, Gautier," he said.

I'm not sleep, *I thought.*

"I'm tired. You wore me out," I lied so he could feel better.

"Shorty, stop lying," he said. He pressed his hard-on against my ass and I turned around to face him.

"I want some more," he said.

For the rest of the day, we had sex. Neither one of us was experienced but it felt good with our bodies joined. Being close to him made me realize how much I loved him. I knew nobody else could ever make me feel the way he made me feel. A few weeks, Salih was able to make me squirt. We were both whipped and it turned into a deadly combination...

"We had fun," he said, breaking the silence.

"We were young in love," I laughed. Salih got up and locked the door to my office. I began to panic because I didn't know what was going to be the outcome of his unexpected visit. He walked over to me and pulled me up. He pressed my body against the desk and slid my joggers down. I rushed out the house but managed to put on a sexy purple lace thong. He massaged my juicy round ass and my ass cheeks spilled out of his hands. A moan escaped my lips and the wetness from between my legs seeped through the material of my thong. My clit throbbed uncontrollably and I couldn't wait any longer. I wanted him to hurry up and enter my body. My hands trembled as I unzipped his shorts. I reached into his boxer briefs and pulled out his meaty, long dick. My mouth watered as I thought about him sliding down my throat. He grabbed me around the neck and seductively licked my lips.

"You knew what you were doing sending me a picture of your pussy," he whispered against my lips. His phone rang and he tossed it across the room. I knew it was his fiancée calling him but should I have cared? Was I breaking up a happy home? My thoughts were interrupted when Salih pushed my thong to the side. He pushed me back onto the desk and opened my legs. I closed my eyes and anticipated his next move. I gasped and dug my nails into his forearms when he eased his thick head inside my slit. My body shuttered as I felt every ridge of him. He pried my legs further apart as he went deeper. The scent of his cologne and the intense pressure between my walls combined made me dizzy. I oozed onto his shaft and almost called his name as he filled me up.

"GODDAMN!" he shouted. His thumb brushed across my clit and my legs trembled. I came before the show started. My wetness dripped down my ass crack and onto the desk. Salih smirked and I rolled my eyes at him.

"That pussy missed King Salih," he bragged. I was ready to protest but he went deeper inside me. I bit my lip as he stroked his massive dick between my walls. My legs wrapped around his waist and I massaged my breasts to take my mind off the pain mixed with pleasure. The desk squeaked as he pummeled into me.

"UMMMMMM," I moaned. He pushed my legs up and held them down while he slammed into me. I wanted to scream out how much I still loved him. I felt a big wave coming and my clit swelled when he rammed himself into my G-spot. My pussy gushed and my muscles tightened around his dick. Salih called me a "bitch," when I fucked him back. It started out slow but it turned into angry sex. I threw my pussy against his pelvis and he moaned my name. My middle finger massaged my pink bud while I slid up and down his length.

"Damn, you're wet!" Salih called out as he stood still and watched my pussy coat his dick with my essence. I was working up another orgasm. My hair was stuck to the side of my face and my breasts were sweaty. It had been a while since a man gave me orgasms back-to-back. I hated to admit it, but I think it was because my body was only familiar with Salih's. Not the one to be outdone, Salih pushed my knees to my forehead and fucked me into the future. I experienced something lethal, something that I couldn't handle as he continuously long-dicked me.

"You wanna give my pussy away, huh? What nigga can fuck you like this?" he asked as he sped up. I was tongue-tied, I could barely breathe because he was in my stomach. I couldn't answer him but my body did when I squirted. Salih groaned out in pleasure as he jerked inside me. He slammed into me again as he erupted. He fell on top of me and stared into my eyes. He was confused, too. I looked away from him but he turned my head so I could face him. He kissed me so passionately my knees buckled. He ran his fingers through my hair as he deepened the kiss. He got hard again and I knew I was in for a rude awakening. The delivery guy came to drop off my food but we didn't open the door for him. We sexed in my office for hours as both of our phones rang.

Hours later...

I went into the bathroom to freshen up and my body was riddled with hickeys. I had fourteen missed calls and most of them were from Aniston. I was getting tired of him. He sent me five text messages cursing me out and disrespecting me. I forgot we had a date at a wine tasting. Aniston would've been perfect for me but he was embarrassed by me. How could a woman like me tolerate such behavior? I wanted someone to love me and be happy with who I was without having to change my physical appearance. Salih knocked on the bathroom door before he came in.

"I'll holla at you later. I gotta go," he said. He left without so much as a goodbye kiss. After I cleaned off, I closed the shop and headed toward my jeep. As soon as I got in, Saz called me.

"What is it?" I asked.

"Ewww, who pissed in your Cheerios?" she replied.

"I'm sorry, Saz. I'm stressed out with everything. Is there something I can help you with?" I asked annoyed.

"No, I was just calling to see if you wanted to go out for a few drinks. We haven't hung out in a while," she replied.

"I have to finish packing while Brooke isn't home," I said.

"You better tell me what's going on with you!" she spat.

"I made a mistake," she said.

"Don't we all," she replied.

"I made a big mistake. I fucked Salih," I admitted. She screamed and it sounded like she dropped her phone. I rolled my eyes because of her dramatics.

"Wait a minute, bitch. Let me get myself together. I wasn't ready for that one. I don't know if I heard you correctly, but what did you just say? You let your baby daddy from hell get some pussy?" Saz asked in disbelief.

"Yes, and now I regret because it won't change anything between us," I said.

"Was it good?" she asked.

"Chileeeeeeeee, he was like milk. He did the body good, honey. I came so much I lost count. It brought back old feelings. I was fine for a while until Dolly decided Salih and I needed to communicate. Why is she torturing me?" I vented.

"Well, she ain't lying. Y'all used her for years and it's getting old. Miss Dolly got a life, too," Saz replied. I made small talk with Saz until I pulled up to my condo. I told her I was going to call her back when I noticed Aniston was parked outside my building. I hurriedly got out of my truck and slammed the door in frustration.

Can my day get any worse? I thought.

Aniston got out of his car and walked over to me with anger sketched across his face. His nostrils flared and he balled his fists.

"I should kill you!" he yelled at me.

"You need to pipe down before my neighbors hear you," I said.

"Do I care about your neighbors? I'm sick of your lies, Gautier!" he yelled at me. His eyes fell on my neck and he grabbed my face.

"Is this a hickey? I knew you was a whore!" he yelled as he squeezed my face. I pushed him away from me and he slapped my face before he choked me. We tussled around the parking lot until one of my neighbors came outside.

"I'm calling the cops!" she screamed. She was a middle-aged Caucasian woman who had yoga classes inside her condo. I went to a few of her classes but I didn't feel comfortable because the other women always made snide remarks about my body. It wasn't necessarily my size but my huge butt and full, round breasts being in spandex.

"Call the cops!" Aniston yelled while he ripped off my shirt. I kicked him between the legs and he doubled over in pain. He called me every name except the child of God. He limped to his car and sped off after he got in. Kristen crossed her arms as she stared me down.

"Me and a few other residents have been talking about the disturbance you brought to this neighborhood with you. I am sending a letter to the leasing office tomorrow morning. Different men show up to your doorstep every month. You are a sweet girl but you cause a lot of trouble. I think you should move before this gets ugly. I have lived here since the community was built and I haven't had any problems until now. I'm warning you," she said.

Use Your Heart and Not Your Eyes

"Kiss my ass, Kristen. I'm only disturbing the peace because I'm the only black face you see when you walk out of the house. This is the first time this happened but it won't happen again because I'm moving!" I yelled at her and she grabbed her chest.

"I'm calling the cops on you, missy!" she said and hurriedly stormed off. I called my mother and told her to keep Brooke overnight because an emergency came up. She asked me thousands of questions but I lied and told her my phone was going dead. The cops came minutes later and I gave them a statement. I told them I was attacked by a stranger because I didn't want to go far into details. Kristen told the cops I assaulted her but I told them it was a lie. They brought up the incident at the shop and asked me if being attacked had anything to do with that. I gave the cops a sob story about me being popular on the internet and it could've been a crazy stalker. After the cops left my condo, I locked the door and grabbed a bottle of wine out the fridge. I sat on my couch with the bottle of wine and my cell phone. I had a lot of messages from people who followed my page. They were asking me if I was okay because they heard what happened to my shop. My life wasn't private anymore and my love life sucked. It was all because I was a woman who the public thought was too comfortable in her own skin. I wanted to break down but I held my composure although the walls seemed as if they were closing in on me. Tyshae sent me a screenshot a few hours later while I sat on my couch watching TV. It was a picture of Salih and his fiancée, Pita having a nice romantic dinner. He looked so happy but I didn't know if it was because of her or because of the mind-blowing sex I gave him. I decided to go out and party with Saz. I would've sunk into a depression if I stayed in the house. I took a shower then did my makeup. I got dressed in a pair of tight jeans and an off-the-shoulder top with bell bottom sleeves. I took a sexy picture in the mirror of my backside and uploaded it to my IG. The caption read: About to make him sweat. I received a thousand likes within two minutes after I uploaded it. My name is Gautier Sadosa and nobody couldn't stop my shine. I had a slight moment but I wasn't changing for anybody. Hiding behind the pain helped seal a lot of open wounds. Why should I reveal my true self if all it did was hurt me?

Tyshae
Cream

"Where are you going?" I asked Eron.

"This is business," he replied.

He was packing an overnight bag and he had only been home for a few days. He claimed he was away at some kind of training but my heart was telling me otherwise. I kept my business private out of fear of being called a hypocrite. See, Eron had a two-year-old daughter that lived in France. I found out about her a few months ago from going through his phone. I had a feeling he was leaving the country to visit his other family. I must say his cheating ways made me a little insecure. I made up a fake page so I could follow his beautiful Victoria's Secret model's page. She didn't post pictures of Eron but I always knew by her pictures when he was with her. Her captions always made it clear she was spending time with the love of her life. She told the magazine she didn't want to reveal that side of her life because she didn't want to expose her daughter or put bad luck on her relationship. Eron must've had something to do with that. Truth is, she couldn't reveal the truth because he had a publicly-known fiancée who he had been with since high school. But Moore wasn't his only mistress. Eron had a few others who I knew about. I knew Eron was a dog when I sent him a picture of my breasts in his DM from my fake page and he still didn't recognize me. His response made me sick. He wanted to know if I wanted him to fly me out so we could get to know one another better. How could he not know my body if we have been together for years? It was because there were so many women, and our bodies probably looked the same. I noticed his choice in women were exotic. Not once did he cheat on me with a sista. My self-esteem dropped so much, I didn't know who I was. I didn't know myself outside of Eron. The only time he spent a week with me was when I had a miscarriage. He even broke down and cried because he blamed himself for stressing me out. Well, he got over his stress quickly because a woman named Amarie was calling his phone a week later. I was told to deal with it because most athletes cheated and there was no way of escaping it. Davian's fiancée told me she didn't care as long as he paid the bills and kept her purse filled with money. How could money matter to me when I loved Eron when he was broke? I had done everything to keep him home but nothing was working. Leaving him was my last resort and the thought alone frightened me.

"My birthday is in a few days," I said.

"That's what Saz and Gautier are for. Do you think I'm going to stay here after you messed up my cars and bleached my clothes? You're fucking crazy, Tyshae! This is the reason why I fuck other women. Black women nag so damn much about nothing and y'all wonder why successful niggas get other women! Learn how to shut the fuck up and stop questioning me. You were accusing me of cheating when I wasn't thinking about it," he fussed.

"Where are you going?" I asked.

"My daughter is sick and she needs me," he bluntly said. I picked up the lamp next to our bed and hurled it at him. He ducked before it smashed into his face.

"I HATE YOU!" I screamed.

"I HATE YOU, TOO!" he yelled back. He grabbed his duffel bag and I darted toward our bedroom door. I fought him as tears ran down my face. I ripped his shirt and dug my nails into his skin. He slammed me against the wall and choked me.

"I'm leaving you, Tyshae. I can't do this anymore. I'm not coming back this time," he admitted. I dropped down to my knees and screamed as loud as I could.

"Call your psychiatrist or something. I can't do this with you anymore. It's affecting my life and you aren't getting any better," he said. I had anger issues and had them for a very long time but Eron was the only one who saw it. It didn't get worse until the fame came. I wasn't mentally ill, but I loved him so much that the thought of losing him made me crazy. I talked to a psychiatrist about it and she told me it came from having low self-esteem. I always thought you had to be overweight, ugly, and many other things people talked about to have low self-esteem but that wasn't the case. I was pretty, had a banging shape, and many men wished they had me, so what was the problem?

"Why would you leave me after all I have been through with you, huh? I loved you when you were broke and didn't have shit! I'll kill your black ass!" I screamed.

"You ain't the same anymore. Your mother filled your head up with a bunch of bullshit. You're a weak woman and no man will ever want you. You have been letting your mother manipulate your mind for years and it's because of her that I can't stay faithful," he said. He snatched away from me and stormed out of the house with his duffel bag in his hand. I sat on the floor and cried my heart out. Gautier wanted me to go to the club with her and Saz but I wasn't in the mood. I had to go somewhere else and vent. There was only one person who really understood me, but we lost contact over the years.

****

Use Your Heart and Not Your Eyes

"What are you doing here so late?" my mother asked when she opened the door for me. I walked past her and headed straight to her kitchen. I went to her liquor cabinet and poured a cup of tequila straight. I guzzled the warm liquor down and gagged when the disgusting taste settled in.

"Tyshae Rakisha Owens, you better get to talking. It's eleven o'clock at night," she said. Me and my mother were almost identical. We were the same height, complexion, and had the same eyes. We were always mistaken for sisters because she looked thirty instead of forty-three.

"Eron left me, Mama. Can you believe that? I did everything you told me to do but it didn't work," I vented.

"I told you to keep that man happy. He's a basketball player and that's what they do. He's young, handsome, and successful. You only had one job, Tyshae. One damn job and that was to stop nagging him. If he wants a white woman, become a white woman. Stop acting so ghetto all the time. Did you use that skin cream I gave you?" she asked.

"The lightening cream isn't working. Nothing is working! Do you not get it? You can't keep a man that doesn't want to be kept," I said.

"I think you need to lose a little weight. Less ass and a bigger boob job. Take that piercing out of your cheek and cover all those tattoos up. You look trashy," she said.

"I am slim. What more do I need to lose? Why can't you accept me for me, Mama? Do you not see how much this is affecting me? We had a decent relationship until Eron got signed to the NBA. All you see is dollar signs because he bought this house for you and the nice car you are driving. You're so focused on the money that you don't realize your daughter is suffering from depression. Who can I talk to if I can't talk to my own damn mother?" I asked. She rolled her eyes at me as she poured herself a drink. She sat at the kitchen island and crossed her arms underneath her breasts as if she was fed up with me.

"Go upstairs, take a warm bath, and get into bed. While you're in bed, you're going to call him and beg him back. Your sister married a wealthy man and she's very happy because she took my advice. You two have it made in today's society. What are you complaining about, huh? Stop acting like a spoiled bitch and do what Eron wants you to do," she said.

"You are sick," I replied and she laughed.

"Do you know how hard it was taking care of two girls by myself? My mother put me out on the streets because I couldn't pay my half of the rent. Your father was locked up and the Feds took everything we had! I had nothing and I'll be damned if I see my girls go through the same thing. My mother loved me when I was able to buy her fur coats with your father's drug money. I told myself I was going to help my daughters survive in this cold world. Listen, Eron loves you. He might have a fucked up way of showing it, but he loves you. All he wants is for you to be understanding and respect his position. Stop nagging him and play your part. Marry him, and if he cheats, take him for everything he has, but you can't do that now because y'all are not married. Use him for what he's worth. Hell, everyone is doing it now. You think half of these women love their ugly ass husbands? Look at Cash Flow, do you think his beautiful wife really wants him? She is building a nest egg for herself and it's best to do it while you're still young and in shape. It's all a hustle, baby. I told you to get pregnant and you messed that up. You let him stress you out until you had a miscarriage," she replied. She got up from the stool and walked around the kitchen island. She grabbed my face and stared into my eyes.

"You're so beautiful and lucky. Accept it and it will pay off. I know you won't be able to live the lifestyle you live by just working at that cheesy shop. You live in that beautiful mansion on the hill with a big backyard pool. You have the fairytale life you always dreamed about. The public knows you as his fiancée and the other women are secrets. That should tell you a lot," she said and I pulled away from her.

"Do you think he'll take me back if I work on myself?" I asked.

"Of course. I'm ready to call him right now," she said. She picked up the phone in the kitchen and called Eron. He answered on the second ring.

"Hey, Eron. Tyshae is here and she needs to talk to you," my mother said into the phone.

"I'm not going back and forth with your daughter, Kim. I'm ready to board the jet so I can go to France," Eron said. Tears fell down my face as I listened to my mother and fiancé talk about me as if I wasn't human.

"This is very important," my mother finally said.

"Aight, I'll get my driver to drop me off there. Luckily, I'm not far away," he replied and hung up.

"Dry your eyes and hold your goddamn head up. No man wants a damn crybaby! You're a grown woman, so act like it," she scolded me. She walked out the kitchen and left me pondering my thoughts. I poured another glass of tequila and took it to the head. Surprisingly, the liquor didn't burn as much as the first time. Gautier texted me but I didn't respond. She wanted to know where I was at so I could party with her and Saz. I didn't want them to know what I was going through, it was too embarrassing. Twenty minutes later, Eron walked into the kitchen with a scowl on his face. Eron was caramel and stood at six-foot-seven. He was just a regular cute boy but what made me fall in love with him was his sincerity.

"This better be good, Tyshae. I almost didn't come but I knew Kim would've called me fifteen times if I didn't show up. That woman is a damn pest," he said.

"I wanted to apologize to you for everything that has been happening. I don't want you to leave me and I'm willing to do anything you want me to do. I won't question you again," I said. He walked over to me and hugged me.

"I would love to be with you but I know this is Kim talking. I can't believe you, Tyshae. I thought we could talk like adults but you're sitting here looking weak. I HATE THIS!" he yelled and slammed his hand down on the counter.

"Where is my old girl at? Do you love me or do you love me because your mother wants you to?" he asked.

"Of course, she loves you," my mother said when she came into the kitchen.

"Mind your business, Kim. I'm talking to Tyshae. She's not a little girl and she can answer for herself," he spat.

"Yes, I love you," I replied.

"I don't believe you," he said and pulled away from me.

"Be out of my house by the time I get back," Eron said to me.

SOUL Publications

Use Your Heart and Not Your Eyes

"And you're lucky this house is in your name because you'd be homeless, too," Eron said to my mother before he stormed out.

"Umph, you got a few days to figure out how you're going to get him back because you can't live here. You made your bed, so lie in it," my mother said and walked out the kitchen. I rushed out the house with tears falling from my eyes. I needed something to take the pain away. I headed straight to the liquor store by my old hood. I got out of my money green Lamborghini and slammed the door. I knew I looked crazy with mascara running down my face but it was the least of my worries. I walked down the aisle looking for my favorite liquor which was Long Island ice tea. The doorbell to the store chimed and I heard a familiar voice.

"Ay yo, let me get two Dutch Masters," he said. I wiped my eyes and grabbed the liquor off the shelf. When I walked to the cash register, I came face-to-face with an old childhood friend. Mason aka Cream was standing at the register looking good enough to eat. He wore jean shorts, a sleeveless Gucci tank top with the matching sneakers. I hadn't seen him in years. Just my luck I'd run into him by coming to a place I hadn't visited in a few years. Cream turned around and smirked at me.

"Oh shit, look who came down from the hills. What's up with you, shorty?" he asked as he hugged me.

"I'm okay and yourself?" I replied.

"I was aight but I feel better now that I'm seeing you," he said. His pretty blue eyes eyed me from head to toe and he sexily licked his pink lips. His blonde hair was cut very closely and was faded on the sides. He had colorful tatted sleeves on his lean muscular arms. Cream was the sexiest white boy I had ever seen but he was too hardcore for me. He was one of the biggest drug suppliers in the DMV area. He was raised in the hood and was the only white kid on the block who talked like the rest of the block boys. His voice was even deep and he had been around the hood so long he didn't look like a white boy, he looked mixed.

"Well, it was nice seeing you," I said. I walked around him and placed my twenty bucks on the counter before I walked out the store. All I wanted to do was go home and get drunk in the hot tub while I listened to SWV. It was nice seeing Cream, but I didn't want him to see me that way. I knew I looked a mess from crying.

"Tyshae, wait a minute!" Cream called out.

"What do you want? I'm kinda in a hurry," I replied.

"Everything good witchu? I gotta pay somebody a visit?" he asked.

"No, I'm fine," I lied.

"Girl, stop lying. Your ass was crying. Is it that basketball player you mess with?" he asked.

"I said I'm fine, Cream," I replied.

"Come take a ride with me," he said.

"Nigga, you gotta be out your rabbit mind if you think I'm leaving my car in the hood," I replied.

"Oh, it's like that? This is your hood, too, and you know we love you around here although you don't be around these parts anymore. You know ain't nobody going to fuck with your shit. I'll merk a muthafucka," he said.

"We can take my car and you can leave your car here," I replied.

"So, you want me to leave my Wraith in the hood?" he joked.

"My car cost more," I said and he laughed.

"Aight, I'll get my homeboy to take my whip. Let me call him really quick since he's up the street," he replied. I should've went to the liquor store on my side of town because I was less likely to run into people I knew. Too bad the liquor store on my side didn't sell Long Island. They only sold top shelf liquor and a fancy Long Island I didn't like. I sat in my car contemplating on what I wanted to do. I was ready to peel off but Cream got inside my car and his homeboy pulled up in the passenger's seat of a black Mercedes. Cream looked at me and smirked; his cologne mixed with a scent of weed filled the inside of my car.

"Let's bounce. I'm hungry," he said.

"Wait a minute, Cream. Do I look like I'm in the mood for some food?" I asked.

"You will get in the mood once you see the food. It's this little spot in Baltimore City that stays open until two in the morning. My homeboy and his wife owns it," he replied.

"Are you dirty?" I asked.

"I took a shower a few hours ago," he said.

"Don't play with me, Cream. You know what I'm talking about," I said.

"Naw, I ain't dirty. Girl, if you don't push this pretty car to the limit and chill the hell out. What are you uptight for? I used to hump on you on the playground a while back. Remember that game, Hide and Go Get It?" he asked. I slapped his leg and he chuckled.

"You didn't change one bit," I said.

"I'm true to who I am. Naw, but for real. You were my little star back in the day. I went away to boot camp and when I came home you was with Eron. Did you ever get my letter?" he asked.

"What letter?" I replied.

"I wrote you and asked if you could be my girl. I ain't going to lie, I was mad when I came home. You part of the reason why I moved to Baltimore with my aunt. I wanted to kill Eron but I didn't want anybody thinking it was some kind of hate crime," he said and I giggled.

"I didn't get the letter," I replied.

"That's cause Kim probably trashed it. She hates my white ass," Cream said and he wasn't lying. My mother cursed me out numerous times when she caught me with Cream. I wasn't sure if it was his color or the fact that he was a troubled kid.

"Kim hates everyone," I replied and he chuckled. Cream popped the top off the liquor and poured it into a plastic cup. He took a sip from it and patted his chest.

"What kind of cheap shit is this?" he asked.

"Long Island," I replied.

"Do you really like this crap?" he asked.

"Yup," I said. He passed me the cup and I took a swig from it. It had been a while since I had the brand of Montebello Long Island Iced Tea. Gautier, Salih, Eron, and I used to sneak to the playground and drink it. Those were the good ole days.

"Do you have any kids?" I asked Cream.

"Naw, not yet. I know you don't because your life is all over the internet," he said.

"I know and I honestly don't like it. I can't go nowhere without my picture being taken," I replied.

"I figured that but don't worry. The place we're going to is laid back. We can go through the back door if you want to," he said.

"Eron broke up with me, so his fans will figure it out sooner or later," I replied.

"That's why you were crying?" he asked.

"That along with other things. Me and my mother got into it. You would think she had my best interests at heart but she doesn't. She wants me to work it out with him after he repeatedly dogged me out. My friends don't know what I have been going through. You are the only person I told," I replied.

"Sometimes a man got to lose someone to realize what he had. He'll come around once he realizes you got somebody else's attention," he said.

"I heard that before," I replied.

"Gautier still wild?" he asked.

"No, she calmed down," I laughed.

"Y'all two were something else. Gautier had too much mouth, though," he laughed. We reminisced about the past as I drove to Baltimore. Fifteen minutes later, I was pulling up to a restaurant with black windows off Pulaski Highway. The place was called Tina's. Cream told me to pull around back and a waiter was outside waiting for us.

"I texted my homeboy, Poppy and told him I was coming through the back. The waiter is going to park your whip in the garage," Cream said. I exited out of my car and he followed behind me. When we entered the restaurant, we walked down the hall into a room that overlooked the restaurant. It was so upscale it looked like a club. The back door led to the top floor and the front door must've led to the bottom floor of the restaurant.

"This is nice," I said looking down.

"He just opened it up a few months ago. It was his wife's idea," Cream said. A cute light-skinned guy walked into the room with two bottles of champagne. He looked to be in his early thirties.

"So, you finally brought someone up here with you?" he asked Cream.

"Poppy, this is my homegirl, Tyshae. Tyshae, this is my right-hand man, Poppy," Cream introduced us and I shook Poppy's hand.

"Yo, this Eron's fiancée, ain't it?" Poppy asked.

"Ex-fiancée muthafucka," Cream replied.

"Fake-ass Tommy," Poppy joked.

"That white boy ain't got as much power as Cream," Cream replied.

"You hatin' nigga," Poppy joked.

"Yeah aight. Where is Katina at?" Cream replied.

"She's downstairs in the kitchen. What do y'all want to eat?" Poppy asked.

"I'm not hungry," I said.

"Get her the lasagna topped with crab meat," Cream said. My stomach growled at the thought of the combination. Those who knew me knew I loved crabs and lasagna.

"Aight and you want the usual? Fried chicken, greens, mac and cheese and cornbread with a side of catfish?" Poppy asked Cream and I giggled.

"What's so funny?" Cream asked.

"Nothing," I replied.

"You want the fried oysters for an appetizer, right?" Poppy asked Cream.

"You got it," Cream replied. Poppy sat the bottles of champagne on the table before he left the room.

"How often do you eat here?" I asked Cream as I sat down.

"Almost every night. I don't have nobody to cook for me. I mean my mother and aunt cook all the time but I like my meat seasoned," he said eyeing my thighs. It felt like the temperature in the room went up and I scooted away from him. He chuckled as he popped open a bottle of champagne. He poured me a glass and I took a sip. It was nice, cold, bubbly and it calmed my nerves a bit.

"This is really good," I said.

"Thanks, this is my brand," he replied. I picked up the bottle of champagne and it was called 8th Avenue. It never dawned on me that it was the street we grew up on.

"Wow, I didn't know this was your brand. I hear a lot of people talking about this; it's very expensive," I said.

"I know it is but people love it. You know my grandfather showed me how to make champagne. I hired a few workers, gave them the steps, and it's been on from there. A billionaire is trying to buy it but I don't know if I'm ready to sell the brand yet. I'm just getting started," he replied.

"Interesting, nobody knows who the brand belongs to," I said.

"I like to stay low-key," he replied. A waitress came into our room and placed the plate of oysters down on the table. She was cute in the face but she had an attitude.

"Can I get y'all anything else?" she asked rudely.

"Naw, we are good," Cream replied. She rolled her eyes at him and stormed out the room.

"You fucked her or something?" I asked.

"Naw, she wants me to, but I ain't messing around with Poppy's workers," he said. My phone rang and it was Gautier calling me. I excused myself and walked over to the corner of the room to talk to her in private.

"Hello," I answered.

"About time, Tyshae! I was worried about you. Are you okay? Where are you?" she questioned.

"I'm out having a drink. What's up with the questions?" I asked.

"Eron tweeted something about being single and focusing on his basketball career," she said. I couldn't believe Eron would do something like that so soon but it didn't sound like him. My heart raced as I thought about another woman posting the status under his account.

"Yes, we broke up tonight," I replied.

"And you didn't call me? You know I would've came over. Where are you now? I'm on my way," she said.

"I ran into Cream at the liquor store, so we are having a drink. I'm okay, Gautier," I lied. I wanted to break down all over again.

"White boy Cream? Be careful, Tyshae, you know he's dangerous," she said.

"Stop worrying about me. Have fun and I'll call you when I get in the house," I replied.

"I will see you at the shop tomorrow morning but please be safe," she said.

"I will, Gautier," I replied and she hung up. Gautier was so overprotective at times. I figured it was because she was the only child and didn't have any siblings to look after. I sat back at the table and Cream was on the phone. I didn't know much about dealing drugs but it sounded like he was speaking in code. I poured another glass of champagne until he got off the phone.

"My bad about that," he said.

"So, what else do you do?" I asked.

"I damn sure ain't a ballplayer. Why ask questions when you already have the answers? Just know I'm in the process of changing my life around," he replied.

"I can get with that," I said.

"What have you been up to, though? Are you trying to pursue your singing career?" he asked. I wanted to be a singer but I let my mother talk me out of it. She told me I didn't fit the description of a singer, whatever that meant. She also told me singers struggled before they made it big, which was true for most singers. I realized how much I lost myself over the years.

"No, I haven't. I'm surprised you remembered that," I giggled.

"How could I forget? You used to sing on the school bus and the bus driver told you to audition at the local talent agency. You were thirteen years old then and had a soulful voice, so I know you sound lethal now," he said.

"I haven't sung in a while but I do sing in the shower. It was just a childhood dream of mine," I replied.

"Are you saying childhood dreams are foolish? If that's the case, I should give mine up," he smirked.

"What was your childhood dream? You never talked about it," I replied.

"Marrying you," he said while staring in my eyes. I shyly looked away and the palms of my hands were sweaty.

"I think it's a coincidence running into you after six years. I think it was fate," he said.

"Just a coincidence," I replied and he chuckled.

"You're still a bougie muthafucka, I see," he joked and I playfully slapped his arm. Cream used to live a few doors down from me with his mother, sister, and younger brother. His sister was half Latino and his younger brother was half black. His mother definitely didn't discriminate. His mother Paula was the coolest Caucasian woman I ever met, but for some reason my mother didn't like her. At the time, Cream was the only kid around my age on my block, so we were always together outside. I smoked my first blunt with him on the playground and he was the first boy I kissed. We somewhat grew apart when I moved to a different neighborhood because Gautier became my best friend. Sadly, I outgrew the friendship I had with Cream which was a good thing because he started hanging with a bad crowd. I saw him around my new neighborhood on the block but we somewhat avoided each other because Eron was my boyfriend.

"Are you sure you sent the letter to the right house?" I asked.

"You gave it to me before you moved. I got a good memory, so I'm sure it was the right house. I'm kinda glad you didn't get it because my life was hectic when I came home from boot camp. I got lost deeper in the streets and my mother got strung out on dope. My sister went off to college and never looked back. It was only me and

Jeremy, so I had to take care of him although we were living with my aunt," he said.

"How is Paula now?" I replied.

"She's clean. She has been clean for three years. Jeremy is going off to college once the summer is over. He got accepted on a football scholarship," he said. Our food came minutes later and we talked over dinner. It was two o'clock in the morning when we left the restaurant. We walked to my car but I wasn't ready to be alone. I was always alone when I wasn't with Gautier and Saz. Being alone in the mansion by myself was depressing especially knowing Eron was out doing what he wanted.

"Goodnight and be safe," he said.

"You don't want me to take you back to your car?" I asked.

"I gotta discuss a few things with Poppy so I'm staying back. You got my number so don't be afraid to use it. Let me know when you get home," he said. He kissed my cheek and walked away from me. I stood by my car and watched him disappear back into the restaurant. It took me an hour to get home. My chest felt like it was going to cave in when I finally realized me and Eron were over. I went inside the house and stood in the foyer. I looked around realizing how empty it was although it was furnished. I kicked my heels off and walked down the hallway looking at the pictures of me and Eron on the walls. I stopped in front of a picture of me and him in high school. His team won the basketball championship game and he held the trophy in one arm and his other arm was wrapped around me. We were young but we were so much in love. You could see it in our eyes by staring at the picture. I snatched the picture off the wall and slammed it onto the floor. I burst into tears as I let out a piercing scream which came from somewhere deep within my soul.

"I LOVED YOU!" I cried. I slid down the wall and buried my face in my hands. I didn't know what to do but I had to figure out my own way. It was time I lived for Tyshae and not anyone else. After I cried the rest of my tears, I went into our bedroom and packed everything I owned. I thought about setting the house on fire but I wasn't cut out for jail. I packed until I heard the birds chirping. I called Gautier because I knew she was awake and ready to open the shop. I told her I needed her help and she was on her way with a U-Haul truck.

"Awww, baby. Are you okay?" Gautier hugged me when she arrived at Eron's house.

"I'm fine," I replied.

"What's going on? You can talk to me," she said.

"Eron and I had a falling out. I just need my space, that's all. Just typical couple arguments," I replied. She peeked over my shoulder and looked at the broken picture frames on the floor.

"It seems deeper than that, Tyshae. Was he cheating on you or something?" she asked.

"No, I already told you we just had an argument. Can you help me with my things? I'm so tired and I feel like I'm ready to pass out," I replied.

"Sure, Saz is opening up the shop, so I'm not in a rush," she said. Gautier was the best friend any girl could ask for. She was dressed in a pair of leggings, a T-shirt, tennis shoes and her hair was wrapped up in a scarf. She came prepared to help me and I appreciated her even more. I just wasn't ready to tell her everything that was happening in my life.

"Girl, you got more stuff than what I expected. Looks like your shopping habit is bigger than mine," Gautier said looking around our bedroom.

"I highly doubt that," I replied. While she was bending over grabbing a few things off the bed, I noticed big passion marks on her neck.

"I guess you had fun last night," I said.

"What do you mean?" she replied.

"Those passion marks on your neck are huge," I said and she blushed.

"Girlllll, you won't believe what happened to me yesterday. Make a long story short, Salih and I fucked inside the office at the shop. And, hunnyyyyyy, it was so good I wanted to shoot him. Do you know how good angry dick is? That man fucked me like he wanted to beat my ass," she said. My mouth hung open in shock. Salih and Gautier were real enemies.

"WOW!" was all I could say.

"Then hours later, him and Pita had a romantic dinner. I should've known better but I couldn't resist him. Yesterday he was the old Salih I fell in love with. I wasn't thinking about nothing else besides touching him again but I'm over it now. My mother is going to help me out with Brooke. Salih will have to go to her house to pick up Brooke. I don't want to be around him anymore. It's time I completely let him go," she said.

"But you two have a kid together. Don't you think this is getting old?" I replied.

"Do you know how hard it is for me to be around that man? It's only until I get my feelings in order. Him being engaged is making it even worse. Why did he have to give me that bomb dick? I couldn't sleep last night just thinking about it, but I also feel like he got what he wanted so now we will be back at square one. Why did I fall into his trap?" she asked and plopped down on the bed in frustration. I sat next to her and rested my head on her shoulder.

"Sadly, all three of us have something in common," Gautier said.

"What's that?" I asked.

"Trying to find ourselves," she said.

"I'm not lost," I replied.

"Yeah, you're right. You and Eron are just going through something but y'all love each other and you always seem so happy. I think it's just me and Saz who are trying to figure out our lives. I have a beautiful little girl but it seems like I'm not good enough for her. I haven't been the best role model," Gautier said.

"You're a great mother," I replied.

"I used to think so, too. But, forget about me. Let's get this stuff out of here because the shop is going to be busy today and nobody will stop our bag," she said. It took two hours to load all of my things inside the U-Haul truck. I took it all to storage except for a few duffel bags. I went to Gautier's condo to shower and change my clothes. It was scorching hot outside so I wore high-waist shorts, a white camisole, and a pair of platform sandals. I did my makeup in the bathroom mirror and opted to go natural with the colors. Usually, my makeup was bold but never too colorful. I took the piercing out my cheek and wore diamond stud earrings instead of large hoops. I combed my stiletto nails through my short hair with moose and gel so it could curl like finger waves. A sense of relief came over me as I stared at my reflection.

It's Eron's loss, I thought.

"No purple lipstick?" Gautier asked me when I came out the bathroom.

"Naw, I'm loving this glittery nude," I replied.

"Me, too, it blends well with your complexion," she said as she was putting on her sandals. She wore a jean short-sleeve romper with a pair of cute slide-on thong sandals. Her weave was in a bushy curly mane. Gautier's hips were to die for and the way her butt giggled when she walked was hard to ignore.

"Salih would faint if he saw all that," I laughed.

"I hope he does," she said.

I grabbed my purse and followed Gautier out the door. I stopped thinking about Eron so I could focus on my clients. Work was the only place I found peace.

****

"I heard you and Eron broke up," a client, Janae said while I was doing her lashes.

"We're taking a break," I replied.

Everyone was asking me about Eron all day at work and it was giving me a headache. I didn't like too much attention which was why I didn't want to tell my friends what was really going on. I didn't want a pity party.

"Stop being nosey, Janae," Gautier said.

"I was just asking, Mother Teresa. You think you're somebody's mama," Janae replied.

"I am as long as you're sitting in my shop. Tyshae is trying to work. You must think you're the only one who wants eyelashes. You don't see the waiting area?" Gautier asked and Janae laughed. Gautier was always popping off but the clients loved it.

"Right, she's being all nosey," Lisa said and the shop got quiet. Janae hurriedly sat up and I got pissed off because I glued the eyelash to her cheek instead.

"Oh, see what we not gonna do is act like you get to talk shit," Janae said to Lisa. Lisa started speaking in her language and Janae jumped out of her chair.

"Wait a damn minute, Crouching Tiger Hidden Dragon. Speak English so we can have a legit argument, hoe! You can take all that sushi makusha eye eye shit somewhere else," Janae spat.

"Would you calm down?" Gautier said to Janae.

"No, I will not calm down. I don't like when they start speaking that shit because I know she's saying something smart. You better get Bruce Leroy," Janae said.

"Bruce Leroy? Janae, have a seat honey. Calm down, do you want a glass of champagne?" Saz asked.

"Yes, please, with frozen strawberries. That little heifer done pissed me off. I haven't warmed up to her yet, so tell her don't do me because I'm not a chore. I will slap her damn face," Janae said then popped her gum. Saz hurriedly brought Janae a glass of champagne and she was happy afterwards. Janae was a regular customer and she always spread the word about our shop wherever she went. She also had the latest scoop of what was going on in the entertainment industry. She worked at a high-end strip club in D.C. where the majority of rappers went. She was their best stripper and although her body wasn't natural, she had a beautiful face.

"So, have y'all heard the latest news?" Janae asked and the shop grew quiet.

"Go ahead and spill it because I know this tea is hot," Saz said while she was giving her client a sew-in.

"So, the baseball player wives are having a show. I can't wait because I know they got some mess with them. Salih's fiancée, Pita, will be in the show, too. I know she's going to bring the mess 'cause that lil' heifer is always poppin' off on IG in her comments," Janae said.

"I can't stand her," Lisa said and Janae rolled her eyes.

"Anyways, y'all know Salih is supposed to be cheating on her with his daughter's mother. Nobody knows who she is but hopefully we will get the tea when the show airs," Janae said.

"And how do you know all of this?" Saz asked.

"My cousin's best friend's sister is married to Darrius and you know Darrius is on the same team as Salih," Janae replied.

"Just because Salih wants his life to be secretive doesn't mean he's cheating," Gautier said.

"I don't know but I do want to know what his baby mama looks like. Hell, he barely posts pictures of the little girl's whole face. He's on that Michael Jackson stuff. He might as well name that child Blanket," Janae said.

"I think the mama is dead," one client said.

"Or she could be ugly," someone else spoke up.

"I don't know what she is but I do know she's too quiet. Y'all must not understand how big Salih is down there. Let's just say things got hectic one night in a private room at the club. This was in the beginning of his relationship with Pita, so he was a little loose back then. That fine ass man got some good eggplant. I was ready to leak the footage but I thought better of it. By the way he slings dick, you know he's crazy," Janae said.

"Oh, really?" Gautier asked.

"Yes, chile. I was running from the dick," Janae said and the shop erupted in laughter. Beads of sweat formed on Gautier's forehead and she balled up her fist. I signaled for her to calm down before she exploded.

"Why are you telling that man's business? Damn, you are messy," Saz said to Janae.

"Messy is my middle name and my last name is Money. Janae Messy Money to be exact," she spat.

"My middle name is Slap A Hoe and my last name is Really Quick," Gautier said and Janae laughed oblivious to what was really going on. I prayed Janae would shut up before Gautier dragged her across the shop. I had to change the subject.

"What kind of events are coming up at the strip club? I swear those parties be live," I said.

"We have a party this weekend. You should come. It's a champagne party for 8th Avenue. I can't wait to see that fine-ass white boy who is going to host the party. I'm down with the swirl this weekend. Oh, and I heard Cash Flow is supposed to be there but he never shows up to events if he can't perform. Y'all better get a ticket before it's sold out," Janae said.

"I wonder if Cash Flow is packing," Lisa said and Saz smacked her teeth.

"There is not enough money in the world for me to find out about that Willy Wonka. Cash Flow is a cross between Flava Flav and Dennis Rodman. You gotta be a desperate bitch to let that man fuck. His wife only wants his money. I heard she was creepin' on him anyway with the basketball player, Davian. Davian is stealing everybody's bitches. If he treated basketball like he does his women, he wouldn't be sitting on the sideline all the time. Davian can't steal a ball for shit," Janae said. I breathed a sigh of relief after I was finished her lashes because she was talking entirely too much. I wanted to snatch the weave out of her head when she mentioned Cream. I wasn't jealous but it was just the principle of it. Cream was someone special to me. After she paid me along with the tip, she left.

"About time that bitch left. Somebody is going to beat her ass one day," Saz's client, Keya said and the shop agreed. I went to the back room to get my cell phone and I had no missed calls from Eron.

Use Your Heart and Not Your Eyes

He wasn't trying to beg me back or see if I had a place to go. I was staying at a hotel until I found something closer to the city. All I needed was a studio apartment, nothing too big. I grew tired of big spaces because it always seemed empty. Saz came into the back room and plopped down on the chair. She looked worried about something.

"What's the matter with you?" I asked.

"Cash Flow keeps harassing me about Yudai so I told him I wasn't going to see Yudai anymore. I have to keep my dates with Yudai very private but how can I do that? I really like Yudai, he's so sweet," Saz said.

"Tell Yudai the truth," I replied as I refreshed my lip stick.

"It sounds easy to do but it's not," she said.

"You can't keep letting him control you. You need to do better for yourself and love yourself. You are a pretty, smart, and loving woman, so Yudai will stick around as long as you're honest with him," I said and she cut her eyes at me.

"You are sooooo annoying!" she spat.

"Excuse me?" I asked.

"Cut the bullshit, Tyshae! Gautier may be blind to your lies but I see right through you. Eron is a cheater and you stuck it out with him but I'm the one who needs to have more respect for myself? Practice what you preach or don't say nothing at all. You must get a kick out of this, don't you? Does it make you feel better about yourself when Gautier and I come to you with our problems? You are so quick to judge when your laundry needs washing. Don't play with me today,"

Saz threatened. Gautier came into the back room because she heard Saz's loud mouth.

"What happened?" Gautier asked.

"Saz doesn't like to hear the truth," I replied.

"I always like to hear the truth when it comes from someone who is genuine," she said.

"You two are always arguing," Gautier said.

"Because I see right through Tyshae's bullshit. Tell Gautier about Eron and his mistresses. You keep talking about Cash Flow and Salih not respecting us but your nigga don't respect your damn ass!" Saz said. Tears welled up in my eyes and Saz's face softened.

"I'm sorry," Saz said.

"Is it true, Tyshae? Eron's having an affair?" Gautier asked.

"Yes, and he has a child by one of his mistresses. Eron has been cheating on me since he was drafted to the NBA. He doesn't come home much and he has another home L.A.," I admitted.

"Ohhhhhh, noooooooo. Why you didn't tell us? You shouldn't have been going through that alone. We're your friends," Gautier said.

"I was embarrassed. Everyone refers to us as 'Relationship Goals' but we are far from it. I was trying to salvage our image," I replied. Saz hugged me as she apologized but I was somewhat relieved. The weight of the world was lifted off my shoulders. I confided in my mother about Eron's mistresses but she told me to accept it and I tried. It was the lowest point of my life.

Use Your Heart and Not Your Eyes

"It's time we start cleaning house. This has to stop with us. We aren't getting any younger and the older we get, the more comfortable we'll be with feeling sorry for ourselves. All of this was a minor setback. We are not property to anyone! Saz is going to sell her hair products, I'm going to expand the shop so we can have one in every city, and you are going to figure out what you really want to do. We need to spend more time building ourselves so we can have less focus on the negativity in our lives," Gautier said.

"Amen," Saz said.

"I totally agree," I said.

"Good, now dry your eyes and fix your makeup. Eron will come back, they always come back when they see strength. He'll be begging you on his knees but hopefully he's too late because you can do better. Hell, I can do better, too. Aniston showing up at my condo made me realize I deserve a good man, not someone who is just happy with fucking me whenever he wants to," Gautier said.

"My situation isn't that easy," Saz said.

"We will take care of that later on, but in the meantime, you should stop dating Yudai because you will make it worse," Gautier said to Saz.

"I know you don't want me to, but I agree with Gautier. Your situation is wayyy different because you can possibly hurt someone else for not being honest," I said.

"Okay, fine. I will leave Yudai alone," Saz said.

"Now, ladies, let's get back to work," Gautier said. She and Saz left the room but I stayed back to make a few phone calls. The first call was to change my number. The second call was to check the balance in my secret savings account. Eron thought I was crazy to spend all the shopping money he was giving me throughout the years.

"Your balance is five hundred thousand dollars," the operator said after I punched in my account number.

Checkmate, nigga, I thought.

I was going to put that money to use and focus back on singing. I knew I had to come out of my pocket but it was going to be worth it. Running into Cream was probably one of the best things that happened to me. I was forever grateful.

Saz
Easier Said Than Done

I headed straight home after I left the shop. Yudai was coming over after his game so we could watch a movie. For the past few weeks, I had been keeping our dates on the down low. What would he have said if I told him I was screwing a possessive famous rapper who had dirt on me? My pride wouldn't allow me to tell Yudai that. He thought so highly of me which didn't happen often. I couldn't ruin the image he had of me. Yudai was a flirt but he didn't pressure me into sex. We kissed a lot but it didn't go any further. It was another quality of him I loved. I took off all my clothes and propped my leg up on the tub. I grabbed a jar of wax and used a flat stick to smear the sticky wax on my vagina. It was a painless remedy I created to save money on waxing. After I did my vagina, I did my arms and legs. I turned up the music on my iPhone dock and played the song "Do You Mind" by DJ Khaled. I poured myself a glass of wine and happily danced around my condo. After the wax dried, I peeled it off my skin like glue. My body was smoother than a baby's ass. I stepped into the shower and washed my body. I washed my hair so it could curl up and air-dry into a cute curly mane. After my shower, I dried off and moisturized my skin in shea butter and mango cream. I got dressed in a see-through black leotard with the robe to match. I stepped into a pair of red Manolo Blahnik heels. I took a picture from the side and uploaded it to our website. I posted that the lingerie came in a size 0-24 and was in stock at the store. I sprayed myself with a little perfume and went into the kitchen. I prepped everything that morning so all I had to do was stick the trays in the oven. Yudai wanted teriyaki steak with roasted garlic potatoes and string beans. I poured myself another glass of wine and seductively danced in the middle of the living room while listening to "Wild Thoughts." The doorbell rang and it was nine o'clock. Yudai was right on time. I hurriedly opened the door and he almost dropped the small bag in his hand.

"GODDAMN!" he said eyeing the outfit I had on. I turned around so he could get a full view.

"What's the occasion?" he asked as he walked in.

"No occasion," I replied. He eyed my bald pussy mound and bit his bottom lip.

"You must want some dick," he said bluntly and my clit throbbed. I wrapped my arms around his neck and stood on my tippy toes to kiss his lips.

"You miss me or something? You can't spoil a nigga like this, shorty," Yudai said.

"I can't help it," I playfully whined and he pulled away from me. He adjusted his bulge before he sat on the couch.

"You ain't ready for this meat stick, baby," Yudai said.

"I'm a grown-ass woman," I laughed and he smirked.

"That's not ready. I'm disrespectful to pussy, reallll disrespectful," he said. I was aroused and my nipples poked through the thin material of my lingerie. He beckoned me to come over to him. I sat next to him on the couch and he handed me a small gold gift bag.

"What's this?" I asked. I didn't want any gifts from him. All I wanted was his time. Cash Flow showed me the bad side of gifts. Gifts controlled some women. It made us dependent on them in the worse situations. Sadly, I got accustomed to expensive things instead of focusing on being treated right.

"It's a little something I saw while I was at my jeweler. Open it up and tell me what you think," he replied. I reached into the bag and pulled out a flat square velvet box. I gasped when I opened it. It was a diamond ring, choker, and charm bracelet set. The ring was a baseball with red diamonds in it. The choker had a baseball diamond pendant hanging from it and my bracelet had diamond baseballs, bats, and baseball glove charms.

"This is too expensive. I can tell by the diamonds," I said. If I didn't know anything else, I definitely knew jewelry. The set was enough to buy a car with.

"I wasn't thinking about that when I got it. It reminded me of you so I was willing to pay whatever," he said. I placed the ring on my middle finger and Yudai put the bracelet around my wrist. I pulled up my hair so he could put the choker around my neck. I had butterflies in my stomach and sweat beads on my forehead.

You should stop dating Yudai until the Cash Flow situation is fully under control, I heard Gautier's voice in my head.

Bitch, you're lucky I'm in another country filming this video or else I'll bust your lip for toting that nigga around you. Don't get too comfortable because I will kill you after I handle my business. That's the only thing that's saving you right now, I heard Cash Flow's voice from a conversation we had earlier.

"I gotta tell you something," I said with tear-filled eyes.

"What's up?" Yudai asked and wrapped his arm around me.

Use Your Heart and Not Your Eyes

Tell him! Tell him, Saz! I thought. I couldn't form the words to tell him. It was suffocating me and I almost had a panic attack thinking about Yudai cutting me off. I thought we were going to just date but we spent more time together than I expected. When he wasn't at a game or practice, he was with me. I was finally happy and didn't want to ruin it. Instead of answering him, I slid down on the floor in front of him. I slowly unzipped his shorts and he watched me. I pulled his heavy dick out of his boxer briefs and he smelled clean. He didn't have any pubic hair around his dick and I loved it. The sight of pubic hair sickened me, especially when it was thick and nappy. I seductively stroked the length of him and he bit his lip. Something about his face contorted in passion turned me on. I licked the tip of him before I slid him into my mouth. He grabbed a handful of my hair and a sexy moan escaped his lips. I bobbed up and down his dick as my tongue licked the head of him.

"DAMNNNNN, SSHHHHHHHH," he hissed. I used two hands to jerk him off while I continued to give him head. Seconds later, he was fucking my mouth. He held both sides of my face as he pushed his dick to the back of my throat. Spit ran down my chin and onto his testicles. I massaged his nuts while he made love to my mouth. He threw his head back and made sexy faces as he enjoyed the feeling. I rubbed my pussy as it violently pulsated. I had never been so turned on from giving head in all my life.

"Get up, Saz! I'm ready to nut," Yudai groaned and I sucked him harder. He yanked my hair and almost snapped my neck as he exploded down my throat. I didn't let up until he was drained. He slipped and called me a, "bitch," because I wouldn't stop sucking. They say you'll see a different man if you don't stop when he tells you to.

"Ummmmm," I moaned as he exploded again. I stood up and he was sprawled out on the couch with his dick lying against his inner-thigh. I rushed to the bathroom to brush my teeth and gargle. Yudai came into the bathroom naked and pinned me against the sink.

"Where the condoms at?" he asked. I opened up the medicine cabinet and grabbed a Magnum XL. I bought the box a few days prior because I knew it was bound to happen. Our chemistry was just that strong. He tore open the wrapper and rolled the condom down his erection.

"After all that, you're still hard?" I asked.

"This is the first time it happened like this. The thought of sliding into you brought my nigga back to life," he replied. He ripped the material that covered my pussy and my heart raced. We were finally about to do it. He sat me on the counter by the sink and pushed my legs back. Luckily, I was flexible enough to get comfortable in that position. I whined when his long tongue licked between my slit. He licked his lips then did it again. His tongue pressed against my mound and he pulled my lips between his. I gushed like a water balloon and my essence tickled my ass as it slid down my crack. His tongue curved upward inside of me after he spread my lips. I wasn't into getting ate but Yudai gave me a new outlook. He treated my vagina like a juicy fruit. He licked, slurped, and sucked until I screamed his name. My eyes popped open when he plunged his big dick inside of me.

"Damn, you're tight," he moaned. My body lazily fell against the bathroom mirror as he had his way with me. His dick slammed into my G-spot with no mercy. He leaned forward and kissed me while he stroked the tightness of my walls. I came when he sexily moaned my name in my ear. Yudai wasn't lying when he said he was disrespectful. He fucked me until my body went limp and my pelvis cramped. My knees were pushed back into my chest. I was curled up like a shrimp while savagely getting rammed by a monster dick.

"My bladder! I'm ready to pee!" I yelled out.

"Girl, this pussy is about to squirt for me," he moaned and went deeper. I squealed like a pig giving birth when I came harder than I ever came before. My lips were dry and numb. I couldn't move my legs and my vagina was extra sensitive.

"Just nut already!" I screamed.

"Shut up," he said. He pulled out of me and yanked me off the counter. He turned me around and lifted my leg onto the counter. He pushed me forward and entered me from behind. With one leg up and the other on the floor, I felt every inch of him. He grabbed my hair and pulled my head back. My breasts clapped as he stroked me. He sucked on my neck as he went harder. I choked on my spit from moaning loudly. If I knew guys my age were slinging dick that way, I would've been dating them. I was attracted to older men but that twenty-year-old was something lethal. I fell forward when I climaxed again. Yudai groaned as he spilled his seeds inside the condom. He fell on top of me and kissed the side of my face.

"Asshole," I mumbled and he laughed.

"You mad?" he asked.

"You violated me," I panted.

"I dicked you down, that's all. Stop complaining," he said and pulled out of me. He flushed the condom down the toilet and stepped into the shower. I took off the rest of the lingerie I still had on to join him.

"I didn't want to rush it but you topped me off so I said forget waiting for it," Yudai said.

"I couldn't resist. I was sexually frustrated," I admitted.

After we showered and dried off, I checked on our food and it was almost done. I went back to my bedroom and Yudai was sprawled out on the bed, snoring. I stayed up until the food was done. I placed the trays on top of the stove and covered it up. I was too tired and sore to eat. I got in my bed and snuggled up against Yudai. We were both sound asleep.

****

I woke up the next morning with Yudai inside me. I wasn't a morning sex person but I was reconsidering a lot of things. He sucked my breast as I climaxed. We took a shower together after our blissful morning. I laid across my couch in exhaustion with a towel wrapped around me. I turned on the TV and Maury was on. Yudai kissed my lips after he got dressed.

"I'll see you in two days. I'll be away in New York. You should come with me. We can do something in the big city," he said.

Ohhhh, that won't be a good idea, I thought.

"I would love to but you know that big party is in a few days and I have a lot of clients who need their heads done. I'm overbooked," I replied.

"Aight, I'll call you in a few," he said. He walked to my door but something seemed off about him. It was almost like he was brushing me off. I called out to him and he turned around with a mug on his face.

"Did I miss something?" I asked.

"I don't know, you tell me. Seems like we have been sneaking around or something. Your body language just gave me a bad vibe. Do you gotta a man or something? Let me know now so I can fall back. I have been asking you out for the past week but we keep ending up here. What's up with that?" he asked.

"What's wrong with being private? Did you see the comments underneath our picture the night we went to the movies?" I asked.

"And you care about that? Everyone gets bashed on the internet, EVERYBODY! It's about having tough skin. I wouldn't have asked you out if I cared about things like that," he replied.

"Can we just take this slow?" I asked and he chuckled.

"Bet, I'll see you when I see you," he said before he left. I called out to him but the door closed behind him. I went back over to my couch and laid down. I stared at the ceiling and many thoughts crossed my mind. I wondered if my upbringing caused me to make childish decisions…

"Hey, Ma. Can I have two dollars for the goody store?" I asked her when I walked into the kitchen. She looked at me and sat her wine glass down on the counter. Bertina was a stone-cold full-figured brick house. My mother had it all, a good job, a great husband, and a beautiful daughter which was me. I had a little sister but she died at two years old from cancer. I didn't remember much of her because I was three when she died. My parents were scared of having another child because of what happened to Paige.

"Didn't you just get paid for babysitting?" she asked and I laughed. I batted my long eyelashes and poked my lip out until she laughed.

"You're a spoiled brat," she said. She went into her purse and gave me twenty dollars. At sixteen years old, I had everything a girl could ask for. I lived in a big house in a suburban area and drove a two-door Volkswagen. I grabbed her face and kissed her cheek. I loved my mother and we had the best relationship. We went shopping on the weekends, we did spa days and went on vacations with just the two of us.

"Bring me two Slim Jim's and don't stay out too late because dinner is almost ready," she said.

"Okay," I shouted out. I walked out the house and my father was pulling up in his black Jaguar. He got out his car with his suitcase in his hand. My father worked for a health insurance agency. He didn't make as much as my mother who was a lawyer, but he did have a decent job. My father, Ronald, was a tall, stocky man. He had a bald head and a full goatee. Both of my parents were dark-skinned which explained my midnight skin.

"Hey, Daddy," I said and hugged him.

"Hey, baby girl. Where are you headed? It's almost dinner time," he said.

"I know and I'm coming right back. I gotta have my hot fries before I go to sleep," I replied.

"Bring me something back," he said and gave me a ten-dollar bill.

Use Your Heart and Not Your Eyes

"Okay, I will. Where is your ring?" I asked him. He looked down at his hand and an odd look was plastered on his face.

"It's in my wallet. My hands keep swelling so I have to take it off sometimes. Thanks for reminding me because your mother would've kicked me out," he joked as he squeezed my cheek. I watched him walk into the house before I got into my car. Something about my father seemed different, like he was spaced out. I stopped at my boyfriend's house before I went to the goody store. He was just someone I kicked it with when I wanted to smoke free weed. Willie was average in the face but he gave me money so I didn't complain. He got my nails and hair done every two weeks. His paycheck from Chuck E. Cheese wasn't much but it was enough for me.

"My mother won't be home until later," Willie said as I blew out the smoke.

"And?" I asked.

"What do you think?" he replied.

"My period is on," I lied.

"Your period is always on," he fussed.

"I can't help I have a bleeding condition. I bleed heavy because I have fibroids. Google it, genius," I said.

"Aren't you too old for fibers?" he asked and I rolled my eyes. Not only was Willie a pest, he wasn't the sharpest knife in the drawer.

"Do you hear that?" I asked Willie while putting my shoes on.

"Hear what?" he replied.

"My mother is calling me," I said.

"You live a few blocks away. How can you hear that?" I replied.

"I have a built-in hearing aid so I hear special noises," I lied.

"Ohhh, yeah. I heard about those," he said dumbfounded and I rolled my eyes. I kissed his forehead and stormed out of his junky room. My next stop was the goody store because I had the munches. After I left the store, I arrived at my neighborhood ten minutes later. I was gone for an hour and I knew my parents were going to be mad because dinner had started. I panicked when I pulled up to my house. Police cars and ambulances were in front. I left my car running as I hopped out. I tried to get inside my house but the police pulled me back.

"I live here! Where are my parents? MOMMY! DADDY!" I yelled. I tried to get away from the officer but he wouldn't let me go in.

"You cannot go in because there is a crime scene," a Latina female officer said to me.

"A crime scene?" my voice trembled.

"We got a call to this residence because gunshots were heard," she said and I collapsed on the ground. My neighbor, Erin ran to me and hugged me. She and my mother were close friends.

"What happened?" I cried.

"She killed them," Erin sobbed.

Use Your Heart and Not Your Eyes

"Who?" I asked.

"I don't know. I only saw the back of her when she ran out the house with a gun," Erin cried. She pulled away from me because an officer wanted to talk to her. I sat on the sidewalk in disbelief until the coroners wheeled my parents out in body bags. My life changed in an hour… An hour was all it took.

Tears fell from my eyes as I thought about my loving parents. After they were killed, I lived with my aunt. She stayed out of my way and I stayed out of hers. We didn't talk much but it worked out for two years. After I graduated high school, I left my aunt's home and never looked back. My grandparents on my mother's side were dead and my father's parents were estranged. I didn't have much family. I used the money my mother left me in her will to get an apartment and from there I went to cosmology school. I hated my father and I tried to forget about him. He was the reason my mother was dead. His mistress was sentenced to life in prison. The police found her hours later trying to board a Greyhound after she killed my parents. The sick part about it was that his mistress was only nineteen. I actually knew her and hung out with her a few times. Her name was Evelyn and she was my father's best friend's daughter. She wrote me a letter a few years back explaining why she did what she did. I didn't fully believe her because she was a manipulator and a murderer. She said my father was lustfully looking at her and it started when she was thirteen years old. Evelyn told me she didn't become intimate with him until she was seventeen. It happened when all of us were on a vacation celebrating her parents' anniversary. My father took her innocence and got her pregnant. She had an abortion three times throughout their relationship but the last time caused her to snap. She wanted to keep the baby but my father told her she couldn't because he wasn't leaving his wife. Evelyn stole her father's shot gun and went to my parents' house. She went into details of what happened at my parents' house before she killed them. She apologized ten times in the letter saying she didn't want to kill my mother but the gun went off. I slipped into a deep depression after I read her letter. I could envision her blowing my mother's beautiful face away. My mother couldn't have an open casket because most of her head and face were gone. My stomach knotted up and I ran to the bathroom to throw up. I got sick every time I thought about my parents and Evelyn. My little brother was four years old and Evelyn's parents were raising him. I saw a picture of him as a newborn because Evelyn's psychotic ass sent me a picture of him with the letter. She wanted me to forgive her so I could be in her son's life but I didn't want anything to do with her. I wished she killed herself, too, after she killed my father. Why did she have to take my mother? I loved my mother more than life itself. I wished I was there so I could've died with her or took the bullet for her. My phone rang as I flushed the toilet. I washed my face and hands before I went to the living room to answer my phone. It was Erin calling me.

"Hey, Erin!" I said happily into the phone.

"Hi my beautiful princess. It's hard getting in touch with you these days," she said. Erin checked up on me daily. She wanted me to live with her after my parents were killed but I couldn't do it because she lived next door to my old house.

"I have been busy at the shop. Maybe we can go out to dinner Sunday. We haven't seen each other in months," I said.

"That'll be great. Are you still seeing Ryan?" she asked. Ryan is Cash Flow's real name. He met Erin a while back, before I found out he was married. Erin hated him and it was another reason why I didn't see her much. She begged me numerous times to leave the married man alone but it wasn't easy.

Use Your Heart and Not Your Eyes

"No, we broke up. I will fill you in soon, but I have to get ready for work," I said.

"Okay, call me later. Love ya," she said before she hung up the phone.

I got dressed for work in something quick and easy because I was running late. I called Yudai on my way to the shop and he didn't answer. I sent him a text but didn't get a reply. His practice wasn't until thirty minutes later, so I didn't understand why he was ignoring me. I walked into the shop with my Tom Ford shades covering my eyes. I didn't want to take them off because my eyes were puffy from thinking about my mother. It had been five years since she's been dead and it felt like yesterday.

"I see you blinging. Girlllll, that set is fire," Lisa said while arching her client's eyebrows. I sat in the chair at my station and crossed my arms.

"Thanks," I replied.

"Yudai bought it for you? I can tell because of the baseball," she said as she blew on a stick with wax.

"Yudai and I just had a friendly date, nothing else. We aren't seeing each other, so I suggest you not discuss my business around your clients," I replied and she rolled her eyes. She whispered something to her client and they both laughed. I wanted to take a hot curling iron and hurl it at Lisa's face.

"You and the girls have been very moody lately. Man problems?" Lisa asked me.

"Are you deaf, Lisa? Didn't I just tell you to mind your business, bitch? I'm not in the mood, so I'm liable to kick your ass,"

I said and she giggled. I was ready to respond but two men came into the shop. One had flowers and the other one had two shopping bags.

"Gautier Sadosa, please," the man with the flowers said.

"That would be me," Lisa joked. If looks could kill, she would've been buried with my father.

"Where is Gautier?" I asked Lisa.

"In her office," Lisa replied annoyed.

"I'll go get her," I said. I walked up the stairs and Gautier was taking new items out of the boxes that were shipped to the shop earlier.

"You have two men looking for you," I said.

"Two men? What do they want? Are they the FEDS?" she asked.

"FEDS?" I asked.

"Just had to make sure Pookie and Peanut didn't snitch on me," she joked and I chuckled. She walked downstairs and I followed behind her. She signed for the items and told me to follow her to the break room.

"What's the matter?" I asked.

"I think Aniston is trying to apologize," she said.

"Aniston's cheap ass didn't buy you anything from Neiman Marcus. Open the box," I said. Gautier had a pair of blue velvet Givenchy knee-length boots, two pairs of expensive shades, and a new Chanel bag. Inside the bag was a gift card to an exclusive weekend spa in Virginia.

"Is it Christmas?" I asked, checking out her gifts.

"This is scary, who is doing this?" she asked.

"Salih?" I replied.

"Chile, please. Salih's ass ain't being this nice to me. This is not the first time I have received flowers. I got some before we had sex, so it has to be Aniston. Maybe that's why he was so mad at me, but still, it's not adding up. He saw passion marks on my neck, so I know he's not buying me gifts," she said.

"Call Salih," I said.

"Nooo, I'm scared," she admitted.

"Text him," I replied and she shook her head.

"What if you have a sick person stalking you? Call him and get down to the bottom of it, or do you want me to call him?" I asked.

"Fine, I'll call him," she said. She pulled out her cell phone from her cute gold fanny pack. She dialed Salih's number and he answered on the second ring.

"Make this quick, Gautier. I'm getting ready for practice," Salih said and she cleared her throat.

"Ummm, I have a question for you," she nervously said.

"I wish you'd stop acting like the phone is tapped and spit it out," Salih said, growing impatient and so was I.

"How was your night last night?" Gautier asked and I covered my mouth to keep from giggling.

"Shorty, what do you need? I paid my child support," Salih said.

"I know but, ummmm," Gautier replied.

"See I knew I shouldn't have gave you some dick. You over there with amnesia. What do you want, Gautier? Do you want more of King Salih, baby?" he asked and I howled in laughter. Gautier swatted at me but I couldn't keep it in. It was hysterical listening to Salih's angry behind trying to be smooth and sexy. It was creepy and cute at the same time.

"You got me on speakerphone?" Salih asked.

"Did you send some guys to my shop to bring me gifts?" Gautier asked.

"Yeah, I gave you some good pipe because now you're delusional," he said and Gautier hung up. Salih called back three times and she sent him to voicemail. The phone to the shop rang and I picked it up.

"Luxury Tea, Saz is speaking. How may I help you?" I asked professionally.

"Saz, this is Salih. Look, I can't talk long, but tell Gautier I sent her the gifts. Tell her she gotta pay me back, though. It was a loan," he said and hung up in my ear. I looked at the phone in disbelief. Salih lost every bit of his mind.

"Who was that?" Gautier asked while trying on her new shades in the mirror.

"Wrong number," I chuckled. Her cell phone rang and her face lit up. She hurriedly answered the phone but she didn't stay on it long. She said a few words to the caller before she hung up.

"You look happy," I said.

"That was Cream, I got in touch with him last night because I wanted him to help me with Tyshae's surprise. I'm trying to cheer her up and you know her birthday is in a few days. It'll be her first birthday in years without Eron," Gautier said.

"You're always up to something. What do you want me to do?" I replied.

"I will keep you updated but I got to go back upstairs to do inventory," she said. After she left the room, I called Yudai again but my call went straight to his voicemail.

What am I supposed to do? I thought. Lisa came into the break room giggling on her phone.

"What do you want me to wear tonight?" she asked the person on the phone.

"Ohhhhh, Daddy. I'm going to suck you dry. When are we moving into our new house? My roommate is trippin' on me again," Lisa said. I was eavesdropping but how could I not? I wanted to know who the mystery man was. I liked Lisa in the beginning but she was rubbing me the wrong way for some reason. She smacked her teeth when she noticed I was looking at her.

"Babe, let me call you back. My mother is calling," Lisa said and hung up. I got up and went back out to the main floor. An entourage came into the shop followed by a camera crew.

This shop is always busy! We need our own show, I thought.

"What is going on?" I asked aloud. The small crowd separated and Pita walked through with her shades on. It was summer time but she had on a fur coat.

"Can I help you?" I nervously asked. I hoped she didn't find out about Salih and Gautier.

"Yes, I'm looking for a stylist named Sazzy. One of my good girlfriends told me a lot about this shop. I want to get my hair done and I want my makeup professionally done. I know it's short notice but I heard this is the new place to be. Come take a walk with me," she said. She wrapped her around me and we walked to the corner of the shop. Pita snatched her shades off and I wanted to slap her for being so rude.

"Sorry about this but I heard this place would look great for one of my scenes. It's classy but ghetto at the same time. Sorta like Black Pink Crew, but anyways, I think it would be more exposure for you all if you film this episode with me. My cousin is going to come in here and I want one of your stylists to attack her because apparently they are sleeping with the same man. While all of this is going on, I should be getting my hair shampooed and bragging about my rich fiancé. So, tell me, what do you think?" Pita asked me.

Okay, maybe we don't need our own show. I was just joking, fix it, Jesus, I thought.

"First of all, it's Black Ink Crew. Secondly, you need to ask the owner," I replied.

"Black who? Anyways, it doesn't matter. Point me to your owner," Pita said.

"GAUTIER!" I screamed.

No wonder Salih is miserable. I would be, too, waking up next to Pita. This is a nightmare, I thought. Gautier came down the stairs and froze when she saw the camera crew and a few other girls.

"What is this?" Gautier asked. Pita pushed me out the way and almost tripped.

"I hope y'all assholes didn't film that!" she said to her camera crew.

"Bitch," one of them said.

"Hi, my name is Pita soon-to-be Mrs. Pita Salih Johnson," Pita said.

"Salih's last name is Jones, but what can I help you with?" Gautier asked, wiggling her fingers.

Please don't hit her! Please don't hit her! I yelled in my head.

"Oh, so you know my soon-to-be husband?" Pita asked.

"I'm a huge baseball fan," Gautier replied.

"Great, so when this is over, he can give you an autograph. But I came here to offer my services to you," Pita said.

"Services?" Gautier asked.

"Your shop has been getting a lot of buzz all over the internet and in the streets. It's the type of environment I need to boost my ratings. It will also boost your clientele," Pita said.

"Let me get this right, you want to use my shop towards ignorance and drama and have it on TV?" Gautier asked.

"I'm sure it goes down here anyway but the brighter side is you'll be paid," Pita said. Gautier looked at me and I shrugged my shoulders. The clients in the shop snickered at Pita because of how pressed she was for Gautier's help.

"I'll tell you what. You can use my shop for two hours if you can get your fiancé to do the scene with you," Gautier said.

Salih is going to kill the both of you! I thought.

"He doesn't want to be in this," Pita whispered.

"Trick him into coming. Once he gets here and sees the cameras, he won't have a choice, now will he?" Gautier asked.

"You're brilliant!" Pita yelled. Pita thanked Gautier and told her she'd hear from her soon before she walked out with her entourage behind her.

"What are you doing?" I asked Gautier.

"Plastic face wants messy, I'll give her messy. Make sure Janae has an appointment that day," Gautier said and I smiled.

"Ohhhhhhhhhh, you're petty. Chile, I need to have my own camera for this one," I said and high-fived her.

Use Your Heart and Not Your Eyes

Hours later….

"Come over here, baby, and give me a kiss," Cash Flow said to me. We were at his private condo. Well, I should say our private condo. I didn't think he was coming back so soon but apparently him and his wife had a falling out. He called me fifty times on my way home from work and begged me to come see him. I went home showered and changed my clothes because he didn't like when I dressed down. He told me I looked like a lumber jack when I wore jeans.

Why am I here? I thought.

I scooted closer to him and he gave me a sloppy wet kiss on my lips; I wanted to puke. Cash Flow caressed my pussy through my panties while trying to talk sexy to me.

"I missed you, beautiful. I couldn't even fuck my wife because all I kept doing was thinking about you. I want to leave her for you, do you believe me?" he asked.

Your swamp lizard-looking ass just wants some pussy, I thought.

"I guess so," I answered dryly. I wanted him to drop dead and even thought about poisoning him. I had no one to blame but myself because I could've left. I tried to leave numerous times and it all resulted in something violent. I never told anyone that Cash Flow had stabbed me in the leg before. It was around the time I found out he was married. Yes, I was worried about him leaking photos, but I could possibly deal with that if that's all he could do to me. I was worried about him killing me and getting away with it. He had money to send someone to kill me or he could do it himself. Cash Flow laid on top of me and kissed my neck. His fingers slipped into my panties. I cringed and trembled when his finger entered me. It felt like rape though I wasn't telling him to stop. Tears slid down my face after he put a condom on and entered my body. I thought about my mother's beautiful face while he pumped into me like a jack rabbit. The noises he made weren't sexy like Yudai's. Yudai's moans were intoxicating; I heard the passion my body was giving him in his voice. The way he whispered my name in my ear as if he was in pain but really my pussy was just that good to him. He was rough but sensual. My pussy got wetter as I thought about Yudai eating my pussy like a pink Starburst which was his favorite flavor.

"That's it, baby. Come on this chocolate turkey wing," Cash Flow said. I came because I was thinking about Yudai. I forgot about Cash Flow being inside of me until I heard his voice. Cash Flow jerked and screamed as he filled the condom up with his nasty sperm. His pink hair was sweated out and the scent of his perm smelled like rotten eggs. He laid on top of me and closed his eyes.

"Did you fuck Yudai?" he asked.

"No," I lied.

"Do you know what will happen if you do?" he asked.

"You'll kill me," I said.

"Exactly, now get up and take a shower. After your shower, help me come up with these lyrics for my new song," he replied and I rolled my eyes.

"Do you have an attitude?" he asked.

"No, but I hope you don't think my services are free!" I yelled at him. He slapped me in the face and I slapped him back. He fell onto the floor and held his face in shock. I thought he was going to get angry with me but he didn't. He smiled at me.

"Damn, that was hot. Look what you did to me," he said, pointing at his erection. I hurriedly got up and went into the bathroom with my purse in my hand. I ran my bath water and took the rest of my clothes off. Cash Flow knocked on the door as I stepped into the luxurious tub.

"I'm going to get help! My record label is stressing me out and my wife is, too. I shouldn't take my frustrations out on you because you're the only one who makes me happy. I'm so afraid of losing you and I can't sleep when I think about the things I did to you, so I pop pills to forget," he said.

You threatened to kill me and slapped me just seconds ago, Chucky, I thought.

"I'll be out when I'm finished my bath," I replied.

"Okay, I'm going to fix you something to eat," he said.

I picked up my phone and texted Yudai for the tenth time. Surprisingly he texted back. He told me to chill out because I was overreacting. He left his phone on the bus and was just getting to it. He also said he was mad because they lost their game. I stayed in the tub for almost two hours texting Yudai. I deleted our message thread and put him on silent when I left the bathroom. Cash Flow was sitting in a chair with a notebook in his hand. On the counter in the kitchen was a homemade burger and fries. I sat at the table and ate my food while I eyed him. He snatched his headphones off and looked at me.

"What's wrong with it? I made it the way you like it," he said.

"It's good, thanks," I replied.

"Do you hate me, Saz?" he asked.

Yes, I do, bitch! I hate you so much, I'll spit on your grave, I thought.

"Yes," I answered honestly. He came over to me and kneeled in front of me. Tears fell from his eyes then he burst into sobs. Cash Flow laid on my lap and cried as I ate my sandwich. Ketchup and juice from the tomato dripped onto his soggy pink hair.

"It will get better," I finally said.

"My mother called me today," he blurted out.

"And what happened?" I replied.

"I told that bitch to eat rocks and choke on my nut. She abandoned me but she thinks she can come into my life to use my money. She didn't ask me how I was doing, she only asked if she could get fifty thousand dollars. Are you going to neglect me the same way she did?" he asked.

I loved you but you gave me your ass to kiss! I thought.

"If you don't like how your mother treated you, why do you treat people who really care about you like shit?" I asked.

"I don't know, baby, that's why I need your help. I don't know how to love anybody," he admitted. I gave him a paper towel so he could wipe his face off.

"You stabbed me in the leg," I said.

Use Your Heart and Not Your Eyes

"Wait a minute now, Saz. I didn't mean to do that! You kicked at me while I was swinging the knife. I was only trying to scare you. I thought we were passed that," he said.

"You drugged me so I could sleep with your label mates," I gritted.

"Listen, baby. The owner of the label gets down like that. You're not the only girl that happened to. It was only for fun. I had to prove to them I was down," Cash Flow said.

"Did it happen to your wife?" I asked.

"She wasn't my jump off, you were, but I caught feelings," he said. I pushed him away from me and headed to the kitchen.

"I should've followed my heart instead of letting my eyes guide me into the wrong direction. I guess we used each other but I got what I deserved for wanting your money. I didn't think I was going to fall for you in the process, but I did. It was the worst shit in my life. My mother worked her ass off so I could have a better life and look at how I repaid her. I let an ungrateful, ugly, rat face gutta snake manipulate me because he gave me diamonds. After all we had been through, do you think I really still love you? I don't want you touching me. I cringe when you look at me. I hate those overly-processed split ends in your hair. Look at you! Look in the mirror because I know you hate yourself more than how much I hate you. YOU RUINED MY LIFE!" I screamed as I threw my glass plate into the wall.

"I'm sorry, Saz. I'm so sorry. I had to be who I was rapping about. Listen, we can start a family together. We can make another baby, and this time you can keep it. I'll leave my wife right now, fuck her. Just please help me. I need somebody to help me," he begged on his knees with tears falling down his face.

"Where are the videos and pictures you had of me? Let's get rid of those first then we can talk about moving forward," I replied.

"There wasn't any. I lied to control you. I only had that one I leaked last year and that's because you dumped me. I can't deal with people abandoning me. Look, just join me for counseling. I feel like I'm really losing you this time. I sensed it while I was on top of you," he sobbed.

Crazy bastard. You just hate to see my strength, I thought.

"When do you go to counseling?" I asked.

"Tomorrow," he said.

"Okay, I'll go, but if you have any videos or pictures of me, you need to tell me right now," I replied.

"I swear I don't," he said.

"Go take a shower and I'll write a few rhymes down to see if they flow," I said.

"Okay, beautiful," he replied. I waited until he went into the bathroom before I pulled my phone out from behind me. I pressed the *stop* button and a devious smile spread across my face.

I got that ass. This is for collateral, I thought.

****

"Why are you nervous?" I asked Cash Flow as we sat in the back seat of a black Yukon. We were on our way to his first counseling session. I stayed overnight with him. A part of me was happy he was breaking down and the other side of me felt sorry for him. The Yukon pulled up to the back of a building in downtown Baltimore. I pulled my hat over my eyes and pushed my shades closer to my face so no one could see me. I wore my hair out so it could cover my face. Cash Flow's bodyguards escorted him into the building and I followed behind them. I immediately sat in a chair when we made it to Dr. Samuels' office. He was a middle-aged black man with a close cut. He wore a tailored brown suit with a cream-colored tie. He sat in a chair across from us and pulled out a leather book to write in.

"Good morning, Ryan Winston, and who is this lovely lady?" Dr. Samuels asked.

"She's my fiancée, Saz Thompson," Cash Flow said and I patted his leg.

"She's my mistress. I'm married to another woman who I will be divorcing soon," he admitted.

"Interesting," Dr. Samuels said as he began to write in his book.

"Your mother should be joining us shortly," Dr. Samuels said.

"Wait, your mother is coming, too?" I asked.

"Yes, that's why I need you here," Cash Flow said and I rolled my eyes. We silently waited for five minutes until there was a knock on the door. Dr. Samuels's secretary escorted a heavyweight woman in who was dressed like she was going to, or coming from, a funeral. She wore all black and the veil on her black hat covered her eyes.

She had a tissue in her hand and silently wept. I wanted to laugh but I held my composure.

"Have a seat, Ms. Winston," the doctor said. She sat in a chair then burst into a fit of tears.

"Excuse me but my arthritis is acting up. I have a rich son who refuses to pay for my medical bills. They are going to take my house from me and I just came from my father's funeral. I also have been eating Vienna sausages for two weeks and now I'm constipated. OUCH!" she screamed and I jumped.

"My hemorrhoids are kicking my ass. It comes from constipation. I'm a nervous wreck. I had a stroke last week. I lost vision in my left eye. Can you please me help me?" Ms. Winston cried and Dr. Samuels began to feel sorry for her.

"Cut that bullshit out! You were on Snapchat last week shaking your ass at a cookout! And your father been dead!" Cash Flow yelled at her. She pulled a knife out her purse and I covered my mouth.

"I'll kill your cabbage patch doll-looking ass! I gave birth to you and you treat me like this? It wasn't my fault I had to go to jail for protecting you. You make me sick! Tell these people how you were growing up. You were crazy and was always doing sick things. You killed the family dog, you set our house on fire from playing with matches, and you stabbed my brother. I took the blame for you. You owe me EVERYTHING!" Ms. Winston said.

"That's because your brother was making me do shit I didn't wanna do, and if you were home, you would've known I needed help, bitch!" Cash Flow yelled.

"Let's all calm down," Dr. Samuels said. Ms. Winston pulled out an inhaler from her purse and Cash Flow threw his arms up in frustration.

"Oh, now you got asthma?" Cash Flow asked his mother.

"I got one lung," she said.

"You two have to take turns talking. Ryan, you go first," Dr. Samuels said in frustration. I bet it was the craziest thing he had seen throughout his career.

"My mother's brother lived with us. She wanted him to stay there because he received a lot of SSI money each month. She used to run the streets and gamble with his money, leaving me in the house with him. He did a lot screwed-up things to me. Nothing sexually but he made me dress like a little girl so he could jerk off. He didn't touch me but it screwed my head up. I had to wear my mother's bra and stuff them so he could think I had breasts. He got off on that sick shit. I kept telling my mother and she did nothing. She told me as long as he didn't molest me, it was fine. She said we needed his money because it was paying the bills. I got so used to dressing like a girl, I went to school in my mother's shirts. The niggas used to bully me and the girls teased me, they called me 'faggots.' I went home and stabbed my uncle in the neck while he was sleeping. My mother took the blame for me. She said she did it because he was abusing me. Truthfully, she knew I was going to be a star. I was a teenager but also a talented rapper. She didn't want to miss out on her meal ticket. She never cared about me, all she wanted was the money. She thinks I owe her something but I don't owe her shit. She took my charge but I don't see it as a favor. She should've prevented it," Cash Flow said. I grabbed his hand and squeezed it as tears ran down his face. I rolled my eyes at Ms. Winston because she was the reason her son was confused.

"I gotta go. This faggot won't give me any money. I came here because I thought he was ready to pay up but all he wants to do is complain. Burnt tooth, fairy ass-looking punk," Ms. Winston said before she stormed out the room.

"Woowwwww," Dr. Samuels said and took off his glasses.

"I wanted Saz to see why it's hard for me to show her I love her. I did some messed up things to her but she hates me. I can see how she looks at me that she hates me. I really love her and I want to change for her before I lose her to someone else," Cash Flow said.

"Do you really love her or are you jealous because you think another man is in the picture?" Dr. Samuels asked and Cash Flow fidgeted in his seat.

"Both. I'm jealous because I love her," Cash Flow said. Dr. Samuels closed his notebook and sat it on the table beside him.

"I'm not trying to attack you, Mr. Winston, but you wouldn't have to be jealous if you really loved Ms. Thompson. Love and jealousy can be relatable, but most men are jealous because of guilt. Guilt which stems from your wrongdoings. What is this other man like?" Dr. Samuels asked.

"Are you asking me or him?" I spoke up.

"Whomever has the answer to the question," Dr. Samuels said.

"He's happy to be seen with her. I know it's friendly and I don't think Saz will cross me like that, but I can't offer her certain things. I have an image to protect far as what my fans expect from me. Saz is not really the model exotic type I rap about," Cash Flow answered.

Use Your Heart and Not Your Eyes

Dr. Samuels cleared his throat and I could tell by his body language he was embarrassed to hear a black man speak so ignorantly.

"Can you be specific when you say exotic?" Dr. Samuels said.

"Asian, Latino, Panamanian and all the foreign girls," Cash Flow responded.

"Black women are the most exotic women on this planet. Why do you think the white man used to leave his wife's bed at night on the slave plantations? Why do you think women pay for shapely bodies and bigger lips? Black women are the most beautiful women on this Earth, I don't care what size they are. I'm not speaking against other cultures, I'm speaking as a black man who was birthed by a strong black queen," Dr. Samuels said.

"This day in age, that doesn't matter. It's about looks and that's what sells," Cash Flow said.

"It's called being brainwashed by social media. Black women don't sell because they are priceless," Dr. Samuels said.

"I gotta bounce. Is this session over? I have a photo shoot and I need to board my private jet in a few," Cash Flow said. He stood up and walked out the office with the door slamming behind him. Tears fell from my eyes and Dr. Samuels handed me a tissue.

"Follow your heart, Ms. Thompson. I am a huge fan of Yudai. I don't know much about him personally but I have followed a few of his interviews and volunteered at the homeless shelter with him. A man who doesn't hide his interest is a man worth taking a chance with. I saw a picture of the two of you. I knew who you were as soon as you walked in," he said and I nodded my head. I thanked him before I walked out his office. I walked out the back door and got inside the Yukon where Cash Flow was on the phone arguing with his wife.

"Bitch, fuck you!" he yelled into the phone before he hung up.

"Sorry about that, Rosara is bugging me out about a pregnancy test. She thinks she's pregnant," he said.

"It's cool," I said and he scooted closer to me.

"Fuck that punk ass doctor. He doesn't know what he's talking about. I love you but you have to understand my career," he said.

"I understand your career; how soon can I get dropped off to my car? I need to go to work in a few," I said.

"We're headed there now," he said.

The drive to his building was a silent one. He was on his phone talking to his publicist and stylist as I stared out the window. Dr. Samuels's voice played over and over inside my head.

"Here you go, take this," Cash Flow said giving me a stack of money. I took it and placed it inside my purse.

"I'll be away for a few days, but when I come back, I'm going to spend time with you," he said and kissed my lips. I got out the truck and slammed the door. When the truck pulled off, I walked in the opposite direction. I left my car in the garage because I no longer wanted it. I called an Uber and the driver arrived five minutes later. While I was cruising through the city on my way to the shop, I saw a woman standing on the sidewalk with a sign and a little girl. Apparently, she was homeless and just lost her job. While sitting at the red light, I put my window down and beckoned her to come over to me. I gave her the stack of money and tears filled her eyes.

"Thank you so much! Thank you!" she said with a deep accent. I waved at her as the Uber driver pulled off. I didn't count the money because it stopped being about the money. Money couldn't void the sadness in my heart. Money couldn't erase the ignorant and embarrassing comments Cash Flow made. Cash Flow wasn't going to change because he had deep-rooted issues within himself. The Uber driver pulled up to the shop and as I was ready to get out, he stopped me.

"This ride is free. That was a beautiful thing you did back there. You're a hero and I bet that little girl and her mother will forever remember your face," the middle-aged white man said.

"Thank you and have a nice day," I smiled.

"God bless you," he said.

I walked into the shop and it wasn't crowded which was a good thing. I didn't like showing up with a lot of people waiting because it didn't look good for business. I went to the break room and grabbed my work vest. I dug into my purse looking for the set Yudai bought for me and I couldn't find it. I began to panic as I dumped all of the contents out on the table.

"What's the matter with you?" Tyshae asked when she walked into the break room.

"I can't find my set," I cried.

"What set?" she asked.

"The set Yudai bought for me," I said.

Use Your Heart and Not Your Eyes

"Where did you have it?" she asked, looking through my things on the table.

"I went over to Cash Flow's condo last night and I put it in my purse on my way there because I didn't want him to see it," I replied.

"Do you think he took it?" she asked.

"No, I would've known if he did. My purse didn't leave my sight," I said.

"Are you sure, Saz? Cash Flow has female tendencies. He could've went through your purse while you were asleep. Matter of fact, I thought we were on a new path? How did you end up with that smurf?" Tyshae asked. I sat down in a chair with my face buried in my hands.

"I screwed up, Tyshae. I slept with you Yudai," I admitted.

"WHAT!" she said.

"I couldn't break it off with him. I caught feelings for him too quick. I mean real feelings. Going to therapy with Cash Flow made me realize how much I really like Yudai and how much he respects me. I have been very emotional these past few days. I'm scared for my life. I don't know what to expect and it's bothering me," I complained. Tyshae sat next to me and grabbed my hand.

"We will get through this together. I think me and Gautier shouldn't pressure you so much. It takes time getting over someone. I guess our hate for him put a lot of pressure on you to the point where you have been keeping things away from us. I'm very sorry," Tyshae said.

"Thank you for understanding. This really means so much to me because I'm just so tired of dealing with everything on my own. Even when my mother was killed, I dealt with the pain on my own because I couldn't talk to anyone. I'm just exhausted," I replied.

"Me, too, but I will say this. Eron leaving me and kicking me out of his house is the best thing that happened to me. I woke up this morning and started twerking," she said and I laughed.

"To what song?" I asked.

"'Bodak Yellow,' that new Cardi B! Owwwwwwwww," Tyshae said with her tongue out her mouth imitating Cardi B.

"Where is Gautier?" I asked.

"She's making sure her new house is up to par. You know Gautier wants everything to be perfect," Tyshae said.

"Let me get to work before Wanda cusses me out," I replied. I went to my station and called Wanda to my chair. She had an attitude with me as she sat down.

"I'm sorry," I said.

"Ummm hmmmm, be glad nobody else can do a frontal like you," she said.

"And that is the truth," I replied.

As the day went on, all I could think about was Yudai's set and where it could've been. Cash Flow would've questioned me if he took it. I figured I dropped it while trying to hide it inside my purse. It was nine o'clock at night and I was on my last client. The bell to the door chimed and Yudai walked in looking like a million bucks. Tyshae looked at me and smiled and Gautier winked at me as she was sweeping the floor. He kissed my forehead before he sat in a chair in my station. His cologne lingered and oozed of sex appeal.

"I thought you was staying in New York after the game," I said.

"I caught an early flight. How long are you going to be? My cornrows are looking a little rough," he said.

"I'm almost done," I replied.

After I was finished my last client, she left behind Tyshae and Gautier. It was my turn to close the shop anyway, so I wasn't complaining. Yudai sat in my chair and he lustfully eyed me.

"Why are you looking at me like that?" I asked.

"Damn, I can't stare at your fine ass?" he replied. He pulled me down and grabbed my face to kiss me. My knees almost gave up on me. He pulled away from me and winked at me.

"I apologize for how I left your crib the other morning. Playing the Yankees is stressful at times because it's one of our biggest games. I was on edge and somewhat took it out on you. If you want to keep it private until we decide to take it further, I'm cool with that," he said.

Tell him the truth! I thought.

"Why are you so perfect?" I asked and he smirked showing his sexy grill.

Use Your Heart and Not Your Eyes

"Not as perfect as you, though," he said and my heart almost skipped a beat. I pecked his lips again before I took his hair out. I smacked his shoulders a few times while I was washing his hair because he couldn't keep his hands to himself.

"Damn it, Yudai. Water is everywhere! Keep still!" I complained.

"You got your titties in my face. What do you expect?" he asked. After I was finished washing his hair, I cornrowed it. I used my clippers and touched him up on the sides. I turned his chair around so he could face the mirror.

"Awwww, shit, a nigga looking GQ," he joked. He reached into his pocket and pulled out a wad of money. He tried to pay me for his hair but I pushed his hand away.

"We are past that," I replied.

"Oh, word?" he said. He placed his hands on the side of my ass cheeks and pulled me closer to him. I wrapped my arms around him and melted in his embrace.

"How about we chill at my crib tonight," Yudai said.

"Okay, I need to swing by my home and get some things," I replied.

"You don't need to," he said.

****

Use Your Heart and Not Your Eyes

Yudai pulled up to a ranch-style mansion two hours away from Annapolis. It was on the outskirts of Philadelphia. It was a beautiful home with four cars parked in his driveway. It was my first time at his house because he was always staying at a hotel in the inner-city. I got out his car in awe.

"This is beautiful. Do I hear water?" I asked.

"Yeah, there's a lake-style pool in the back of the house," he replied.

"Oh my God, I want to see it," I said in excitement. We walked around to the back of the house and there was a beautiful pool in the back which resembled a lake; the scenery was breathtaking.

The light in the back of the house came on and a short brown-skinned woman came out of the sliding doors. She wore a long silk Dashiki and her hair was wrapped up in scarf.

"Yudai, who is this woman?" his mother asked with a slight accent.

"This is Saz, Ma. Saz, this is my mother, Ekemma," he replied.

"Hello," I shyly waved. His mother crossed her arms and eyed me up and down.

"What's her business here?" she asked.

Nigga, I know damn well you don't live with your mama, I thought.

Yudai kissed his mother on the cheek and he said something to her in French. I knew it was French because I went to school with a few African girls who spoke it. I should've known he came from a different background because of his name.

"Excuse my rudeness, I thought you were up to no good. He expressed how much he likes you. I'm going to go in and check up on your father, you two be safe and you know what I mean," she said before she stormed back into the house.

"That was awkward," I said and Yudai chuckled.

"My parents come here to housesit when I'm away but I actually like them living here. I'm very close with my parents and I know you thinking I'm a mama's boy," he said and I chuckled.

"It's cute," I replied and squeezed his cheek.

"Yeah, aight," he replied.

"Where is your accent from?" I asked.

"I don't have one. I was born in Maryland and my father is American. My mother moved to the U.S. when she was a teenager. She met my father at work and they hit it off. Her English is still rocky but she taught me and my sisters French, so I speak to her in French a lot," he said.

"So, that's why you hung low?" I joked and he burst into a fit of laughter.

"Mandingo tribe, huh?" he asked and I nodded.

"Let's go further down where it's dark," he said.

"Your parents might be watching," I replied.

"This is my house, shorty, and it ain't like I'm doing it in their faces. So, what, you scared?" he asked.

"Your young ass is always talking smack," I replied.

"And I proved to you I can back it up. Had that ass begging me to stop," he said.

I'm going to fall in love with you, I can feel it, I thought.

I walked to the end of the pool where it was dark. I kicked off my shoes and took off my leggings. I sat on the edge and put my feet into the water. Yudai took off his clothes and shoes and got into the pool only wearing his boxer briefs. He was gorgeous and although that's not usually a term used to describe a man, he was. His physique and body art gave him a pretty boy thug appeal. He stood between my legs and massaged my thighs. I figured Yudai was respectful to women because he saw how his father treated his mother.

"I was thinking about you all day today," he admitted.

"Thinking about getting your piece wet, huh?" I asked.

"Naw, I mean it's past great but I was thinking about your silly ass attitude. I like how we vibe when we talk. The shorties I have come across was always extra in trying to impress me when really, I like laid back females. Don't get me wrong, though, you bougie as fuck but you got a little sass to it. I got you stored in my phone as Sassy," he said. I looked away from him and he lifted my head up. He seductively licked my lips then pulled away from me with a devious smile on his face.

"Nigga, I know damn—ahhhhhh," I screamed when he yanked me into the water. I flailed my arms and kicked my feet.

"I'm drowning!" I screamed and Yudai cracked up laughing.

"HELP!" I yelled.

"Girl, cut that shit out, stand up," he said. I stopped flailing around and stood up in the water. I was so embarrassed I wanted to fight him.

"I should kick your ass!" I yelled.

"My mother will come out here on that tip. Don't say nothing if she shoots you with a needle out a wooden straw. Those things hurt," he said. I tried to get out the pool but he pulled me back.

"You mad?" he asked.

"Yeah, I'm mad. Gautier just did my eyelashes," I complained. Yudai pushed his body against mine and I felt his hard-on. He slid my boy shirts to the side and slide in his finger into me.

"Get away," I moaned.

"Shut up," he replied.

"Ohhhh, this feels good," I moaned against his lips. He inserted another finger inside of me and his thumb circled around my clit. His lips brushed against my neck and he kissed it.

"Ummmmmmm," I whined as my body climaxed. Yudai was familiar with my body already and that was a dangerous thing. It took him just one night when it took others before him months or sometimes never. He pulled his fingers out of me after he was finished.

"Let's go in the house," he said and we climbed out of the pool. I tiptoed behind him and followed him to the side of the house. I couldn't wait to get out of my wet, cold clothes. The air conditioner made it worse.

"It's cold in here," I whispered.

"Why are you whispering?" he asked.

"Your parents are here," I said.

"But this is my house, so chill out. Damn, you got me paranoid," he replied. I followed him down a long hallway past a few life-size African statues until we stopped at double doors with "Y" handles.

"Really?" I asked and he chuckled.

"Why not?" he replied. He pulled the doors open and his room was the size of my condo. A king size bed sat in the middle of the room and there was a small aquarium behind his bed on the wall. The whole wall was a gigantic fish tank with pretty exotic fish.

"This is dope," I said.

His room didn't have much furniture in it but it was enough. It was clean, and although it was plain, it was still a nice room. His bathroom had two toilets, a Jacuzzi, and walk-in shower that could fit five people or more inside.

Yudai helped me out of my wet clothes and laid them across the sink. I stepped into the shower and he stepped in with me. I playfully mushed his face with a handful of soap. He turned me around and gave me a loud smack on my ass that stung.

"OUCH!" I yelled.

"Yo, you stay playing with me. Keep on, Saz," he threatened and I poked my lip out.

"Awww, mama's baby is about to cry," I joked and he slapped me on the ass again.

"Aight, I'll stop," I screamed in laugher.

After we showered and dried off, I got dressed in one of his T-shirts. I got underneath his comforter, and my body sank comfortably into the mattress. I yawned from exhaustion. Yudai got in bed with me and turned the TV on which hung from his ceiling.

"What's up with your product? Are you selling it yet?" he asked.

"No, not yet. I have to find a name for it and I need to do other things," I replied.

"Sazzy's," he said.

"That's plain," I replied.

"But it's catchy and, besides, the name is so simple I think it will market better. You must want one of those long ass names that can't even fit on the bottle and is hard to pronounce. My sisters be losing their hair stuff and can't even tell you the name of it when you try to help them find it. Why do y'all women do that?" he asked and I giggled.

"Because we do that," I replied.

"My sister, Imani used to come into my room like, 'Yudai, did your simple-headed ass see my hair stuff in the pink bottle.' The whole time I was throwing it in the trash because she kept popping off with her mouth," he said.

"Don't mess with a woman's hair products," I replied.

"I don't, my sisters jumped me as soon as I stepped off the school bus," he laughed.

"Sounds like you had fun growing up," I replied.

"Yeah, although we were a poor, it was cool because we had each other," he said.

"Poor?" I asked.

"Yeah, we had a roof over our heads and food on the table but the materialistic things, not so much. Our parents raised us with love," he said. I laid on his chest and he rubbed his fingers through my hair and massaged my scalp. Yudai and I sat up and talked about everything until we fell asleep.

BOOM! BOOM!

I jumped and looked around the room. Yudai came out the bathroom brushing his teeth.

"YUDAI! Tell your company to fix herself up and help prepare breakfast!" his mother said.

"She's coming," Yudai called out and I looked at him.

Use Your Heart and Not Your Eyes

"Sometimes my sisters come over to cook breakfast but they are not here," he said.

"What am I going to wear?" I asked.

"Put on my baller shorts. Are you shy or something?" he chuckled.

"I'm scared," I said.

"Get up and stop tripping," he said. He pulled the covers off me and I climbed out of bed pouting. He playfully smacked my butt as I walked to the bathroom. He had an extra toothbrush on the sink for me. After I took care of my morning hygiene, I slid on a pair of his shorts and left his bedroom. When I walked into the kitchen, his mother was cleaning fish.

"Good morning, Mrs. Hasan," I said.

"You can call me Ekemma. I'm still young," she said.

"I don't know how to clean fish. I never ate it for breakfast," I said.

"Yudai and his father likes fried fish in the morning. I don't quite understand it myself but they like it with grits," she said. I picked up the fish by its tail with my nails and almost gagged.

"This is disgusting," I mumbled and she smacked her teeth.

"Chile, you will get used to it if you are planning on spending more time with my son. I'll show you how to clean, and don't worry, I'll give you some gloves so you won't mess up your nails," she said. She reached into a drawer and pulled out a pair of plastic gloves and I was embarrassed.

"I'm okay, I need a filling anyway," I lied and she laughed.

"Saz, honey, it's okay. You don't need to impress me. Just be yourself, I don't bite. I use gloves myself when my set is fresh," she said. Ekemma wasn't as mean as she looked, she was actually nice. It brought back memories of cooking with my mother. After we cleaned the fish, I skinned a batch of potatoes before I chopped them up.

"What are your intentions with Yudai?" she asked.

"We're just dating right now," I replied and she chuckled.

"It seems more than dating to me. My son never brought a girl around this family. I was actually surprised last night to see you. He must really be smitten by you. How long have you two been dating?" she asked.

"Over a month," I replied.

"And you're already meeting the family. What did you do to my son?" she laughed.

Your son has been doing things to me, I thought.

"I wasn't expecting it to happen so fast. I still can't believe it myself," I replied.

"I met his father at a hotel. I was a housekeeper and he worked in the kitchen. We fell in love in a week. My family didn't want us together, it made us closer," she said.

"Why?" I asked.

"My father was strict. He wanted me with a Nigerian man. Yudai's father was everything he hated. Lyle was a troubled teen who ran the streets. He was a part of a gang and the only reason he got a job was to avoid going to jail. I was twenty years old when I had our first child. My family disowned me because I wasn't married. Till this day, I don't regret nothing," she said.

"Where is your family now?" I asked.

"They moved back to Africa a few years ago. I haven't spoken to them in years, they never met my kids. They kicked me out when I was pregnant. I lived with Lyle and his mother until we had our second daughter. The apartment was too small for all of us. I couldn't get good jobs because my English wasn't so clear. I still have trouble with certain words but thank God it isn't that bad," she said.

"Sorry to hear that about your family," I replied.

"I was very heartbroken but Lyle and his family comfort me," she said.

A tall light-skinned handsome man with hazel eyes walked into the kitchen with a tissue in his hand. He coughed into the tissue and his eyes was running. It didn't take much for me to figure out it was Yudai's father. Yudai resembled him. The only difference was their complexion. Yudai was a tab bit darker.

"I told you to stay in the bed. Why are you spreading your germs around?" Ekemma asked her husband.

"Good morning," his father said to me.

"Good morning, my name is Saz," I said.

"I'm Lyle. I would shake your hand or give you a hug but I have a cold," he said. Yudai came into the kitchen and his father placed him in a headlock. His mother yelled at them in French.

"Chill, Ma," Yudai said.

"Get out the kitchen! You want to play, go outside," she spat.

"Come on, Pops, let's play a game in Madden really quick," Yudai said.

"Hurry up so I can kick your ass," Lyle said as they headed out the kitchen.

Ekemma and I talked and got to know each other while we prepared breakfast. I was exhausted from standing up in the kitchen cooking a meal for four people. You would've thought we were cooking for a big family. The front door opened and I heard heels clicking against the floor.

"Smells good in here, Mother!" a female called out. I wasn't expecting to meet Yudai's sisters. Sisters were hard to get along with, sometimes harder than the mother. Two women came into the kitchen and they were plus size. The taller one was prettier and shapelier than the shorter one, although they both had wide hips. I could tell the shorter one was going to be a problem because of how she looked at me.

"Hi, my name is Zoya. I loovveeeee you and your friends. I follow y'all on IG," the taller one said.

"Thank you and I love those shoes," I said, admiring her style. The shorter one squinted her eyes at me.

"Speak, Imani," Ekemma said to her daughter.

"I'll speak to her when I realize she's not a gold digger," Imani said.

BITCH!

"Why do you always have to be an evil wench? You know darn well Yudai can spot a gold digger from a mile away," Zoya said.

"So can I and I have," Imani said.

"Saz is a popping hairstylist throughout the city. She doesn't need our brother's money," Zoya said. Zoya took my hand and pulled me toward the kitchen table.

"Girl, sit down and be comfortable. Imani is the oldest so she tries to be like our mother. Pay her no mind, but I'm glad to finally meet you in person. Yudai is always talking about you. I actually called the shop today to schedule a hair appointment with you but nobody answered," she said.

"Gautier probably didn't make it in yet," I replied.

"We usually help with breakfast but me and Imani just got back to town. She went with me for a photo shoot," Zoya said.

"That's awesome, what was it for, if you don't mind me asking," I replied.

"Modeling. I'm modeling for bigger girls. If you ever need me for the boutique, just let me know. I'm not trying to sound pressed, but let's face it, the media sleeps on girls like us. I screamed when I found out you and Yudai were dating," she said.

"Awwww," I said. I liked Zoya, she reminded me so much of Gautier.

"When did you start modeling?" I asked.

"This was my first professional shoot. I also want to be an actress, too, so I figure I do this to get my foot in the door for more exposure," she said.

"I wish you nothing but the best," I replied. Yudai came into the kitchen and went into the fridge.

"Y'all not messing with my lil' shorty is y'all?" Yudai asked and I blushed. He sat next to me and kissed my cheek.

"I hope y'all are using protection. Lord knows we don't need her putting you on child support," Imani said.

"Mind yo' business, Imani. This ain't got nothing to do with you. Get your daughter, Ma, because she's being disrespectful to my company in my house," Yudai replied.

"No, it's okay. I don't mind answering her questions. Yudai will never have to worry about me trapping him because I don't want kids," I admitted. Ekemma looked shocked and so did Yudai.

"Wait, so you don't see a future with Yudai? Yudai wants kids," Imani said and Zoya shook her head.

"We are just dating. We are still in the process of getting to know one another," I replied.

"But you didn't stop him from hitting it. Typical gold digger. Take what you can from him but don't see a future with him," she said.

"ENOUGH!" Ekemma said to her daughter.

"How do you know they are sleeping together?" Zoya asked Imani.

"Yudai is pussy whipped. Look at him. He barely knows her and she's already sitting with the family for breakfast. She's even cooking dinner with our mother which I think is too much considering she's still getting to know him. Y'all are moving too fast," Imani said.

"Go home, Imani," Yudai said.

"He's picking her over this family already," Imani said.

"Stop being a bitter bitch!" Zoya yelled at her.

"Watch y'all's mouths!" Ekemma said.

"I think it's time for me to leave," I said and got up. I knew Yudai was too good to be true. Who wants a man who has a sister like Imani? I went to Yudai's room and got dressed. Thankfully, he washed and dried my clothes while I was asleep.

"You don't gotta leave," Yudai said. He tried to touch me but I pulled away from him.

"I have an appointment in an hour," I lied.

"You don't have to lie to me, Saz," he said.

Use Your Heart and Not Your Eyes

"Why did you bring me here? Your sister embarrassed me in front of your mother. She practically called me a slut in so many words," I vented.

"Imani is just mad because I didn't end up with her best friend's little sister," he said.

"Best friend's little sister?" I asked.

"This girl I was kicking it with in high school but I wasn't feeling her in that way. Imani is close with her so maybe she feels like she's being loyal to her. Listen, I don't know and don't give a fuck what they have going on. I like you," he said.

"So, what's the girl's name?" I asked, feeling jealous. How dare the bitch still be close to the family.

"Makeisha," he replied.

"You still talk to her?" I asked.

"She texts every now and then but that's about it," he replied. I rolled my eyes at him as I slipped my shoes on.

"Take me home," I said.

"You gotta be bullshitting me," he replied.

"No, I'm not. Take me home or I can catch an Uber. My gold-digging ass does have a job," I spat and he chuckled.

"I don't want to argue with you," he said.

"Who is arguing? All I want is to go the hell home and get ready for work," I replied.

"Bring yo' ass on then," he said with an attitude. I snatched my purse off the floor and opened the bedroom door. I said goodbye to his family before I left the house. I stood outside by the front door and he took his time. I was waiting for twenty minutes before he walked out his house.

"About time!" I said.

"I had to eat to breakfast. You should've sat your ass down with everyone else and ate. I know you're hungry," he said. He unlocked the door to his white Porsche and I got in the passenger's seat. The ride home was quiet. I checked my DM's and my Facebook page to avoid talking. I wasn't necessarily mad at Yudai. I just wished he could've gave me a heads up about Imani. Imani went overboard with her questions as if she was Yudai's mother. The bitch needed to learn her place.

"Why are you mad at me?" Yudai asked, breaking the silence.

"Why you didn't tell me about your evil ass sister?" I asked.

"I didn't expect that myself. I never brought a girl around my family. Makeisha came around but as Imani's friend. She caught me off guard, too, so I don't understand your fucked-up attitude right now," he said.

"She embarrassed me," I replied.

"She embarrassed herself. I apologize for how that went down but it won't happen again," he said.

You damn right it won't because I will not be in the same room as her again, I thought.

"It's cool," I said.

We made small talk the rest of the ride but it was still awkward. When he pulled up to my building, I kissed his cheek before I got out of his car. He rolled the window down.

"Ay, yo, Saz!" he called out to me and I turned around.

"Hit me up when you get out of that funky ass attitude," he said. He rolled the window up and pulled off.

Now you're mad! I thought. I rushed to my condo because I couldn't wait to tell Gautier and Tyshae about Imani's evil ass. For some reason, I kept thinking about the chick named Makiesha. I felt like there was more to it than what Yudai was telling me despite having secrets of my own.

I think I fell in love with his ass. No, it's too soon. But can't you fall in love at first sight? Yeah, you can but is that only in movies? I argued with myself in my thoughts. I sat on the couch in frustration because my feelings were all over the place. I finally realized Yudai had my heart.

What do I do now? I thought.

I took a quick shower and got dressed for work. I wore a pair of ripped jeans with a matching jean ripped top. I brushed my hair up into a big curly ponytail and added my big silver hoop earrings. I didn't have time to do my makeup, so I just put gloss on my lips. I slipped my feet into a pair of red bottoms and grabbed my purse before I headed out the door. I searched the parking lot for my car and was ready to report it stolen until I remembered I didn't have a car. I caught an Uber to work thinking of my next vehicle. While I

Use Your Heart and Not Your Eyes

sat in the back seat of the Uber, a cute Audi Q7 truck pulled up next to us.

My next vehicle, I thought in excitement.

Salih
The Truth

I walked up to Gautier's mother's house and rang the doorbell. I was running late in picking up Brooke because I had a game that was a few hours away. Gautier's mother, Alita opened the door with a scowl on her face. It was almost eleven o'clock at night. She didn't like me and made it known. I guess she thought I dogged her daughter out for no reason which was far from the case.

"I know it's late but I had a game this evening," I said.

"Brooke is asleep," she said.

"She can sleep on the ride to my loft," I said and she rolled her eyes. She walked into the kitchen and I followed behind her.

"Where is Gautier?" I asked because she should've been there so I wouldn't have to deal with her mother's attitude.

"Why are you concerned about my daughter, Salih? She's out being a happily single woman and hopefully doing single woman things," she said.

"Are you trying to piss me off?" I replied.

"Why would I do that if you hate her? I honestly don't see why Gautier was in love with you. You talk to her like garbage and you're ashamed to tell people who your daughter's mother is. Matter of fact, I feel like you're ashamed of your own fucking daughter for Christ's sake. You're a poor excuse of a man. I hope and pray Gautier finds a good man who can make a great impact on Brooke. The poor child is so damn confused and it angers me! She's being bounced around because of your immature ass attitude. One minute, she's at your mom's then she's here and there's so much back and forth. When will you stop being a little boy and realize how much foolishness you are inflicting in my daughter's life? You don't want her to date, yet you have a fiancée. You have been verbally abusing her over the years and it's me she cries to. I honestly don't you want in their lives because you make them unhappy," Alita fussed.

"Tell Gautier to call me and thanks for everything," I said and walked out her kitchen. I didn't want to disrespect Alita because she stepped up the first year of Brooke's life. She played the father for that whole year and it was the biggest thing I regretted. Gautier and I had unprotected sex for years and she didn't get pregnant until she cheated on me. In my mind, my logic was true about Brooke not being my daughter when she was born. I walked into Brooke's room and she wasn't asleep. She was sitting up in her bed holding her teddy bear.

"Hey, princess. Why are you up so late?" I asked and picked her up.

"Grandma was fussing," she said. I held her close to me and rocked her in my arms. I wanted to tell her I was sorry for neglecting her but she wouldn't understand because she was a baby at the time. Brooke kissed my cheek and wrapped her arm around my neck.

"Grandma's mean," she said.

"She's protecting you and your mother," I replied.

"She hurt your feelings. You look sad," she said.

"I'm tired, baby. Daddy's tired," I replied. I was tired of the way I had been doing things. I put her shoes on and walked down the stairs with her in my arms. Alita was sitting on the couch reading a book.

"Give grandma a kiss," Alita said. I put Brooke down and she ran to her grandmother and gave her a kiss.

"Thanks again," I said to Alita and she rolled her eyes at me as I closed the door. Brooke jumped down the steps and almost slipped.

"Stop doing that before you break something!" I said and she giggled.

"I'm afletic," she said and I chuckled.

"Athletic, baby girl," I replied. I opened my truck door and placed her in her car seat. Gautier pulled up in front the house. She got out of her truck wearing her work vest and she looked sleepy.

"I wasn't expecting to see you here," she said.

"Late game," I replied. She opened my truck door and kissed Brooke on the cheek.

"Are you coming with us?" Brooke asked her mother in excitement.

"No, baby. Mommy has to take care of a few things. Be good for Daddy and I'll see you tomorrow," she said before she closed the door.

"Why are you lying to her?" I asked and she rolled her eyes.

Use Your Heart and Not Your Eyes

"Am I invited to you and your fiancée's house?" she replied.

"I have another crib. I think you should come so we can talk about this situation," I said. Gautier squinted her eyes at me as if I was up to no good.

"I'm not fucking you again, so let's get that straight now. I'm also not in the mood for any more of your games, Salih," she replied.

"I can hit that again if I want to and we both know that, so we ain't gotta waste our breaths on arguing about that. It's time we put everything on the table," I said.

"We have tried that for the past four years! It never works with you. It's either your way or no way at all. Look, I'm busy planning Tyshae's birthday and I don't have time to entertain your ass. Call me tomorrow when you're ready to drop Brooke off," she said. She tried to walk away from me but I grabbed her arm.

"Let's go, Gautier," I said with seriousness in my voice. She snatched away from me and opened up the passenger's side door. Brooke was already asleep. When I got inside my truck, Gautier grilled me.

"Lose your attitude before I knock some sense into you," I said.

"I would like to see you try," she replied.

"You and your mother trippin' on me," I said.

"Can you blame us?" she replied.

"No, I actually don't," I said as I backed up.

"Don't damage my truck, so be careful how you back up. Lord knows you don't mind damaging things," she complained.

"Yo, please shut the fuck up. I'm trying to be cordial with you but you're trippin'. At the end of the day, WE hurt each other," I said.

"You need to learn how to let things go," she said.

"But yet you call me a deadbeat because I didn't know Brooke was mine? Stop putting all of this on me. What did you tell your mother about us? For some reason, she thinks I just up and left you pregnant. Why didn't you tell your mother the truth? She stays coming at my throat because she doesn't know the full story. That's another reason why I directed my anger toward you. You are playing the victim card too much. Yeah, I did some foul shit and said foul things, but I had a reason. It might not have been the best solution, but you think I don't feel some type of way listening to your mother curse me out over the years? She told me she hopes another man raises Brooke. I swear, Gautier, I almost snapped when she said that bullshit. After everything she said to me, I still couldn't fix my mouth to tell her the truth about why I didn't think Brooke was mine. She thinks you're an innocent woman not knowing you have some flaws, too," I vented.

"I told her," Gautier lied.

"This is why we don't get along. Yo, don't lie to me!" I yelled. I hurriedly looked in the mirror to make sure I didn't wake up Brooke.

"Okay, I didn't tell her. I was mad at you, so I got some kind of comfort behind her lashing out on you. I truly apologize for that but I think you're a great father to Brooke," she said. Her cell phone rang and she stared at it.

Use Your Heart and Not Your Eyes

"Tell your nigga you are busy," I spat and she smirked.

"It's my mother calling. I bet she's wondering why my truck is at her house and I'm not," she replied.

"You can't tell her you're with me, can you?" I asked.

"Why should I do that when you're an engaged man?" she asked.

"But it was cool when I had you cumming a few days ago, huh?" I replied.

"I was vulnerable," she said.

"Here we go with the victim card again," I replied.

"Where are we going?" she asked as she yawned.

"To my loft," I replied.

Gautier dozed off and the rest of the ride was silent. Forty minutes later, I was parking in front of my building. I woke Gautier up and she looked around.

"We're here," I said and she rolled her eyes. I got Brooke out of her car seat and carried her to the building with Gautier following behind me.

"What if someone spots us?" she asked.

"It's only two lofts in the building. I own both of them for privacy," I said. I punched a code in and the door unlocked. We caught the elevator to the loft upstairs which was bigger than the other one.

"This is lovely. I would've never known this building had something like this inside," Gautier said as she looked around. The five-story brick building was very plain and old looking on the outside but the lofts were renovated. The building used to be an old doctor's office and it was a wreck when I first saw it. I bought the building for twenty thousand dollars and had it remodeled. The two lofts combined were worth over a million dollars.

"It's huge," Gautier said as she looked around.

I took Brooke to her room and laid her down in her Barbie-style queen-size bed. Gautier came into the room and looked around.

"Her room is bigger than my room at the condo. She has her own bathroom, too? It's Barbie everything in here," Gautier said.

"She's a princess," I laughed.

I followed Gautier out the room and into the living room. She kicked her shoes off and sat on the couch across from me.

"So, what are we doing?" she asked.

"Communicating without our mothers," I replied.

"Are you going to stop controlling my life?" she asked and I leaned back into the couch.

"I don't control your life. I only want you to set a better example for our daughter. You got too many niggas in your life and it's not a good look," I replied.

"Cut the bull crap. Just admit how jealous you are, so we can move forward. You know darn well Brooke doesn't see any guy I talk to. I keep that away from her," she said.

"You want me to be jealous over you," I chuckled.

"How can we be cordial if you keep pretending like you don't care about me? Just say you're jealous," she said.

"I'm not jealous," I replied and she smacked her teeth. My phone rang and it was Eron calling me. I walked out the living room to answer my phone.

"Yoo," I answered.

"Did you go to my house to see if Tyshae moved out? I want that bitch out of my crib by the time I get home," Eron said. I pulled the phone away from my ear to make sure I was talking to the right person.

"Nigga, who in the fuck do I look like to you? I got my own problems and you know I'm not getting involved in your shit. Why would you kick her out anyway? That's Tyshae, the girl you have been with since high school. Yo, I thought you were just joking earlier when I talked to you, but you're serious?" I asked in disbelief.

"No, I'm trying to move my shorty in there by the end of the week," Eron said.

"Bruh, you can't be this dumb. How can you move your side-bitch into a home you shared with your fiancée? You couldn't get a different house?" I asked.

"Nawwww, man. My funds ain't how it used to be. Women ain't cheap," he said.

Use Your Heart and Not Your Eyes

"How are you going broke?" I asked, not understanding him.

"Now you're sounding like my accountant. I'm only asking if you can swing by there to make sure she's gone. I tried to call her but she changed her number," Eron said.

"If she changed her number, I'm sure she's not in your crib. Sounds like she's done with you, too. Yo, you foul for how you did Tyshae," I said. I knew for a long time Eron was cheating, but what could I say? I wasn't a saint when it came to Pita, but Pita wasn't with me before I had money. Tyshae was with Eron every step of the way. She got on my nerves at times and was always in my business, but shorty didn't deserve that.

"Here we go with this bullshit again. You're a hypocrite, bruh. You have been treating Gautier like trash for how long?" he asked.

"Why are you bringing up old shit? And I did what I did because she did some foul shit. Tyshae ain't do nothing but ride with you and you kicked her out the crib? Nigga, that's lame. You could've at least waited until she found another spot," I vented.

"Can you check for me or not? I know Dolly will do it for me," Eron said.

"Nigga, I'll fuck you up if you involve my mother in your shit!"

"She ain't involved in your shit? What's up with you? Usually you side with me but lately you have been on some other shit. Talk to me, bruh," Eron said.

"Ain't nothing wrong with me, muthafucka. I'll holla at you later, I got something to do," I replied.

"Oh, yeah, I have been meaning to tell you that Moore's friend has been asking for you," Eron said. I slept with Eron's baby mother's friend a year ago after a fashion party in Paris. After she thought she was pregnant, I left her alone. I didn't want to have kids scattered everywhere. I strapped up that night but the condom ripped because her pussy was dry.

"She should've bought a new pussy along with her new ass. I don't want any parts of that hoe. She tried to trap me the same way Moore trapped you," I replied.

"Moore didn't trap me," he lied. I was ready to respond but Gautier snatched the phone out my hand.

"I just wanted to tell you how disgusted I am with you. Tyshae was with you when you were wearing Salih's hand-me-downs. She was with you through it all and you did her like she was one of your hoes. It's all good, though, because I'm going to make sure she moves on to someone better, clown," Gautier said into the phone. She and Eron got into a heated argument and he called Gautier a "bitch." I took the phone from her.

"Watch your mouth, nigga. Who are you talking to like that, bruh? Calling her a bitch is way out of line," I said.

"I see what this is, fuck you, too, nigga!" Eron yelled into the phone before he hung up. I sat my phone on the kitchen island and Gautier grilled me.

"Who tried to trap you? You have been calling me hoes and sluts when really you ain't no better with your dirty-dick ass," she said before she left out of the kitchen. I followed behind her and we started arguing. Gautier called me every name she could think of. Tired of arguing with her, I went into my bedroom to take a shower. She followed behind me questioning me about having more kids.

"Would you shut up? Damn, just shut the fuck up!" I yelled.

"I need to know if Brooke has any other siblings. If you are anything like Eron, I'm sure she does," she said. I took off my clothes and walked into the bathroom.

"We can talk in the shower," I said.

"Do you want more kids?" she asked.

"Where is this shit coming from?" I replied. At times, I wanted to slap Gautier because of her mouth, but I didn't hit females. I wish I did sometimes because she always brought me to that point.

"I want to know," she said.

"Aight, I have three kids nobody knows about. I have one older than Brooke by a year and the other two are under a year old. Now, can I take my shower in peace?" I asked.

"I hate you," Gautier said with tear-filled eyes.

"The feeling is mutual," I said.

"You cheated on me when we were together?" she asked.

"Yeah and she gave me a little boy," I replied. Gautier stormed out the bathroom and into my bedroom. I followed behind her.

"Come on, baby, why are you mad? You wanted the truth, so now I'm giving it to you. One of my baby mamas lives in the other loft in this building. Do you want to meet her?" I asked Gautier. If looks could kill, I would've been buried with my dick cut off. I sat on my bed and watched her pace back and forth yelling and screaming.

"Okay, Gautier. You can calm down now. I was just kidding with you, damn. Why are you always emotional?" I asked and she mushed me.

"Why would you play with me like that?" she shrieked.

"I thought it was going to shut you up. I told you the truth and you kept asking me, so I lied and you're still trippin'," I said. I grabbed her by the belt loop of her pants and pulled her over to me. I unzipped her pants and pulled them down her hips.

"So, you ain't going to help me take these tight-ass clothes off you? Why can't you wear loose pants? You know the ones construction workers wear? You show too much ass," I complained and she smacked my hand away. She got undressed and stood in front of me wearing a bra and a see-through thong. The thong was sucked in between her pussy lips giving her a sexy camel toe. My dick hardened as I imagined how wet she was. Gautier's pussy was the best pussy I had in all of my twenty-four years of life. She was tight and soaking wet every time I was inside of her. As soon as I entered her while we were at her shop, I almost exploded. She fit me like a glove. I pulled her thong to the side and massaged her pink bud with my middle finger. My sentiments were true, she was leaking like a broken faucet. A moan escaped her lips and I couldn't hold back any longer. I pulled her onto the bed then pushed her meaty thighs back where I could get a full view of her fat cat. A deep gasp escaped her lips when my tongue slid into her tightness.

"SHAT!" she screamed. My fingers dug into the flesh of her thighs as I sucked on her pussy. I separated her wings while my tongue splashed around in her wetness. Gautier's pussy was gushing onto my lips and pre-cum drizzled out my dick. I pressed my tongue flat on her clit then pulled her lips into my mouth for a kiss. She bucked her hips forward and I held her legs down.

"It feels toooooo gooddddddd," she moaned. My tongue parted her lips and flickered across her clit. Her nails dug into my shoulders and her lower body rose off the bed as she climaxed on my lips. I didn't give her a chance to redeem herself as the head of my shaft parted her lips to enter. She squeezed her breasts as I gently stretched her open. She bit her lip and closed her eyes as I slid further into her and she winced in pain. I was planted deep inside of her. I laid on top of her with her leg hanging over the crook of my arm. It was Gautier's favorite position; she liked pain mixed with pleasure. I started out with deep long strokes until her body adjusted to my size. After she was relaxed, I pounded her into the mattress. I wrapped my lips around her nipple and sucked on it as I rammed my hardness into her G-spot. My dick was coated in her white cream. I pushed her other leg up so I could get all the way in. I was deeper inside her. I gently choked her while I hungrily sucked and licked her full lips. I clutched a fist full of her weave and pulled her head back so I could kiss her neck. I didn't forget her sensitive areas. Her body still responded the same way, probably even more than it ever did.

"I missed you so much," she whimpered as I stroked her walls.

"I missed you, too. Damn, Gautier. Fuck, baby," I moaned. She screamed my name as she came for the third time. I pulled out of her and laid on the bed. My dick stood straight up with her essence covering it. She climbed on top and eased her pussy down on my shaft in a squatting position. I gripped her hips and almost chewed my bottom lip off when she slid up and down my length. I wanted to explode as I watched her pussy swallow my dick. She massaged her breasts and moaned as she rode me. I had flashbacks of us when I had sex with her for the first time. Seeing her on top brought back deeper feelings.

"Ride that shit, go ahead! Fuck! Go faster!" I coached her as I slapped her ass. She slammed down on my dick and tightened her walls around me. The room spun and I got dizzy. Every drop of blood in my body traveled to my dick. She knew I was on the verge of exploding. She slowed down and placed her palms on my chest. She seductively rode me as her meaty ass cheeks clapped together. It was the sexiest thing known to man. I dug my fingers into her hips and closed my eyes as I exploded inside of her.

"AAAARRRGGGGGGGHHHHHHHHHHHH!" I groaned as a heavy load filled her up. She laid on my chest and I kissed her forehead.

"You're setting me crazy," she said.

You set me crazy, too, shorty, I thought.

We headed to the shower after we caught our breaths. Inside the shower, we went for another round. Matter of fact, we went at it until we heard birds chirping. I fell asleep on top of her with her breast stuffed inside my mouth.

Hours later...

"Wake up! Brooke is up!" Gautier said while my head rested on her chest.

"Shut up, damn. I'm tired," I replied groggily.

"Daddy!" Brooke called out. I hurriedly jumped up and went crashing onto the floor because the sheet was tangled around my body. Brooke came into my bedroom and Gautier hurriedly covered herself up. Brooke ran to her mother and hugged her.

"Good morning, Mama's baby. Are you hungry?" Gautier asked Brooke.

"Yes, I want some pancakes," Brooke said. Gautier got out of bed with a sheet wrapped around her.

"Mommy is going to freshen up. Go watch cartoons and I will call you when breakfast is ready," Gautier said. Brooke excitedly left my bedroom and Gautier blushed when I looked at her. Waking up to her and Brooke in the house opened my eyes. My family is what I have been missing. If I didn't have any feelings for Gautier, it would've been easy to walk away.

"She might be confused," Gautier said.

"She won't be," I replied and walked into the bathroom. After I took a shower, I checked my phone. I had twenty-one missed calls from Pita along with ten text messages. I was ready to send her a text but she called me again.

"Yeah," I answered while putting on my baller shorts.

"Where are you?" she screamed into the phone.

"Minding my business. Is there something I can help you with?" I asked.

"As a matter of fact, there is. The wedding planner is coming by shortly!" she yelled.

"Reschedule it because I'm not coming there no time soon," I replied. I heard something break in the background.

"Get your ass home now, Salih!" she screamed.

"The last time you screamed like that, the Botox settled in your face and made it stuck. I'm not rushing you to the surgeon again, so you will be on your own," I said.

"I swear to God I'm done with you!" she burst into sobs over the phone. I felt a tad bit guilty for treating Pita that way.

"I'll make it up to you," I said and she stopped crying.

"Be here by noon," she said and hung up. Gautier was looking at me when I looked up.

"What time are you taking me to my mother's house so I can get my truck? I have things to do today," she said.

"Like what?" I replied.

"We're surprising Tyshae tonight. I still haven't found anything to wear and Saz needs to do my hair," Gautier said.

"We can leave shortly," I replied. Gautier went to the kitchen and my phone rang again. I thought it was Pita calling back when I snatched my phone off the bed but it was Yudai.

"Yo, what up?" I answered.

"Your fiancée called my phone all night last night looking for you. Take your ass home," Yudai said.

"Stay outta grown folk's business," I chuckled.

"Yeah, aight. Pita cursed me out this morning. She told me to go back to Africa. That's some racist shit, bruh. I almost disrespected her but I didn't on the strength of you," he said.

"She must've got your number from one of our teammates' wives. I'll talk to her dumb ass later on. I'll see you later at the team meeting," I replied.

"Bet," he said and hung up.

I headed to the kitchen and Gautier was fixing a plate of pancakes, eggs, and sausage for me.

"Someone is going to be hyper," I said because Brooke had a lot of syrup on her pancakes.

"I'm going to shower while y'all eat. Hopefully, you will be ready to take me to my truck when I'm done," Gautier said. I was ready to ask her what the problem was but thought better of it. I didn't want to expose Brooke to any more of our arguments. Brooke helped me clear off the table after we finished breakfast. I took her to her bathroom to help her brush her teeth and wash her face.

"Who is Pita, Daddy?" Brooke asked me.

"Where did you hear that from?" I asked.

"I heard Mommy talking about her to Aunt Shae on the phone. Mommy said Pita was plastic like a Barbie doll. Can I play with her today?" she asked and I chuckled.

"Pita is a friend of mine," I said.

"Is she pretty like my Barbies?" Brooke asked.

"No, but your mother is. Don't tell her I said that, okay? It's our secret," I said and tickled her. She ran out the bathroom after I washed her face.

"Mommy! Daddy said you're pretty like my Barbies," she screamed.

Damn, baby girl. You just ratted me out, I laughed to myself.

****

"Give Mommy a kiss and be good for your father. No more sweets today," Gautier said to Brooke. We were outside of Gautier's mother's house. Alita was looking out the window at us.

"Hurry up before Alita comes out here and beats your ass for staying out with a boy last night," I joked. She closed the back door and gave me the finger.

"I can't get a kiss?" I asked.

"My mother is looking," she whispered through the passenger window.

"I know, that's why I want one," I replied.

"You always have to be a jackass." Gautier smirked as she walked away. I watched her round backside sway from side to side as she walked into the house. I pulled off and headed to my mother's house. Thirty minutes later, I was pulling up in her driveway. I got out and helped Brooke out her car seat. My mother opened the door wearing a housecoat with a scarf around her head. She angrily blew cigarette smoke out her mouth as she watched me.

"Good morning," I said.

"Don't 'good morning' me. I spent two hours plotting on murdering your fiancée this morning. She called me twelve times last night! But this morning, she must've bumped her head. She cursed at me and told me if it wasn't for you, I would still be in the ghetto on welfare. That woman better not, and I mean better not ever in her life come around me or call me again. Gautier never disrespected me and it's been times where me and her argued, but she never spoke to me that way. I was planning on quitting smoking but that heifer made me want something stronger. Who got some kush?" she asked.

"Oh, I'm sorry. I didn't see Brooke. Come here and give Nana a kiss," my mother said as she put the cigarette out. Brooke ran to her and hugged her.

"We're going shopping today and getting our nails done. I missed my baby," she said.

"You should've thought about that before you woke up and decided I couldn't communicate with Gautier through you anymore," I said.

"Shut up, Salih before I slap you. You are on my bad side for the rest of the week. I can't believe you stooped so low with your taste in women. Gautier really did a number on you," she fussed as she walked into the house.

"Mommy stayed with me and Daddy. She was sleeping in his bed," Brooke said in excitement. My mother put Brooke down and told her to go in the living room so we could talk.

"I don't feel like talking, I gotta go somewhere really quick," I said.

"Get your ass in that kitchen," she gritted.

I walked into the kitchen and she followed behind me.

"Give me the scoop," she said.

"Come on, Ma. Why are you being nosey?" I smirked.

"I have been dealing with you and Gautier's shit for how long? I let y'all use me for how long? Oh, I gotta right to be nosey about this. Now, tell me what happened. Did y'all make up?" she asked in excitement.

"We still have somethings to talk about," I replied.

"Let me guess, you slept with her?" she asked and I grilled her.

"Don't look at me like that. Pita had a feeling you was out sleeping with another woman. It's called female intuition and it looks like she was right," she said.

"I mean, it didn't happen like that. One thing led to another. Don't mention this to Gautier. I know how you do, you can't hold water. You even got my daughter snitching on me," I said.

"I hope y'all do the right thing. I want y'all to get married and have more babies. Everyone makes mistakes, so you need to forgive her," she said.

"Why should I?" I asked.

"Because you love her. If I thought you didn't love her, I would've accepted Pita's airheaded ass a long time ago. Plus, Gautier is like family. She used to help me cook breakfast every weekend. When you went off to college, she still came over and spent time with me. Believe it or not, she helped me out of a depression. It was always me and my boys, but after y'all left, it was just me. She checked up on me every day. I told myself that she is the kind of woman I want my son to marry. What else is wrong with her other than that one mistake she made when she was nineteen years old?" she asked. I couldn't respond because she was right. Gautier had a good heart despite everything else.

"I'll be back later on to get Brooke. I have a meeting and a game later," I said.

"Okay, but just remember time doesn't wait for no one. If you want her, you better go get her before a good man comes along," she replied. I kissed Brooke goodbye before I left my mother's house. Pita called my phone five times but I didn't answer because I was on my way there. Twenty-five minutes later, I arrived at the house. I hurriedly got out of my truck and unlocked the front door.

"PITA!" I yelled out. I walked around the house looking for her but didn't spot her anywhere. I noticed the sliding door to the pool was open. I stepped outside and she was sitting in a lounge chair by the pool wearing a thong bathing suit.

"I should slap the spit out of your mouth? Why did you disrespect my mother? You talked about her being on welfare? Bitch, your whole family is full of illegal immigrants. You must've forgot about the small house you lived in when I met you. You're a celebrity because I fucked you. You called Yudai and told him to go back to Africa? If I find out you voted for Trump, I swear on my brother I will ruin you," I vented. Pita snatched her shades off and smirked at me. She picked something up off the table and threw it at me. It landed by my feet and I picked it up. My heart almost stopped and my legs turned into noodles. It was a positive pregnancy test.

"We used protection," I said.

"We didn't use protection two months ago. Remember when we went to Barbados? We got high and drunk and had sex on the beach. I should've known something was going to come out of it because you never gave it to me like that before. It was almost as if I was another woman," she replied. I sat in the chair next to her and thought about that night. It all came back to me…

Two months ago, in Barbados…

Pita was straddling me on a private beach by our hotel room. It was our two-year anniversary and I wanted to do something special for her. She was wet and naked from swimming. I brought my lips to hers to give her a shotgun from the blunt I was smoking.

"What's the matter, baby? Are you upset about something?" Pita asked as she massaged my dick through my shorts.

"Naw, I'm just thinking," I replied.

I was thinking about Gautier and some guy named Aniston that she was dating. Eron told me earlier that day he overheard Gautier and Tyshae talking about Aniston over the phone. I didn't know why it was bothering me but it was. I picked up the bottle of white Henny and gulped it down. Images of Gautier letting my brother's killer make love to her flashed through my thoughts. Before I knew it, I was almost done with the whole bottle.

"Calm down, Salih. I don't want you getting tired before I surprise you," Pita said. She kissed me and my dick hardened underneath her. I caressed her face and maybe my mind was playing tricks on me because I saw Gautier's face.

"It's supposed to be me and you against the world," I slurred.

"It will always be us," she said. I rolled her over and ended up on top. I kissed her lips and she wrapped her legs around me. I pulled my dick out and entered her. She gasped as I gave her deep, slow thrusts.

"SALIH!!" she screamed my name.

"You feel that, baby? That's how much I have been missing you," I slurred.

"Come in this pussy, baby," she moaned.

I knew it wasn't Gautier I was making love to, but in my mind, I made myself believe it was her. I pulled out of Pita and ate her pussy like my life depended on it. She screamed and moaned as her legs trembled. Her pussy gushed in my mouth like a juicy grape. Her moans were too loud and almost turned me off because she sounded like a wounded pig. I pictured the faces Gautier used to make and her sexy moans when I was on top. Gautier used to moan in my ear to make me explode. After I was done eating Pita out, I turned her over and entered her from the back. I pounded into her until we both climaxed. After we were finished, I carried her to our hotel room and fucked her against the wall. Two hours later, we were in bed. Pita was sound asleep but I was wide awake staring at the ceiling fan. I slid on a pair of shorts then grabbed my cell phone. I walked out of the sliding doors which led to the beach. I smoked another blunt as I scrolled through Gautier's pictures on Instagram.

I can't believe I still love your hoe ass, *I thought…*

"Damn," I said aloud after thinking about that night. Pita got out of her chair and kneeled in front of me.

"Please tell me what I can do to fix us. Why are you treating me like this? We were so happy when we first met, but now you can't stand to look at me," Pita said.

"I came to realize that we still don't know much about each other. I'm always away and you're always shopping and having photo shoots. What are we supposed to do? We both know this will never work. We used each other. You got what you wanted out of me and I used you to get over someone," I said truthfully. Tears fell from her eyes and I wiped them away.

"I'm going to be a single mother all because you have been playing with my heart!" she screamed at me.

"We played each other. Neither one of our hearts is in this relationship," I replied.

"I don't want to be alone and pregnant," she said. I brushed my hand down my face because it was a tough situation. I missed out on Gautier's pregnancy and didn't want to become that man again. At the end of it all, I planted the seed and I had to watch it grow.

"Have you been to the doctor's?" I asked.

"I just found out last night. Why do you think I was calling everyone? You should've been here with me," she said.

"You're right but we can't cry over spilled milk, can we?" I asked and she rolled her eyes.

"We need to get through whatever problem we have to work this out. I'll be damned if you leave me after this," she said. She got up and walked into the house, leaving me pondering my thoughts.

"Damn, bro. I wish you was here to help me figure this out," I said as if Damien could hear me. I laid back in the chair and closed my eyes thinking about my life. I should've never got involved with another woman until my feelings for Gautier went away. I was definitely paying the price for it.

Tyshae
Strawberries and Cream

I sat on the edge of the bed inside my hotel room with tears running down my face. It was my birthday and I spent most of the day alone. Although Eron hasn't been a good boyfriend, he didn't miss out on any of my birthdays. It was nine o'clock at night and I was supposed to get dressed for a party. I didn't feel like partying and I also didn't want to run into Cream because I hadn't called him since we had dinner. My happiness went up and down. One minute I was happy that Eron left me then the next minute I would break out in sobs. I picked up my cell phone and called my mother. She hadn't been answering my phone calls, not even on my birthday.

"What, chile?" she finally answered.

"Hey, Ma. I was wondering if I could come over. I want to talk to you," I said.

"Talk about what? Talk about how you're still being a spoiled damn brat? Are you and Eron back together yet?" she asked.

"No," I sobbed.

"You can't come to my house until you get your man back. Maybe this will make you grow up. Don't call me until you fix it!" she said and hung up on me. I called her back from the hotel phone and she answered sweetly, not knowing it was me.

Use Your Heart and Not Your Eyes

"You're a sorry excuse for a mother! I'm going to make you regret turning your back on me. Do you hear me? YOU ARE DEAD TO ME!" I screamed into the phone before I hung up. I was thinking about calling my sister but we hadn't talked in a year. We were never that close because she acted too much like our mother and we bumped heads a lot. Kimmy was a gold digger and only married her husband because he had money. He was short, unattractive, and had an odor. He was a nasty slob and I couldn't understand how she laid up with him. What was wrong with wanting to be independent? I had many talents, I could sing, do nails, tattoos and piercings. What was the point of it all going to waste just to live off someone else's success? The more I thought about it, the angrier I became. I called Saz and Gautier because I was on the verge of losing my mind. I sat on the couch in the living room area with a bottle of wine and a Black & Mild. I picked up the smoking habit when Eron's cheating became worse. It took Gautier and Saz almost an hour to arrive at my hotel room. They were dressed in club wear and I still wasn't ready. Saz wore a cute white bondage dress with red pumps and her makeup was natural. Her hair was styled in a cute curly ponytail and her baby hair framed her forehead perfectly. Gautier wore a white sleeveless bell bottom romper with red heels. Her weave had added inches which reached past her butt. It was bone straight with the classic part in the middle. She dyed the tips of her ends honey blonde which went well with her complexion.

"It's your birthday, girl, we are fittin' to turn the hell up," Saz said.

"Can we just stay in and watch movies?" I asked. Saz and Gautier looked at each other as if I said something crazy.

"Tyshae, honey. The lord knows we really love you but we will jump you if you don't get ready. And why are you smoking Black & Mild's? That's not cute at all, honey bunches," Gautier said.

"At all," Saz cosigned.

"You two are all I have," I cried.

"Step away from the wine and cigars," Saz said. Gautier sat next to me and wrapped her arm around me.

"Listen to me. Eron doesn't matter anymore. You have friends who are like your sisters that will drop anything to see about your well-being," Gautier said.

"Everything except for getting dicked down," Saz said. I threw a pillow at her and she laughed.

"Saz got some new eggplant in her life and doesn't know how to act," Gautier said.

"Hell, look who's talking. You slept with Salih how many times?" Saz asked and I looked at Gautier.

"Y'all did it again?" I asked and she blushed.

"Please don't remind me of that powerful stroke. That nigga was hitting my pussy like he was playing baseball, shat," Gautier fanned herself.

"Well, at least y'all are getting some. I haven't had any dick in six months," I admitted and Saz choked on her wine.

"Ewwww," Saz said.

"Six months? Did you at least touch yourself?" Gautier asked.

"I haven't tried masturbation," I admitted.

"Is she our friend?" Saz joked and I gave her the finger.

"You mean to tell me you haven't had an orgasm in six months? Chile, that's why you're always uptight. I'm not telling you to be a thot, but you better pluck that feather and keep it moving," Gautier said.

"It's kinda gross. I just don't think a woman should touch herself if she got a man and I had one until now," I replied.

"You have been single for six months, hunty. Damn, you could've had the pool guy hit it," Saz said.

"Your pool guy was fine," Gautier said.

"He was eighteen years old," I replied.

"And?" Saz asked.

"What could he do for me?" I replied.

"Showed you how to play with the pussy at least, don't sleep on younger guys. Yudai has eggplants," Saz said.

"Hold up, how does he have eggplants?" Gautier asked Saz.

"He has the type of dick that make you want to give him your eggs to plant inside your womb. That's baby daddy right there," Saz said. Gautier and I howled in laughter.

"Y'all hoes need Jesus," I chuckled. That's all I needed, my friends. They hadn't been in my room for ten minutes and managed to lighten my mood.

"Look what we got you," Saz said holding up a gift bag.

"Aww, what is it?" I asked.

"Look inside," Gautier said.

I reached into the bag and pulled out two boxes. One box had a white two-piece stretch outfit. The top was made like a sports bra with strings attached so I could tie it around my torso. The pants had strings on it, too, so I could tie it around my hips. It was a skimpy outfit but I loved it. In the other box was a pair of red Gucci stilettos along with the matching clutch.

"Ohhhhhhhhh, this outfit is lit! I was thinking about getting it but I didn't because Eron would've been mad. Awww, I love y'all," I said in excitement.

"There's one more box in there," Saz said. I picked up a skinny box which was hiding underneath the other two boxes. I opened the box and pulled out a fire red lace front wig.

"BIITTTTTTCCHHHHHHHHHHH! You made this lace front for me? I'm about to faint! This looks like the style Cardi B was rocking," I screamed in excitement.

"I made it earlier. It took me hours to make that. I knew how much you admired that style and I figured it would look good with your red shoes and clutch. We are fittin' to be cute or whateva," Saz said.

"Let me hurry up and get dressed. Ohhh, I'm going to walk out here looking like a new bitch. Tyshae, who? Call me Shae tonight because I'm fittin' to show off. Move out of my way, bitches. Birthday girl is coming through," I said and rushed to the bathroom. I took a twenty-minute shower then got out and moisturized my body. I sat in a chair in the living room while my friends pampered me. Gautier did my make-up while Saz put my wig on. An hour later, I felt more than good. I stood in the mirror admiring my outfit and hair. Gautier and Saz took pictures of me and I couldn't wait for Eron to see me looking brand new. I wanted it to eat him up inside because he was missing out. I turned around to get a full view of my backside. I had to make sure my butt sat up perfectly.

"Stay just like that. Beautiful pose," Saz said as she took my picture.

"Body goals," Gautier said.

After I put on a couple pieces of jewelry, we left out of my hotel room. A red stretch Maybach was parked in front of the hotel when we walked outside.

"Wait a minute. I thought we were only partying. What's all of this?" I asked Gautier.

"Just living it up tonight," she replied.

A cute Asian-looking driver opened the door for us. I melted into the seat as soon as I sat down. Saz poured us a glass of champagne and turned the music up. I already had a slight buzz from the wine I was sipping in my hotel room but I finished the glass of champagne in one gulp anyway.

"Don't get drunk before the party," Gautier said.

"Hell, if she doesn't, I will," Saz replied.

The ride to the strip-club wasn't a long one. We arrived twenty minutes later. The driver got out and opened the door for us. When we stepped out the limo, cameras flashed and I put on a fake smile. I didn't like to be caught off guard but it was a big event for Cream's champagne, so a lot of people were in attendance. The bouncers opened the doors to the club after we finished taking pictures.

"SURPRISE!" everyone shouted. I wanted to kick my heels off and run. I covered my face to keep from shedding tears. I should've known Gautier and Saz was up to something. Cream walked through the crowd dressed in all white, wearing a pair of red Mason Margiela shoes. He hugged me and wished me a happy birthday.

"I should fight y'all," I said.

"Strawberries and Cream. Notice everyone is wearing red and white. I remembered your favorite fruit and realized it would go well with cream," Cream said. I gave him a friendly peck on his lips and he smirked.

"Go ahead and have fun, we will be in your section in a few," Gautier said then winked at me. I rolled my eyes at her because it was evident what she was trying to do.

"Are you coming, Saz?" I asked.

"I'm going to hang out with Gautier. It's your birthday, so have fun," Saz said. She leaned forward then whispered in my ear.

"Bittcchhhhhhhhh, you better ride his fine ass. You have our permission to be a thot tonight. Just remember to strap up," she said then kissed my cheek. They disappeared into the crowd and left me standing with Cream. He grabbed my hand and walked me upstairs. On our way there, a few familiar faces and guests wished me a happy birthday. Although I wasn't expecting everything that was happening, I was thankful. Cream nodded at the bouncer guarding his section and he opened the rope. I sat on the plush black leather couch and Cream sat across from me.

"You look good," he said.

"You look handsome yourself," I replied.

"Why are you sitting over there then? I don't bite, Strawberry," he said.

"Ugh, I can't believe you're calling me my childhood nickname," I joked.

"We had some fun times," he said.

"We sure did," I replied.

"I could've been your first but you were too scared," he said and I waved him off.

"It amazes me how much you haven't changed," I laughed and he chuckled.

"I'm a different man except when it comes to you. This party is a new stepping stone in my life. It's your birthday and I'm also ready to get out of these streets, if you know what I mean," he replied.

"Congrats to us. It's a new stepping stone for me, too. Not only am I celebrating my birthday, I'm celebrating my freedom and yours, too. Seems like we both were tied down to things that wasn't good for us over the years," I replied.

"You're right about that. I lost too many friends to the streets, I should've been out but things held me up. If I had you, though, I don't think I would've got so deep into it. Your presence is enough for me to wanna be right for you," he said.

Maybe true love was in front of me the whole time, I thought.

I thought back to the day when my mother found out about Cream…

"You were out with that white boy again, huh?" my mother asked me as soon as I stepped into the house. I spent all day with Cream at the park close to our neighborhood.

"Who told you?" I asked.

"Don't worry about it, Tyshae! I refuse to have my thirteen-year-old around that trash! The boy is trouble and you keep going around him. I'm moving away from here," she said.

"But, Ma! Why are we moving?" I cried.

"Why do you think? He's in a gang and I don't want you affiliated with that shit! This hood has nothing but gang members. I don't want my daughters getting caught up," she said. I stormed out of the house as she called out to me. I saw Kimmy standing on the sidewalk talking to a dope boy. I knew it was her who ratted me out. Kimmy was three years older than me and we somewhat looked identical. The only difference was she was darker and thicker. Kimmy was also a neighborhood slut which she failed to tell our mother about. I pushed her into a car and she tripped and landed on her ass.

"I should kick your ass, bitch!" I yelled at her. She got up and charged into me. She pulled my hair and I slapped her in the face.

Cream's mother ran out her house to break us up. The boy Kimmy was talking to was cheering her on to beat my ass.

"Stop fighting!" Paula screamed. She pulled us apart and Kimmy's lip was bleeding.

"That's why you're not going to see your little white boy again, bitch!" Kimmy said and walked away. Paula pulled me into her house and I sat on her couch in the living room. She held my chin up to look at my face.

"Your sister is jealous because you're prettier than her," Paula said. Nobody in the hood liked Kimmy or my mother because of their snobby attitudes. I couldn't understand it because I was nothing like them. Cream came into the house to check up on me. He was fourteen years old but the streets, his height, and physique made him appear older.

"What happened? Why were you fighting?" Cream asked.

"My sister told our mother about us hanging out," I cried. Paula shook her head and walked out the living room. Cream sat on the couch next to me and wrapped his arm around me.

"Are you in a gang?" I asked.

"Who said that?" he replied.

"Don't worry about it, are you in a gang?"

"Not really, it's not official yet," he said and I scooted away from him.

"My mother doesn't want me around you anymore," I replied.

Use Your Heart and Not Your Eyes

"Your mother doesn't give a shit about me being in a gang, it's because I'm a white boy. Kimmy is fucking every gang member in the hood," Cream said.

"I'm scared," I said.

"Let's go to my room and talk," he said. He grabbed me by the hand and we walked upstairs to his room. I sat on the bottom of the bunk bed and he took his hoody off. He pulled a gun from the back of his pants and hid it underneath his bed.

"Why do you carry a gun?" I asked.

"For protection," he replied.

He sat next to me on the bed and we silently stared at the wall before he broke the silence.

"I hate that your mother doesn't want me around you. You're the only person I can tell everything to. Why does she want to take you away from me?" he asked.

"I don't know but I don't want her to. You're my only friend," I replied. He leaned in and kissed my lips. It was different than our normal kiss which was only a peck; it was a kiss where his tongue slipped into my mouth. A weird feeling formed between my legs. A moan escaped my lips when Cream's hand slid up my shirt and palmed my small breast. We spent ten minutes making out until he decided to take it a step further. He unbuttoned my pants and slid his hand inside of my panties. I laid back on his bed and closed my eyes. Another moan escaped my lips when he slipped a finger inside of me.

"Can I take these off?" he asked and I nodded my head. In my mind, I was seeking revenge against my mother. I wanted Cream to do what he wanted to do to me so it could make her miserable. After

my pants and panties were completely off, Cream pulled his sweat pants and boxers down. As soon as he laid on top of me, a loud bang was at his door followed by my mother and his mother arguing.

"Where in the fuck is my daughter?" my mother yelled. Cream hurriedly got dressed and ran downstairs. I got dressed and ran downstairs behind him. My mother was standing in their living room with a scowl on her face.

"I told you stay away from him and this is how you repay me? It doesn't matter because soon you two will no longer be neighbors. Let's go home before I whip your ass," my mother said. She grabbed me by my sweater and yanked me out the house. Cream tried to reach out to me but his mother pulled him back and closed the door. When I got home, my mother whipped me with a belt as Kimmy watched and laughed. I saw Cream the next day at the bus stop. We talked but we didn't say much to each other. I told him where I was moving to but his mind seemed to be somewhere else. Later on that day, when we got out of school, Cream got caught with a gun and was sent to a boy's boot camp...

"I missed our friendship," I said after reminiscing.

"You mean our teenage love. We had more than a friendship and your mother knew it. That's why she was afraid of you hanging around me," he said.

"Teenage love?" I asked.

"Yeah, I was in love with you. I mean I don't know how you felt about me but I know how I was feeling about you. I was even stealing strawberries for you from the grocery store. Your eyes lit up every time we sat and ate them at the park," he replied. He got up from his seat and sat next to me. He poured me a glass of his champagne and scooted closer to me.

"Sorry for not texting you," I said.

"It's cool, I figured you wasn't going to. I know you're going through something," he replied. I looked into his pretty blue eyes and they still looked at me the same from when we were younger.

"We won't have to worry about anyone coming between our friendship again. I left my mother in the past," I said.

"I like this new hairstyle. It fits you," he said referring to my hair.

"Thank you," I blushed.

A few of Cream's friends came into our section and he introduced me to them. I could tell they were street guys but I wasn't uncomfortable around them. I was able to be myself opposed to being around Eron's teammates' snobby wives and girlfriends. Gautier texted me to see if I was okay and I sent her the "cool" emoji.

"I'm going downstairs, I will be right back," I told Cream.

"Aight, and come right back. Don't go down there to be hot in your ass, neither," he said and I winked at him.

With yo' fine ass, I thought.

The bouncer opened the rope for me and I made my way downstairs where the strippers were entertaining the party. I found Gautier and Saz sitting in their own private section.

"Ugh, you were supposed to stay upstairs," Saz said with a wad of money in her hands. A pretty redbone woman with a banging body was shaking her ass in Saz's face while Saz tossed money at her.

"Get it, bitch! Make it clap," Saz shouted over the music.

"Is Saz into women?" I asked Gautier and she doubled over in laughter.

"Saz just likes to have fun. These strippers are bad," Gautier said placing a five-dollar bill inside the stripper's G-string.

"Ohhh, look who walked in," I said, pointing at the door. Salih walked into the club with Yudai and a few other guys. Saz immediately straightened herself up as if she wasn't just shaking her ass with the stripper. I should've recorded her but it was too late.

"Why are you acting scared?" Gautier asked Saz.

"Hush your mouth, it's time to act like a lady with class," she replied. Salih and Yudai walked into the section with gift bags.

"I don't like your ass like that, but happy birthday," Salih said as he handed me the gift bag.

"Thanks, asshole," I replied as I hugged him. Yudai handed me a gift bag and I hugged him, too.

"What's up, shorty. Are you still mad?" Yudai asked Saz and she playfully rolled her eyes at him. Gautier sipped her drink pretending like she didn't see Salih. Salih sat next to Gautier. I was shocked.

Use Your Heart and Not Your Eyes

"How tight are those pants? Stand up so I can see," he said to Gautier.

"Don't embarrass me," Gautier spat.

"You'll get embarrassed if you don't stand your ass up," Salih replied. They got into a small argument but it wasn't like their usual arguments. It was a playful flirtatious one. Yudai and Saz walked off and I wondered what they were up to. I opened up Salih's gift. It was a cute cross-body Louis Vuitton bag.

"Awww, thank you. I can use this to put my cash in at the salon," I said.

"Open the purse up," Salih said. I opened up the purse and there was stack of money. I didn't have to count it to know it was around ten thousand dollars.

"Don't say I didn't get you anything for your house warming," he said. Salih was rarely nice to me. It seemed as if he was paying for what Eron did to me.

"I'm moving, too, where is my gift?" Gautier playfully asked him.

"I gave it to you last night," Salih replied and Gautier blushed.

I opened Yudai's gift and it was cash in an envelope. I trashed the gift bags and kept all my money inside of the purse Salih got me. I prayed to God nobody didn't rob me as I walked around with fifteen thousand dollars in cash. I left Gautier's section to go back to Cream. As I was walking through the crowd, I spotted Janae whispering in Cream's ear. I walked over to them and she screamed at me in excitement.

"Happy birthday, girl! Look at you looking all good," she said. Janae was a stripper at the club. She was wearing a white G-string with glitter strawberry patches covering her nipples.

"Thanks," I replied.

"Am I going to see you after the party is over? I got a hotel room downtown," Janae flirted with Cream.

"Janae, honey, Cream is booked tonight and so is our room. Ain't that right, baby?" I asked Cream and he bit his bottom lip.

"We can leave now," he said. Janae rolled her eyes and hurriedly walked away. Cream wrapped his arms around my waist and rested his head on my shoulder. I felt the hardness of him pressed against my ass.

"Look what you did to me," he said whispering in my ear and it caused my clit to throb.

Six long months, Tyshae. Birthday sex wouldn't hurt. It's not like he's a stranger, I thought. A hostess was walking around with a tray of champagne. Inside the champagne glasses were whole strawberries. Cream grabbed two glasses of champagne for us.

"Are you staying with me tonight?" he asked and I nodded my head. He grabbed my hand and led me back to his section which was filled with more gifts for me. There were all kinds of shopping bags and envelopes waiting for me.

"Really?" I asked Cream.

"Yeah, I'm making up for lost times. Plus, some of these gifts are from the guests, too. You can open them after we cut the cake," he said.

I had the best birthday a girl could ask for. A lot of our Instagram followers were inside the building, too; the club was jam packed and it made me party harder. A few hours later, everyone sang "Happy Birthday" to me. The hostess brought out a three-layer strawberry short cake with a champagne glass in the middle. Surprisingly, inside the champagne glass was a shot of my favorite Long Island drink. I thanked everyone for bringing me gifts after I blew out the candles, but I was too tipsy to open my gifts. I thanked Cream again for making his event about me, too. I felt the need to do something special for him in return. I went to the bathroom and freshened up my makeup. After I was finished, I went to the DJ's booth and whispered something in his ear.

"The birthday girl wants to sing a little something before the party is over. So, everyone please come closer to the stage," the DJ announced and I thanked him. He handed me the mic and the beat to the song, "Use Your Heart" by SWV blared throughout the club.

As we stare we both seek and hope to find
Real love, purified...

I sang the song with my heart and soul as the crowd cheered. I gave a shout out to all my friends including Cream when I finished singing.

"Thank you all for everything. I love y'all," I said into the mic before I gave it back to the DJ.

"Goddamn, she sang that song. Okay, everyone last call for alcohol, the club is closing soon and don't forget to tip the strippers. They gave one hell of a show tonight. Almost made me cheat on my wife," the DJ joked.

"Come the hell through, Tyshae!" Saz slurred as Yudai held her up.

"I almost forgot how beautiful your voice is," Gautier said as she hugged me.

"Can I send my gifts home with you? I'm staying out," I said.

"I already took care of that. Have fun and be safe. Let me know the details in the morning," Gautier said. I kissed her cheek and hugged Saz goodbye. I took a few more pictures with Cream before the club let out. I got in the back seat of his Yukon limo and kicked my shoes off. He placed my feet in his lap and rubbed them.

"That feels so good," I said as I rested my head on the seat. My eyelids grew heavy and I ended up falling asleep.

"Tyshae, wake up." Cream shook me. I opened my eyes and looked around.

"Where are we?" I asked.

"At my crib in Towson," he replied. I looked out the window and we were parked in front of a newly-built building. I could tell by the valet driver in front of the building that it cost a grip to live there.

"You want me to carry you?" he asked.

"I'm fine," I replied as I slipped on my shoes. The door opened to the limo and we stepped out. The lobby inside the building reminded me of an upscale hotel. We stepped onto the elevator and Cream pushed button eight which was the highest in the building. The elevator doors opened to another set of elevator doors. Cream punched in a code on the wall and the doors opened. We stepped inside a spacious two-level studio-style loft. The windows were so big it seemed as if the home didn't have any walls, just windows. The kitchen was the highlight of it all. It was a stainless-steel kitchen which was made like something inside of a restaurant. The place was so nicely decorated, I automatically felt like I was at home. Cream took me on a tour through his house. The upper level was his bedroom. I sat on the plush California king size bed and got comfortable. Cream stripped down to his boxer briefs. I never thought leg art on a man was sexy until I saw Cream's. His body art was beautiful but the bulge between his legs almost gave me an orgasm.

"What's wrong with you?" he asked.

"Oh, nothing," I replied and looked away. He grabbed my hand and placed it over his shaft.

"A white boy can't be packing heavy weight?" he asked.

You make Eron look like a baby, I thought.

"Come and join me in the shower," he said.

I shyly undressed in front of him. The only man who saw me completely naked was Eron. It didn't seem too bad because I was familiar with Cream. I don't think I could've done it if it was another man. Cream lustfully eyed my full breasts and the bald peach between my legs. I covered my breasts and he moved my hand away.

"Why are you shying around me?" he asked. He wrapped his arms around me and pulled me into him. My heart raced and butterflies formed in my stomach.

"I'm not shy," I lied.

Use Your Heart and Not Your Eyes

"We can go to bed," he said. His patience made me want him even more. I pulled his face to mine and kissed him. His hands squeezed my ass cheeks and a moan escaped my lips. I couldn't remember the last time my body was touched in that manner. I seductively traced my tongue over the outline of his lips and he moaned into my mouth. He picked me up and placed me against the wall. His warm, wet mouth covered my hardened nipple. He pressed his hard-on against my center and I wanted it right then and there. I slowly wound my hips on him so he could feel how wet he made me. He carried me to his dresser and pinned my legs against my forehead. My pussy gushed when he stuck his tongue inside me.

"OHHHHHHHHH!" I moaned.

His tongue trailed up and down my slit while his mouth covered my mound. He massaged my breasts as his tongue went deeper inside me. Sounds of him smacking and slurping on my vagina echoed throughout his room. My legs wrapped around his neck and a hoarse cry escaped my lips. I screamed his name as my body went through an unknown feeling. It was a feeling I never felt before. Tears filled my eyes and my legs trembled as I panted. I squealed as my essence came exploding out of my pussy.

"ARRGGHHHHHHHHHHH!" I cried. I tried to push Cream's head back because my pink bud was too sensitive. He pushed my legs further up and I was in a folded position. His tongue circled around my anus before he covered it with his lips. It was by far the weirdest thing I ever felt, but it felt so good. It drove me insane. I stuck my finger inside of my pussy to boost the feeling. I wasn't sure if I was masturbating the correct way but it was working. Cream spread my cheeks wider and snatched my fingers from between my slit. He stuck a finger in my anus while his tongue jabbed into my pussy. I laid limp as my body exploded and my essence ran down the crack of my ass.

"FUCK ME!" I screamed. He left me panting to get a condom from his nightstand. He pulled his thick and long dick out and I couldn't wait for him to invade my body.

"SHHHHHHHHHHHH," I hissed as he pressed his dick into me.

"Damn, Shae. Fuck," he groaned as he squeezed his girth into my tightness. He rubbed my soaking wet clit then stuck his wet fingers in my mouth. I sucked his fingers as he pounded into me. I gripped the edge of the dresser when he threw my legs over his shoulders. I winced in pain, he was too deep.

"Rub your pussy, baby," he said. I rubbed my clit and the sensation drove me insane. I made noises that I wasn't familiar with. Cream fucked me with so much passion, I forgot about everything that happened in my life. I wanted to be held captive in his bedroom for the rest of my life. I screamed his name as I exploded for the third time. He picked me up and laid on the bed with me on top of him. I turned around to ride him backwards. My nails dug into his knees as I bounced and grinded on his dick. My wet buttocks clapped and Cream squeezed and slapped them.

"Slow down, Shae!" he moaned, but I couldn't. I couldn't get enough of the great sex. Eron was always quick and selfish when it came to sex. Cream wasn't my first but it felt like he was because my body never had a full orgasm until he opened my legs.

"ARGHHHHHHHH!" Cream shouted when I sped up. He snatched my wig off but I still couldn't stop. He sat up and gripped the back of my neck to slow me down. He cupped my chin and licked the side of my face. It sent chills down my spine and my nipples got harder. They were so hard, they hurt. I slowed down and Cream pushed himself upwards inside me and grinded into my spot. I closed my eyes still straddling him. I could feel him in my stomach. I rested my head on his shoulder and slowly moved my hips in the motion of his rhythm.

"ARRHHHHH, CREAM. UGGHHHHHHHH. SHHHHHHHH," I cried as I came harder than the other times. He groaned in my ear letting me know he was coming, too. It took us a few minutes to come back to reality. We actually had sex and it was so amazing. I rolled off Cream and he laid on his back sprawled out. I don't know how I missed it, but he had a strawberry-shaped pussy tatted on his lower stomach with my name in the middle of the slit. The strawberry was dripping with what looked like cream. It was a very detailed and explicit tattoo but I liked it.

"What made you get that?" I asked and he chuckled.

"I got it when I was nineteen. I always thought about you," he said. He climbed off the bed and went into the bathroom to flush the condom. I followed behind him and gasped when I looked in the mirror.

"Damn it! My wig," I said and Cream chuckled.

"Ain't nothing wrong with the du-rag," he joked.

"It's a cap," I laughed.

"You still look good to me," he replied. I wrapped my arms around him and kissed him. I couldn't get enough of him.

"I hope you don't disappear on me again. I mean, we ain't gotta rush anything. We can still be friends as long as you keep it real with me because I will always keep it real with you," he replied.

"I'm not going anywhere, Mason," I teased and he slapped me on the butt.

Use Your Heart and Not Your Eyes

"I haven't been called by my government in years," Cream said.

We took a shower together and played around in the bathroom. I ran out the bathroom with a towel wrapped around me and Cream chased after me. He caught me and slammed me onto the bed. He laid on top of me and kissed me.

"You are still childish," Cream said and I mushed him. We always played around with each other. I used to provoke him just so he could chase me when we were younger. There was something about the way he grabbed me.

"You still like it," I said.

"You always had me chasing you. When are you going to let me catch you?" he asked seriously while staring into my eyes.

"I'm not running anymore," I said.

****

I woke up to breakfast in bed. Cream wasn't a good cook but he tried. My eggs were runny and my toast was burnt.

"What's the matter? I googled the shit and this is what it told me to do," Cream said, pointing at my plate.

"Well, at least you used seasoning," I joked and he cracked a smile.

Use Your Heart and Not Your Eyes

"So, you got white people jokes this morning, huh? Tell me something, Shae, why is your pussy so tight? I mean virgin tight. I guess your ex wasn't a black stallion, huh?" Cream said.

"I can't stand you," I laughed.

"I tried," Cream said.

"I know you did and that's all that matters," I replied.

"What are your plans for today?" he asked.

"I have to work but afterwards I'm free," I replied.

"Good, because I want to take you out," he said then winked at me. I sat my plate on the nightstand next to his bed and tossed the covers off my naked body.

"Can I get some more of that white stallion before I go to work?" I asked.

"You ain't shy no more, huh?" he asked, reaching into his drawer for a condom.

"Nope," I replied.

I turned over and got on all fours and Cream knocked my spine into different places. I was instantly whipped and I didn't know if it was a good or bad thing.

A few hours later...

I walked into the shop like I owned it. My heels clicked against the marble floor as my hips swayed from side to side. I flicked my hair back and popped my gum as I headed toward my station. Gautier and Saz stared at me and everyone else in the shop was looking at me, too. I sat in my chair and crossed my arms and legs.

"Come through, Eva," Gautier joked.

"Eva?" I asked.

"Girl, remember in that movie, *Deliver Us from Eva?* Eva got some good eggplant and she strutted up in that shop like she owned it," Saz said.

"Looks like someone got some good dick last night," one of the clients said.

"Why can't I just be happy?" I asked.

"Honey, only one thing can make a woman this happy early in the morning," Lisa said.

"I had a wonderful birthday," I said.

"You mean birthday sex," Saz's client said.

Gautier motioned me to go to the break room. I got up and headed toward the back with her and Saz following behind me.

"Spill it," Saz immediately said when she locked the door. I dropped down low and playfully shook my ass.

"This hoe must've had some dope fiend dick," Gautier joked. Saz playfully threw a few ones at me as if we were still at the strip club.

"Cream had me creaming. It was so beautiful," I blushed as I sat in a chair.

"I figured it was. We were trying to call you all night to make sure you were okay and you never called us back. I told Saz you were getting broken in. I knew he was going to tear it up the way he was looking at you while you were singing," Gautier said.

"Wait, what are you talking about? Who was singing?" I asked.

"You got on stage and sang last night. You haven't been on Twitter or Instagram this morning? They have been talking about you all morning. People are tagging Eron in their comments about you glowing already with your new boo. You and Cream were very close last night, you could definitely see some unfinished business between y'all two. You are literally the highlight of everyone's day today," Saz said.

"Oh no, what if Eron thinks I have been with Cream the whole time?" I said.

"About that," Gautier said and handed me her phone. Anger filled my heart when I read Eron's tweet. I guess he couldn't take the pressure of his fans tagging him in the pictures of Cream and me. Eron tweeted that he broke it off with me because I had been cheating on him with Cream.

"Social network is a gift and a curse," Gautier said.

"They are calling me a hoe!" I said in frustration.

"I used to like Eron but now I hate him more than I hate Cash Flow. You have been with that bastard since high school. He cheated on you and now he's making you look bad. I want to kill him," Saz said. I smiled wickedly when an idea popped up in my head.

"Eron wants to play dirty. Okay, I got something for his little dick ass," I said. I reached into my cross-body purse for my cell phone. I hurriedly got on Instagram and went live. I told the world my truth. It probably didn't mean much to my followers but I wasn't going to let Eron keep destroying my character. I was a good woman regardless of my insecurities; he should've left me or helped me through them instead of making it worse. I told my followers about his secret child and the model he was cheating on me with. I told them everything and didn't feel bad about it. I was certain I wasn't the only woman who lost herself in a relationship. After I was finished my live video, I placed my phone back inside my purse in disbelief.

"I can't believe I just did that," I said.

"I can. Eron shouldn't have painted a false picture of y'all's relationship. He made himself look like the victim. He didn't have to respond to his fans. If he was a real man and really loved you, he would've told them the truth. Better yet, he would've just kept his damn mouth shut," Gautier said.

"I was thinking we should go on vacation. We keep talking about it but we never plan it," Saz said.

"Sounds like a plan," Gautier said.

"Sure does," I replied.

"I'll book it today. When are y'all trying to go?" Gautier asked.

"Soon," Saz said and I nodded my head in agreement.

"Okay," Gautier replied.

My phone rang and it was my mother calling me. I told my friends I needed to talk to her in private and they left the break room. I answered the phone thinking she was going to apologize to me but she didn't.

"Eron is very upset with you!" she yelled into the phone.

"That's why you're calling me? You don't want to apologize for how you have been treating me?" I asked.

"You brought this on your damn self. I told you to stay the hell away from that white boy. Have you been sleeping with him this whole time?" she asked me.

"You are insane," I spat.

"I didn't raise you to be a white man's whore!" she yelled.

"You didn't raise me at all!" I screamed into the phone.

"Cream is no good. He's a drug dealer! Eron is successful, why on Earth would you do that to yourself? And now you want to be a singer? I saw a video of you singing. You have lost your mind since Eron left you," she said.

"No, I had some good dick since Eron left. I'm grown in case you haven't noticed, so you can't tell me what to do anymore. I'm going to continue dating Cream, and who knows, I might give you some blue-eyed grandbabies in the future," I said and she gasped.

"Karma is a bitch, Tyshae," she threatened me.

"I know it is, Mother. You and Eron will have a day in hell," I replied before I hung up.

I left out of the break room to get my day started. I didn't have many clients which was a good thing because I was sore and exhausted. Cream sent me a text telling me to have a good day and that he hoped to see me later. I instantly blushed; I still couldn't believe Cream was back in my life like he never left. Janae came into the shop wearing a sports bra and pair of leggings. She was a cool chick but at times she went overboard with her mouth.

"Hey, everybody!" Janae said as she sat in Saz's chair.

"Heyyy," a few people replied back to her.

"Soooo, you have been kicking it with Cream?" Janae asked me.

"Yeah, we have history," I replied.

"Girl, what made you cheat on Eron with Cream? I mean Cream is fine and all, but Eron's success is legit. I heard rumors about Cream being in a gang," Janae said. Gautier walked over to Janae and crossed her arms.

"See, what we are not going to do is rain down on Tyshae's happiness this morning. Leave her the fuck alone and mind your business for once. You didn't get enough tips last night? Who pissed in your Cheerios this morning?" Gautier asked.

"She must be mad that Cream didn't make her cream last night," Saz said and high-fived Gautier. Janae rolled her eyes knowing she couldn't take it there with Saz.

"Y'all are lucky nobody else in this city can lay my weave better than Saz. I'm not feeling y'all's attitudes," Janae said.

Use Your Heart and Not Your Eyes

"You must didn't see Tyshae's live video. Eron is a cheater, so therefore we are sticking behind her," my client, Opal said.

"Whatever, all I know is that Eron is more established," Janae complained.

"Cream has his own champagne line which is getting buzz from all over. Once it starts selling in other countries, it's a wrap. Cream is about to get foreign money," Saz said.

"Whatever," Janae said. Janae was in her feelings because she couldn't get what she wanted. Just a few days ago, Cream was everything and more to her. It didn't take much to realize she was a hater. Janae changed the subject and started gossiping. She had the shop in an uproar as she talked about some of the people's fashion.

"I peeped you and Salih getting real close last night. I heard y'all used to date in high school. Is that true?" Janae asked Gautier.

"We grew up in the same neighborhood is all. People get older and go separate ways," Gautier replied.

"You mean people start getting money and forget where they came from," Janae said.

"Where do you get this stuff from?" Saz asked.

"That's what I want to know, too," Gautier asked. Once Janae got the scoop on something, it was liable to spread fast like a virus.

"Well, my cousin's baby mama's brother used to kick it with some dude named Sisco. Apparently, Sisco killed Salih's brother and they said you had something to do with it. I even heard you had a daughter by Sisco. My cousin told me in the club last night when they saw you and Salih talking," Janae said.

"Tell your cousin to get his facts straight because that's a big lie!" Gautier said.

"Sisco called my cousin last night from his cell phone, you get it? Cell phone?" Janae asked but nobody laughed.

"Ewww, y'all are so uptight this morning, but anyways. He told my cousin he fucked you and your daughter might be his. How old is your daughter anyway, and why don't you bring her around?" Janae asked.

"Why don't you fix those lumpy ass shots in your ass, bitch?" Opal asked Janae. Janae stood up in a fighting stance. Opal, who was much smaller and shorter than Janae, snatched her hand away from me while I was giving her a filling.

"Girl, I'm from East Baltimore, so don't play with me. I'll cut your fucking throat up in here," Opal said. Opal was as hood as they come. She had the scars on her body to prove it. She was a stripper, too, and I heard her and Janae had some kind of beef going on in the past at a club they worked at.

"You are jealous because I stole your clientele, trick," Janae spat.

"That's because I'm a stripper, not a prostitute. You must've forgotten how I whipped your ass last year in the dressing room. Don't play with me, Janae, because I'm not with the shits. I'll stomp a hole in your forehead," Opal said.

"Y'all can take that outside," Saz spoke up.

Use Your Heart and Not Your Eyes

"Naw, I'm good. This lumpy ass made twenty stacks last night in the club, so I ain't trippin' over these washed-up hoes," Janae said. Opal sat back down to get her nails finished.

"I'm going to catch her ass, you just watch. I really love y'all, so that's the only reason why I'm behaving. I don't want the shop to get a bad name because y'all are doing so good and people follow y'all," Opal said and I thanked her. Two hours later, the shop was empty. I sipped my glass of wine as I listened to Gautier venting about what Janae said.

"I can't believe this is happening. I made one mistake in my past and I'm still paying for it. I bet this is why nobody from our neighborhood leaked information about me and Salih ," Gautier said.

"Also, because you hid the pregnancy. Salih went away to college and they forgot about y'all being a couple. It's very understandable why nobody put two and two together. So, trust me, nobody will believe Salih is the father," I said.

"That's the point, Tyshae. I'm tired of hiding it. We hid it so much that people will suspect I had a baby by Salih's brother's killer," Gautier said.

"I think it's time you and Salih expose the truth since Brooke is getting older. No sense in having her attached to someone who killed her father's brother," Saz said.

"I will figure this all out after we come back from Mexico," Gautier said. We decided to go to Cancun for three days for a quick getaway.

"Yayyy, I can't wait. Y'all better have those passports ready. We leave next weekend and it takes four to six weeks to get a passport," Saz said.

"SHIT!" I shouted out.

"What?" Saz asked.

"I left my documents in my file box. My file box is in Eron's closet," I said.

"He's still out of town, so go get it. We can't get our money back," Gautier said.

"Do you still have the house key?" Saz asked me.

"Yeah, I do," I replied.

"Go ahead and get it. We'll cover for you in case a client comes in," Gautier said. I hurriedly grabbed my purse and car keys. I prayed Eron was still out of town since he usually spends a week or more with his daughter's mother.

****

When I pulled up to Eron's house, I got out and unlocked the door. I rushed to the bedroom and went inside the closet. At the very top shelf, my box was still there. I opened it up and scanned through it; my birth certificate, social security card, and passport was still inside. I made sure I didn't leave anything else behind before I left the bedroom. When I got to the front door, I heard a noise coming from the kitchen followed by a familiar voice.

"Yes, I'm here. When are you coming home? I miss you," the voice said as I got closer. I couldn't believe my eyes and my heart shattered into a million pieces. I stood in the entry way of the kitchen watching her and listening to her talk to my ex-fiancé.

"Nasty bitch," I finally said and she dropped the phone. My sister, Kimmy turned around and I wanted to throw up. She was pregnant and it looked like she was past due.

"What are you doing in my house?" she asked me.

"Your house? Bitch, this ain't your house!" I yelled at her.

"It's been my house since he kicked you out," she said.

"You are married," I replied and she laughed.

"I'm divorced. I left my husband a year ago. Mother doesn't even know yet," she said.

"How can you do this to me? I know we weren't close, but how could you sleep with my man? Are you carrying his child, too?" I asked.

"Get out of my house," she said and grabbed a knife.

"I'm leaving. I would kick your ass but you ain't worth it. Being pregnant by Eron is your karma. You will see how much of a man-whore he is. I bet you don't know where he's at, do you?" I asked.

"Training camp, where else would he be?" she asked.

"With his daughter's mother, bitch. Trust me, you will see. You think he loves you, huh? You wanted my life and now you got it. Sleepless, lonely nights will come for you, too," I said.

"I'm carrying his child. Something you couldn't do," she teased.

"It was a blessing in disguise. I wish you well, sis," I laughed. I hurriedly left the house with my box in my hand. I got inside my car and sat there for what seemed like forever. I surprised myself when I didn't cry. I felt like I wanted to but I didn't. Instead of being mad, I should've been blessed. I thanked God for giving me strength. I wasn't going to cry and fight over someone who didn't love me. Eron wasn't worth it and neither was my sorry-ass sister. The way I looked at it, they were each other's karma. If Kimmy was still the same as before, she was going to drain Eron's pockets dry. Her baby was her meal ticket since she was no longer with her husband. Eron fell into her trap and it was too bad because he should've had a faithful dick. My phone rang and it was Cream calling. I blushed as I thought about his kisses and the way he touched my body. I immediately answered the phone.

"Hello," I answered.

"What's up, beautiful, are you hungry?" he asked.

"What do you have in my mind?" I asked.

"Come and join me for lunch if you're not busy," he said.

"Send me your location," I replied.

An hour later, I was at Capital Grille in Chevy Chase with Cream. He sat across from me smiling.

"Why are you smiling?" I asked.

"There is a reason behind this lunch date," he said.

"Your sneaky ass."

"I talked to Yarmin Ross today," he replied.

"That owns Millionaire Records?" I asked.

"Yup," he said.

"Okay, what happened?" I replied.

"He's looking for a female artist to sing a hook on one of his artist's songs. He saw your video and said you are the perfect fit. He's digging your voice and your style," Cream said.

"I don't know about that, I mean, I was drunk," I replied.

"Naw, Strawberry. I'm not buying that drunk shit. The liquor gave you courage to do it, but that's how you felt. I think you should give him a call to see what's up. You're not signing under his label or nothing like that. He just wants you to sing a hook," Cream said.

"What's the deal with you and Yarmin? He could've just called the shop, everyone knows the number," I replied.

"I was just at the studio kicking it with him. He and I go way back if you know what I mean," Cream said pointing to the gang-related tattoo on his hand. He knew Yarmin because they were both in the same gang.

"We're not gang banging anymore, so you don't have to worry about getting caught up. His label is one-hundred percent legit. I wouldn't point you in that direction if it wasn't a good move," he said.

"Can I think about it?" I replied.

"Of course, don't rush nothing you're not sure about. I only want you to follow your dreams," he said.

"What about your dreams?" I asked.

"I'm staring at it," he replied.

We sat for two hours, eating and talking. Cream wasn't surprised about Kimmy and Eron. He said he always knew Kimmy was grimy. After we finished lunch, we took a walk on the strip. We received a lot of stares because Cream was holding my hand.

"I don't think people are feeling us," I laughed as we stood by a crosswalk.

"Fuck them," he said and squeezed my ass. A white older woman looked at us in disgust. I pulled Cream's face closer to mine and gave him a big, wet sloppy kiss.

"My schedule is clear for the day. The shop isn't busy. What are your plans?" I asked.

"I had a few things to take care of, but they can wait," he replied.

"Good because you are stuck with me," I said.

I spent the rest of the day with Cream. We ended up back at his home and things got heated up. I was sprawled out on his kitchen island getting my soul snatched from me. Cream's tongue had a mind of its own. After he was finished eating me out, he gave it to me deep in missionary style. I couldn't understand how someone could feel so good. We took a shower together after we tired each other out in the kitchen. I laid on his solid chest while he palmed my ass. He kissed my forehead and I playfully wiped it off.

"Fuck you then," he joked.

"Nasty mouth," I replied.

"That's because it was on your pussy," he said and I pinched him.

"Stop, girl, damn. You know I'll turn blue," he said. I was ready to respond but my phone rang. I answered the unfamiliar number.

"Hello," I answered.

"You're a dead bitch!" Eron yelled at me and I sat up. My mother must've given him my number.

"Excuse me?" I asked.

"Are you trying to ruin my image? I saw your video from earlier! Bitch, I will sue you for slander," Eron screamed into the phone.

"Sue me after all you have done to me? You got my sister living in a house I was just living in a few days ago. You lied on me and told everyone I was cheating on you when you know it was the opposite. You are such a lame-ass nigga! I'll get my cousins from my father's side to whip your bitch-ass!" I yelled into the phone and it got quict on his end.

"I don't want you with that white boy," Eron finally said. He didn't call me because of my live video. He couldn't stand to see me happy so soon. I guess he thought I was going to beg him to take me back.

"Too bad because I'm not going to stop seeing him. Don't call my phone no damn more! The next time you do, I'm going to record you and send it to your slew of bitches," I replied.

"Hang the phone up, I'm tired of hearing that muthafucka whine," Cream said and Eron heard him.

"Tell that broke wigga he can't fill my shoes," Eron seethed and Cream snatched the phone away from me.

"Speak to me, muthafucka. Run that shit by me again, I can't fill what?" Cream asked, getting pissed off. Eron yelled something into the phone then hung up.

"Punk-ass muthafucka," Cream said and tossed my phone to the end of the bed. I thought it was going to be the end of me and Eron when he dumped me, but I thought wrong.

Saz
Jealous Over You

I couldn't stay mad at Yudai. After all, it wasn't his fault his sister was rude. We ended up at my home the night of Tyshae's party. We were drinking and had the wildest sex ever. We woke up on my floor by the front door naked. Cash Flow had been trying to get on my good side. He was back to sending me flowers and "I love you" messages. His attitude did a three-sixty since he had that session with Dr. Samuels. My life finally seemed peaceful but I still couldn't find it in my heart to forgive Cash Flow for the things he did to me. Yudai and I were still staying out the public's eye so our dates consisted of spending time in my condo. One thing was for sure, Cash Flow would never come to my home because he stuck out more to the public with his colorful clothes, emoji-tatted face, and pink hair. I cringed at the thought of his pink hair.

I was prepping the table for dinner when the doorbell rang. I opened the door for Yudai. As soon as he saw me, he wrapped his arms around my waist and gave me a deep kiss. He palmed my ass as he sucked on my lips. Yudai was a very sexual person. A few mornings I woke up with him eating my pussy. I didn't have to ask and he didn't have to ask me, he took it whenever he wanted and I didn't stop him.

"I can't get enough of you," he said. I closed the front door and he followed me into the kitchen.

"What's for dinner?" he asked.

"Lasagna, asparagus, garlic bread, and Caesar salad. For dessert, we are having homemade rice pudding," I said.

"You can't spoil me like this," he joked.

"You spoil me," I replied and he did. Yudai was always bringing me gifts. One night, he walked into my condo with three shopping bags. Yudai knew what to get me and I think having sisters played a big role in that.

"Your set is still being cleaned?" Yudai asked about the jewelry he bought for me. He asked me about it one night and l lied to him. I was sick to my stomach after I lied to him, but I couldn't tell him I lost it because I didn't want Cash Flow questioning me about it.

"Yeah, I have been very busy and didn't get a chance to pick it up," I replied.

"I'll pick it up for you. Where is it at?" he asked.

"By the shop. Don't worry, I'll get it before me and the girls go to Cancun this weekend," I replied. He went into his pocket and laid a few bills out on the table.

"I don't need any money," I said.

"Who said you did? It can be emergency money or something. Is dinner ready? I'm starving," he said.

"Yes, it will be in a few minutes," I replied. He kissed my cheek before he walked out the kitchen. Something on the counter buzzed. It was Yudai's cell phone. We weren't in an official relationship but I still wanted to know if he had other girls on the side. I peeked at the phone and the name "Makeisha" was on the screen. Makeisha was his sister's friend and she was also someone Yudai was serious with. To say I was jealous was an understatement.

"Your phone!" I called out to him. He came into the kitchen and picked it up. He declined the call and I rolled my eyes at him.

"What's up with you?" he asked.

"You can talk around me," I replied.

"I know I can because I don't have shit to hide. I declined the call because I didn't feel like talking. Why are you looking at my phone anyway?" he asked.

"Because I thought it was mine!" I said.

"Shorty, you mean to tell me you thought my phone was your bright ass pink phone? Stop lying and keep it real," he replied.

"I was curious because you told me I was the only one getting your time," I said.

"That's the truth," Yudai replied.

"What's the deal with you and her? Y'all still fucking or what?" I asked straight to the point.

"No, I haven't touched that girl in months. She started calling me after she saw a picture of us," Yudai explained and I rolled my eyes.

"Show me a picture of her," I said.

"Yo' ass crazy," he replied and I crossed my arms.

"Are you serious right now?" he asked. I cocked my head to the side and jerked my neck so he could know how serious I was. Yudai pulled up a picture of her on IG then passed the phone to me. She was pretty and thick but very shapely. She looked mixed with Asian or something. She reminded me of a plus-size Karrueche. I slid the phone back to him and he smirked at me.

"She's cute. What's the story behind her? I know it's more because she seems very close to you," I said.

"We were dating, it could've been serious but things happened between us. I knocked her up and she got rid of it. I haven't spoken to her since. I don't believe in abortions. I couldn't force her to have the baby, but she went about it all wrong. She waited until she was five months pregnant to get rid of it. Our families knew about the pregnancy, so she had the support. Money wasn't an issue because I had just signed my contract. Come to find out she did it because she didn't like the attention I was getting from females. I sorta lost respect for her. I can't even look at her when I see her. I mean, why would she allow me to hear his heartbeat and do that to me? She took being insecure to whole other level. It's one thing to be insecure, but it's a problem when your insecurities hurt people that care about you," Yudai said. The last comment hit too close to home.

"Women deal with hurt differently," I replied.

"You don't play with a life like that. She killed my son. An abortion should be in early stages, not in second trimester," he said and I agreed.

"You'll make a great father," I said.

"One day but no time soon. If it happens, it happens, but I damn sure ain't trying," Yudai said. His phone rang again and it was her calling. Yudai picked up his phone and turned it off. It was almost as if she knew he was with me.

"Let me know when you want to go back to her," I said.

"Naw, I found something better. Now hurry up and fix my plate. I'm trying to watch a replay of our game from earlier. I think those niggas were cheating," Yudai complained.

"But y'all won," I replied. Yudai's team played the Washington Nationals earlier that day.

"Barely," Yudai said.

A few minutes later, we were sitting at the table eating dinner. I didn't have much of an appetite, so I played around in my food. I was always in and out with my happiness; one minute I was fine then the next minute I began feeling low again. Often times, I wished my mother could come back to life because it was so much easier with her alive. I couldn't help but to think how drastically my life had changed since she was murdered.

"What's up with you? Please don't tell me you are still tripping over that phone call. Now you got me feeling like I really done something to you. I'm either away for a game, practicing, or with you. I don't have much free time but the little time I do I have is with you," Yudai said. It was guilt eating me up because I couldn't give him the little bit of what he expected from me. I thought about letting him go until I became a better woman because I had some deep-rooted issues. It was just so hard because I didn't want to be that woman to make Yudai feel a certain way about love. I also didn't want him to turn out like Salih. Women can fall in love again after being hurt, but men were different. All it takes is one female to give them a different view about relationships and they would carry that burden forever.

"Nothing is wrong with me," I lied.

"I don't think this shit is going to grow between us if you can't never say shit. I'm not a fucking mind reader, Saz," Yudai said, getting annoyed.

"Why do you have an attitude?" I asked.

"Why do you think? One minute you're happy then the next you space out," he replied.

"Get off my back," I said.

"Fuck you," he spat. He got up from the table and headed toward the door. I ran after him and pulled him back.

"I'm sorry, I was thinking about my mother and a few other things. It just seems like I can't piece my life together since she was killed. It's almost as if my life ended with hers. I'm an emotional wreck sometimes," I admitted. Yudai closed the door and locked it. I hugged him and he rubbed his fingers through my hair.

"My bad, shorty, I didn't mean to come at you like that," he said.

"Can we lay down and watch TV in bed?" I asked.

"Cool," he replied.

We went to my bedroom after he finished eating his food. I got undressed down to my bra and boy shorts before I got in bed. Yudai took off all his clothes, he was only wearing boxer briefs. I noticed a slight change in his weight. He was filling out perfectly, making him look a little older.

"How much weight did you gain?" I asked him and he chuckled.

"Twelve pounds. It's all your fault. You cook big meals and dessert," he replied. We laid around in bed for the rest of the night watching movies. Usually Yudai pulled my panties to the side when he was in the mood but he wasn't touching me. I did everything to get him in the mood. He was hard but he wasn't moving. I brushed my ass against his dick and still got nothing. Frustrated with him, I slung the covers off my body and went into the kitchen to get a bowl of rice pudding. I closed the fridge and jumped because Yudai scared me. He pressed my body against the fridge, towering over me. His hand slipped into my boy shorts and he cupped my pussy.

"Why you not in bed?" I moaned.

"I got out to piss but I saw you bending over on my way to the bathroom. How bad do you want it?" he asked into my ear.

"I don't," I lied. He gently grabbed my neck and shoved his tongue down my throat. My rice pudding slipped out my hand and on to the floor. My floodgates opened as I anticipated his pleasurable entrance. He slid my boy shorts down and got on his knees to taste me. He threw my leg over his shoulder and licked my slit. I unhooked my bra so he could reach up to my massage my breasts. My nails ran through his thick mass of curls as his tongue made love to my center. He moaned against my pussy and it made me wetter. I grinded onto his face and screamed his name as I was nearing an orgasm.

"YUDAIIIIIIIII!" I moaned. He slurped and kissed my center as my essence ran down my inner thigh. My pussy was an ice cream cone on a summer day as it melted and dripped down Yudai's chin. I exploded on his tongue and he moaned from the taste of me. He stood up and kissed me with my cum dripping down his lips. I pulled him into the bedroom and went into my drawer to get a condom. He freed his thick, long bat from his boxers and I spread my legs for him.

"Put them behind your head," Yudai said. I did what he told me to do. It was his favorite position because he liked watching my pussy swallow every inch of him. He kissed my pussy before he pushed the tip of his head through my opening. I bit my bottom lip because it wasn't easy going in. Seconds later, he had me pinned down on the mattress, screwing my brains out. He bit my bottom lip and pulled my hair. He was so nasty when it came to sex it completely turned me out.

"UMMMMMMMMMM, BABBBYYYYYYY!" I moaned.

"Is this my pussy?" he asked while deep stroking me.

"Yes, baby!" I moaned. He pressed his body flat on top of mine and I gasped because he was all the way inside me. He gripped my hair and sucked on my neck as he slowed his thrusts. My eyes were closed and my mouth was gaped open. The noise from him splashing in my wetness got louder as I squirted. My pussy squeezed him and he almost lost it.

"This pussy is so good, shorty. I'm going to make you mine," he groaned into my ear. I wanted to elbow him for talking and fucking me the way he was and making me come. I exploded again and he exploded right after me. He collapsed on top of me and rested his head on my shoulder.

I'm so much in love it's scaring me and I don't know what to do, I thought.

The next morning…

"I'm going to miss you," I said hugging him on my tippy toes.

"FaceTime me later on. I hope you show me a titty or something when you do," he said and kissed my lips.

"I will, call me after practice," I said. He pecked my lips again before he walked out my front door. I locked the door and headed to the bathroom. I showered then got dressed for the day. I got on the Uber app for a ride to the shop. I was too busy to go to the dealership. By the time I left the shop, the dealerships were closed. The Uber driver arrived at my building thirty minutes later. Luxury Tea was just opening when I arrived. Gautier was on the phone smiling from ear to ear when I walked into the shop.

"I wonder who that is," I said and she playfully rolled her eyes at me.

"I gotta go. Talk to you later," Gautier said and hung up her phone.

"You didn't have to hang up," I said and she blushed.

"Yes, I did because you're nosey. Anyways, that was Salih on the phone with his fine ass," she fanned herself.

"Ewwww," I said and she playfully mushed me.

"Brooke and I spent the night with him again last night at his loft. I don't know how long this is going to last because he's still an engaged man. I feel guilty about it but when I'm around him, he belongs to me. I don't know how this is going to end but it makes Brooke so happy," Gautier said.

"Salih will figure it out. I'm just glad the nigga ain't being an asshole to you anymore," I replied.

"Oh, he's still an asshole. We argued this morning because he's just finding out we are leaving for Cancun in a few days. He had the nerve to tell me I couldn't pack my own bag because he doesn't like the clothes I wear," Gautier replied. Tyshae walked into the shop sipping on an iced coffee from Starbucks.

"Good morning, best frans," Tyshae happily sang.

"Do you have some cream up in that coffee?" Gautier asked and Tyshae flicked her off. The door to the shop opened and Cream walked in with a purse in his hand.

"Good morning, ladies. Shae, you forgot your purse," Cream called out to her.

"Dick was that good this morning?" Gautier whispered to Tyshae.

"Thank you, baby," Tyshae said to Cream.

"I'll be here around seven. Y'all have a good one," Cream said before he bopped out the shop.

"Looks like we all had a good night last night," I said and everyone agreed.

Lisa came into the shop with red teary eyes. She walked past us to her station and grabbed a tissue. She sat in her chair and burst into tears.

"Ask her what's wrong," I whispered to Gautier.

"You're the nosey one. You ask her," Gautier whispered back.

"Is everything okay?" Tyshae asked Lisa.

"Yes, I'm fine," Lisa snapped.

"No need to be a bitch about it," I replied.

"I'm not being a bitch but y'all don't need to be in my business! Do I look okay to y'all?" she sobbed.

"Do you want to talk about it?" Gautier asked.

"The man I was seeing dumped me. He left me because I told him I was pregnant. My family will disown me behind this. No husband, no baby. Am I supposed to get rid of my baby? I don't want to do that," Lisa said.

"Why are you having unprotected sex with a man that belongs to someone else?" Tyshae asked.

"The same damn reason why you were fucking a man who was having unprotected sex with everyone else. Love makes us do crazy things," Lisa said.

"Wait a minute, Lisa. You can go home if you feel the need to attack us for being concerned," Gautier replied.

"I'm sorry, I just need to get myself together. We were supposed to move in together," Lisa said.

"Who is the man?" Tyshae asked him.

Use Your Heart and Not Your Eyes

"He's nobody special. Can I come with y'all to Cancun? I need to get some fresh air, too," Lisa said. I looked at Gautier and Tyshae and they shrugged their shoulders. I didn't want Lisa to hang with us but Tyshae told her it was okay.

"Thank you all so much. I really need this," Lisa said and hugged us. I rolled my eyes and Gautier told me to behave. I didn't want to share my friends, they were all I had. Lisa was cool to work with sometimes but that's as far as it went. Lisa went into the bathroom to fix her makeup.

"So, y'all just recruiting bitches?" I asked.

"Stop being a brat. The girl needs to get away. We all know what it feels like to be wronged by a man. Let her have her moment," Tyshae replied. The door opened and a few clients walked in.

"Okay, let's get to work," Gautier said.

We were so busy, I didn't eat anything. Everyone was trying to get their hair and nails done before we went on vacation. I could barely text Yudai because of how busy I was. By the time I got off, it was midnight. Gautier dropped me off at home and I couldn't wait to get to my fridge to eat some leftovers from the night before. While I was heating up leftover lasagna, my cell phone rang.

"Hello," I answered the unfamiliar number.

"Open up the door," the caller said. I began to panic because he showed up at my home. I rushed to the door and opened it. Cash Flow was standing in front of me with two shopping bags. I wanted to scream because of his outfit. He wore pink shorts, a lime green shirt with a pair of tan Ugg boots. I almost fainted when I looked at his hair. His hair was dyed yellow and he had a hoop earring in his ear. Usually I kept my mouth shut but I couldn't hold it in any longer.

"What in the hell do you think you're doing? Why do you look like a runaway teen on meth? Your hair is damaged and you have split ends," I fussed.

"Shorty, this outfit cost me three stacks. You need to get hip," he said and kissed my lips. He walked into my condo and looked around.

"After all the money I gave you, you settle for this shoe box?" Cash Flow asked in disgust.

"It's in my budget, not yours. How did you find out where I live?" I asked.

"I have my resources. This place doesn't have much security," he said.

"I'm not a celebrity," I replied.

"But you're my bitch. I got you a few things while I was out on business. I hope you like it," he said.

"Make yourself at home while I go freshen up," I replied. I hurried to my bedroom and hid all of Yudai's things in the back of my closet. I placed his toothbrush in the medicine cabinet and hid his shower gel behind a rack of towels. I walked back into the kitchen and Cash Flow was trying to unlock my cell phone. I snatched my phone from him and he smacked his teeth.

"What are you looking for?" I asked.

Use Your Heart and Not Your Eyes

"Did you cut it off with that baseball player? Look, Saz, I'm trying to be nice about the situation considering how bad I have treated you, but I'm ready to bring out the monster again. I know you were with him when your thot bucket-head ass friend had her birthday party. I keep tabs on you," Cash Flow said.

"We are just friends," I replied.

"So, explain to me why you just went to the back to hide that nigga's shit," he spat.

"I don't have to explain shit to nobody but the man upstairs. What are you doing here?" I asked.

"I need you to check something out for me," he replied. He pulled out a piece of paper from his back pocket and I snatched it from him.

"What is this?" I asked.

"Lyrics to a song called, 'Eat A Pickle,'" he replied and I laughed. I leaned forward clutching my stomach as tears pooled from my eyes. Cash Flow smacked me on the back of my head.

"Cut that shit out!" he yelled in frustration. I sat in a chair at the kitchen island and read the piece of paper.

Eat a pickle, trick, choke on this dick
Your man ain't shit and he plays polo stick
Weeka weeka boo, the fool is you
I got a hunnit g's for that sloppy toppy
Give it to me please stove top stuffin'
Eat a turkey like you want a pickle, bitch...

Use Your Heart and Not Your Eyes

"Ummmm, yeah. I'm very confused about this one. Have you ever thought about being a clothes designer instead of rapping? I know a lot of drag queens would shop at your store," I said. Cash Flow came across the kitchen island and wrapped his hand around my throat. He pulled a gun out and placed it to my temple.

"I'm trying to be nice to you. I turned my life to God, but I will put a hole in your dome if you make fun of my talent and my fashion again. There is only one nigga like me in the game! Bitch, I'm worth millions more than your pop tart ass. Fix my lyrics and hurry the fuck up," he said. He pushed me and I fell off the stool. If he didn't have a gun, I would've slapped the spit out of his mouth.

"I'll see what I can do," I said.

"That's my baby. Now, pull those pants down so I can smell you. I missed you," he replied.

"I'm tired," I said. He pulled the gun out again and pointed it at me.

"Do it!" he replied. I pulled down my pants and my thong. Cash Flow told me sit on the counter and I did. He opened my legs and inhaled the scent of my pussy.

"I missed you," he said. He stuck his tongue inside me and I laid still wanting it to be over. Cash Flow was good in bed when I was in love with him but now it was creepy being with him. I was completely over him but he was forcing himself in my life. He pulled his dick out and jerked off as he ate my pussy. He purposely exploded on my counter after he was finished. I hurriedly sat up and ran to my bedroom to wipe his thick saliva off my vagina. For some reason, he got a kick out of hulk spitting on my pussy. I thought he was changing but it was all a façade to lure me back in. I walked out the bathroom and he was eating my lasagna.

"I think we should work on having a baby," he said.

"You have officially lost your damn mind! Get the fuck outta my house!" I screamed.

"I'll shoot you," he threatened.

"I'd rather be dead than keep dealing with your crazy, confused, wanna-be Barbie ass. Shoot me and get it over with because I'm about tired of your threats. I tried to believe you were going to change but nope, you are still a punk ass bitch. I bet you're scared to fight a real man. If you want to fight like two bitches, do it without a gun. I'll whip your Bratz doll looking ass in two seconds. Let's get it," I replied. Instead of getting mad, he lustfully stared at me.

"Damn, you're hot when you get mad. How about this, when I finish this next tour, we should work on having a little mini me. You can stop working at ghetto style kitchen hair salon so I can take care of you. What do you think? After you give birth, we will get married. I got our lives all mapped out, baby. I left my wife today. If you don't believe me, check out all the gossip blogs. I came over here to celebrate with you. No more hiding us, we are exposed to the world," he said.

"You left your wife?" I asked pissed off.

"Yeah, I left her. I really do love you, Saz. I just want you to be more understanding toward my character and music career. I didn't want to pull a gun out on you, but love makes niggas do crazy things. You know I don't like to be made fun of," he replied.

"I don't get what you're saying," I spat.

"I'm your man now. It's official," he smiled. He got up and kissed my cheek before he headed back to my bedroom.

"Hurry up, I want to take a bubble bath with you while we figure out baby names. I can't wait for this one, Saz. I'm ready to be a family man," Cash Flow said. I picked up my phone and googled Cash Flow's break up. I dropped my phone on the floor and the screen cracked. Out of all the lies he told, he was finally telling the truth. A year ago, I would've been ecstatic, but he was late—very late. I cleaned Cash Flow's semen off my counter and fought back the vomit that threatened to come up my throat. I wanted to kill him and thought about ways to get rid of him. I went to my bedroom and he was getting undressed. I walked past him and went straight to the bathroom. He followed behind me, singing and dancing like we were the world's happiest couple.

"My assistant found a new house for us. While I was away working, I was putting our lives together. You're the only woman I shared my life with. Nobody else knows about my childhood but you. That should mean something," he said.

Yeah, it means something. You're a crazy fruit rollup, I thought. I looked down at his feet and got light headed. Cash Flow's toe nails were polished yellow with a big emoji designed on his big toe. I don't know how I missed it but his nails were polished red. He ran our bath water then left out the bathroom. He came back with a stack of money in his hand and tossed the bills into the tub.

"Yeah, shorty. We about to bathe in money. I call it a money bath, ya' heard?" he asked in excitement. I got undressed and stepped into the water of soggy bills. I couldn't wait to tell my friends about Cash Flow. Cash Flow tried to tickle me but I wasn't in the mood.

"Can we hurry up and finish this bath? I have to wake up very early," I said.

"Aight, Saz. Damn, you're ungrateful," he replied.

A few hours later...

I laid in bed unable to sleep as Cash Flow snored and farted. I got out of bed and grabbed a blanket from out the hall closet. I went to the living room and crashed on the couch. I looked out the window by the couch and it was pouring raining. It was three o'clock in the morning and I had to be up at seven. I picked up my phone and called Erin. I was supposed to meet her for brunch but I couldn't make it. She answered the phone half asleep.

"What happened? Is everything, okay?" she asked.

"I need your guidance," I sniffled into the phone.

"What's the matter, baby?" she asked.

"I'm suffering from depression. I just want to talk," I replied.

"Okay, I'm on my way. Meet me downstairs in thirty minutes," she said and hung up. I slipped on a pair of pajama pants and tennis shoes. I grabbed my phone and house keys before I left my condo. Erin was there in less than thirty minutes. I got into her car when she pulled up. She was in her mid-forties but she still looked good. Erin was a slim light-skinned woman with long sand-colored locs. She had small freckles on her face and a little gap between her front teeth. Nonetheless, she was an attractive woman.

"What's the matter, Saz? You know you can always come to live with me instead of being out here all alone," she said.

"I know but I don't want to see my old house," I replied.

"It's on the market to be sold. The family that lived there just recently moved," she replied.

"I miss her so much," I burst into sobs and she wrapped her arm around me.

"I miss her, too, she was my best friend, my only friend," Erin replied.

"It's hard trying to move on with my love life. I have been trying to fill that void and ended up with a man who doesn't respect me and now I can't get rid of him. I fell in love with someone else. Cash Flow left his wife for me so now it will be hard to get rid of him. He thinks I owe him. I want him dead so bad it scares me. Who can I go to for help? A restraining order against him will ruin my image and the shop's image. He has a lot of fans and they will do everything in their power to destroy me although I'm already destroyed. I just need a way out without exposing so much of my life to the media," I said.

"You young folks are so focused on social media that y'all are willing to die because of it. Who cares what those people think? Your safety comes first. That man is a lunatic. Look at him, he's very ignorant. You're a talented, gorgeous young girl who deserves so much more. Does the young man you're dating know about this?" she asked.

"No, and that's what's eating me up. He doesn't know anything about Cash Flow. I wasn't expecting things with Yudai to get serious, but they did. Cash Flow keeps threatening to kill me and I believe it. He killed his uncle when he was a teenager and his mother took the rap for it because she knew he was going to be famous. He comes from a dysfunctional family and the fame is making it worse. He feels like he can do anything and get away with it because he has money. Sadly, he can get away with anything," I said.

"Is he beating you?" she asked.

"He hit me a few times but he verbally abuses me most of the time. He's always threatening me with a weapon, telling me he's going to kill me. I have a feeling he's going to end up killing me and my murder will go unnoticed," I replied.

"My sister's husband is an attorney. Give me a few days to figure this out but in the meantime, you might have to ignore him. Get a new number, don't just block his calls because he can always use a new number to call you from. Don't stay at your home. Do you have any friends you can stay with until this blows over? More than likely he's a coward and won't do anything physical to you around anyone because they'll be a witness. If he tries to come around you after you cut all ties with him, it will help build a case. As long as you're entertaining him, it's his word against yours and he knows that. You can't say he's stalking you if you are letting him into your home," she said.

"I let him in because he will kill me if I don't," I replied.

"We will figure this out but don't let him know what you're planning on doing," she said.

"Okay, I can do that," I replied.

"Sure, you can. Cash Flow does what he wants because you allowed it for so long and now it's outta' hand. Problems don't disappear if you ignore them, they become bigger problems," she said.

Use Your Heart and Not Your Eyes

"Thank you so much. I was ready to have a nervous breakdown," I replied.

"Losing a close parent can set a sane person crazy. You're not the first and won't be the last. You should try coming to church with me one Sunday," she said.

"The same church my mother went to?" I asked and Erin nodded her head.

"Sorry, but I can't. I'm not ready," I replied.

"It takes time," she said.

I kissed her cheek and hugged her.

"Go to Cancun and have fun. Don't worry about anything. I'll figure it out," she said.

"I will," I replied. I got out of her Mercedes and closed the door. I waved her goodbye as she drove away. Cash Flow was sitting on my couch smoking a blunt when I walked into my condo.

"Why did you leave the bed?" he asked.

"The same reason why you left the bed. I wanted to smoke," I replied.

"You could've smoked in here," he said.

"No smoking is allowed in the building," I replied.

"Why am I getting this bad vibe from you all of a sudden? Pretty boy got you feeling yourself, huh? Just a few months ago, you were a bird bitch," he scoffed. I rolled my eyes at him and walked into my bedroom. I got into bed and he came into my room yelling and fussing at me.

"You went downstairs to see that nigga! I saw you getting out a Mercedes," he said.

"You're crazy," I replied. He jumped on my bed and started kicking me. His toe went into my mouth and I bit him. He reached for his gun and I hurriedly tackled him onto the floor. I sat on top of him and sent bone crushing jabs into his face. He headbutted me and my head hit the nightstand. He grabbed my hair and dragged me across the floor. I screamed for him to stop because I felt my hair being ripped from my scalp.

"You were obedient when I treated you like shit! This is how you wanna act after I left my wife for you?" he yelled. I punched him in the nuts and he doubled over. I kicked him in the face and he fell back into my dresser. I dashed toward my phone to call for help but I wasn't fast enough. Cash Flow tackled me onto the floor and repeatedly slapped my face until I was dizzy. Our fights weren't as bad in the past because I didn't fight him back. I saw a stiletto shoe underneath my bed and grabbed it. I hit him in the face with it and blood squirted everywhere.

"ARGHHHHHHHH!" he cried as he rolled around on the floor. I went inside my closet and got a pair of Timbs. I hurriedly put them on and I stomped him. My room was a mess.

"I HATE YOU!" I screamed and kicked him again. I kicked him until I tired myself out. Cash Flow laid unconscious on the floor. I hid his gun inside a vent before I went into the bathroom to look at my face. My face wasn't as bad as I thought it would be. I had a few scratches, a bleeding lip, and a black eye that makeup could cure. I got into the shower to soothe the aches and pains my body felt. Cash Flow stumbled into the bathroom with blood leaking down his face.

He stood in the mirror and looked at his face. Both of his eyes were swollen and his lip was bleeding.

"I can't believe you did this to me," he cried.

"Get the hell out of my house before I whip that ass," I replied. He dropped down to his knees and wrapped his arms around me.

"I can't leave you. We can forget this happened, okay?" he cried and I pushed him away from me. He angrily stood up with a balled fist.

"Get the fuck out before I kill you and don't you ever come back. I swear on my life, I'll kill you. Enough is enough and I don't want you anymore. WE ARE DONE!" I yelled.

"I'll be back when you calm down," he said. He snatched a towel off the sink and cleaned his face off. Seconds later, he was fully dressed.

"You're going to regret this, bitch," he seethed. He snatched a pair of my Gucci shades off the dresser and placed them over his eyes before he walked out my condo. The door slammed behind him and a picture fell off my wall. I looked around my room and threw my hands up in frustration. It took two hours to clean up the mess in my room. Cash Flow's blood was embedded in my carpet. I grabbed a runner from the hallway and covered the stain up with it. I laid across my bed and closed my eyes. I was exhausted and relieved that Cash Flow finally got what was coming to him.

****

Use Your Heart and Not Your Eyes

I went to work hours later like nothing happened. I wore my makeup a little heavier.

"Our flight leaves tomorrow morning. I sooo can't wait," Gautier said as she passed out iced coffees.

"Me, neither," I replied. I sat in the chair because my body was still sore from Cash Flow dragging me.

"Are you okay?" Gautier asked.

"Yes, I'm fine. I slept wrong," I lied.

"Girl, I know that feeling. I'm always sleeping wrong," she said. I checked my phone to see if I had a missed call from Yudai but I didn't. It was strange because he always texted and called in the morning. I sent him a text telling him we needed to talk. I finally mustered up the courage to tell Yudai everything about Cash Flow and me.

"I don't think we are going to be that busy today since yesterday was so hectic," Tyshae said.

"Awww, look. Yudai's car just pulled up," Gautier said. My smile faded when Yudai barged into the shop with murder in his eyes. He snatched me out the chair by my vest and dragged me to the bathroom. He locked the door and I immediately started crying. I felt it in my soul something bad happened. Gautier and Tyshae were knocking on the door for him to open it up. They feared he was going to hurt me.

"Yo, what the fuck is this?" Yudai asked, showing me his phone. It was pictures of Cash Flow wearing the set Yudai bought me. He had a video and I was scared to watch it. I had a feeling Cash Flow recorded me, and to make matters worse, it was a recent video of us at his secret home. It was the day he begged me to go to therapy with him. Too bad he cut that part out the video. The video was from a security camera in Cash Flow's living room.

"That nigga called me early this morning and told me he was fucking my bitch and how icy your jewelry looked on him. This is why you wanted us to be on the hush, huh? I asked you what happened to the shit I bought you and you straight up lied to my fucking face!" Yudai yelled at me.

"I can explain," I sobbed.

"Shorty, check this out. Ain't shit to explain because you're a sneaky ass trick. You even had the audacity to ask me about my ex when you were fucking that whack ass colorful nigga! You were trying to play me or something? You wanted a nigga to take care of you the whole time! You ain't shit but a groupie ass bitch. I can't believe I fell in love with your hoe ass. That nigga clowning me on the internet wearing my shit, Saz," Yudai said.

"Baby, listen. I thought I lost the jewelry and was scared to tell you," I replied.

"He said his whole label fucked you," he vented.

"I was drugged," I replied.

"Bitch, I ain't trying to hear that shit. That's a groupie favorite line when they get caught hoeing around. Yo, lose my fucking number. You were only good for pussy anyway. My sister told me you were a gold digger," Yudai said. He opened the door and walked out the bathroom. I ran behind him and grabbed his arm.

"STOP!" I screamed and pulled on his shirt.

"Get the fuck off me," he snatched away from me and I followed him outside. I tried to keep him from getting in his car but Gautier and Tyshae was trying to pull me away from him. A small crowd formed around us and I was making a complete fool out of myself.

"Please, don't leave me! I swear I will tell you everything. Let's just talk about this," I begged.

"Get her before I embarrass her," Yudai said to Gautier.

"Saz, honey. People are looking at you," Gautier said.

"Fuck them!" I screamed. Yudai broke away from my grip and got into his car. He sped off, leaving me in the middle of the street in tears. Tyshae and Gautier pulled me into the shop and took me upstairs.

"Can you explain to me why that nigga came in here like Lim from *Soul Food*?" Gautier asked.

"Cash Flow told him everything!" I sobbed.

"We knew this was going to happen," Tyshae said.

"Not right now, please, not right now," I trembled.

"What made Cash Flow suddenly do this?" Gautier asked.

"He came over last night. He put his hands on me, so I whipped his ass until I knocked him out. I told him I was done and I really meant it this time. I don't care if he kills me anymore. My life ain't shit anyway. I want to join my mother. I should've been in the house with her when she was murdered," I cried and Tyshae covered her mouth.

"Nooo, Saz. Don't say that. We love you," Gautier said.

"This hurts so bad," I sobbed.

Lisa came upstairs to tell us a few of my clients were downstairs waiting for me but I couldn't move.

"Tell them Saz is sick and she's going home early," Gautier replied.

"I can't live like this anymore. I can't do it," I said.

"We have your back, Saz," Tyshae said.

"Please, call him and tell him to come back," I cried.

"Let him cool off. Lord knows that boy is pissed off right now. He had us scared for a second," Gautier said. My phone rang inside my fanny pack and Tyshae grabbed it.

"What do you want, lame? Leave Saz the fuck alone! What point don't you get? Do you want us to pay you a visit and beat the rainbows out of your ass, unicorn? Naw, I'm not putting her on the phone so you can keep your whack ass apology. She's done with you, Ass Flow, so get gone!" Tyshae yelled into the phone.

"I don't care about my man leaving me, bitch! Worry about your lame ass lyrics and your emoji keyboard-looking face. You're just jealous of her because you can't fit her clothes. Why were you wearing her jewelry anyway? You wish Yudai was your man, don't you? Call your cousins! Call them, muthafucka, and tell them to line the hell up outside the shop. You must have forgotten me and Gautier are from the hood. I'll get your chain snatched, Shit Flow," Tyshae said and hung up.

"See, I'm ready to pay someone to merk that nigga. That nigga gotta die," Tyshae said, getting pumped up.

"Sit your prissy ass down," Gautier said and Tyshae rolled her eyes.

"He ran me hot. He had the nerve to say his wife sent those things to Yudai from his phone. Just like a female to throw stones then hide his hands. I can't stand a bitch-made man. I'm popping Sis on sight when I see him," Tyshae ranted.

"Yudai said Cash Flow called him, so he's lying. He wanted Yudai to stop talking to me. Cash Flow is crazy if he thinks I'm going back to him. He ruined my life," I said.

"Calm down, Saz. It will blow over. Yudai will calm down," Gautier said.

"Yudai permanently cut people out of his life, so he will never talk to me again," I replied. I called his phone and it went straight to voicemail. I threw my phone against the wall and it shattered.

"I need to go home," I said.

"I'll take you," Tyshae said.

****

Tyshae stayed with me at my condo all day. Gautier and Lisa held down the fort at the shop. I laid on my couch with a blanket wrapped around me while drinking a glass of wine.

"Gautier needs to hurry up with the food," Tyshae said.

"What are they saying on Instagram about me?" I asked Tyshae.

"Nothing, Cash Flow didn't leak anything. I think he just wanted Yudai to see it. Cash Flow is still a married a man, so his wife can take everything from him because technically he cheated. He ain't that stupid, trust me. He knows Yudai wouldn't blast you like that. Fake niggas recognize real niggas, too. Have you noticed a lot of our issues stem from social media? We are letting it control us. We are so focused on what people think instead of thinking about ourselves. Those people are strangers, what more can they do besides post and tweet about us? I deleted my personal account and kept my business account. I'm done with it," Tyshae said.

"I can't believe everything happened so fast. It seems like just yesterday that Yudai walked into the shop for the first time. We instantly hit it off and somewhere down the line, we fell for each other so quickly. I'm going to miss him and it might take a while for me to come out of this funk. All I want to do is explain my side of the story. If he walks away, so be it, but at least he will know the truth," I said.

"He will come around. I don't agree with his actions but I could tell he had some deep feelings for you, I heard it behind his anger. If he didn't care, he would've chalked it up to the game and moved on. Waiting for him to come around is the hard part, but that's what your friends are here for. We are supposed to heal each other's wounds," Tyshae said.

"I have never in my life felt so beautiful until I met Yudai. I drift off from the world when I think of him. He has a rugged but sensual type of love. Oh, and the sex was amazing. Everything about him is just perfect," I said, getting emotional again.

"I'm suffocating," I cried.

"Let it all out, Saz. I felt suffocated, too, when I caught my sister in the house I once shared with Eron. She's pregnant by him," Tyshae said.

"WHAT!"

"I have been meaning to tell you and Gautier but I couldn't because I wanted to forget about it. I'm supposed to be an emotional wreck but I can't find it in my soul to shed a tear for that punk-ass nigga," she said.

"Sorry to hear that. What is wrong with niggas these days?" I asked.

"We let them get away with too much. I should've left Eron when I found out he had a baby. The signs are always there but we be so much in love that we ignore them. We are always looking for a reason to stay when the truth is in our hearts," Tyshae said.

"You should pour these things out into your songs. You're a very deep woman. You can be the next Mary J. Blige. I hope you do something with your singing," I replied.

"I'm still thinking about it, but in the meantime, let's listen to some Mary J. Her song, "My Life," would always be one of my favorites," Tyshae said. The doorbell rang and Tyshae went to get the door. Gautier walked in with a bag of food. Brooke ran into my living room and jumped on my couch.

"Can you give me a wig like aunt Tyshae's?" Brooke asked. I picked her up and hugged her.

"Don't jump on Saz's furniture, Brooke! Lord knows that couch probably cost twenty thousand dollars," Gautier joked.

"You can jump on anything you want to jump on in here," I told Brooke. Brooke was an adorable little girl but she was grown for her age. She wasn't one of those bad kids that talked back and cursed, she was a prissy kind of grown. She was into her nails, hair, and clothes. Although she was spoiled rotten, she wasn't a brat. She was a fun little girl.

"I want a pink wig like Shae's for my fifth birthday. Can you put some glitter in it? I want to look very pretty," Brooke said in her cute little voice.

"Okay," I replied and kissed her cheek.

"You better not have my baby looking like Lil Kim. She can have a cute little Dora Explorer type of wig or something," Gautier said. Brooke went over to Tyshae and sat in her lap.

"Can I try it on?" Brooke asked Tyshae.

"Okay, that's enough. Go sit at the table so we can eat," Gautier said. She picked Brooke up and walked her over to the table.

"Which one of us is going to tell Gautier Brooke is not a doll baby. She's always holding her," Tyshae laughed.

"You can't help but not to. Look at her, she's so adorable. I want to steal her," I said.

"Go ahead so Salih can shoot your ass," Tyshae laughed.

Gautier fixed our plates but I wasn't in the mood to eat.

Use Your Heart and Not Your Eyes

"Get over here and eat. You don't want to lose any weight from starvation. That isn't healthy," Gautier said.

"I will eat later. You can put my food in the microwave," I replied.

"Do you want me to pack your bags for you or are they already packed? We have to be at the airport by six in the morning," she said.

"They are packed already," I replied.

Gautier left an hour later to take Brooke over Dolly's house. Tyshae stayed back with me and watched a few movies. I picked up my cracked iPhone to see if I had any messages from Yudai and I had none. I called him again and it went straight to voicemail.

What am I going to do? I thought.

Salih
Déjà Vu

The team sat in the dugout watching the score board. We were down by one score and the bases were loaded. Yudai was up to bat. He was having an off game as if his head wasn't in it. He hadn't had a hit all game and the game was now in his hands. The pitcher threw the first pitch and it was a strike.

"Fuck!" Yudai cursed.

He put his hand up and stepped out the batter box to get himself together. He took a deep breath and stepped back up. The pitcher delivered a fast ball. Yudai swung his bat and hit the ball but it wasn't hard enough to fly over the first baseman's head. The first baseman caught the ball and it was the end of the game; the Phillies won. Yudai snatched off his helmet and threw it against the wall inside the dugout.

"Good game, we can't win them all," I said to Yudai.

"Good game? He played like a rookie today!" Andy said.

"What happened out there? Your head wasn't in the game! You should've stayed seated if you didn't want to play," our teammate, Daniel fussed at Yudai.

"Y'all need to chill the hell out. This ain't the first time we lost and it won't be the last. All of us fucked up at one point," I said.

"Take up for him because that's your buddy," Andy spat.

Use Your Heart and Not Your Eyes

"How many times have you missed the ball? You haven't been catching shit lately," I replied. The team cleared out the dugout and Yudai was still seated.

"Nigga, what's up with you?" I asked.

"Why?" he asked.

"Oh, now you got an attitude with me? Lil nigga, we are boys. You gotta tell me something because you didn't give a fuck about the team today and that ain't like you. Are you having girl problems or something?" I asked.

"That bitch ain't shit. She made me look like a clown," he vented.

"Saz?" I asked.

"Yeah," he replied.

"What she do?" I asked.

"She was fucking me and Cash Flow at the same time. He sent me a video of the shit, but that ain't all of it. Shorty gave that nigga the set I bought for her. I know we weren't official but she was playing games with me. It's my fault, though, I fell for her fast. I always thought she was bad. I saw pictures of her on IG before I met her in person. I been checking for her on the low for months," Yudai said. I sat next to him and stared ahead as we watched the stadium clear out.

"Gautier is my baby mother," I admitted and he looked at me.

"Saz's friend Gautier?" he asked.

"Yeah, she was my girl a few years back. I went off to college then my brother was killed, so I kinda drifted away from shorty. Make a long story short, I left school to visit her. I knew where her mother kept the spare key, so I used the key to surprise her. It was late and I knew her mother was at work. Anyways, I walked in and caught her fucking another nigga. I didn't do nothing, though, I went to my mother's house and grabbed a gun my brother kept hidden underneath his bed. My mind was already messed up because my brother was dead and my shorty was getting broke off by another nigga, so all I saw was blood. If it wasn't for my mother catching me, I would be in jail. She told me she couldn't lose another son. She broke down in front of me so I gave her the gun. Weeks later, I found out the guy Gautier was fucking had a street beef with my brother. He was the one who killed my brother. He got locked up for serving an undercover cop and they found a gun on him. They traced it to my brother's murder. Gautier didn't know I saw her, I was ignoring at that point. Fed up with me ignoring her, she came to my school to tell me she was pregnant. I curved her because in my mind it was the other nigga's baby. When I got signed, I wanted a DNA test because I didn't want it to affect me in the long run. I bribed Gautier into signing a form stating that she remained anonymous in my life. I loved her and hated her, the worst combination," I said.

"Damn, that's deep," Yudai said.

"Talk to Saz. I have been where you're at. We tend to ignore shit thinking it's going to disappear but it doesn't. It took almost five years to sit down and talk about it with Gautier. Our daughter is getting older and I didn't want her growing up surrounded by negative shit. Don't fuck around and turn into an 'ain't shit nigga' like I did because of a female. Does Saz know that you know?" I asked.

"Yesterday morning I went to the shop and snatched her ass up. I said some foul things to her, but it's crazy because when she started crying, I felt sorry for her. She was pulling on my clothes and begging me to talk to her. Gautier and Tyshae had to pull her off me so I could leave. Shorty was a wreck. This love shit just ain't for me, but I appreciate this talk, though," he said. We dapped then left the dugout.

A few hours later...

"Daddyyyy," Brooke yelled out when I walked into my mother's house.

"Have you been good for Grandma?" I asked.

"I'm always good," she replied.

"Get your shoes, Brooke. Hurry up before we're late," my mother shouted out.

"Where are y'all going?" I asked.

"We are going to the movies," Brooke said. I reached into my pocket and gave Brooke a hundred-dollar bill.

"You missing one," she said.

"Little girl, you better get your shoes," I replied.

"I'll call you when we're done and you can meet me," my mother said when she walked into the living room.

"Aight, cool. I might crash here for a few hours and take a nap," I replied. I kissed their cheeks before they left the house. Pita called me and I answered the phone after the second ring.

"Hello," I answered.

"When are you coming home, I'm craving chicken," she whined.

"I'll be there when I wake up from my nap. When is the appointment?" I asked.

"My doctor can't see me until next month. Why do you keep asking me?" she snapped. Annoyed by her voice, I hung up the phone. Seconds later, Gautier was FaceTiming me. I got comfortable on the couch before I answered. I hurriedly sat up when I realized she was wearing a bathing suit.

"You walking around like that?" I asked.

"Yesssss, we are having so much fun, baby. Where is my princess?" she replied.

"She went to the movies with my mother. Let me see what you got going on," I said and she smiled.

"What do you want to see?" she asked. She placed the phone closer to her breasts.

"Stop playing all the time. When are you coming back?" I asked.

"You miss me?" she asked.

"None of your business," I replied.

"I thought we were cool," she giggled.

"Naw, we ain't cool until you take that shit off. Ain't nothing wrong with wearing a T-shirt on the beach," I said. She poked her lips out and rolled her eyes at me. I stared at her natural beautiful face and wished things could've worked out better for us.

"Why are you looking at me like that?" she asked.

"Why do you think?" I replied and she blushed.

"Gautier! Hurry up! The beach party is ready to start," Tyshae called out in the background.

"Tell Brooke to call me," she said.

"Aight," I replied and the line went dead. I somewhat didn't want her to get off the phone but I didn't want to stop her from having fun. I did enough damage to her social life. A text came through my phone and it was her. The text read:

If you didn't want me to go to the beach, you should've said it. I would've stayed in my room to talk to you.

I didn't know what was going on between us. I hadn't told her about Pita being pregnant yet. I actually didn't want to tell her because we were getting along. We still argued but it wasn't nothing compared to our past arguments. I texted Gautier and told her to have fun.
Damn, I ain't got shit to do, I thought.

The next day...

"Yo, are you aight?" I asked Eron.

"Nigga, do I look aight?" he spat and I waved him off.

Davian invited us to his strip party. He invited Yudai, too, and Yudai declined until I told him it was a strip party. We were inside a luxury rented mansion. The strippers were on floating devices inside the indoor pool. The party was lit and turned out better than I expected. Davian walked around the party wearing a silk robe, swimming trunks, and Gucci loafers.

"That nigga think he's a dope boy," Yudai said and I chuckled.

"Stunting like he be in the game. That muthafucka is off the court so much, he's the team mascot," I replied.

"Did Tyshae come back from Mexico yet? Can you call Gautier?" Eron asked me.

"No, who do I look like to you?" I asked.

"My homeboy, my right-hand man," he replied.

"I'm not getting in the middle of that. Why would you waste your time knowing she moved on with the white boy?" I asked. Eron was ready to respond but he was cut off from the crowd screaming. Cash Flow and his label mate, Ice Grill walked into the party with their bodyguards behind them.

"These lame-ass niggas," Eron said.

"I can't believe people buy their music," I replied.

"The rap game has changed. All you need is a catchy beat with no real bars or lyrics," Yudai said. Cash Flow snatched the mic from the DJ when he stood up on the small stage.

"What's poppin', fam? Are y'all ready for the show?" Cash Flow asked and the crowd screamed.

"Drop the beat," Cash Flow said to the DJ.

"Me and Ice Grill got some new fire for y'all called, 'Eat a Pickle.' So, I want all of y'all to shut the fuck up and listen to these kick ass bars," Cash Flow said.

"Bruh, is this nigga for real?" Yudai asked. Tears came from Eron's eyes as he howled in laughter.

I fucked his fat bitch
She said she's on a diet
I told her be quiet, fuck a salad, eat a pickle

Cash Flow was taking jabs at Yudai.

"I bet two stacks you can't throw that bottle and hit one of those niggas," Eron said.

"A broke man should never bet a professional pitcher to throw anything. You might as well pay me my bread now, nigga," I said. Eron went into his pocket and slammed the money down on the table. We were sitting in the front of the audience, so I had a better aim. I picked up a beer bottle and focused in on Ice Grill because he wasn't close to the crowd. I cocked my arm back and hurled the bottle at him. It smacked him on the side of the head and the DJ cut the music off.

Use Your Heart and Not Your Eyes

"Which one of y'all niggas threw that?" Cash Flow asked, looking around. Cash Flow walked over to us and got in Yudai's face.

"Did you throw that bitch-ass baseball, boy?" Cash Flow asked into the mic. Yudai swung and knocked Cash Flow into a speaker. It got hectic after that. Cash Flow's bodyguards jumped on Yudai. I picked up a chair and hit one of the bodyguards with it. Davian pulled out a gun and shot in the air.

"Get those niggas out of my party!" Davian said to his security. The security bum rushed Cash Flow and his team to kick them out.

"Are y'all ready for some real rap music?" Davian asked into the mic. A few local rappers came out on stage and performed one of the city's hottest songs called "Money Boy." The crowd was hyper than before.

"You straight?" I asked Yudai. He smirked at me and held up Cash Flow's diamond "Cash Flow" chain.

"He must've forgot I'm from B-more. We snatch nigga's shit," Yudai said and Eron slapped hands with him. No cameras were allowed inside the party, not even cell phones. If you had a phone on you, you couldn't get in. Davian got caught up in so much stuff with women, he couldn't risk another scandal. A stripper came over to Yudai and whispered something in his ear. He smirked at her then she grabbed his hand and led him through the crowd.

"That little nigga about to fuck something," Eron bragged.

A stripper came up to me and she was cute, but I told her I was straight. She wanted to give me a private dance. I knew how the strippers operated, they targeted the heavy hitters first then made their way down the money train.

"He doesn't know what he's missing. Let me show you how a real nigga spend money," Eron said to her. He followed behind her and I went to the bar. While I was at the bar, a woman upstairs caught my eye. I didn't see the front of her but the back of her was familiar. Matter of fact, she was wearing a dress I bought her. Davian whispered something in her ear and she anxiously looked around as if looking for someone. She didn't know I was at the party. She probably called me to see about my whereabouts but my phone was in the car. I stood in the corner so she wouldn't see me and watched her. Davian tried to brush her off but by the look on her face, she wasn't having it. He looked angry with her, maybe she was blowing up their spot. Something in my gut told me Pita was up to something but how could I fault her? I cheated on her the majority of our relationship. I only hoped she wasn't trying to pin a baby on me if another man could be the father. Davian walked out of Pita's face and she was pissed. She stormed down the stairs, headed to the door. I hurriedly walked through the crowd and met her at the door. She looked surprised to see me.

"What's up? I didn't know you was coming here," I said.

"Oh, hey. I tried to call you but I'm assuming your phone is in the car," she nervously said.

"Why are you not at home if you're carrying our child?" I asked.

"I wanted to come out for some fresh air, plus I'm meeting a few friends here," she replied.

"Go home," I said.

"Are you coming with me?" she asked.

"Yeah, because we need to talk," I replied.

I searched for Yudai and Eron to tell them I was leaving. I found them in a private room upstairs with eight of the baddest strippers I had ever seen. I told them I was leaving and they waved me off. Yudai was intoxicated; two strippers were on his lap kissing each other while grinding on him.

"You want me to drop you off?" I asked him.

"Naw, I'm good," Yudai replied.

"Leave the little nigga alone. He's in good hands when he's with me. I'm about to teach him how to be a real man. You got soft on me, bruh, we always partied and fucked bad bitches together," Eron said.

"I'm out, make sure he's straight," I said to Eron.

"He's good, stop acting like his father, nigga," Eron spat.

I left the party and Pita was waiting outside for me. Davian had a valet service, so we had to wait for our cars. I got inside my Bugatti and sped off. I got home before Pita did. I got out of my car when she pulled up to the front of the house.

"What was that about?" I asked.

"What was what about, Salih? Now you care about me?" she asked.

"I need to know if the baby you are pregnant with is really mine, that's all I care about right now," I replied. Pita slapped the hell out of me.

"How dare your cheating ass accuse me of anything!" she screamed.

"Why are you still here if I'm a cheater? I'm not begging you to stay here. The only reason I'm trying to be cordial with you is because you're pregnant. The love ship has been sailed. The innocent act, please cut the shit out. You act like you haven't stepped out before. I'm never home, so I know some other nigga was entertaining you," I said. She walked up the steps and punched the code in to the house. She kicked her heels off when she got inside.

"I know you're fucking one of those girls at the shop. I found receipts! Flowers, edible arrangements, and a lot of other items were sent to that ghetto ass shop, Luxury Tea. So, which one is it? I know it isn't Eron's ex-fiancée. I know it isn't the one Yudai was dating, so that leaves the fat sloppy bitch that's always posing in a bathing suit or the wanna-be black Chinese bitch. I bet you thought I was stupid but I know everything!" she said.

"You are trippin'," I replied and walked out her face. Pita followed behind me yelling and screaming.

"Yo, shut the hell up. We aren't together. You wanted me around because of the pregnancy and that's what I'm doing. I only questioned you because a pregnant woman shouldn't be at a fucking party!" I replied.

"And you're an engaged man! You shouldn't have been there, either," Pita said.

"We are not engaged anymore. What part don't you understand?" I asked.

"We ain't gotta love each other but we are getting married for this baby. You think I wanna be a single parent? You can leave that to the bitches in the hood and the thousands of strippers who get knocked up for a meal ticket. I will ruin your ass before that happens. Your fans would be disappointed in you if you left me like this and we both know it. Salih Johnson is such a hero, yada yada. All of that will change in the blink of an eye. The world will always side with the damsel in distress. A pregnant one at that," Pita said.

"Yoooo, my last name is JONES!" I yelled at her and she jumped.

"You wanna have my last name and don't even know it. You were better off trapping me by sticking a hole in the condoms. I would've respected you more. At least I would've known right then and there you were after my money. But to pretend to love me and care about me? Shorty, this is low, very low," I said.

"Goodnight, Salih. Go to your other home like you have been doing," she said.

"You ain't gotta tell me. I'm going to make an appointment for you myself since your dumb ass can't do it," I replied. I grabbed a few things and walked out my house.

****

Yudai showed up at practice looking sluggish. He wore a pair of shades and he could barely stand up straight.

"Someone partied hard last night," a teammate said.

"Davian's party was lit last night. I was in there, too," someone else said.

"He has the best parties and the baddest strippers," someone else cosigned.

"Bruh, you aight?" I asked Yudai.

"I had too much to drink. I have been throwing up all morning," he said.

"Did you do any drugs?" I whispered.

"Hell no, what do I look like?" he asked.

"Just checking because we get random drug tests," I replied.

"I heard you snatched Cash Flow's chain," Daniel said to Yudai.

"I don't discuss rumors, bruh," Yudai replied and Daniel waved him off.

"What did you do with the chain?" I asked him.

"Sold it for a few stacks to a nigga from my old hood. He's going to use the diamonds in it," Yudai replied and I chuckled.

"I bet his bitch-ass went to the cops. Too bad it could've been anybody," I chuckled. Yudai held his stomach as he rushed across the field. He leaned over the fence and threw up. Yudai was excused from practice. Luckily, we didn't have a game that day. After practice, I went to a nearby restaurant in Baltimore. I waited for thirty minutes until Davian arrived. He held his hand out for me to dap him but I wasn't in the mood. I wanted to get straight down to business.

"Damn, it's like that?" he asked and sat across from me.

"Are you fucking Pita? Man to man, I need to know because she's claiming she's pregnant and I'm not taking care of another nigga's seed. I don't love her, so if you want her, go for it. I'm trying to keep a clean reputation, ya feel me?" I asked. Davian shifted in his chair then brushed his hand down his face.

"Look, man. I don't know how to tell you this but Eron is fucking Pita. She tried to go in the room he was in with the strippers and I stopped her. I told her you were at the party and she left," he said.

"Nigga, I swear on my brother I'll bust your shit for lying to me," I replied.

"Come on, bruh. Look at the girls I fuck with. I like those hood ratchet chicks. Pita too bougie for me and, besides, she ain't all that to me. Eron is banging her, she was at his hotel room when we had an away game a few months ago. I shouldn't be telling you 'cause Eron is my boy, but I'm not trying to be in the middle of this. I got enough baby mamas to deal with. I asked him about it and he told me it was payback for fucking some chick he was feeling in high school. He said you got the chick pregnant, too. He didn't tell me her name, he just said you knew he was feeling shorty because he always had to stick up for her. That's all I know," Davian said.

My head was racing with a million thoughts. Eron was supposed to be like my brother. Deep down he was mad at me for being with Gautier. When I thought about it, Eron always took up for Gautier but he never said anything about liking her. After all those years, he still felt some type of way. My brother said something a few years back about Eron but it went over my head…

Use Your Heart and Not Your Eyes

We were sitting in front of the house kicking it. I was sitting between Gautier's legs and Eron was sitting on the steps with us. Damien pulled up in his Crown Vic and got out with a brown paper bag. Inside the bag was a few bottles of Henny.

"What are y'all niggas doing? Where is Ma at?" Damien asked me.

"At work, where else?" I asked.

"What's in the bag?" Gautier asked Damien.

"Some grown nigga shit. I got a few wine coolers, you have to get them from my back seat, though," Damien replied. Gautier stood up and brushed her round bottom off before she walked to his car.

"I will holla at y'all later. I gotta meet up with Tyshae," Eron said, giving us dap. Damien sat next to me when Eron walked away.

"You can't let your girl hang around you and your homeboy like that if it makes him uncomfortable," Damien said.

"What do you mean by that?" I asked.

"The nigga just be uncomfortable around y'all and I don't trust it. Homeboy or not, something ain't right with that," he said.

"Yo, you just paranoid," I replied.

"Aight, don't say I didn't warn you. My shorty can't even come around my niggas. I will have to merk one of them for looking at her ass or something," he replied...

314
Use Your Heart and Not Your Eyes

"Yo, you aight? You zoned out for a minute," Davian said.

"Yeah, I'm straight. You want a bottle or something?" I replied. Davian wasn't a close homeboy but he was tolerable. I didn't have anything else to do so I sat back and chilled.

"Eron's ex fiancée on the beach looking good as hell. I bet that nigga is sick," Davian said and showed me a picture of Tyshae wearing a thong bathing suit.

"She was rocking with him for years," I said.

"Some women you gotta be faithful to and some women don't deserve it. I cheat on my woman because she ain't shit, neither. I wifed a hoe then caught feelings for her. Now look at me, I'm addicted to hoes," Davian said. An hour later, I left the restaurant. Eron called me and I silenced the phone. I wasn't surprised he slept with Pita, I was shocked behind the reason why he slept with her. I couldn't imagine him having some type of feelings for Gautier. She was mine and he was like my brother. I went to my loft and turned on the TV. I thought about picking up Brooke but thought better of it because Alita always gave me hell. I was somewhat pissed my mother took Brooke to Alita but she said Brooke wanted to see her other grandmother. I fell asleep watching reruns of *Power*.

I woke up to someone ringing my doorbell. I looked at the clock and it was a little after midnight. I looked on the security camera in the kitchen to see who it was. Gautier was standing at my door with her luggage. I opened the door and she walked in half asleep.

"Where is Brooke?" Gautier asked.

"Over your mean ass mother's house. I thought you wasn't coming back until tomorrow," I replied.

"The girls got sick from eating the food and they didn't want to go to the hospital in Mexico. As soon as we landed, we went to the hospital. I stayed with them for a little while to make sure they were okay. I told their asses not to eat from the food stand at the market. It smelled horrible," Gautier said. She kicked her shoes off and laid on my couch.

"Come over here so you can lay next to me," she said. Gautier was clingy, but I was used to it. There were times when I was studying and she had to lay on me with her arms wrapped tightly around me. I sat on the couch and she laid on my chest.

"You must miss me or something," I said and kissed her full lips.

"No, I just want the warmth because it's freezing in here," she said.

"We gotta talk about something," I replied and she sat up.

"What is it?" she asked.

"Pita is pregnant," I replied. Gautier scooted away from me and crossed her arms.

"Congratulations, I mean she's your fiancée after all," she said dryly.

"She might be pregnant by Eron," I admitted.

"What? Eron is fucking everybody now? Let me get this straight. Eron, your best friend, is screwing your fiancée and Tyshae's sister?" she asked. I know Eron cheated on Tyshae with

Kimmy years back. Actually, it was his senior year in high school. I didn't know he was still seeing her.

"I don't know what Eron is doing. My concern is Pita and this pregnancy. I don't know if she's pregnant for sure. I fucked up, Gautier, big time. That bitch is trying to destroy my character because I don't want to marry her," I said.

"Destroy your character? How can she do that?" she asked.

"How do you think? I'll look like a fuck nigga if I leave her now," I replied.

"You left me while I was pregnant, so what is so special about that bitch?" Gautier asked.

"Would you calm down?" I asked.

"No, I'm not calming down. You left me and I struggled with Brooke for a whole year, but you feel some type of sympathy for that bitch? She fucked your best friend, so it might be his baby. I don't know why I came over here," she said. She stood up and I pulled her back down. She snatched away from me. I understood where she was coming from but I didn't want to be that man again.

"I was young when you got pregnant. It was mistake, and till this day, I still feel messed up behind it. I missed Brooke's first words and first baby steps. Overall, I missed her birth. I want to stick around just in case the baby is mine because I don't want to miss out on anything. What is wrong with that?" I asked.

"You gave me hell for years but that bitch gets a free damn pass? I'm out of this muthafucka," Gautier said.

Use Your Heart and Not Your Eyes

"That's because I don't care about her as much as I care about you. You crushed me, she can't. It's a big fucking difference, so stop being childish about it. I could've not told you and let you find out from someone else," I fussed.

"Let's face it, you will always make me pay for what I did. You're still trying to hurt me, huh?" she asked.

"Yo, what? What does me being there for my seed have anything to do with you?" I asked.

"The same damn reason why you punished Brooke for the shit I did to you! This is about everything!" Gautier yelled.

"How?" I asked.

"I'm not good enough for the world to know I carried your child for nine damn months but Pita is? Your child with Pita will have a normal life. I signed a damn form but that bitch doesn't have to? Where is her Salih treatment at?" Gautier asked with tears falling down her face. I stood up to hug her but she pushed me away.

"I thought we were getting past everything but clearly we're not. At least I got closure out of all of this. I can finally move the hell on and be with someone who is proud to show me and Brooke off together," Gautier said.

"No other man will raise my damn daughter. I love my daughter and you know it," I gritted.

"But you love your perfect life even more. I guess we both got what we wanted which was great sex. The honeymoon is over, back to our real lives," she said.

"This is my real life. If we go back to where we were, we will be living a lie," I replied.

"Sometimes a lie is better than the truth," she replied.

"So, what are you saying, Gautier?" I asked.

"I'm saying goodbye," she spat. She grabbed her luggage and left out of the door.

I sat on the couch in disbelief.

I don't know what to do, I thought.

I walked into the kitchen and poured myself a drink. The past few weeks with Gautier and Brooke completed me. In the blink of an eye, it was all gone again. I called my mother and she answered the phone on the second ring.

"What do you want? I'm ready to strip for my boo," my mother said.

"I'm confused," I replied.

"Goddamn it, Salih. You called me this time of night to tell me something I been knew since you were a little boy?" she asked.

"Cut it out, Ma," I chuckled.

"What's the matter?" she asked.

"I pissed Gautier off," I replied.

"Boyyyyyyyy, what the hell is new? You always piss her off, shit. You're pissing me off! Wait a minute," she said.

"Did you find that Tevin Campbell song, yet?" she asked the man she was with in the background.

"MA!" I said.

"What? Make this quick, I have to prep myself for this split I'm going to surprise him with. You know your mama is getting old and squeak a little bit," she replied.

"I'm ready to come over there and fuck that nigga up. What are you doing splits for? I hope you got a life alert necklace nearby," I said.

"I ain't that old for a life alert necklace. I'm ready to hang up," she said.

"All jokes aside, I'm confused. I think I want to be with Gautier again," I replied.

"So, why are you confused?" she asked.

"Pita is pregnant," I replied. My mother hung up on me. I called her back and it went straight to voicemail. I stayed up until the sun came up. Gautier was heavy on my mind. I knew what I had to do. I had to man up and make it right.

Gautier
The Transition

I sat in my mother's kitchen playing around in my bowl of cereal. I cried all morning thinking about Salih fathering another child. I know it was childish of me, but it seemed as if me and Brooke weren't good enough. The fact that he knows the baby may not be his is what put the icing on the cake. My mother walked into the kitchen with a cup of coffee in her hand.

"He hurt you again, huh? I knew it was going to happen when you and Brooke started spending the night with him," my mother said.

"I don't want to talk about it," I replied.

"When are you going to stop letting him make a fool out of you? That man is engaged, Gautier. You're not entitled to him because y'all have a daughter together. People co-parent every day," she said.

"People who don't want to work it out co-parent. After all of this time, we still love each other. Don't you get it? I won't let another man close to my heart if I can't have him. Why do you think I haven't gotten serious with anyone yet?" I asked.

"Listen to yourself. You haven't gotten serious with anyone but he has! He is going to marry another woman and build a family with her!" my mother yelled at me.

"I KNOW!" I screamed with tears falling from my eyes.

"She's pregnant, Ma," I burst into sobs.

"Now do you see why I hate him so much. I'm sick of this shit," she fussed.

"Leave him alone, please," I replied as I wiped my eyes.

"Leave him alone? He's a sorry excuse for a man. He went off to college and left you here with a damn baby to raise by yourself. He flaunts that woman around like she's his trophy but hides you in the dark. You deserve way more than his sorry ass. He better not ever come near my house or I'll expose him myself," she ranted.

"I'm not innocent in all of this," I replied.

"There you go again, blaming everything on yourself," she spat.

"I haven't been honest with you. Salih caught me with another boy in your house. He caught us having sex and he didn't think Brooke was his. The boy I had sex with is the one who killed his brother. Not only did he kill him, but he bragged about having sex with me and how easy it was. Salih was never ashamed of me, he was ashamed of what I did to him," I said.

"Why didn't you tell me?" she asked.

"I was mad at him and got a kick out of you downing him. He may not be good to me but we both know he's a good father," I replied and she rolled her eyes.

"Okay, I see where this is going. Just know you deserve better and should never settle. I want you to have a better life than what I had. I was young and fast, I had you by a street boy who couldn't stay out of jail. I don't know if your father is dead or alive. You're smarter than that, though, just be careful out here," she said.

"I will, Mother," I replied.

"How was Mexico?" she asked.

"It was okay for the first day then afterwards, it went downhill. Saz barely wanted to party and Lisa couldn't do certain things because she's pregnant. It was pretty much me and Tyshae turning up. Just know I will never go to Cancun again. It was wayyyyy too many young folks," I said.

"I have been meaning to tell you. Someone at the church has been asking about you. I didn't want to tell you right away because I had to do my research. I had to make sure he wasn't married and on the down low, if you know what I mean. Anyways, he follows your page and speaks highly of you. He's very handsome and has a good job. He's an electrician. He's twenty-eight years old, has no kids and never been married," she said.

"Are you trying to play matchmaker?" I laughed.

"I want some more grandbabies but I want you to be married first. I think a regular nine-to-five man is what you need. Salih will always have to meet up to the expectations of his fans. You deserve more attention," she said.

"I guess you're right. I'm not replacing Salih's place in Brooke's life, though, but I do want something stable. I'm going to start dating again," I replied.

"Dating and making booty calls are two different things, Gautier," she said with her eyebrow raised.

"What are you saying?" I asked.

"I'm saying you have been spreading your legs instead of getting to know a good man," she replied.

"Are you calling me a hoe?" I asked and she laughed.

"No, but I do know the men you were talking to were only for sexual purposes. You can't fool me," she said.

"You have a point. What's the man at your church's name?" I asked.

"Jamel and he's fine. He comes to church with his mother sometimes. I'm going over to his mother's house for dinner, do you want to come?" she replied.

"I guess, I don't have anything else to do," I said.

I played with Brooke and watched a couple of movies with her until it was time for us to get ready for dinner. I wore a cute mid-sleeve tan maxi dress with ruffles around the neckline. I styled my hair into a high ponytail with a swoop bang. I took time with my makeup and perfected it. I slid my feet into a pair of tan tie-up Steve Madden sandals with cute colorful puffy balls that hung from the strings.

"You look pretty Mommy. Are you going with Daddy?" Brooke asked, standing in the doorway of the bathroom.

"No, baby, we are going over Grandma's friend's house," I replied.

"Is Daddy coming?" Brooke asked.

"No," I replied.

Use Your Heart and Not Your Eyes

I dressed Brooke in a cute black and white polka dot sundress with black tie-up sandals. I brushed her hair into a bun and placed a polka dot bowtie around her bun. I added a little lip gloss on her lips.

"Call Daddy so he can see my new dress," Brooke said. I FaceTimed Salih and gave Brooke the phone.

"What's up, baby girl? Where are you ready to go? Is that lip gloss on your lips?" he asked.

"We are going to dinner with Grandma. Are you coming?" she asked her father.

"Not this time, baby. It's a girl's outing," Salih said.

"Are we staying with you later?" Brooke asked.

"Let me ask your mother. Put her on the phone," he said. Brooke gave me the phone though I didn't want to talk.

Why does he have to be so damn fine? I thought as I stared into the phone.

"Are y'all coming over?" he asked.

"No, Brooke can," I replied.

"I want you to," he said.

"I have a date," I replied.

"Stop fucking playing with me. A date with who?" he asked.

"None of your business," I replied.

"You will always be my business. Matter of fact, go ahead on your date. That nigga ain't me, he ain't getting far with you," Salih replied.

"Pick Brooke up from my mother's house later if you want to see her. Other than that, we don't have a damn thing to talk about," I spat.

"Fuck you then," he said and hung up.

I turned around to make sure Brooke didn't hear us but she wasn't in the room. I sat on the bed and wondered if I should go with my mother to her friend's house. She stood in the doorway staring at me.

"You must've heard us arguing," I said.

"I heard y'all on my way upstairs. I don't want to force you into anything," she said.

"You're not, it's time for me to try something new. Besides, ain't nothing wrong with making him a little jealous. Maybe he would work harder for it," I said and she laughed.

"Let's go," my mother said.

****

I pulled up in the driveway of a two-car garage home. The house looked brand new and the garden was beautiful. It was in an upscale neighborhood. The door opened and a short middle-aged woman walked out the house wearing a blue and white sailor dress. Her hair was a little old-fashioned but she had a pretty face.

"Good evening. I'm Stephanie and you must be Gautier. Your mother is always bragging about you at the church. I need to come and check your salon out. I heard many great things about it," she said.

"Nice to meet you, Stephanie," I replied.

"You all come on in, I just took the turkey wings out the oven," she said. I grabbed Brooke's hand and followed Stephanie into the house. We walked into the living room and a few of her family members were sitting on the couch watching TV. Brooke saw a little girl sitting on the floor playing with Barbies, so she immediately took off.

"Make yourself at home. I'm going to help Stephanie in the kitchen," my mother said. I waved at everyone and they waved back. A handsome man sitting in the loveseat smirked at me. He had long locs with blonde at the tips. His goatee was shaped up nicely and he had a sexy pair of bedroom eyes. He wasn't dark-skinned how I usually liked my men, but nonetheless, he was handsome. He stood up and walked over to me.

"My name is Jamel. I've heard great things about you. Wow, you are amazingly beautiful in person," he said.

"Thank you, I heard many great things about you, too," I replied.

"Want to grab a drink and go to the yard and talk?" he asked.

"Okay, I'm going to let my mother know so she can keep an eye on Brooke," I replied.

"Aight," he said and winked at me. When he turned to walk away, I almost had a heart attack. Jamel's ass was huge! I went into the kitchen to get my mother.

"Excuse me, Ma, can I talk to you for a second?" I asked.

"Sure, I'll be right back," she said to Stephanie. My mother stepped out into the hall.

"Why didn't you tell me Jamel's ass was so huge?" I asked.

"Really, I haven't noticed," she replied.

"You haven't noticed? How can you miss it? Ma, that man's butt is bigger than mine and you know I got a donk," I whispered.

"We all have flaws. Go talk to him and I will keep an eye out for Brooke," she said and walked away from me. I walked out the back door and Jamel was sitting by the pool with a cocktail. I sat next to him and he smiled at me.

"So, tell me about yourself," he said.

"I'm twenty-three years old, I'll be twenty-four on Halloween. I have a little girl and I own a salon and a boutique. My life is very simple, what about you?" I asked.

"I'm twenty-eight years old and I'm an electrician. I have no kids but I'm looking to settle down. I transitioned seven years ago and I must say it was blessing. I've never been happier," he said.

"Transitioned from what position?" I asked and he laughed.

"Oh, no, not that. I used to be a woman," he said.

"WHAT?" I asked.

"I used to be a woman, I had a sex change. Wait, is that a problem?" he asked.

"You damn right it is," I replied.

"Wait, you were dating Aniston, right? We were in the same transitioning class before we had a sex change. I'm so sorry, Gautier, I thought you were comfortable with transmen. It was the only reason why I asked your mother about you," he said in embarrassment.

"Aniston the personal trainer is a woman? She had a dick?" I said.

"I'm assuming you didn't know women could get prostatic penises," he said.

"It was big," I replied.

"We can choose the size we want it to be. I shouldn't be telling you this because it's supposed to be private, but I'm going to give you the name of this app. It's for women who like to date transmen. You can see for yourself," he said. I ran into the house and picked Brooke up. I went to my car and placed her in her car seat.

"What happened?" my mother asked when she ran out the house.

"Jamel is a woman," I said.

"What?" she asked.

"She's a woman, a transman. Maaaaaa, why would you do this to me?" I asked.

"Oh noooo, baby. I didn't know," she replied.

I thought about Aniston and it all made sense. He was clingy like a female, threw tantrums like a female, and full of himself like a female. Everything screamed female. Disgusted and humiliated was an understatement.

"I'm going to go in and tell Stephanie something came up," my mother said and went back into the house. Brooke was having a fit because she was playing with a little girl.

"I want to play with Maddie," Brooke said.

"Maybe some other time, okay," I replied.

I took my mother and Brooke back to the house. I told them I had to take care of something before I pulled off. I drove like a bat out of hell on my way to Aniston's house. I came to a halt when I stopped in front of his house. His Lexus and motorcycle were in the driveway, so I knew he was home. I got out of my car and rang his doorbell. He opened the door shirtless, wearing a pair of boxer briefs. I stared at his body trying to figure out how it was possible and that's when I noticed it. He had two scars underneath his chest where his breasts once were. He pulled me into him and he even smelled like a man.

"I knew you were going to come around. Did you miss me?" he asked. I pushed him into the wall and smacked him.

"Son of a bitch! Why didn't you tell me you were a woman?" I asked.

"Who told you that? That's a lie," he said.

"I ran into someone who knows you and they told me, Aniston. That's not something you keep from people. You humiliated me!" I screamed at him.

"I am a man. I made you feel good, didn't I? Baby, let's talk about this," he said.

"You threw that brick through my shop's window, didn't you? That's some real female shit and it has your name written all over it. I know it was you and you will give me the money for that. I will sue your ass for everything and expose you for tricking me into believing you were a man," I said.

"I thought you loved me," he said.

"Bitch, we were only fucking! Run me my money or else. I swear to God you will pay for this," I replied. Aniston fell on the floor and burst into sobs.

"You must've skipped a dosage of your hormone pills because you're acting like a bitch right now. Get your ass up and pay me for the window you destroyed at my shop," I said.

"Please, Gautier. Don't do this to me. I want to be with you but you were messing with other men. You made me feel less of a man, like I couldn't satisfy you," he said.

"You are less of a man! Don't you get it?" I asked.

"NOOOOOOOOOO!" he cried.

"I wasted my time coming over here. Keep the money, but you need to expose yourself. What if someone falls in love with you and wants a baby? What are you going to do, Annabelle? You cannot go around destroying hearts like this. I thought I was giving my body to a man. You owe me an apology and many others," I said.

"This is what happens when you open your legs for anyone. You just never know what you might get. Most of the women I fuck are hoes, why should they care if I'm a real man? Your fat ass was only looking for a nut," he said. How could I respond to that? I should've been more concerned about who I let in my body instead of looking for a quick nut to ease my pain. See, I should've learned my lesson when I lost Salih but instead I buried myself in a deeper hole. I wasn't a hoe, though, I was a hurt woman who used sex thinking it was better than experiencing love. My motto was, "fuck em' then duck em." Nothing good has come from it. Sometimes, we become so vulnerable to our insecurities, we fall victim to ourselves. Everything I have done was a silent cry for love. Not just any type of love, but love from the man who I had loved all my life. I walked out of Aniston's home and got back into my car. I headed home with Salih still on my mind.

****

The next day, I was back at the shop. Tyshae, Saz, and Lisa were all feeling better. They only had the twenty-four-hour virus. Saz was still moping around because Yudai wasn't talking to her. Tyshae was glowing behind the text messages Cream was sending her and Lisa seemed to be in a good mood, too. The phone at the shop rang and I answered it.

"Luxury Tea, Gautier speaking," I answered.

"Hey, Gautier. This is Pita, I was wondering if you were still down for my casting crew to come to your shop. We are going live tomorrow at four and this will be perfect for first day's ratings," she said.

Going live? Chile, you are setting yourself up, I thought.

"I forgot all about it. Look, Piñata, I changed my mind about that. I'm not in the mood," I replied.

"I can sue you for this. We had a verbal agreement," she said.

"I changed my mind! Do not come to my shop," I replied.

"Why not? Afraid of being exposed for the hoe you are? I know you're fucking my fiancé. I saw the bank statements and I also saw the gifts being sent to your shop in your name. Instead of being enemies, we can make money off this little scandal. I think me and you going at it will be a better idea, the old idea is canceled. Salih is playing us, why not play him and get rich?" Pita said.

"You're absolutely right. I'm tired of his shit, let's get this money," I replied.

"That's the ratchetness I'm talking about. I can always count on y'all ghetto bitches for a couple of bucks," she said and hung up.

"Who was that?" Tyshae asked.

"Pita bread," I replied.

"What does she want?" she asked.

"She wants to do the show, remember? Call all our regulars and tell them to get down here. This bitch wants a show and I will give her one," I replied.

"What do you have planned?" Tyshae asked. I pulled Saz and Tyshae to the side and gave them the rundown. I wasn't going to humiliate Pita but the way I saw it, every woman was for herself when it came to love.

"What's going on?" Lisa asked when she came out the bathroom.

"Nothing, we're just talking about something. Make sure you do your makeup to perfection for tomorrow, I'm doing a video for promotion," I replied.

"Okay, can you give me some spiral curls?" Lisa asked Saz.

"You better be here early in the morning before my clients start arriving," Saz said.

I went upstairs to the boutique and put together everyone's outfits. I was making sure my girls were looking cute for TV.

Salih
Payback

I was sitting in the passenger's seat of Pita's car while texting Gautier for the twentieth time. She was ignoring my calls and texts and it messed up my whole mood for the remainder of the day. Pita took a car selfie of us and posted it on her page. I snatched her phone from her and tossed it in the back seat.

"Do I look like I want to take some damn pictures?" I asked her.

"You're an asshole," Pita said.

"Shut the hell up and drive so I can go on about my day," I replied. I didn't tell her about Eron yet. I wanted to know if she was really pregnant first. She called me early that morning and told me she had an appointment. I met her at the mansion at three o'clock and she was overdressed like she was going to a club.

"Where are you going?" I asked when she turned down a back street.

"It's a short cut, so chill out. What has gotten into you?" she asked.

"I'm tired of you, that's what has gotten into me," I replied.

"That's no way to talk to your pregnant and glowing fiancée," Pita pouted. I wanted to slap her head off her neck. Ten minutes later, Pita pulled up to Gautier's shop. Four vans pulled up in front of her car and I looked at her.

"Shorty, please don't tell me you set me up to be filmed," I said. Pita rolled her eyes at me as she put lip gloss on her lips.

"We talked about this already, baby. Entertainment sells, now get out of the car and pretend you are accompanying me while getting my hair done," she said.

"I'm not getting out. Bitch, you crazy," I spat. My phone beeped and it was a text from Gautier. She told me to get out and play along because it was going to be worth it. Going with my gut instinct, I got out the vehicle. I waited on the sidewalk for Pita. Once she stepped up, I grabbed her hand and we walked into the shop.

"Good afternoon, how can I help you today?" Gautier asked. I couldn't help but to stare at her wide hips in her tight palazzo pants.

"I have a four o'clock hair appointment," Pita said.

"I'll be right back to get the stylist for you," Gautier said. The camera man zoomed in on Gautier's ass as she walked away.

"So, that's the bitch you're fucking, huh? I saw you looking at her ass when she walked away. Is that who you were texting on our way here? You told her we were coming, didn't you?" Pita screamed.

"What's going on out here?" Gautier asked when she came back out.

"So, you really wanna act like you don't know me, huh? I knew I recognized your face from somewhere. You have been sending my fiancé pictures to his DM," Pita screamed and dramatically knocked over a stack of magazines. The doors opened and a few girls walked in behind Tyshae.

"Ohhhhhhh, bitch! I know you didn't come to my job! You fucked my man and got pregnant by him bitch," Tyshae screamed at Pita. Gautier looked at me and winked. I sat in the chair and watched the drama unfold. Pita was right. The shit was very entertaining.

"Ummm, what?" Pita asked.

"Yeah, Shae, that's the hoe that I saw coming out of Eron's hotel room a few months back. I told you she was fucking her fiancé's best friend," one girl said.

"You got this all wrong," Pita said.

Tyshae pulled out her cell phone and called Eron on speakerphone.

"About time you came back to your senses. You miss daddy? Look, baby, I know I fucked your sister and moved her in, but I was only mad at you for not being there when I needed you. Let's forget about all of this so we can move forward," Eron said.

Bruh, you gotta be the dumbest nigga, I thought.

"I'll come home under one condition," Tyshae said and looked into the camera.

"What's that?" Eron desperately asked.

"Tell me the truth about Pita," Tyshae said. Pita tried to snatch the phone from Tyshae but a girl stepped in and pushed Pita back.

"Cut the camera off!" Pita screamed but the camera men kept filming because it was a live recording and the ratings were probably rolling in.

"I smashed her one time. She snuck into my hotel room when I was drunk. I swear, baby, I'm done cheating on you. Just come back home so we can talk," Eron said. Tyshae hung up and grilled Pita.

"I'm ready to fuck this bitch up!" Tyshae screamed and charged into Pita but Saz held her back.

"Salih, I swear Eron is lying. Do you believe?" Pita cried. She forgot about the cameras; she was worried about her meal ticket.

"What do you want me to say? We have been broken up for a year. We agreed to live under the same roof until you got your business up and running," I replied.

"You set me up, bitch! You set me up!" Pita yelled at Gautier. She tried to hit Gautier but one of the girls held her back.

"Get this bitch out of my shop!" Gautier yelled out. Pita was escorted out the shop followed by the camera crew.

"Okay everyone, back to business. Someone is ready to come in and film our work. They will be here in thirty minutes," Gautier said. I stood up and walked over to her.

"You foul as hell for this," I said.

"You can thank me later. I publicly helped you get rid of the bitch and exposed Eron's nasty ass at the same time. Don't get too excited, though, I did this for Tyshae at Pita's expense," she said.

"I'm sorry," I replied. She rolled her eyes and walked away from me but I grabbed her arm.

"People are watching us," Gautier whispered.

"Let them watch. I apologize for everything I have done to you. I'm working on being a better man. I still had a lot of growing up to do, we both do," I said. She looked around and everyone was staring at us. A cameraman came back into the shop to film us.

"I forgive you, but you still gotta put in that work. Nigga, this beef ain't over yet," she said I chuckled.

"Aight, bet. Can I take you out?" I asked.

"I get off at eight tonight and you better not be late," she replied. I gave her a kiss on her lips and she blushed. I walked out the shop and Pita was outside ranting and raving. She ran up to me and hit me while still being recorded.

"I HATE YOU!" she screamed.

"You fucked my best friend!" I yelled at her.

"It was only one time. You were out cheating on me," she said.

"Cut the shit, Pita. We haven't been happy for a very long time. The game is over, so walk away," I replied.

"You have been cheating on me with that fat bitch!" she screamed.

"She's my daughter's mother! Those receipts and all that other stuff you found was for my daughter. Me and Gautier decided to keep it out of the public eye," I said.

"You told me she was dead," Pita replied.

"No, I didn't. Cut the shit out, you knew she was my daughter's mother. You used this storyline for your ratings. You tried to set me up to make me look like a bad guy," I said. The people on the sidewalk looked at Pita in disgust. I told a little lie, too, but so be it. Pita was willing to humiliate me for her personal gain. I came too far to go out like a sucka. Pita got in her car and sped off. Gautier gave me her car keys so I could escape the crowd of people that was forming around me. They were asking me questions about Gautier and how I felt knowing my best friend slept with my fiancée.

When I pulled up to my mother's house, Eron was getting out of his car in anger.

"You ratted me out!" Eron yelled at me.

"Nigga, fuck you. You ratted yourself out. I'll knock your bitch-ass out, muthafucka. Run up on me again," I replied.

"You could've warned me," Eron said.

"I didn't know it was going to happen," I replied. My mother came out of the house and stood between us.

"Let's go in the house and talk," she said.

As soon we got inside, Eron swung on me. I punched him in the face and he fell over my mother's coffee table. She screamed for us to stop as we tussled around the living room. I slammed him onto the floor then wrapped my arm around his throat.

"STOP!" my mother yelled. I pulled away from Eron and he gasped for air.

"Punk-ass nigga," I said. Eron got up and sat on the couch.

"I can't believe you, bruh. We have been boys for fifteen years and you played me. You let Tyshae make a fool out of me," Eron said.

"Naw, playboy. You did that to yourself. You smashed my fiancée because you had some kind of vendetta against me. I always had your back despite everything you have done," I replied.

"You knew I was feeling Gautier. I always stuck up for her when you used to fat shame her. I wanted to be an athlete then you wanted to be an athlete. Everything I did, you just had to do it better. Homeboys don't compete, bruh," Eron said.

"Nigga, you sound like a bitter baby mama. Matter of fact, you started acting different when I signed a contract that was double the money you signed for. This shit ain't about me, you just can't accept the fact my life turned out different than yours," I replied.

"I can't believe this is over Gautier," my mother said.

"It's not over her. Eron is going broke because he keeps splurging on different bitches. He's blaming everybody for his fuck-ups instead of owning up to it. I don't owe you nothing, bruh," I said to Eron. He stood up and wiped the blood from his mouth.

"We ain't brothers no more," he said then stormed out the house.

"Money will change your life. Y'all were like brothers," my mother said.

"Yeah, but things change. Eron keeps spending money on different women and now he's mad at me because my pockets are still straight," I replied.

"You don't need friends like that. Look on the brighter side, at least you kicked his ass. You always had a good arm. Come in the kitchen so I can fix you something to eat. I saw that live video with you, Gautier, and Pita. It was streaming on Facebook. The cat is out the bag now," she said.

"Yeah, Ma. The cat is finally out the bag," I replied.

Late that night...

I walked out the bathroom into my bedroom. Gautier was braiding Brooke's hair in my bed. I pulled the covers back and climbed into bed.

"Hurry up, damn. She's straining her neck," I said. Brooke was asleep with her head lying in an awkward position.

"Do you want to do her hair?" Gautier snapped.

"You got jokes, huh? Forget all that, though, what happened with your date? The other day, you were trying to stunt out on a nigga. Your hair was done up all nice and shit. Where that nigga take you to?" I asked.

"Why are you always in my business?" she asked.

"I wanna know what kind of dude was entertaining my baby mama," I replied and she smirked.

"Promise you won't laugh," she said.

"Shorty, if you don't get to telling me something," I replied.

"My mother was telling me about some guy at her church. He's single, handsome, and got a good job. He's just an average decent man. Anyways, his mother invited my mother over for dinner. I had nothing to do so me and Brooke tagged along—" she said and I cut her off.

"I should slap the hell out of you. You took my princess with you to meet some clown-ass nigga?" I asked getting agitated.

"Can you let me finish?" she asked.

"Hurry up with it," I replied.

"So, I walked into his mother's house. His name is Jamel by the way. He was sitting in the living room kicking it with a few church folks. I was like 'damn he's fine.' He walks over to me and we introduced ourselves. I could tell he was a good dude, so I accepted his invitation to the yard so we could talk. He told me his life has been complete since he transitioned," Gautier said.

"Transitioned? Fuck was that nigga talking about?" I asked.

"Babe, promise you won't laugh," she said.

"I'm not, what was that nigga talking about?" I asked.

"He used to be a she. Transitioned as in transman," she said. I cracked up until my eyes watered.

"Hold on, shorty. You were talking big shit and ended up meeting a woman? That's what your ass get for trying to stunt out on me. What happened next? This should've been filmed too," I said.

"He apologized for coming at me like that. He figured I was okay with the lifestyle because I was dating Aniston," she said.

Use Your Heart and Not Your Eyes

"Hold up, Aniston the personal trainer?" I asked.

"Yes, Aniston was a woman, too. Babe, her dick was almost as big as yours," Gautier said.

"She made you squirt?" I asked and she smacked her teeth.

"No, dumb-ass," she replied.

I took Brooke to her bed when Gautier finished her hair. I went back to my bedroom and Gautier was dancing around my room wearing lace panties with bowties in the back.

"Here we go with this," I said.

"Ain't nothing changed. Just the years between us," she replied. She turned the music up a little bit on the Bluetooth speaker.

"You wanna dance with me?" she asked.

"Naw, I'm trying to fuck you in those skimpy panties you got on," I replied. She threw her arms around my neck and kissed my lips. The sweet scent of her perfume filled my nostrils.

"Do you forgive me? I want to hear you say it," Gautier said.

"Yeah, I do. You forgive me?" I asked.

"A little bit," she giggled and I palmed her ass.

"How can I make it up to you?" I asked.

"By giving me your heart again," she said.

"You always had it," I replied.

"I still love you," she said.

"I will always love you," I replied.

"Are you still trying to fuck something?" she asked, licking my lips. She reached into my boxers and massaged my erection.

"Stop playing and take those panties off," I said, reaching for them. She smacked my hand away then pulled back from me.

"I'm going to sleep. You better jack off or something. I have to get up in the morning," she said. She got into my bed and I slid in behind her. I wrapped my arm around her and kissed the back of her neck.

"I'm hitting it out the frame when you spread that pussy for me again. You used to fucking robot dick. I got nothing but real pipe," I said and she laughed. Funny how life turns out. I had Gautier back but I lost my best friend, someone who was like my brother. If I had to do it all over again, I still would've picked Gautier. My real brother was in the grave. Fuck Eron.

Saz

Picking Up the Pieces

One month later…

The issue with Cash Flow died down after the fight we had for a few weeks. Out of nowhere he started calling me again and harassing me about a chain Yudai snatched. I wanted to get my number changed but too many of my clients had it and I was still waiting on Yudai to come around. My friends were happy so I stopped showering them with my issues. I was still going through it but I was hiding it behind a fake smile. I gave up my condo and ended up moving into Gautier's new house. Gautier was never home. She stayed at Salih's loft every day, even when he was away at a game. Cash Flow spray painted my mother's tombstone with the word "Dead Bitch." He said he didn't do it but who else could've done it? I stayed in bed for two days and cried my eyes out. Erin was doing the best she could to try and help me, but the attorney said I needed real proof. I had a recording of Cash Flow but I couldn't use it because it was done in private. My story was never going to be heard. I climbed out of bed not wanting to get ready to go into the shop. I showered and got dressed in a pair of leggings and a T-shirt. I brushed my hair into a ponytail, grabbed my purse then headed out the door. I walked outside and hit the alarm to my new Audi truck. I got inside my truck and backed out the driveway. Most of my nights were spent awake thinking about Yudai. I stalked his page daily just to see his face. It seemed as if he got finer with each picture. His sister, Zoya reached out to me to see how I was doing. She wanted me to come out with her and her mother for lunch but I declined. I didn't have anything against them, I just didn't want Yudai to think I was using them to get back with him. I parked my truck when I arrived at the shop. We were already popular in the city, but the video with Pita put us on the map. People from all over wanted to come to the shop. We were offered a few deals from a few networks to make a show based out of our shop. Gautier was skeptical about it because she didn't want us to turn against each other for ratings.

"Good morning, Luxury Dolls," I said when I walked into the shop.

"Good morning," Tyshae and Gautier sang back.

"Are you down to go out with us tonight? We were invited to radio station 92.3's party tonight. It will be fun considering we haven't been out since we went to Mexico," Tyshae said.

"I don't have anything to wear," I lied.

"We have a boutique upstairs, and how do you not have anything to wear?" Gautier asked.

"I got rid of a lot of things when I moved out my condo," I said.

"We should go shopping. I need some new clothes anyway. I gained ten pounds since I started dating Cream," Tyshae complained.

"That's good dick weight," Gautier teased.

"I guess we can go shopping later," I said.

"Are you sure you're okay?" Gautier asked.

"Yes, I'm fine. Trust me," I replied.

Janae walked into the shop with a few girls trailing behind her.

"Heyyyyy, everyone! Who is going to the party tonight?" Janae asked.

"We are," Gautier said.

"Can you hook my nails up?" Janae asked Tyshae.

"Okay, go to my station," Tyshae said.

"After I'm done with my nails, can you style my weave? I need to look good tonight because you know the fashion police is going to be in attendance," Janae said.

"I gotchu," I replied.

I sat in the chair in my station and waited for my clients to come in. It was still early so the shop was empty. I didn't want to go out; I'd rather sleep or watch TV. I was content with being by myself. I actually preferred it that way. I wanted to call Yudai or text him but my pride wouldn't allow me to continue making a fool out of myself. Lisa came into the shop eating a muffin. She gained a few pounds since we went to Mexico. Her stomach wasn't round but she had a pregnant glow to her. We still didn't know who her baby father was. Eron came into the shop with a bouquet of flowers. He had been coming around since Pita's first episode. Speaking of Pita, she trashed Salih's mansion after he left her. Pita was still doing her show and the ratings were dropping. Only one episode was hot and that was the first episode with Gautier and Salih in it. Pita's fans instantly forgot about her. Instead, they were trailing Gautier's coattail which made her more popular than she already was.

"What are you doing here?" Tyshae asked Eron.

"Can we please talk? I'm sorry," he said.

"I've moved on, Eron, and you did, too. Kimmy isn't good enough for you anymore? Oh, let me guess. You want me back because you're going broke? I'm only good enough for you to struggle with, huh?" Tyshae asked.

"It ain't even like that. I know you will ride for me no matter what," Eron replied.

"The girl doesn't want your sorry ass anymore. Get gone, please, so we can have our morning female gossip," Janae said to Eron.

"Shut your hoe ass up. I bet I could fuck you right now if I wanted to," Eron said.

"Your money ain't long enough, honey. Hell, I'm scared of that penis anyway. You got how many baby mamas now?" Janae asked. After Eron's affair with Pita got out on live TV, more woman popped up saying Eron was their baby's father. It was rumored he had eight kids, all by different women. Six of them were taking him down for child support. He had to give up his mansion and a few of his cars to live comfortably.

"I need to talk to you, Tyshae," Eron begged.

"We're family in this shop, so whatever you have to say to me, you can say to them," Tyshae said.

"I'm ready, baby. I want to make this right. Will you marry me?" Eron asked. I dropped my head and covered my face. I was embarrassed for him.

"My nigga, why on Earth would she leave a man who believes in her dreams for a man who caused her nothing but nightmares? Who in the hell would want to deal with all your baby mamas, especially since her sister is one of them?" I asked.

"Mind your business, Saz," Eron said and I rolled my eyes.

"Please stop making a fool outta yourself. I'm asking you nicely," Tyshae said to Eron. He got mad at her and slapped her in the face with the flowers. I jumped out of my chair and attacked him with my clippers. The girls pulled me away from Eron as he yelled and held his bleeding ear.

"You will pay for this, bitch," Eron said to me before he walked out. The girls roared in laughter after he rushed out the shop. I sat back in my chair and crossed my legs as if nothing happened.

"Saz, honey, your ass is crazy," Janae laughed. The two girls that came in with Janae were sitting on the couch whispering and laughing about something. I knew they were strippers, all Janae's friends were strippers. They were pretty girls; one was light-skinned and the other one was caramel. The caramel one was thicker, around a size fourteen in the hips. She sported a short haircut and tattoos covered her arms and legs.

"Did anybody go to Davian's party a month ago? I can't stop talking about it. That was party was soooooo lit. Y'all know I racked up," Janae bragged.

"We were in Mexico," Gautier replied.

"Oh, that's right, I forgot. I hope Davian has another party because I cashed out. I made so much money. I haven't been at the club in a month. I'm taking a vacation for a little bit," Janae bragged.

Use Your Heart and Not Your Eyes

"Tell me about it, Nae. I left with Yudai's fine ass. Girrllllll, have you ever been fucked by a young boy? He almost sent me to the hospital," the caramel stripper chimed in. Janae was signaling for her to be quiet but she kept going on and on about Yudai. Surprised was an understatement since Yudai didn't party much. I guess he found a new thing to do since we weren't on good terms.

"You should've poked a hole in the condom, then you would've been set for life," the light-skinned girl said.

"He had his own condoms, besides, we're still fucking so it might come into play," she bragged.

"Girl, you crazy! Stop lying on that boy," Janae said. She was trying to keep the situation from escalating.

One thing about hair salons or any other shops where a lot of women frequented, there was always some gossip.

"I can call his fine ass up right now and he'll answer. I don't lie on my pussy, baby," she replied to Janae.

"Call him up then hand me the phone so I can cuss his ass out for fucking your nasty ass," I said.

"Excuse me?" she said.

"You heard me, bitch," I replied.

"She was just joking, Saz," Janae lied.

"I'll whip your ass, too, bitch," I said to Janae.

"I just want my nails and hair done. There is no need to get rowdy with me. If you want those hoes to leave, they can leave.

They are not fucking up my money tonight. I need to look good for the neighborhood," Janae said.

"We rode with you!" one girl yelled at Janae.

"So, what! I can't find another shop in this area to do my nails and hair. Y'all bitches are being messy. I'm the only one who can come in here with the mess. Take it outside or something. I was trying to tell you to be quiet but you kept bragging," Janae fussed. The two girls stood up and rolled their eyes at Janae. Yudai's jump-off grilled me.

"He would never bang a fat bitch like you," the caramel one said.

"We're almost the same size, hoe. Keep talking," I said and got out my chair. Lisa and Tyshae pulled me back.

"She's not worth it," Lisa said and I snatched away from them.

"I'm cool," I said. I sat in my chair when the two strippers walked out the shop.

"Where did you find those hoes at?" Gautier asked Janae.

"They strip with me sometimes, but they wanted their nails done. I warned them about that mess. Who didn't know about Yudai and Saz?" Janae asked.

"Awwww, Janae is growing up. She's trying to be a peacemaker," Gautier teased.

"Whatever, I didn't like them hoes like that anyway. It can only be one messy hoe in the room. I wear that crown," Janae stated proudly. I went to the break room and called Yudai. He finally answered the phone. I knew it had something to do with the stripper. I was sure she called him before I did.

"Your stripper girlfriend is trying to trap you. I'm giving you a heads up since you're out here fucking anything," I said.

"I find that funny considering you should've gave me a heads up, too," he replied. I hung up the phone and went back out to the floor. I didn't have the energy to argue with Yudai. I actually didn't have the energy to do anything.

I had six clients and was finished by six o'clock in the evening. Gautier was still doing makeup and Tyshae was doing nails. I told them I would meet them at the mall because the shop was getting too rowdy for me. I couldn't tolerate the noise anymore; the loud talking and laughter gave me a headache. I walked in and out of the stores unable to find anything to wear. I gave up and went to the food court. I got something to eat from Panda Express and took it to a table. While I was eating, a pretty dark-skinned woman came up to me.

"Someone is sitting there," I lied when she sat across from me.

"Saz?" she asked.

"And who are you?" I replied.

"I guess you wouldn't remember me because I didn't look like myself. My name is Tupa," she said with an accent.

"You might have me mixed up with someone else. I don't know you," I replied.

Use Your Heart and Not Your Eyes

"A few months ago, you gave me money. I was standing on the sidewalk begging for help with my daughter," she said.

"I'm so sorry for my rudeness. I've kinda been in a funk lately. How have you been? Wow, you are extremely gorgeous," I said and she smiled.

"Thank you. You are, too, I must add. I have been wanting to come to your shop to thank you for helping me but I didn't want to invade your personal space. I had a feeling I was going to run into you one day. You helped me out so much, I want to thank you. I came here years ago from Africa to go to school and live a better life. I lived with my aunt and her husband. For many years, he has been coming into my room at night while she worked her third shift at a nursing home. I ended up pregnant with my daughter. My aunt kicked me out after I gave birth. I told her my daughter belonged to her husband. She didn't believe me, her own flesh and blood. He admitted to sleeping with me but he told her I drugged him and took advantage of him. I never made it to college. I ended up a homeless teen mom for many years. I had jobs but couldn't keep them because of transportation. My daughter didn't have clean clothes and the kids teased her and she is only in Pre-K. That day you saw me, I gave up. I was ready to take my daughter to church then kill myself. You saved me," she said with tears falling from her eyes. I couldn't stop my tears, either.

"I used the money to get a hotel room. I cleaned myself up and went looking for a job. I had the money to send her to school with clean clothes. I didn't find a job that day but I ran into a woman who was looking for models. She asked me if I ever tried and I wasn't sure of it. She gave me her information and I held on to it for weeks until I finally called her. I had to figure out something quick before the money was gone and we were back on the streets. I called her and we set up a day to audition. I had no experience but they said my pictures were remarkable. I landed the job and now I'm able to afford my first home. If nobody ever told you before, I'm telling you now. You are an angel. I love you, Saz," she said.

"You're an angel, too, Tupa. You don't know how much you saved me just now," I replied.

"I have to get going, I have to pick up Kamina from school. We will see each other again, I promise," she said.

"How old are you?" I asked.

"I am twenty years old," she replied.

"Come to my shop so I can style Kamina's hair," I said.

"I will, she will love that. See you soon, Saz," she replied. She walked away and a sense of relief came over me. I didn't think helping a homeless person out would've made such a big impact. Instead of reading an article in the newspaper about her dead body being discovered, I was going to read about her in a magazine.

You go, girl, I thought.

My phone beeped and it was Gautier. She and Tyshae were at the mall and wondering where I was at. I texted them and told them I would meet them by Saks.

"Your hand is empty," Gautier said when I approached them.

"I wasn't in the shopping mood, but I ate so now I'm good. Who is ready to spend some money?" I danced around.

"Are you high?" Tyshae asked me.

"No, why you ask that?" I replied.

"You have been moody lately. Oh, let's not forget crazy, too," Tyshae said.

"I feel little better. Let's hurry up so I can get dolled up. We should take a limo to the party," I said.

"Whatever makes my baby happy," Gautier laughed.

"Her spoiled tail," Tyshae said.

We stayed in the mall until it was time to close. I bought a cute cream-colored knee-length dress with a pair of spiked nude pumps. As soon as I got home, I showered then did my makeup. I didn't have time to do my hair so I opted for a thirty-inch deep wave lace front wig with a side part. I added a nude lipstick to my lips which sparkled like diamonds. I curled my eyelashes and added little rhinestones on the tips of them. I turned the music up on my iPod and poured a glass of wine. While I was in a good mood, I took a picture of my wig. I was always promoting my wigs and hair products. My wigs were like dope to a dope boy and I was selling them fast. Tyshae texted me and told me to walk outside. I finished my glass of wine, grabbed my clutch then headed for the door.

"Oh, no she didn't. Why you didn't do my wig like that?" Tyshae asked when I got inside the limo.

"I just got this hair and played around with it. I wasn't expecting to wear it but my hair was looking a mess. Why y'all didn't tell me I was looking busted?" I asked.

"Honey, you have been looking busted for weeks. We thought you were aware," Gautier said.

"Salih didn't complain about your dress?" I asked.

"I got dressed while he was in the shower. I hauled ass out the house," she laughed.

"Cream didn't approve of my see-through dress, so I had to change," Tyshae said.

"See-through dress?" I asked.

"It was sheer and it sparkled. I wore nude panties and a bra underneath," Tyshae shrugged.

"Hoe, you were naked," Gautier said and we laughed.

Cardi B's "Bodak Yellow" played in the limo.

"Tell the driver he foul for that one. I'm about to snatch my wig off!" I yelled as I danced in the seat.

"These are bloody shoes!" we yelled in unison. Me and Gautier were wearing red bottoms. Tyshae passed me a glass of Henny on the rocks. Gautier pulled two fruit loops edibles out of her purse.

"Where did you get that from?" Tyshae asked.

"A client gave it to me. Anyone want a piece?" Gautier replied.

"I'm scared. Last time I was so paranoid, I hid under my bed. I thought someone was breaking into my condo but it was Cream taking a shower. I told Gautier I wasn't messing with that anymore," Tyshae said.

"Give me a piece," I said and took it from her.

"Don't eat the whole thing," Gautier said but it was too late. It was so good, I couldn't help it.

We arrived at the party almost an hour later because of heavy traffic. It looked like the whole city was trying to get there, too. I had a buzz when I stepped out the limo. The fashion police were at the front door exposing fake red bottoms, Gucci, and many other name brands. It was all for fun but a lot of people left from embarrassment.

I thought the place was going to be a little bit upscale being as though a lot of people were coming.

"I should've worn what I had on earlier to this muthafucka. I know they are lying about having the party here," Gautier said as we looked around.

"Fashion police, my ass, where is the health inspector?" Tyshae asked.

"We might as well have fun. Hell, I'm feeling good. I'm trying to party!" I said and walked through the crowd. Our VIP section chairs were rundown. All three us had to squeeze on a small couch.

"They probably were being cheap and hired the wrong event planner. I refuse to believe the radio station had any parts of this," I said. The hostess got on stage and apologized to everyone for the club looking the way it did. The liquor was free for the rest of the night.

"I'm cool with that," Tyshae said.

My palms began to sweat when Yudai walked in with friends from his old neighborhood. I should've known he was coming since the party was in Baltimore. A few girls were following behind them and I got jealous when the girls sat in the section with them. One girl sat on Yudai's lap and I was livid.

"He doesn't know you're here," Tyshae said.

"Fuck him," I replied.

Cream walked into the club with a few guys with him. He came over to our section. Tyshae stood up and sat on his lap and he wrapped his arm around her waist.

"What's your name, shorty?" Cream's friend asked.

"Saz, what's your name?" I asked.

"Bogie. You fly as hell, shorty. I'm digging your style," he said. Bogie was attractive but he was a little on the short side.

"I'm digging your outfit, too," I replied.

"Appreciate it, can I take you out sometime to get to know you a little better?" he asked. Gautier's eyes darted over to Yudai and she fake coughed. She was warning me about Yudai looking at us. I looked over at him and he was looking right at me. I rolled my eyes at him and continued talking to Bogie. Bogie was actually funny and managed to make us all laugh. Gautier was texting Salih who was home with their daughter. I could only imagine what type of questions he was asking her out of jealously. After all the liquor I consumed in the club, I had to release my bladder. I stood up and rushed to the bathroom with Gautier following behind me. I stood in line and danced around until I walked into the nasty stall. I pulled down my thong and squatted over the toilet. I heard someone throwing up and cringed. There was something about vomit that sickened me. I wiped myself then flushed after I was done. Gautier came out the bathroom wiping her mouth with watery eyes.

"Are you okay?" I asked.

"I had to vomit all of a sudden," she said.

"Are you pregnant?" I asked.

"Girl, are you crazy?" she replied.

"I'm just asking, I mean there is a possibility, right?" I asked.

"No," she said.

"Salih used protection when y'all first had sex at the shop? If he didn't, it's possible you are. You know how those symptoms start coming in after six weeks or so," I said and she just stared at me.

"Are you okay?" I asked.

"I haven't had a period in almost two months," she admitted.

"You might want to lay off the liquor," I said.

"Do you want to leave?" I asked.

"Yeah, we can. My stomach isn't feeling right," she said.

We walked out the bathroom and went back to our section. Gautier told Tyshae we were leaving but she wanted to stay back with Cream. Bogie walked us outside because he wanted my number. As I was giving him my number, Yudai walked out the club.

"Yo, Saz, let me holla at you," Yudai said.

"Nigga, where your manners at?" Bogie asked Yudai.

"In my back pocket, nigga," Yudai said.

"It's okay, Bogie. I'll get your number from Cream," I said. Bogie grilled Yudai before he went back into the club.

"You were ready to leave with that nigga?" Yudai asked.

"And if I was? It's none of your business. I have been calling and texting you for how long and now you're concerned?" I replied.

"I had to clear my head. Is there something wrong with that?" he asked.

"You weren't clearing your head, you were busy fucking strippers," I said.

"And? What were you busy doing? Lying and trying to hide me like I'm some clown-ass nigga that only wanted to fuck you. We were both busy doing shit," he said.

"Go back inside, the groupies are waiting," I replied.

Gautier and I got into the limo, leaving Yudai on the sidewalk. He looked like he wanted to say something but he walked away and went back inside the club. Gautier laid her head on my shoulder, "He still loves you. Salih acted the same way. Hopefully, he will grow out of it sooner than later," Gautier said.

"I still love him, too," I admitted.

"Bogie was cute but he doesn't fit you at all. I can see you now running all over that man," Gautier joked. The driver took her to Salih's loft then took me home last. I stumbled into the house feeling the effects of the edible I ate. Gautier wasn't lying about it, they didn't kick in right away, but when it did, I was stuck. I took my shoes off and headed to the kitchen. I felt like I was dying of starvation. I went through the fridge and grabbed a pack of lunchmeat and bread. I sloppily made six sandwiches and ate them all. The doorbell rang and I fell onto the floor.

"Somebody is trying to kill me. Somebody is trying to kill me," I said aloud. I grabbed a knife off the counter and sat against the fridge. The doorbell rang again followed by a knock.

Cash Flow, I thought. I stood up and walked to the front door. I squeezed my knife as I thought about jabbing it into his heart.

"You are going to die!" I screamed when I opened the door. I lunged toward him with my knife but he was quicker. He wrapped his arm around me and I dropped the knife on the floor. He covered my mouth and dragged me into the house. I knew he was going to find me, he always does. He dragged me into the living room then pushed me down on the couch.

"Shorty, you gone crazy! You almost stabbed me," the voice said. I looked up and tried to focus my gaze on the man in front of me. I had double and cloudy vision.

"I'm so hungry," I said. He kneeled in front of me and forced me to look at him.

"Do you feel drugged?" he asked.

"I'm so higghhhhh. I ate something with weed in it. My chest is about to explode," I said.

"Damn it, Saz. You can't eat that and drink," he said. He went into the kitchen and came back with a jug of milk. He forced me to drink the milk and I tried to fight him.

"Noooooooo, I don't like milk. Please, don't make me drink it," I screamed.

"Stop screaming like I'm killing you and drink the damn milk," he fussed. He placed the milk to my mouth and I gulped it down. Seconds later, I was throwing up and it got on Yudai's shoes. He took his shoes off and helped me into the bathroom.

"Where am I? Where am I? Get me out of this house, get me out of this house," I yelled.

"Calm down, you are hallucinating," Yudai said.

"Why did you bring me to my parents' house?" I asked. Yudai helped me out of my clothes after he undressed. He ran our bath water and helped me into the tub. I rested on his chest and he wrapped his arms around me.

"You gotta relax, shorty. Take deep breaths because I can hear your heart beating fast," he said.

"I can't," I whined.

"Yo, you are baked," he said. I relaxed my body as I took deep breaths in and out. My chest was about to explode and I began to panic all over again.

"I'm having a heart attack," I said.

"Anxiety attack, it's just the weed," he replied.

The water helped a little bit. We took a shower after our bath. I dried myself off when I stepped out the shower and Yudai followed me into my bedroom. I pulled the covers back on the bed and slid in. He slid in behind me. His body next to mine was soothing.

I really do miss Yudai. I know he's not really here. It's better than feeling alone, I thought before I closed my eyes. It was all a hallucination.

I woke up hours later with cotton mouth. I felt a pair of arms around me and began to panic. I pushed the stranger off the bed and he went crashing onto the floor. I was completely naked and I wanted to scream for being set up again. I was drugged and taken advantage of before and I couldn't believe I fell for it again. I rushed into my closet and grabbed my robe. I was ready to call the police until I saw Yudai sitting on my bed rubbing his head.

"Yo, your ass is fucking crazy. First you tried to stab me and now this?" he asked.

"How did you get in?" I replied.

"I asked Tyshae last night at the party for your address. I practically had to beg her for it," he said.

"How did you know I moved?" I asked.

"Salih said something about you and Gautier being roommates," he said.

"Are you hungry?" I asked.

"Yeah," he replied. It was awkward for the both of us. We had a lot to say to one another but neither one of us could say anything. I walked into the kitchen and smelled a strong scent of Pine Sol coming from the living room.

"Did you clean up?" I asked.

"Yeah, your throw up. The shit was enough to make a blind person see. I can't stomach it," he said. He sat at the kitchen island as I nervously prepared breakfast. I couldn't believe he was in my presence but there was still an elephant in the room. I cooked pancakes, sausages, eggs, grits, and oatmeal. Yudai loved oatmeal with brown sugar and fresh fruit. I laid the food out buffet style and gave him a plate so he could dig in. I sat across from him and watched him.

"This feels different," I admitted.

"Because we both have a lot to say to each other," he replied.

"I don't know what to say other than I'm sorry for lying to you," I said.

"I apologize for calling you those names. I tend to blow up when I'm pissed off. That's the main reason why I avoided you, I was still mad. I wish you would've said something, though. We spent many nights in bed talking about everything. I felt played," he said.

"I know but it wasn't that easy. I was scared of him at one point in time. He abused me and threatened to kill me. I lost count of how many times he held a gun to my head. When I got with you, I wanted to leave that part of my life behind. We were in a good place and I didn't want to ruin it," I said. He stopped eating and looked at me with hurt-filled eyes.

"That nigga put a gun to your head?" Yudai asked and I nodded my head.

"Saz, that's some serious shit. I would've had that nigga merked if I knew all of that. I know some niggas that would've bodied his ass for a few stacks," he said.

"I didn't want you to ruin your career behind him. He's not worth it," I replied.

"Not knowing about y'all could've ruined my career. He came at me on some sucka shit and I was ready to slip back into my teens when I had a street mentality," he replied.

"He called you after I whipped his ass. He came over to my place the day before you came to the shop. I was fed up with him and I wanted out for good. We got into a big fight. I gave him an old-school ass whipping. I guess he couldn't handle it," I said. Yudai got up and walked around the kitchen island. He wrapped his arms around me and kissed my neck. I melted into his embrace. I was emotionally attached to him.

"I didn't realize how much I missed you until I saw your lil' gorgeous ass last night," he whispered in my ear.

"Go sit back down. I'm still mad at you for banging that nasty-ass stripper," I said and pulled away from him.

"Lacy?" he asked.

"I don't know her name," I replied. He sat back down across from me and I rolled my eyes at him.

"I admit, I smashed her once," he said.

"She said twice," I replied.

"Once but the second time she gave me the head. It wasn't nothing serious. We exchanged numbers, talked here and there, but I swear that's as far as it went. I wasn't smashing nobody else when we were chilling," he said.

"Where do we go from here?" I asked.

"I don't know, you tell me. Is he the only nigga you were fucking besides me?" he asked.

"Yes, I swear. What are you going to do about Lacy? She was ready to get that ass beat. She told the whole shop about y'all," I said, getting mad again.

"I ain't wifing no stripper, so we ain't gotta worry about that. It was just sex," he said.

"You ate her pussy?" I asked.

"Fuck naw! Yo, you still trippin' off that weed, huh? I'm not putting my mouth on woman's pussy if I can't take her home to my family. That's too intimate," he said.

See, that's why you're special to me, I thought.

"What are you doing today?" I asked.

"Catching a flight to Chicago. We have a game tomorrow afternoon," he said.

"Can I go?" I asked.

"You want to go with me out of state?" he asked.

"Yeah, I'm trying to make sure I don't miss out on a good thing again," I replied and he smirked.

"Come over here, shorty," he said. I shyly walked over to him and he pulled me by my robe. I stood between his legs as he palmed my ass.

"Why are you blushing?" he asked.

"Because you make me nervous sometimes. Not in a bad way," I replied. He leaned forward and kissed me. I wrapped my arms around his neck and kissed him back.

"You could've went out with my sister and mother for lunch. I was cool with it," he said.

"I didn't want you to think I was intruding. You said you was done with me, so I took it to heart," I replied.

"I said a lot of things I didn't mean. I couldn't stomach watching him fuck you. We probably could've talked about it if he just called and told me he banged you, but a video? You can't expect a nigga to bounce back from that right away. I'm still pissed off because I saw it," he said.

"Wait, I want you to listen to something," I replied. I grabbed my iPhone and went to the videos. I played the video of Cash Flow talking in the background. He admitted on the recording he drugged me so his label mates could have their way with me.

"This might not stick because he wasn't aware of me recording him," I said.

"Naw, shorty. It might not stick but it will cause a lot of girls to speak up. I'm sure you weren't the only one who fell victim to this bullshit. Their sales will decline and the label will suffer. It will hurt those niggas, trust me. Report your phone stolen. Call your service company and tell them you lost your phone at a party. I'll get one of my homeboys to leak this and it won't be traced to you. If he decides to take you court, he can't say you did it. Do you want me to do this?" he asked.

"Yes," I replied. He turned my phone off and placed it on the counter.

"I'm ready to take care of this. I'll call you later," he said. He left the kitchen and went to my bedroom to get dressed. He kissed me goodbye before he left. I took a shower and got dressed for work. I had a feeling something good was finally about to come out of everything.

****

"So, y'all made up?" Tyshae asked me while I was cleaning my combs.

"He's still bothered by the video but he's coming around. I don't care how long it takes. I'm just glad I was able to tell him my side of the story," I replied.

"That boy wouldn't let me have fun last night. He kept asking me for the address. I was going to give it to him anyway, I just wanted to see him sweat a little," Tyshae said.

Use Your Heart and Not Your Eyes

"Where is Gautier," I asked.

"She said she had to take care of something," she replied. The door to the shop opened and a pretty light-skinned girl with a banging shape strolled in wearing sweat pants, tennis shoes, and a T-shirt. She looked familiar but I couldn't remember where I saw her.

"That's Davian's fiancée, ain't it?" I asked because I wasn't sure.

"Yeah, that's Remeka. I wonder what she wants because she doesn't come to this side of the city. Let her tell it, it's too hood for her," Tyshae said.

"Can we help you with something?" I asked.

"Yeah, you can! Tell that Chinese bitch to come out here," she said.

"Oh, wait a minute. We ain't bringing that damn drama to our shop," I replied.

"It's too late! That bitch has been fucking my man for months. He told me everything this morning. I'm not leaving here until I have a conversation with that hoe. She thinks he bought her a house. Davian ain't buying nobody a damn house," Remeka said.

"I thought Lisa was fucking Eron," Tyshae admitted and I agreed. Lisa walked into the shop and I looked at the clock. It was nine o'clock in the morning which was the time she was supposed to be in. It was one of those times where I wished she came in a few hours late.

"Hold on, girl. Let me call you back," Lisa said into the phone. She hung up the phone and grilled Remeka.

"What are you doing here?" Lisa asked Remeka.

"I want to know why you can't leave my man alone. Do you think he's leaving me for an industry hoe? Well, bitch, you better think again. Davian isn't going no damn where! Stop calling his phone, texting him, and calling me from a blocked number. I guess you thought he was going to help you get off your roommate's couch, huh? He used you for easy pussy and there's many others like you. We are getting married next month, so your services are no longer needed. Let this be the last time I come to this shop because the next time it won't be nice. I'm bringing my cousins and sisters up here on your ass," Remeka said.

"You can bring those bitches up here if you want to. That'll be the day I bring my gun to work. You said what you had to say, so goodbye. Ain't no jumping up in here, bitch. We stick together like family," I said.

"Y'all can get got, too. Think it's a game," Remeka threatened.

"Bye, hoe!" I spat.

Remeka called us a bunch of dirty bitches before she left the shop. Lisa sat on the couch and burst into tears. Tyshae looked at me and I shrugged my shoulders.

"I'm getting an abortion," Lisa said.

"Are you sure about that?" Tyshae asked.

"I made an appointment a few days ago. I thought Davian really loved me but he didn't. He's seeing Janae now," Lisa said.

"WHATTTTTT!" we said in unison.

"I found out last night. She posted a picture of a man lying in bed with his face covered up. I noticed the tattoo on his arm and it was Davian. We got into a huge argument about it. I texted him all hours of the night and Remeka must've read them. I don't know what she's talking about when she said I call her from a blocked number. It could be anyone," Lisa said.

"Let Janae deal with Remeka and her cousins and sisters then. We are getting a lot of publicity now and don't need any drama. Take this as a lesson learned, move on, and stop fucking other people's men," I said.

"I thank y'all for sticking up for me. I haven't had female friends until I became a part of this family," she said.

"It's cool, now put your vest on because the clients are about to start rolling in," I replied.

"And please don't say anything to Janae about Davian. Let her deal with the mess since she's always in everyone else's mess," Tyshae said. Gautier sent me and Tyshae a message saying that she wanted us to come to Salih's house when we left the shop.

"What is going on?" I asked as I read the message.

"I don't know but I'm not sure if I want to go to Salih's house. Can you imagine how he'll treat us," Tyshae said.

"Salih isn't that bad," I replied.

"You didn't grow up with him. Something is wrong with that demon," she replied.

We closed the shop down early after we finished our clients. I followed Tyshae to Salih's house which was almost a thirty-minute ride from Luxury Tea. I looked up at the building and texted Gautier. She gave us the wrong address. The building we arrived at looked vacant. Tyshae knocked on the window of my truck and beckoned me to get out.

"Salih lives here? No way he lives here. This place looks vacant," I said, looking around.

"I already talked to Gautier. She's in this building," she replied. We walked to the building and Gautier was standing by the door waiting for us. She was wearing house clothes and her eyes looked woozy.

"Are you sick?" Tyshae asked Gautier.

"Just come in," Gautier said.

We stepped into the building and it looked extremely different than the outside. We caught an elevator up to the top floor. I was in awe when we stepped off.

"This is bigger than the lofts in New York. Damn, this spot is nice," I said, looking around.

"I had to decorate it because it was too plain," Gautier said.

"This place is PHAT!" Tyshae said, looking around. Brooke was sitting on the floor in the living coloring. She ran to me and hugged me. I picked her up and kissed her cheek before I handed her to Tyshae.

Use Your Heart and Not Your Eyes

"Is everything, okay?" I asked Gautier.

"I went to the store this morning to get a pregnancy test," she replied.

"Okay, what did it say?" Tyshae asked.

"I didn't take it yet. I'm scared," she said.

"You better take it now and get it over with," Tyshae said.

"Okay, I feel better now that y'all are here," Gautier said. We sat in the kitchen, drinking a glass of wine while Gautier was in the bathroom. Ten minutes past and she was still in the bathroom.

"What's taking her so long?" I asked and Tyshae shrugged her shoulders. The elevator door opened and Salih stepped off.

"Who invited y'all?" he asked.

"Here we go," Tyshae said.

"Is that my wine? Damn, you could've at least brought a bottle of Cream's champagne over here," Salih said.

"We're not staying long," I replied.

"Chill out, I'm just kidding. Where is Gautier? I was trying to call her phone but she didn't answer," he said as he picked up Brooke. Gautier walked out holding the pregnancy test. She hid it behind her back when she saw Salih.

"What are you doing here?" she asked.

"I live here. I came home to get my luggage," he said eyeing her.

"This is going to be good," I said and Tyshae agreed.

"What are you hiding?" he asked.

"Floss," Gautier said.

"Okay, Pretty Woman," I said and Tyshae giggled. Gautier rolled her eyes at me.

"Stop lying, I saw it. What does it say?" he asked.

"What does what say?" she replied.

"The pregnancy test, Gautier. Is it positive?" he asked and she looked at us.

"What are you looking at them for? You are the one who took the test," he said. He put Brooke down and walked over to Gautier. He reached behind her and snatched it out of her hand.

"Ohhhhhhh, bitch. She's in trouble," I whispered to Tyshae. Salih stared at the test and somewhat smirked.

"Is he mad or happy?" I asked Tyshae.

"Knowing him, probably neither," she replied.

"Come here, Brooke," Salih said. She walked over to him and he kneeled in front of her.

"Listen to Mommy while I'm gone. We don't want to upset her because she's carrying your little sister or brother, okay?" he said.

"Okay," Brooke said in excitement.

"Awwww, we are going to be godmothers again," I said.

"You saying that like I want y'all to," Salih said and I gave him the finger. He went to his room and came back with his luggage.

"I'm going to call you as soon as I land," he said to Gautier. He kissed her lips then kissed Brooke's cheek.

"Remember what Daddy said, Brooke," Salih said.

"See you later," Tyshae and me said as he left out the door.

"Go play while Mommy talks to Saz and Tyshae," Gautier said. Brooke ran back to the living room to finish coloring.

"Your hot in the ass behind. Got pregnant fast, huh?" I asked.

"I feel like I'm dreaming," Gautier said.

"I'm happy for y'all. It was bound to happen. You are stuck with that man and there is nothing you can do about it. Neither one of you could move on, that's what you call real love," Tyshae said.

"I'll sip to that," I replied.

"Pita might be carrying his baby, too, so Salih might have two babies on the way," Gautier said.

"God is working in your favor. That ain't his baby, I'll bet money on it. If it was his baby, she would've went to her doctor's appointment and stopped playing around. What is she trying to hide?" I asked.

"The due date," Tyshae said and we laughed.

"We will have to wait and see. But I am really looking forward to this time around. I have my friends, Brooke, family, and Salih," Gautier said.

"Congrats to you! Now we're just waiting for the wedding and everything will be set," Tyshae said.

"I would love to stay and chat, but I'm flying to Chicago for Yudai's game. I'm finally going to see him play. Everything is out on the table with us, so no more hiding. I'm going to be cheering for my baby tomorrow," I said as I grabbed my purse.

"Don't come back pregnant," Tyshae said.

"You'll be pregnant before me, Strawberry," I said. I kissed their cheeks before I stepped on the elevator. I couldn't wait to pack for my trip.

Chicago, here I come! I thought.

Tyshae
Til Death Do Us Part

I sat across from Yarmin Ross and his rapper, Money Bags. I decided to give the music industry a try. It took me a while to think about it but I finally made my mind up. Cream was sitting next to me as we listened to our new track called, "Savage Wife." Yarmin and Money Bags bopped their heads to the music that was playing inside the studio.

"This shit is going to blow up," Money Bags said. Money Bags was a young cutie. He was around twenty-two years old. He was tall and slim with long pretty locs. He was dark-skinned and had a pretty, but boyish, face. If he shaved his goatee, he could go for a lesbian because of his looks.

"I knew it was going to be hot. I called Cream right after I heard your voice," Yarmin said. Yarmin wasn't a flashy producer. He wore basic clothes but his jewelry spoke volumes.

"We are dropping this at midnight. Are you sure you don't want to sign to this record label?" Yarmin asked.

"Let's see how this goes. I'm just trying to get my feet wet first," I replied.

"My doors are always open for you," he said and shook my hand. I hugged Yarmin and Money Bags as I thanked them for giving me the opportunity. Cream gave them dap before we left the downtown studio.

"I can't believe this!" I screamed when we got on the sidewalk.

"I can believe it, beautiful," he said. I wrapped my arms around him and kissed his lips.

"Thank you," I said.

"Of course, you know I gotchu. Now, let's grab something to eat. I'm starving," he said.

"You're always hungry," I replied.

"It ain't an issue when I'm eating that peach, though," he said and I pushed him.

"Why you gotta be nasty?" I asked.

"How? I'm just a man who likes to enjoy the taste of his woman's fruit," he said.

"Your woman, huh? How are you just going to put claim on me?" I replied.

"Because I can and I just did. You always been mine. Eron's bitch-ass doesn't count," Cream said.

"So, I'm your woman now?" I asked, feeling giggly inside.

"My woman," he repeated.

"And you're my man, huh?" I asked.

"Yeah, girl, you got jungle fever," Cream said.

"Let's go so we can feed you," I replied.

"Now we're talking," he said.

We went to a nearby Japanese steak house for dinner. Cream almost ordered the entire menu.

"This is why I'm gaining weight," I complained as I munched on grilled shrimp.

"That's happy weight, Shae. You're still slim to me, your ass is just bigger, though, but you know where that came from," he said looking down at his dick.

"You're so full of yourself," I laughed.

"Am I lying?" he asked.

"I'll give you a cookie for that," I replied.

I heard familiar voices coming from behind me. When I turned around, Eron and my sister were ready to be seated…across from us. It was a very awkward moment for me. I didn't plan on seeing him on one of the happiest days of my life. The cat was out the bag and everyone knew Eron left me for my sister. He received backlash for it but due to his financial status, it wasn't as bad as being broke.

"Oh, hey, Tyshae. I didn't see you sitting there underneath that wig," Kimmy said.

"Hey, sis. Don't order too much off the menu, I'm sure neither one of you can afford the tab. Looks like you two will be dining off appetizers and sparkling water," I fired back.

"We can't live as lavish as you, trap queen. Drug money grows on trees. Isn't that right, Cream? What are you two celebrating? Finding a new connect?" Kimmy said.

"Don't respond to her, Shae. She's miserable, look at them," Cream said.

"How is Paula doing, Cream? Is she still smoking crack and sucking dick to get high," Kimmy teased. Cream clenched his jaw and his face almost turned red. I was tired of Kimmy's mouth. I walked my plate of food over to her and smashed it against her face. Eron jumped up and got in my face as Kimmy cried about me ruining her two-thousand-dollar shirt. Cream jumped up and stood in front of me.

"What are you going to do, white boy?" Eron asked Cream. I saw Cream reaching to his hip and hurriedly jumped in the middle.

"Let's just take our food to go," I pleaded with Cream.

"You heard your house negro. That's what he is, right? He's your master," Eron said. Cream slammed his fist into Eron's face and the people in the restaurant screamed for help.

"Son of a bitch!" Cream yelled as he sent another bone-crushing blow to Eron's face. Cream was a fighter, Eron wasn't. Cream had to learn how to defend himself being the only white boy in the hood. He could take an ass whipping and give one without feeling any way about it. The staff and I tried to pull Cream off Eron but it wasn't working.

"The cops are coming!" I yelled at Cream. He pulled away from Eron and dropped a few hundred on the table. I followed him out of the restaurant and we hurriedly got in his car. He pulled off before the police could get there.

"I'm going to drop you off at the mall and keep going. I have a gun on me and I don't know if they reported my license plate," he said. I was paranoid and scared. I began to cry.

"I don't want you going to jail!" I screamed.

"I won't if I can ditch this gun," he said. He came to a halt in front of the mall and told me to get out. As soon as my foot hit the concrete, he sped off. I heard police sirens going in the direction of Cream's Wraith. I sat on a bench and cried my eyes out. My hands were shaking as I had flashbacks of Cream getting locked up when we were younger. It was almost like déjà vu. He was on probation; a gun charge could send him to jail for ten years. I picked up my phone and called Saz but she didn't answer. I forgot about the date she was going on with Yudai. I wanted to call Gautier but she was pregnant and I didn't want to stress her out. Calling my mother was out of the question. I didn't have many people, just my friends and Cream. I took an Uber home, and as soon as I got in the house, I turned on the news. I didn't see anything about Cream. I went on Instagram, Snapchat, Facebook, and Twitter and found nothing. I went into the kitchen for a glass of wine to calm my nerves. I called Cream's phone but it was off. I cried like a baby as I stared at the wall; I cried myself to sleep.

Hours later...

I woke up to the sound of someone knocking on my door. I ran to the door and opened it without a thought because I knew it was Cream. I came face-to-face with Eron.

"What are you doing here?" I asked. He slammed my face into the wall and I slipped on the floor. I tasted blood in my mouth as it dripped down my nose. Eron closed the door and locked it.

"Thought I was your white boy, huh?" Eron asked.

"Please, leave!" I said. He picked me up and slammed me into the wall. Eron weighed a hundred pounds more than me and was very tall. He slung me around like a rag doll. I figured he was stalking me because he knew where I lived. He must've followed me home from the shop one day. Eron was going through something and was taking it out on me.

"We can talk about this, please, just stop," I begged. He slammed me onto the couch and I laid still, afraid he might hurt me.

"All I wanted was for you to come back to me. I fucked up and I apologized, but it still wasn't good enough. How many times have I cheated on you? How many times have I left you and came back weeks later? What was so different about this time, Shae? I was going to come right back but your hoe ass couldn't wait. You just had to go and fuck that white boy. You made me look like a fool in that restaurant. You thought your little broke jokes were funny, huh? That nigga got more money than me, huh? He can take care of you but I can't anymore? Is that why you don't want me?" he cried. I wanted to answer but I was afraid to.

"ANSWER ME, BITCH!" he yelled and pulled a gun out on me.

"I'll kill you before I see you with another man. Til death do us part, Shae. You made me look like a fool at the shop in front of your friends. You think I'm a clown-ass nigga?" he asked.

"No," I cried.

"My life isn't shit without you, Shae. I slept with other women but I didn't love them. I only loved you," he said.

"You slept with my sister and she's carrying your child," I replied.

"I thought you was going to ride with me forever. I made you, Shae. I was the first one who fucked you. Everything you have is because of me. I put you on the map. Nobody was checking for your ghetto country ass. I gave you a makeover, I upgraded you from Reeboks to red bottoms," he said. He pointed the gun to my stomach and laughed.

"Bitch, you couldn't even carry my child. If you could've, I wouldn't have had to fuck other women," he said.

"What did I do to deserve this, Eron? What did I do besides love you and be faithful? I gave you my life and you gave me your ass to kiss so many times. You broke me down to pieces. I tried to become the women you cheated on me with and you still fucked other women. I tried to make you happy countless times and you didn't care. I lost our baby because of the stress you put me through. None of this is my fault. You brought this on yourself. You got famous and shitted on those who cared about you. You even fucked Pita, your best friend's fiancée. I loved you so much, I kept your secret. You set Damien up to get robbed because you were slinging drugs. It was you who owed Sisco money and you lied and told him Damien had you robbed of his product. I overheard y'all talking. Salih went years thinking Gautier did it, but it was you. I said nothing because I LOVED YOU!" I screamed and he pulled the trigger. The bullet pierced through my stomach.

"I didn't want to set him up, Shae, but Salih had everything. He had a brother, Gautier, and most importantly, he had a mother. I had nobody! It was either me or Damien, and I chose me. Sisco was going to kill me, Shae. You knew he was going to kill me," Eron cried. I laid on the couch as blood seeped from my wound. Tears slid out of my eyes because I felt my life slipping away. Eron couldn't emotionally kill my spirit, so he took another route—he wanted to end my life. I knew Eron was a bad seed with a jealous heart, but love makes you see past a lot of things. The signs were always there, but I thought if I gave him my love, it would've changed him. It didn't change him, it made him worse, because he had mistaken love for a sign of weakness.

"I'm tired of fighting my demons, Shae," Eron said. He put the gun in his mouth and pulled the trigger. His brain splattered on my face as his body fell onto the floor. My cell phone rang and I knew by the ringtone it was Cream. I crawled on the floor to my phone and answered it.

"He shot me," I cried.

"WHAT!" Cream screamed through the phone.

"Eron shot me. I don't think I'm going to make it. It burns so bad, Cream," I said.

"Listen, baby. I'm right around the corner. Stay on the phone. Please, stay on the phone," his voice trembled.

"I love you, Cream. Thank you for coming back into my life. You made me so happy," I said. I couldn't hold on any longer. The phone dropped out of my hand and the last thing I heard was Cream screaming my name...

I woke up and looked around the room but my vision was blurry. I was heavily sedated but I knew I had people surrounding me. I tried to talk but I couldn't. My words were slurring.

"Tyshae, oh thank God. Thank God," Cream said.

"She's up?" Saz asked.

Gautier and Salih came over to my bed and everyone looked like they hadn't slept in days.

"I'm going to get the nurse," Yudai said.

"Can you hear us?" Saz asked and I nodded my head.

"You've been sedated for a day. You lost a lot of blood and passed out from shock, but the doctors said you will have a speedy recovery. It was only a flesh wound, thank God," Gautier said. The nurse came in to check on me. I was so high, my hospital bed felt like it was moving. I closed my eyes because I got dizzy. Suddenly, I threw up because of the medication.

"It's okay, that happens sometimes. The meds make some patients dizzy as if they are on a merry-go-round," the nurse said. My friends left the room while two techs cleaned me off. I felt a little better but I was still woozy.

"Is she up? I want to see my daughter! Get your ass out of here," my mother said while Cream was standing in the doorway.

"Would you calm the fuck down, Kim? She's resting and you don't have to bring that shit up here. She's been through enough with you and your filthy-ass daughter," Cream said.

"I will have you removed from this room, serial killer. I know you were responsible for this. You're trying to use my daughter because she's a singer now. Tyshae, baby. You're coming home with me when you get out of the hospital, okay?" my mother asked me. She didn't care about me, she heard the song on the radio and saw dollar signs.

"She's coming home with me, Kim," Cream said.

"We will see about this," my mother said. She pushed past Cream and came over to my bed.

"Ohhh, Tyshae, sweetie. I'm so sorry this happened. I told you to leave Eron alone," she said, caressing my face. I moved my head away from her because she was making me feel uncomfortable. I cried to my mother many times about Eron's infidelities and she told me to stick with it. She didn't love me and I was finally content with that. She treated her daughters how her mother treated her. I couldn't make any excuses for her because she knew it was wrong when her mother did her the same way. My sister came into the room with her fake tears, crying about how sorry she was.

"I didn't know he was going to do that to you. I was a victim, too. He abused me and forced me to be with him," Kimmy lied.

"So, we're supposed to sit here and pretend like y'all give a fuck about Tyshae? Let me guess, y'all heard her song on the radio? She's not giving y'all any damn money. She doesn't owe y'all jack shit. You ought to be ashamed of yourselves. You didn't want her in your house and her own sister is carrying her ex-boyfriend's baby. She's doesn't need fake love right now, she needs real love to help her through this, and we have been here! Where in the hell were y'all?" Gautier asked my mother.

"Calm down, shorty. Don't stress yourself out," Salih said to her.

"I am calm, Salih. I will be calm when that poor excuse of a mother gets the hell out and takes her trash with her," Gautier said.

"I know her wide-load ass ain't talking to me," Kimmy said.

"She was talking to the both of you. Y'all need to leave," Saz said.

"She's my sister, we are real family," Kimmy said.

"Go home!" I whispered.

"She told y'all to go home," my mother told my friends.

"GO HOME!" I said a little louder.

"We are here for you," my mother said.

"Where were you when Kimmy was fucking Eron?" Saz asked.

"I didn't know about that until after Tyshae left!" my mother said. I actually believed her. I knew when my mother was lying.

"I'm going home, Ma. Call me when she gets home," Kimmy said before she left. She didn't care about Eron. She wasn't sad one bit that he committed suicide. A few detectives came in and everyone cleared my room. They asked me about Eron's behavior and I told them everything. From the time he walked in until I passed out. Twenty-minutes later, they left my room. I couldn't fight back the tears anymore. Everything happened so fast. One minute, I was leaving the studio with Cream then the next minute, I was clinging on to life. I hoped Eron burned in hell for what he did to me. Cream came into the room alone so we could talk.

"This is my fault, Shae. I exploded yesterday, but I couldn't help it. The things he said messed my head up. When I look at you, I don't see color. I see a woman I have been in love with since I was a teenager. I should've been there, baby," Cream said with tears falling down his face. I grabbed his hand and kissed it.

"You are here now and I'm alive. That's all that matters," I replied.

"I was pulled over a little after I dropped you off but I had already ditched the gun. They were searching my car, so that's why I couldn't answer the phone. Kimmy told the police I was ready to shoot Eron. I swear I hate your sister, Shae," he said.

"She will see her day in hell, too," I replied.

****

I was released from the hospital three days later. I went to Cream's house because I heard how much blood was in my living room. I was sleeping next to Cream when I had a dream Eron shot me in the head. I woke up out of my sleep and felt something wet between my legs. I was twenty-four years old and peeing in the bed.

"What's the matter, Shae? Everything okay?" Cream asked when he sat up.

"I had a nightmare and I wet the bed. This is so embarrassing. Throw me over a bridge. I'm useless," I cried. Cream hugged me and kissed my forehead.

"It's not that big of a deal. I'll clean it up," he replied. He picked me up and took me to the bathroom. I couldn't take a real shower yet, only bed baths because of my bandage. Cream cleaned me off as I sat on the toilet seat and cried. He dressed me in his T-shirt and shorts. He took me to the spare bedroom so he could scrub his mattress. He slid back into bed and wrapped his arm around me.

"I'm sorry," I said.

"It's cool, Strawberry. I ain't trippin' and neither should you. I wouldn't have cared if you shitted on the sheets. I'm thankful that you're alive. When I found you lying on the floor, I thought you were dead. I don't care what I have to do to help you," he replied.

"I love you," I said.

"I love you more," he replied.

"I would make love to you but I need to wash my ass properly before I try and get all sexy," I said and he chuckled.

"I'll break you off properly when you heal," he said. I kissed his lips and he palmed my butt.

"I think you should move in with me," he said.

"Are you sure?" I replied.

"Yeah, it ain't like we are strangers. With that good pussy, I might not never leave the house," he said and I pinched him.

"Good, because I wouldn't want you to," I said.

"When the time is right for us, I'm going to marry you," he said and I blushed.

"Then we can have some babies?" I asked and he chuckled.

"Hell yeah," he replied.

****

A week later, everyone was inside Cream's house. It was Sunday and Gautier wanted to cook dinner for me. Cream's mother, Paula was helping Gautier with the greens and pot roast.

"Look at Gautier cooking with Martha Stewart," Saz said.

"Shut up before Paula hears you," I replied.

"Girl, Paula got a body on her. No wonder Cream got a little black in him. Those people are light-skinned," Saz said.

"Do you ever stop?" I asked Saz.

"Nope, I'm happy right now. You're getting better and Yudai is making me wetter," Saz said.

"Did you eat an edible?" I asked.

"I had a little piece," she giggled.

"What do you know about that seasoned salt?" Saz asked Paula and Paula laughed.

"I know more shit than you, doll baby," Paula said. Paula still looked the same from back in the day. Her long blonde hair hung down her back. She was slim but curvy. She didn't have much butt but she had hips and breasts.

"Run me my money," Salih said to Cream.

Use Your Heart and Not Your Eyes

"You are cheating," Cream said back.

"Both of y'all niggas are cheating," Yudai spat.

"Why are they playing dice in the middle of the living room?" I asked Saz.

"'Cause my baby is hood. Look at him with his pretty thugged-out ass. Girlll, we snuck a quickie in on our way here. Babbbbyyyyyy, I offered him the eggs. I'm going to be pregnant next year," Saz said. I snatched her glass of wine from her and sat it on the table.

"No more wine," I said.

"I heard that, Saz. What is up with the eggs?" Yudai asked.

"You don't know? Shorty is trying to trap you," Salih replied.

"Would you shut the hell up. Who asked you?" Saz asked Salih.

"It's just a term we joke about. Like 'ohhh, lil' daddy can get the eggs,' meaning he's bae for real," Gautier said.

"Saz, keep talking shit about these eggs. Her lil' ass is going to be stuffed like a turkey. I'll give her ass a whole cage full of hens," Yudai said and I burst into laughter.

"Your sperm ain't that strong, baby. You're still a spring chicken yourself," Saz replied.

"Yeah, aight. Keep talking shit, Saz. You ain't got to show off. Excuse my language, Ms. Paula Dean, but Saz can't handle the bat. She can't make it to first base, either," Yudai said.

"Paula Dean? Really muthafucka?" Cream asked Yudai.

"Saz told me your mother's name is Paula Dean," Yudai said and everyone looked at Saz.

"I'm high," Saz said.

"There is nothing wrong with a little humor," Paula said. We went outside on the patio to catch the nice fall breeze. The men stayed inside and played PlayStation.

"Thanks for coming, Paula. It was a pleasure seeing you again," I said.

"Anytime, baby. I always wanted to visit Cream but he's always ripping and running. Now he has a reason to keep himself still," she said.

"'Savage Wife' is number one on iTunes. That's what I'm talking about," Gautier said as she looked at her phone.

"That song is hot. I set it as my alarm clock," Saz said.

"The girls at the shop miss you. Hell, everyone misses you. Too bad you deleted your social network," Gautier said.

"I'm going to get back on there after I heal mentally. I still see his face when I close my eyes sometimes. I can't believe Eron did what he did," I replied.

"He probably had a lot of issues going on but couldn't talk about it. Maybe sleeping with a lot of women was a sign for help. We all react to things differently. We stop loving ourselves and end up hurting people who care about us in the process," Saz said.

"Well spoken, Saz," Paula said.

"Can I talk to Gautier alone?" I asked Saz and Paula.

"Sure, I need to smoke a cigarette anyway," Paula said.

"I'm going to check up on the food," Saz said. They walked into the house and closed the sliding doors.

"Saz is going to sneak a quickie off with Yudai. They fuck everywhere," Gautier chuckled.

"I have been holding something back from you for a long time. I know you might hate me but life is too short to keep secrets from your close friends," I said.

"Okayyy," Gautier said nervously.

"Eron set up Damien to get killed because he owed Sisco money. He told Sisco Damien stole his product out his backpack. I know it was wrong, but Eron was my boyfriend at the time and I couldn't rat him out. He didn't know I knew and he shot me because I told him I knew. Please don't hate me for this," I said.

"Damn, Shae. That's deep considering you watched Salih blame me for all these years," she said. We stared ahead and watched the cars drive past in the busy city.

"I'm still your friend," she said and I wiped my eyes.

"We all made mistakes when we were younger and carried it with us to adulthood. Me and Salih are working it out after all this time and I swear I don't feel like digging it back up again. Let's keep it buried because we are all happy now. It's time for us to move on from this madness. It will be between us, let's forget you told me," she said.

"Thank you," I replied.

"Now, let's go in to eat," Gautier said.

When stepped back into the house, Paula was taking a tray out the oven.

"I thought Saz was going to help you," I said to Paula.

"Her and Yudai went down to the car to get something," Paula replied.

"Her ass is going to be pregnant, watch," Gautier said.

My mother called me but I ignored her call. I had buried her with the rest of my past as I stared at my future. Cream looked at me and blew me a kiss. I thanked God for giving me and my friends second chances.

Epilogue
Gautier

One year later...

I woke up to Salih Jr. crying. I tapped Salih and told him it was his turn to feed him.

"Aight, I'm coming!" Salih angrily spat then slung the covers off his body. He stood up and stretched and I lustfully eyed his tall, chocolate body. He stepped into a pair of shorts and left the room to tend to our three-month-old son. I stared at my wedding ring with admiration. Salih and I had a secret wedding in Maldives with only close friends and family at the wedding. We got married a month after I gave birth to baby Salih. He proposed to me at our baby shower. I wasn't expecting us to get married any time soon, but we did it. Pita's baby ended up being Andy's, Salih's teammate. Salih sold the house he had with her and moved us to a mansion in Potomac, Maryland. I bought another shop in the D.C. area. The grand opening was only a week away. My mother and Salih were finally getting along which was important to me because I wanted my family to be close-knit. Salih didn't talk about Eron much, but I knew his death bothered him. He was slowly coming back around from it. Salih walked into the room carrying our son who looked exactly like him.

"He wakes up as soon as my dick gets hard. I was ready to slide in before he started crying," Salih complained.

"Give him to me," I said.

"Naw, we aight," Salih replied. He kissed Baby Salih's forehead. The baby yawned as he drifted off to sleep.

"He's going to be a baseball player, too. I can't wait, baby. You and Brooke can continue on y'all little shopping sprees. Me and Jr. are going to sit back and chill," Salih stated. He was excited when he found out we were having a boy. I hadn't seen him that excited in years.

"Let's pray he doesn't get your attitude," I said.

"What's wrong with my attitude?" he asked.

"It's horrible," I replied.

"Y'all niggas just don't understand the type of nigga I am," he smirked. He placed the baby in his bassinet in the corner of our room then he climbed into bed. He slid my negligee up to my hips and passionately kissed my neck.

"I'm thinking we should have another one so that way the kids won't be too far apart," Salih said.

"You have lost your...ohhhhh," I moaned as he entered me.

"Damn, Gautier," he groaned into my ear. I wrapped my legs around him as he slid up and down between my tight, wet walls. I licked his lips and he squeezed my breasts. I was on the verge of coming instantly and it hadn't been more than a minute. Salih covered my mouth as he went deeper. I closed my eyes as the orgasm rippled through my body.

"You're going to wake the baby up," he whispered but it was too late. The baby screamed at the top of his lungs. He was spoiled and it wasn't because of me. Salih held him so much he couldn't sleep in a crib. It was Salih's first time experiencing the early stages of newborns, so I kept my mouth shut. I didn't want to make him feel uncomfortable and take away that feeling from him. I'd rather him learn on his own. Salih pulled out of me and went into the bathroom to wash his hands. He came back and picked up the baby. He held him close to his chest and rocked him.

"I can hold him so you can sleep," I said.

"I got this, shorty, get some rest," Salih said. He kissed my lips before he headed out our bedroom. In the past, Salih was a hurt man, but underneath it all, he was a remarkable man, too. He was a great father and a loving husband. He was still jealous but that part of him wasn't going to change. I got out of bed and grabbed my robe. I walked down the hall to the nursery and Salih was sitting up in the rocking chair fast asleep. I gently took the baby from him and laid him down in his crib. I took a blanket and covered up Salih. I kissed his lips before I went down the hall to Brooke's room. I opened her door and she was asleep with half the covers by her feet.

My beautiful family, I thought. I walked down the hall and passed the family portrait of us. All four of us were wearing Jerseys with Salih's number on it, which was eighty-seven. I couldn't wait to fill the hallways of our home with many family photos of our new legacy.

Saz

"What's the surprise?" I asked as Yudai's hands covered my eyes.

"Can you wait? Damn, you're nosey. Watch your step," he said.

Yudai picked me up from the shop because he had a birthday surprise for me. It was a long surprise. We were in the car for almost an hour. I heard a door open and he gently pushed me in.

"SURPRISE!" they yelled. He uncovered my eyes and I gasped. I was standing in an empty house with my friends and Yudai's family.

"Oh my God. What is going on?" I asked.

"This is our new home," Yudai said. I looked around and the house was huge. We were finally official. We had been in a relationship for over a year. The year was a smooth one for me. Cash Flow and his label mates were serving time in jail. Their dirt finally hit the fan when the video of him admitting to drugging me surfaced. Over twenty girls came forward and said they were drugged, too, at their parties. The majority of them were fifteen to seventeen. Cash Flow pissed his mother off when he didn't pay her. She snitched on him by claiming he molested his five-year-old cousin. I wasn't sure if it was true, but it was enough to get him a longer sentence. The record company he was under was sold to Yarmin Ross, the same producer Tyshae ended up signing to. She was no longer working at the shop but visited whenever she could. Cash Flow's wife, Rosara left him and ended up dating the rapper, Money Bags. She knew he was seeing me the entire time but she didn't confront me because she didn't love him. Turns out she wasn't pregnant by Cash Flow, I know she was happy that she dodged that bullet. She came into the shop and gave me my jewelry set back. She apologized about everything I went through with Cash Flow. Sadly, he had done the same things he did to me to her and he was paying for all of it.

"I'm ready to cry," I said and fanned myself. Zoya handed me a tissue and I wiped my eyes. Erin held a double chocolate three-layer cake in her hands with twenty-two candles. They sang "Happy Birthday" to me as I blew out the candles. Yudai's sister, Imani was in the crowd, too. She waved at me and I waved back. We were cordial because of Yudai but me and Zoya became close. Tupa and Kamina were at the party, too. She brought Kamina to me on the regular so I could do her hair. Kamina was the sweetest little girl. She and Brooke formed a cute little friendship at the shop.

"Happy Birthday, girl. This is for you," Janae said as she handed me a gift bag. I rubbed her small baby bump. She was pregnant with a girl. Davian left Remeka and settled down with Janae. They got married a few months ago. I couldn't believe Davian actually settled down and stopped cheating. There was somebody for everybody.

I hugged Yudai and kissed his lips while the guests took pictures of us.

"Come around back," he said. He grabbed my hand and led me out back where a cookout was going on by the pool. Gautier and her mother were working the grill. Salih was stocking coolers with beers and soda. A DJ was setting up in the backyard and I was screaming in excitement.

"We are about to partyyyyyy!" I sang as I danced around.

"We can party later. Let's see the rest of the house. Everyone just got here, so we are still setting up," Yudai said. He grabbed my hand and took me on a tour through the house. It had five bedrooms, six bathrooms, and a basement. I screamed for joy when Yudai opened a door to a salon-style room that was big enough to turn into a small salon. I also had a makeup station.

"This was Gautier's idea," Yudai said.

"What did I do to deserve this?" I asked out loud.

"Made me fall in love with you," he said.

"I'm ready to cry but I just did my eyelashes and don't want to ruin them. We will be living together?" I asked.

"Yup, under the same roof," he smirked, showing his diamond grill.

"Now you can give me the eggs," he said.

"I'm ready to give your fine ass the whole dairy aisle," I replied.

"Ain't nothing but space and opportunity, shorty. What are you trying to do?" he asked, grabbing his dick. I locked the door and lifted my knee-length skirt. I slid my thong down and pulled Yudai into me.

"We got five minutes," I said as I unzipped his jeans and released his dick. He lifted my leg up and sucked on my bottom lip.

"All I need is three, shorty," he replied and entered me. He fucked me against the wall and gave me the three best minutes a woman could ask for. We weren't married yet and didn't have any kids, but those plans were up in the air. In the meantime, we were enjoying each other's company. After we finished our quickie, we headed back downstairs with our guests. I partied like I never partied before. Not only was I celebrating my birthday, I was celebrating peace and love in my life.

Tyshae

"What does it say, Shae?" Cream asked from the other side of the bathroom door. I opened the door with the pregnancy test in my hand. I smiled at him and he smiled back.

"Is it positive?" he asked.

"YES!" I screamed. He picked me up and spun me around the room. He lifted my shirt up and kissed my stomach. I giggled in excitement because of how happy he was. I had to see a psychiatrist after I recovered from my gunshot wound. I was having problems sleeping. Cream, my friends, and music helped me through it. My songs sounded better, maybe because of the hurt and pain I felt behind everything I went through. I realized singing helped ease the pain, so I signed a deal with Yarmin Ross. Cream gave up the streets like he said he would. He launched a vodka and wine line. He found ways to turn his street money into legit money. He has lived up to everything he promised me.

"Will you marry me?" he blurted out. I sat up and looked at him in shock.

"Are you serious?" I asked.

"Yeah, what type of question is that?" he replied. He got up and left out the room. He came back with a small black velvet box.

"I had a feeling you was pregnant, so I went out to get this. I wanted to make everything official. Will you marry me?" he asked.

"You damn right, I will!" I screamed. He slid the ring on my finger and it was huge. It was a single diamond teardrop-shaped ring.

"This is so beautiful. I have to call my friends and tell them. A bitch is fittin' to be married!" I screamed and Cream laughed. I hurriedly grabbed my phone off the dresser and called Gautier. I placed her on hold then called Saz who was breathing into the phone.

"Were you fucking?" Gautier asked Saz.

"Not anymore, unlike y'all old hens, I'm still a young chicken," Saz joked.

"I'm pregnant!" I blurted out and they screamed into the phone.

"And I'm getting married!" I blurted out and they screamed again.

"Shut the hell up!" Yudai yelled at Saz.

"Nigga, you shut the fuck up! Best fran is pregnant and getting married," Saz spat back.

"Oh, my bad. Tell her congrats," Yudai said in the background.

"I can't talk too loud. Yudai was asleep and I scared his ass when I screamed. We need to celebrate. What are we doing?" Saz asked.

"Weekend trip getaway," Gautier said.

"Can I plan your wedding?" Saz asked me.

"Yeah," I laughed.

"And I will help, too. This is going to be fun," Gautier said.

"I go on tour next month. It's perfect timing because I won't be showing yet," I said.

"Cream is going to be a daddy. Awww, I bet he was excited," Saz said.

"He was but I know Paula will be very happy. I will have to wait until later to tell her because she'll scream my head off," I replied.

"Lisa just got dropped off at the shop by her new man," Gautier said.

"Who?" I asked.

"Aniston," Gautier said and we howled in laughter.

"I forgot to tell y'all. I talked to Janae at Saz's party and she told me Kimmy was strung out on drugs. She hooked up with some man and he turned her out. She's locked up for stealing an iPad from best buy. Now, my mother is raising her son by Eron. Ain't that something?" I asked them.

"Her karma," Gautier said and Saz agreed.

I sat on the phone with my friends, basking in happiness. I had a great man, good record sales, and loyal friends. I dropped Kimmy and my mother out of my life for good. I had learned a valuable lesson in knowing my self-worth. Fat, tall, skinny, or short, all women had insecurities. The key to overcoming them is learning how to love yourself. True love will prevail if you use your heart to love instead of what you see. What we see is not always the truth. Just because a man has a lot money, doesn't mean he will treat you the way you deserve. A plus size women can have insecurities that doesn't have anything to do with her weight. A slim light-skinned girl with a pretty face doesn't always have it all. Social media only shows one type of beauty when beauty comes in all shades and sizes. Overall, the key is to be happy with who you are and the pieces to the puzzles will fall into place.

The End

If you think these ladies had a story to tell, wait until you see what Gautier's new, Luxury Tea in D.C has in store...

Made in the USA
San Bernardino, CA
06 March 2020